Once Upon a Viking

DEMELZA CARLTON

Three tales in the Romance a Medieval Fairy Tale series

Appease: Princess and the Pea Retold

DEMELZA CARLTON

A tale in the Romance a Medieval Fairy Tale series

One

To six-year-old Princess Sativa, betrothed seemed like such a strange word. Mother had told Sativa that it was a fancy word that meant promised. She was promised to the prince, and he was promised to her. When she'd asked what kind of promise, her mother had only smiled and said, "The unbreakable sort."

So now Sativa sat in the place of honour in

her father's hall, beside her promised, Prince Reidar. She wasn't sure what she wanted to do with him. Big boys like him usually spent all their time in the practice yard, sparring with swords and shooting arrows into targets. He had a sword strapped to his side, too, like one of her father's knights. It was smaller than their swords, though, for he was only a boy.

It certainly bothered his mother, though. Queen Regina looked like she'd drunk vinegar instead of wine every time he bumped her with his sheathed sword. More than once, Sativa had been forced to smother her laughter, or risk a quelling glance from her own mother.

Sativa yawned, remembering to cover her mouth before her mother saw. She wouldn't have been so excited about attending this feast if she'd known it was so boring. She'd eaten her fill of the food, and she wasn't allowed any wine, so why did she have to keep sitting there? Normally when she'd finished her dinner, she could go play with her little sisters, or the castle kittens, but her mother insisted she must spend the whole dull day with the prince. Her betrothed.

He'd arrived here on his horse yesterday, and he'd scarcely said a word to her since.

She eyed him carefully as he ate another piece of meat. He had a tongue and teeth, same as her, so he should be able to talk. While she watched, she caught him smothering a yawn. He was as bored as she was!

"Do you want to see my horse?" Sativa asked Prince Reidar.

Reidar turned to Regina. "Mother, may I?"

"Kings do not ask permission, they command," came the reply through Regina's gritted teeth. She eyed Sativa with distaste.

Reidar drew himself up. "Mother, I am going with my betrothed to see the horses," he announced grandly.

Regina nodded once.

"Mother," Sativa began.

"You may go. A feasting hall is no place for children, and it grows late," Mother said. She peered fearfully at the hall's high windows, where the afternoon sun slanted in.

Sativa forced a smile. Her mother had been afraid of the dark for as long as she could remember. Not for herself, but for her children. Apparently Sativa's fairy godmother, Dalia, had told her that her daughters would be stolen from her by evil that swooped out of the darkness. Queen Dorota had lived in nightly dread ever since. "Yes, Mother," Sativa said.

Sativa led the way out of the hall, hearing Reidar's heavier footsteps behind her.

"His name is Philip, and he's really only a pony. Father says I may have a proper sized horse when I am bigger." Sativa glanced back over her shoulder. "As big as you, I think."

"When you are my queen, you will need a proper horse to ride. How else will you go hunting?" Reidar said.

"Queens don't hunt, Mother says. Killing is a job for men."

Reidar laughed. "My mother hunts as well as any man, or so my father says. So do many of the ladies at my father's court. They call it sport, pitting oneself against a noble beast, then bringing its carcass home for the victory feast. When you come to my castle, I will make sure you learn to hunt."

Forbidden pleasures and a new horse. Maybe her betrothal wasn't such a bad thing.

"What else do you have in your castle?" Sativa asked. "Will I get to wear beautiful gowns like my mother does?"

"Fit for a queen, I am sure. You shall choose them," Reidar said.

Betrothal sounded better and better.

Sativa led the way out to the fields beside the castle, but there wasn't a horse to be seen. "Where are they?" she asked in dismay. She found a guardsman at the castle gate. "Where are the horses?" she demanded.

"This time of day, the horses are all in their stable, having dinner, young mistress," the guardsman said.

Sativa wasn't supposed to enter the stables, but with her mother and everyone else at the feast, no one but she and Reidar would ever know. "We must speak of this to no one," she said imperiously as she led the way.

Two

His mother was wrong, Reidar decided as he followed the little princess. Sativa would make quite a queen one day, if her six-year-old self was any indication. As long as no one did anything to dampen her fire between now and their wedding, which would be at least a decade away. She had her mother's fair colouring, so she'd probably grow up to look like her. Regal and feminine and fiery — everything his kingdom needed in a queen, for if the border wars continued, she would need to rule while he kept the neighbouring armies at bay like his father was doing right now.

She might not hunt yet, but she at least rode. That was good, and she knew her way to the stables well enough. His sisters would not be so sure, leading the way around his father's castle, but the princess of a bigger, more prosperous kingdom like this one, living in a castle surrounded by such a huge town, would need to be more assured than the girls at his father's seaside castle back home.

"This is Philip," Sativa announced, waving at a fat pony that looked very much like a hairy barrel with legs. A hairy barrel that snorted, blowing his mane up off one baleful eye that stared disdainfully at Reidar for a moment before it disappeared beneath the descending mane. "He likes apples." She fetched an armload of fruit from the apple barrel, her shoes scuffing through the straw.

Then her face screwed up, and she sneezed. And sneezed again. Reidar counted seven in all before he began to grow concerned for her health.

By the time the sneezing fit had subsided, her eyes and nose were running and Sativa needed to hold onto a post to stay on her feet.

Reidar's heart sank. Perhaps his mother was right, after all. He'd need a strong queen, not a weak one, and Sativa's health mattered. She wouldn't just have to rule the kingdom in his absence – she'd have to give him an heir or two to ensure the succession, too.

"Are you well?" he asked.

She sniffled loudly and wiped her nose on the back of her hand. Then she seemed to remember herself, and she pulled out a handkerchief to clean herself up in a more ladylike fashion.

"It's the straw," she said thickly. "It makes me sneeze something awful. My father found a physician who had seen something like this before, in a son of some sultan of a desert land far to the south. He called it rose fever, because the prince sneezes at flowers. Me, I sneeze at straw. Not all straw. Just the stuff we have here, which the farmers insist on growing as pasture because it makes our fields the most fertile in the region. Pea straw, they call it. He said I should go to the desert, where it is dry, or by the sea, where it is too salty for such straw to grow."

Reidar couldn't help it. He laughed. "No wonder your parents wanted us to be betrothed. My father's castle is on a cliff overlooking the sea. The salt breeze blows day and night, so that all you can smell is the sea. When you are my queen, I shall build you a tower, and the topmost room shall be your bower, so that you will never need to sneeze at straw again."

"It sounds like heaven," Sativa admitted. "A place with no straw, where I can breathe. Do you truly mean it?"

Reidar pulled a ring off his smallest finger and held it out to Sativa. "Take this as a symbol of my unbreakable promise. I swear that one day, when I am old enough, I will return to save you from this place, and carry you off to my castle to be my queen."

Sativa smiled. "Just like a hero in one of my nurse's fairytales." She slipped the ring onto her finger, and for a moment, the amber caught the sunset light, glinting gold as the silver setting glowed around it. "I will wait for you, my prince," she promised.

Three

Regina found Reidar, as she always did. "So you already know, then," she greeted him.

Reidar traced his finger around the jewels on his father's crown. His crown now. "Yes, I know. Father is dead of his wounds from some skirmish in the border lands, and they are bringing his body home for a proper burial at sea, as befits the King of Viken."

"You will need to find a wife, and have heirs as soon as possible." Regina continued, as though he hadn't spoken.

Reidar rose. "I shall. Have someone summon Rudolf home. He shall be my heir until someone more suitable is born. And send an envoy to Kasmirus, to bring me my bride."

"Rudolf? The boy was sent south for good reason. His claim to the throne is second only to yours, my son. Some might say his claim is stronger, if only because his father was the eldest son. Best to keep him where he is, or he will steal your throne out from under you before your father's ashes are cold." Regina nodded in satisfaction.

But Reidar would not be dissuaded. "You see conspiracies where there are none, Mother. Rudolf will be sent for, because his father is dead, too, and he must swear fealty to me as his new king. If he refuses, then that is something I must deal with. All the more reason to marry."

Regina's eyes blazed. "There are fertile girls aplenty at court. I will see that they are dressed in their best tomorrow, so that you may make your selection."

Reidar shook his head. "A queen must do more than breed. She must rule, and bring alliances and armies when I need them most. You must go to Kasmirus, and bring back my bride."

Regina laughed. "I am too old to travel, my son. Better for me stay here. Besides, I had heard that King Boreslas lost his daughters to a dragon. Your bride is in the belly of the beast, if I am not mistaken."

"That's the tale they tell at the docks, now? Sailors selling stories of dragons eating maidens in foreign lands? Sounds like a fairytale to me, Mother. All the more reason to send an envoy to Boreslas. He owes me a bride, or an answer." He surveyed the sea from the tower windows. He could see to the horizon from up here, though not the land where Sativa lived. If she still lived. "I give you leave to prepare for my father's funeral, and for my coronation. When my bride arrives, you may also plan my wedding. My father trusted you to rule while he was at war, and it was fitting. But now I am king…and I shall do things my way."

All colour drained from Regina's face. Had she truly thought she could control Reidar as she had his father? More fool her.

Reidar ignored her, and summoned a servant. He gave orders for the court to assemble for sad news, for he knew they must be told of his father's death.

For the king was dead. Long live the king.

Four

Princess Sativa played with her amber ring as she waited for her father to notice she'd arrived. For years now, it had been too small to fit on her fingers, so she wore it on a thong around her neck.

Her heart went out to her grey-haired father, for now he looked like an old man.

Her father had aged a lot since the dragon came. First the loss of her mother, then the dragon plaguing the city, and then the final blow of losing her sisters in one fell swoop, just as the seeress had predicted, though Queen Dorota had not lived to see the dragon devour her daughters.

Sativa's sneezing had kept her indoors, away from the parade where her sisters had died that day. It was bittersweet, to know her affliction had saved her from a fiery death. If the dragon had only torched the fields of straw instead, perhaps she would have seen some bright spot in the animal's advent, but no. It stole sheep and maidens, and only burned knights who tried to slay it.

Or it had until last night, when everyone within a hundred miles had learned of the dragon's death. How it had happened, no one knew – not even those watching from the city walls, for there'd been so much fire and smoke no one had been sure the dragon was dead until a man walked through the gates, carrying a maiden, and announced that he'd killed the beast.

And now her father wanted to hold a feast

for the man? It was too much. They were still in mourning for her sisters. To host this sort of celebration when…

"Sativa, my dear! How go the preparations? Do you need a new gown to wear?" Her father was so cheerful it could only be a lie.

Yet she forced a smile that matched his. "The castle kitchens are cooking up the feast to end all feasts, they say, they are so happy the dragon is dead. But I thought, so soon after the loss of my sisters…something more sombre might suit…" She caught the look of horror on her father's face and lapsed into silence.

For a moment, she stared into eyes that mirrored hers. All the guilt and devastation at such a tragic loss, the wish that it had been her instead, and the complete and utter despair of having to live knowing the girls were gone, shone through his irises.

"Your sisters would have wanted a celebration. The biggest, grandest feast ever held in our halls to mark the death of that foul beast. They would want it to be remembered. It is the end of mourning, for today we celebrate a triumph over the devil himself!" Father said fiercely. "You and all the court will wear your brightest raiment. We will commemorate this day! A thousand years from now, they will still talk about how the dragon was slayed!"

Sativa hoped that sometime in the next thousand years, someone found out how the dragon had been slayed. So far, the only part of it they'd found was its head.

"Yes, Father," she said dully. She would do as he asked, because he was the king, and if he gave in to the despair she knew filled his heart, they would all be lost.

Five

"I find that hard to believe, Sir George. You've slayed monsters that were more troublesome than a dragon?" Father asked.

The dragonslayer – a shoemaker, Sativa had been horrified to discover, who her father persisted in addressing as though he was a knight – looked down at his food, abashed. It took him a moment before he managed to say, "Your Majesty, every monster is troublesome. Your dragon is certainly the biggest beast that

I've ever faced, but size is not all that matters. Some of them are so cunning, or there are so many of them, or they are so intent on killing you…why, it's a wonder I'm still alive. There was this pair of unicorns up near your western border…"

Sativa beckoned a server over to refill her cup. She half-listened to the shoemaker's story, which seemed to include pigs, giants and his paragon of a squire, who had saved his bacon more times than he could count. Every time he mentioned his squire, his gaze swept the hall, settling on a table at the back, where the squires sat. Most of them squabbled over the food, focussed only on stuffing their faces with more meat than most of them had seen in months, judging by their ravenous appetites, but there was one on the end, smaller than the rest, who sat aloof from the fighting.

The small squire turned to look at the dais where Sativa sat, and she found herself staring back in the most unladylike way. The squire was no squire at all, but a woman, wearing leather armour that had clearly been made to accommodate her breasts.

She had saved the shoemaker's life?

Surely not. Had she been the maiden the shoemaker carried off the field yesterday? She must have been hurt fighting the dragon, yet she showed no signs of any injury now.

Sativa shivered. Something about the girl's eyes, even across the hall, chilled her very soul.

She began to pay attention to the shoemaker's story in earnest now, eager for details on what this woman had done.

"Truly, I couldn't have killed the dragon without her," the shoemaker concluded.

Father laughed. "You are too modest, Sir George. But the time has come to make you more than that." He rose to his feet, more unsteady than usual. He'd drunk more wine to maintain the cheer he insisted upon for this event.

"My subjects!" the King shouted. "Lords, ladies, knights, men! We are here to celebrate a great victory. Sir George has defeated the dragon that oppressed us for so long." He raised his cup in a toast, then drank. "And he shall be rewarded!"

The crowd cheered and drank with him, but Sativa merely bowed her head. With all eyes on her father, no one would notice that her cup stayed on the table where it belonged.

"Kneel, Sir George!"

The shoemaker stumbled a little and Sativa prayed that he would not embarrass her father by sprawling at his feet. Someone must have heard her prayer, for the shoemaker managed to regain his balance and make his way to her father without any further mishaps.

Now Sativa drank as the shoemaker droned his way through his vows of fealty to her father. Someone must have coached him, she suspected, because he didn't stumble over the words as he presented her father with his sword.

Her father made him more than a knight — when the shoemaker rose, he was a lord.

This seemed to make him even more

nervous – it took him a couple of tries to get his sword back into his scabbard, so that when he succeeded, a cheer rose up from the hall for the newly minted lord.

Even Sativa managed a smile at this.

"And as a final reward for his heroism, I have decided to bestow my only remaining daughter, Princess Sativa, on him in marriage this very night. My personal confessor and priest will marry them in the castle chapel after the feast, and if I'm not mistaken, Lord George will have an heir on the way before the night is through!"

Sativa's smile died.

Six

Reidar sent his advisers away for the day, rubbing his temples. Wearing a crown was a heavier burden than he'd thought, even on the days when the gold circlet didn't sit on his head. Keeping the people of the borderlands safe while repelling invaders and dealing with a dozen attempts to steal his crown…and that was just this week.

He was sorely tempted to find some way to let the would-be usurpers wear the crown for a day, so that they might take on the cares that came with it. On the morrow, they could return to their normal lives with no desire to ever wear that treacherous circlet again.

But he couldn't, in conscience, do it. One man with too much power could wreak a lot of havoc in a day.

Or even one woman.

Reidar sighed. "Mother? I sent everyone away so that I might have some peace. Why are you still here?"

She stepped out of the shadows. The Queen Mother should not lurk so, but no one would have been brave enough to say such a thing to Regina. Not even her son.

"I have a matter of great importance to speak to you about. Alone," she said.

Reidar spread his hands wide in invitation. "Very well, Mother. Speak."

She glanced around. "Not here. There is something I must show you first." She beckoned imperiously, and stalked out of his solar.

Sighing, Reidar followed.

She led him to her own apartment. "Now, line up! Let him see you!" she ordered as she went in.

Reidar wanted to turn around and not follow her any more, but as the king, he could hardly admit to being afraid of what he might find in his mother's chambers. So he sighed again and stepped inside.

"Which one do you like best?" Mother demanded.

She'd lined up a bunch of children. Highborn, by the look of them, and all girls, though it was hard to tell at this age. They had no curves to them for they were all too young to be women yet.

"What for?" Reidar asked tiredly. "I don't need a cupbearer. If you want another lady-in-waiting, it would be better for you to make your own choice. I have no idea what to look for in a female companion."

That was a lie, but he managed to utter it with a straight face. He looked for the ship carrying Sativa every morning and every night, but there had been no sign of it yet. Still, he would ascend the tower again tonight, in the hope that he would see it.

"You like them pretty and young, yes? Well, pick which one you want!" Mother said impatiently. "You need an heir!"

The girls giggled at this, and some of them blushed. Maybe some of them were women, though just barely.

"I'm not marrying some girl scarcely out of the nursery so I can get her with child! Mother, I have a bride, who is on her way here now. Send these girls back to their mothers, where they belong. I will sire no bastards on the daughters of my sworn bannermen. There is no honour in such things. Better to hand the kingdom over to one of the usurpers across the border than fail in my duty as king. I promised to protect my people, not seduce their children!" Reidar glared at the girls, who quailed under his gaze. He softened his expression — it wasn't their fault they were here. They were good, obedient daughters who would one day make fine wives for other men of the court. "Girls, go home," he said.

He waited until they were gone before he rounded on his mother. This time, his voice was cold. "Mother, I am betrothed to Princess Sativa, and until I hear word from her father that she is dead, I shall keep my promise. But even were word to arrive at this very moment that she truly is in the belly of this dragon of which you speak, I still would not take a child to be my queen. We may have been children at our betrothal, but more than a dozen years have passed since then. I have no doubt she is a woman grown, and everything I could expect for my queen. She will not break her promise, and I will not dishonour her or myself in breaking mine." He stared at the doorway the girls had run through in their haste to escape. "Would you have my people think me a paedophile?"

She swelled indignantly. "I would have them think you are a king, seeing to his succession."

Reidar sighed. "As a queen yourself, I need not remind you that these things take time. Nine months, at least, and sometimes longer. How long was it after your marriage that you gave birth to me?" He met her angry gaze for a moment before he turned on his heel and left.

He didn't need to hear her answer. It had been seven years. Seven years of trying, and giving birth to his sisters and all the other children who had not survived long enough to leave their cradle, before he had come along.

If his people had to wait seven years for his heir, then so be it. They had a young, strong king. They would have Rudolf, a man with enough royal blood to stand in the heir's place until then. Now, if their neighbours would just stop attacking them for no good reason, Reidar might be able to get his people a little peace. For he knew he should have no peace from his mother until he was wed. And maybe not even then.

Seven

In the flurry of activity around the new Lord Shoemaker, Sativa slipped away before her welling tears fell. The crown princess could not cry before the court.

She barely made it to the corridor before tears blurred her vision, but there was no one to see her distress as she fled to her chamber. A chamber she had once shared with her sisters, but was now cold and empty.

No one had lit a fire in here, and horror

enveloped Sativa as she realised why. She was not meant to return here tonight – she was supposed to spend the night in her new husband's chamber. Crushed under the body of some shoemaker, as they consummated a marriage she did not want. Had not agreed to. Would never agree to, while she was betrothed to Prince Reidar of Viken.

Her fingers flew to the ring she wore on a thong about her throat, a solid reminder of the boy she had not seen since their betrothal. The prince would be a man grown now, strong enough to challenge the shoemaker for his rightful bride.

The thought of Reidar made her smile through her tears. He would ride up on his charger, wearing armour like the knights who'd come to fight the dragon. Only he would come to fight for her honour, and her love. He would make short work of the shoemaker, before lifting Sativa herself in his arms and carrying her off to his kingdom.

Her heart swelled at the thought. Yes, yes!

Reidar would save her.

Sativa darted to the table and seized a quill, then searched for a clean piece of parchment. She would write him a letter, telling him about the dragon and the shoemaker and Reidar would come…

Too late.

Because her father would have her marry the shoemaker tonight. Tonight, the lowborn boy would take her maidenhead and make her miserable. Would Reidar even want someone so tainted when he arrived weeks later? What if she was carrying the shoemaker's child?

Sativa shuddered. She would not give her body to a man who did not deserve it. Who did not love her. Better to be devoured by a dragon, like her sisters had been, than that.

As long as she stayed in the castle, she would not escape this marriage. Her father would force her to it, for he could not go back on his word.

But Sativa refused to go back on her word. She'd promised to wed Reidar, and she would.

She'd leave the castle tonight, and by the time her father realised she was missing, she would be far from his walls. There was no time for farewells, and who would listen, anyway? Her sisters were dead, and her father had given her away like some bauble. No, there was nothing for her here.

Down went the quill. Instead, she collected what coins she could find. Her sisters had no need for money now, and she had no idea what the price would be for passage to Reidar's kingdom, she told herself as she pawed through the chests containing her sisters' belongings. For if he could not come to her, she would go to him. With him, she would be safe.

She bundled together some spare clothes, then donned a cloak in the hope that it would hide her. Sativa paused for a moment to say a silent farewell to her sisters' spirits and the home she had known for all her life, before she turned her back on it forever.

Eight

Sativa had managed to saddle her mare, Salt, and fasten the saddlebags to the animal, when she heard approaching footsteps. Swearing silently, she slid into the stall with Salt, praying that the intruder would go away. She held her breath as she peered through the gaps in the stall wall.

Whoever it was did not respond to prayers, for they came into the stable. One of the squires, she thought at first, until the squire came into view.

Sativa almost swore again as she recognised the flaming hair of the woman the shoemaker had been staring at all night. The one who'd been so indispensable at slaying all those monsters. She would not let her lord's bride escape.

"Who's there?" the woman demanded, sliding her dagger from its sheath. "Show yourself!"

Sativa sidled deeper into the stall, hoping the woman wouldn't see her. She refused to be dragged back to the hall, to be a prize for the shoemaker. The straw shifted under her boots and Sativa nearly fell on her behind, but caught herself in time. Salt lifted her head from her dinner and snorted at Sativa, blowing fragments of straw everywhere.

Sativa gasped in horror, the worst thing she could possibly do.

The tickle started in her nose, building until it was unbearable, as if an angry bee had lodged up there and wanted out. Sativa couldn't stop it. She couldn't.

She sneezed.

Damned pea straw.

The door to the stall flew open, and the flame-haired woman stood in the breach, blocking Sativa's escape.

Sativa kept her head down, hoping the woman wouldn't recognise her, doing her best to keep the horse between them.

"Princess?"

Too late. The shoemaker's woman was an observant one.

"Why are you not at the feast, celebrating with everyone else?" she asked.

Because there was nothing to celebrate. Not any more. And this woman would not stop her. Sativa took a deep breath, fighting back another sneeze, and told the woman so.

Her dark eyes widened in surprise. And disbelief. For who could blame her? A princess's life must seem like paradise to a commoner.

Sativa continued, "I am not a prize to be

won. I will not be handed to that shoemaker in marriage like some pretty bauble." She wanted to say that she would challenge anyone who tried to stop her, but Sativa was no fighter. This woman walked like a cat on the hunt – the way swordsmen stalked each other in the practice yard. So Sativa closed her mouth and glared instead.

The woman didn't seem to notice. "George is no mere shoemaker," she said slowly. Then she gave the tiniest smile. "True, he was once a master shoemaker. But he is also a hero, a slayer of monsters and giants. He has saved maidens and whole towns from monsters. And he slayed a dragon at the very gates to your city. Your father has seen fit to make him a lord and give him lands to match. Any girl would be lucky to be allowed to marry such a man." Her voice swelled with pride as her smile beamed across the stable.

This woman wanted to be the lucky girl, Sativa realised. She wanted to marry the shoemaker, and from the way her eyes flashed, she considered Sativa her rival.

Could they come to some sort of arrangement? If the woman let Sativa go free, then she would be free to marry the man she wanted.

"I will not be a prize," Sativa said. When the woman didn't seem to understand what she meant, Sativa continued, "He does not love me. Though I sat beside him, he scarcely even looked at me. He had eyes for only one person in the feasting hall. You. The one he calls his squire, but you are more than that, aren't you? You are his lover."

Any normal woman would blush at such bluntness – Sativa even felt her own cheeks grow hot – but this woman looked like she wanted to laugh.

Instead, she glanced around, before lowering her voice to say, "I am not his lover. I am his partner, in that we slayed the dragon together. We have slayed many beasts together, but I think his hero days are done."

"Lover or not, his heart belongs to you,"

Sativa stressed. Would the woman force Sativa to lower herself to her level and make a bargain with a commoner? Sativa tried again. "You shall not stop me. I ride to the coast, and my betrothed. A man who loves me, or at least he did once."

For who could know what Reidar thought of her now? She had not seen him since their betrothal.

A smile flickered across the woman's face so fast Sativa thought she had imagined it. Then her expression turned serious as she looked the princess up and down with a practiced eye.

"Take only what you need with you," the woman said. "Food, water, weapons, and clothes that are suited for rough travel. Nothing that will mark you for what you are, because there are men on the roads who will take advantage of a lady. They will see you as even more of a prize."

Sativa drew in a deep breath, wanting to shout at the woman that she was no one's prize.

The woman finished, "You would be safer in your father's castle."

Sativa saw red. Safer married to a shoemaker? Forced to share his bed? "What would you know of it? A girl pretending to be a squire knows nothing of the cage that is a royal court."

This time, the woman laughed. A ladylike laugh, Sativa realised uneasily, just like her mother had taught her. And then she dropped the tiniest curtsey, as though she wore a gown and not a man's garb. The kind of curtsey a princess might offer her equal.

After a moment, the woman wiped her eyes. "Forgive me, Your Royal Highness, but I was raised in a royal court, a princess in all but name, alongside Queen Margareta's own children. And I could take my place at her side again tomorrow, if I wished. But I will not leave these walls without my armour, my weapons, and enough money and provisions for the journey, because I know there are monsters out there." She drew a dagger from its ankle sheath and held it out to Sativa. "Take it, Princess, for I promise you will have need of it."

Sativa swept aside her cape, revealing two sheathed daggers strapped to her girdle. "I am not a fool." Even if she now felt like one. How had she not noticed the woman's cultivated speech? And why would a woman so highborn want to marry a shoemaker?

The woman fumbled through her bag and pulled out a cloth bundle that she thrust at Sativa. "Then at least take these. Court dresses will be no use to you on your journey."

Sativa glanced down. She still wore her feast dress – how could she have been so stupid? She should have changed into something less showy. She should have bribed some other girl to wear her gown, to pretend to be her at the feast.

Here before her was another girl. But would she wear the gown?

Sativa took the clothing. "I thank you. But I must repay you, and I will need all the coin I have for my journey, as you say. Wait."

She worried that she was making a terrible mistake as she stripped off her silk dress and put on the other girl's clothes. They were made of cloth as fine as anything else Sativa wore, and hardly scratched at all. A blessing. But to dress as a man…Sativa had to force herself to leave the stall, stepping out into the strange woman's scrutiny.

"They are finer than they look," Sativa managed to say. She bundled up her gown and thrust it at the woman. "Here, consider this a gift."

"I have no need for silk," the woman replied, dismissing it as nothing more than an ill-fitting gown. She was a fine lady indeed in her homeland. "Oh, no. I cannot wear this."

Sativa was growing desperate. Every moment she delayed, she came closer to being caught. "Every priest in the city is so drunk they cannot tell the difference between one woman and another. Yet in an hour, my father will command one of them to conduct a wedding, marrying me to the shoemaker. If you wear this, they will think you are me. Marry the man, if that is your wish. By morning, it will be too late for anyone to do anything. I will be gone and you will be his wife." Sativa's eyes implored her. "Please."

"My lady? Are you here, or am I too late?" a male voice called.

The shoemaker.

Sativa's breath caught in her throat. He was looking for her. "He cannot catch me here. He will stop me!"

To her credit, the woman did not hesitate. She took the gown from Sativa's unresisting fingers, tucked it under her arm and winked at the princess. Then she marched out of the stables.

"Lord George," Sativa heard the woman say.

"Thank God," George said. "I thought you'd left. Melitta, I swear I didn't know about the princess. I must speak to the king, tell him I cannot…"

Sativa waited until their voices had died away before she turned to fasten her saddlebags and check that she'd saddled her horse correctly. She rarely had to do it without the help of a groom, but needs must. Finally, she summoned the courage to leave the stables, leading Salt.

There was no one in sight as she swung onto the mare's back, but movement caught her eye and she stilled.

A door swung open, and a lady stepped out. A lady in a shimmery silk gown, with embroidery that drank the light of the torches in the courtyard, glowing gold as if by magic. It was Sativa's gown, but it was Melitta's now.

A man bowed low before her. The shoemaker. "My lady," he said throatily.

Sativa's breath caught in her throat. No man had ever spoken to her with such emotion in his voice. If Reidar loved her half that much, she would be a fool to delay. She wished the shoemaker and his lady well, but she could not stay to see more.

Sativa spurred her horse into a trot, not daring to look back as she departed into the welcome darkness.

Nine

"Even if your girl hasn't been eaten by the dragon, the beast will take her from you all the same," Regina announced as she swept into Reidar's solar.

Reidar set down the report he'd been trying to read. "Explain yourself, Mother," he said, trying not to grit his teeth. He failed, naturally.

"Word has reached the city that he has increased the reward. Whoever slays the pesky dragon shall have half the kingdom and be named the highest lord in the land." Regina spread her hands wide. "Well, we all know what that means."

Reidar sighed. "No, I do not. Speak plainly."

Regina gave an exaggerated sigh, as if to demonstrate she'd been doing it for far longer than her son, and was far more skilled, too. "Half the kingdom is the usual dowry that comes with a princess's hand in marriage. If your girl lives, she's the other part of the prize."

"King Boreslas would not do something so dishonourable as to break the betrothal without offering me some sort of recompense. He would not offer my bride as a prize without consulting me." Reidar picked up his scroll and pretended to concentrate on it.

"Perhaps the letter has gotten lost. There are plenty of pirates on the sea between here and Kasmirus, my son. Six ships have not arrived in port, and there was no storm to delay them." Regina nodded in satisfaction, as though she was the siren who had lured these ships to their doom.

Reidar almost laughed at the image of his mother, sitting on a rock without her clothes, singing for ships full of common sailors.

"When our neighbours stop raiding our borders, and you stop wasting my time with tavern gossip, perhaps I shall have time to wipe out the pirates," Reidar snapped. "Perhaps you should take a ship out and fight the pirates yourself. I'm sure they would find you a formidable enemy." He didn't hide his fierce grin.

"You're as insolent as your father was," Regina snapped back.

Now Reidar truly did laugh. "It must be something that comes with kingship, for you've never told me that before. Now, leave me alone, Mother."

Regina marched out the door.

Insolent. Well, she'd called him worse. Only now did he let the rest of her words sink in, and Reidar began to worry.

Desperate times called for things no man

would normally do. Breaking a betrothal was a small thing, when your whole kingdom was beset by a dragon as dangerous as Boreslas' one was reputed to be. A king who would offer half his kingdom to the slayer of such a fearsome beast was a desperate man indeed. Perhaps Reidar should offer Boreslas some of his own best warriors to assist him. He had lost many men fighting the dragon, and it was the mark of a good ally to help when needed. Perhaps when the winter snows set in, and his marauding neighbours decided to stay home, he would venture across the water with a band of warriors. He could defeat the dragon and claim his bride, who would look on him as her hero, for he would have saved her father's kingdom.

He laughed softly at himself. Why, he'd grown quite sentimental for a moment there. Almost as though he was in love with Princess Sativa, the woman he hadn't seen since she was a child. Was she comely, now, with the kind of curves a man wanted? Would she still have her childish fire, refined to something more queenly? Would she have turned from rebellious daughter to obedient wife? Somehow, Reidar doubted it. Oh, she might be beautiful enough to put the sun and moon to shame, and she was born to be a queen, but if she was to rule here she would need every spark of stubbornness she'd possessed as a child, stoked up to a roaring blaze. The women of Viken were as fierce as their men, and Sativa would lead by example as their queen.

Or he would have to give in to his mother's increasingly strident demands that he marry a Viken girl. And in choosing one, he would offend the families of all the girls he'd overlooked.

Not for the first time, he prayed that his envoy would bring his bride safely to him soon. Unharmed, uneaten, unmarried.

Then he returned to the report in his hands, because as long as a monarch lives, his job never ends.

Ten

Sativa watched the sailors loading up the ship, wincing as the captain bawled orders, before she summoned the courage to address the man.

"I seek passage to the sea, and onward to Viken," she announced.

The captain grunted, then turned to face her.

Sativa was tempted to turn away from his scrutiny, but what was this man to cow her?

She stood firm and jingled her purse. "I can pay."

"We already have a passenger," he said. "What's your name, girl?"

Girl. Sativa longed to tell him who she was, but she wouldn't get far if she did. She glanced down at her borrowed clothes, then jerked her chin up. "Lady Melitta. I helped Lord George slay the dragon."

The captain's eyes widened. "If you don't mind sharing, mayhap we do have space. I'm Captain Ziemowit. You can call me Ziemo, my lady." He executed a stiff bow.

Praying that she wouldn't be called to slay anything, Sativa followed him aboard. At the back of the boat was a wooden cabin, not much larger than Salt's stall. Sativa had to duck her head to go inside.

"What is it, Captain?" a fretful female voice asked. "Will no one let me mourn in peace?"

"We have another passenger. An important lady. She avenged your husband, she did, and all those others the dragon took." Captain

Ziemo cast Sativa an adoring look. "I watched the battle from this very deck. While the menfolk fell, she stood firm and faced that dragon to its death."

So Sativa's suspicions were true. The squire had been the true hero. Sativa wished she'd thanked the woman, but it was too late now.

"Very well," the woman said, rolling over in her bunk to squint at Sativa. "I have no maid, so the other bunk is free. It is no less comfortable than mine, for I have tried them both. I am Lady Nekane, or I was, before the dragon killed my husband, Sir Hurik. If he had but waited a day..." She sighed heavily. "Now I must go to my sister, for I have no one and nothing else. He spent all our funds on new armour to protect him against the dragon, but it was not enough."

Sativa inclined her head to the widow. "I am sorry for your loss. No doubt, your husband waits for you in heaven now, at peace with all the other lost heroes."

"Yes, yes!" Lady Nekane said, then

dissolved into tears.

The captain shook his head and backed out of the cramped cabin. Sativa followed him.

She pulled out her purse. "How much do I owe you?"

Captain Ziemo waved away her coins. "Nothing, my lady. My ship is at your disposal. The least I can do for the dragonslayer. The honour of meeting you is enough. We have a full cargo, and she has paid for the cabin. If you do not mind the weeping. If you do, I could put her ashore and tell her to find passage on another ship."

Abandon a widow in such grief? Never. Sativa shook her head. "Fate has been cruel enough to her. Let her stay."

The captain bowed. "As you wish, my lady. I shall have your things brought aboard. Where are they?"

Sativa hefted the small sack she'd removed from her saddlebags. "This is all I have. I travel light, for I am going home." She prayed this would not be a lie. Reidar's castle would be her home. It had to be.

Eleven

By morning, Nekane's constant crying had nearly driven Sativa mad. Sativa wanted to scream at the woman that she'd lost all four of her sisters and almost been married off to a stranger because of the dragon. At least her late husband had chosen to fight the beast. But Sativa understood grief better than most, after losing so much more. Grief paid no heed to reason or sense, especially when it was so fresh. Why, Nekane had not been a widow for more than two days.

So Sativa spent most of her time on deck, staying out of the way of the crew as they occasionally adjusted the sails. There was less of this than she expected, for the current carried them seaward.

When the endless fields gave way to forest, Sativa wanted to cheer, because she wasn't sneezing any more. But it grew hot and still between the trees, with no breeze reaching the river, so the sailors rolled the sail up and tied it the beam at the top of the mast, and there they stayed.

Sativa approached the captain. "What are they doing?" she asked.

He shaded his eyes from the sun and looked up. "Catching the breeze, perhaps, or admiring the view. 'Tis cooler up there than on deck. I'd be up there myself, but someone must steer the ship."

There was a cool place on the ship? Sativa tugged her sweat-soaked tunic away from her skin for what felt like the dozenth time. She longed to be in the tower room she'd shared with her sisters, wearing little more than linen shifts in the heat. But there would be no such days again. Her sisters were dead, and she would never go back.

"They'll make space for you if you wish to join them, my lady," Captain Ziemo said, evidently mistaking the look of longing on her face. He cupped his hands to his mouth and shouted, "Move aside there. The lady is coming up!"

Sativa opened her mouth to protest. Surely it was too high and too dangerous. Her mother would have screamed aloud at the very thought. And her father…

No longer cared. He'd handed her over to the shoemaker.

Lady Melitta would do it, a sly thought whispered through her mind. It was true. Lady Melitta would be up the mast in no time. Why, the woman had defeated a dragon and who knew what else. The captain would think less of her if she did not.

Sativa swallowed and made her way to the mast. It was just a dead tree, she told herself. She'd climbed plenty of trees as a child, until her sisters had tried to copy her and Viola had broken her arm in a bad fall. Then her mother had banned them all from such things. Since her mother died, Sativa had never felt the need to disobey her. Until now.

Someone had cut notches into the mast, which made it a much easier climb. Sativa had to stretch for some of them, for they'd evidently been cut with a man's longer limbs in mind, but she managed until she grasped the sail. That's when she made the mistake of looking down.

Sativa swore.

The men around her laughed. "I didn't know ladies knew words like that," one of them said.

Sativa felt her face grow hot. If she were still alive, her mother would be ashamed of her.

"Don't look down, lady," a boy who could not be more than ten years old told her. "Hook your elbows over the yard and hang onto the shroud." He demonstrated, and so did the others.

They all looked like men being crucified, Sativa thought uneasily, as she dug her fingers into the folded sail. But crucifixion took days to kill a man, and they wouldn't be up here that long, she told herself.

And there was a breeze up there, she was pleased to find, as it caressed her face. She was level with the treetops, and she could see the forest stretching for miles on either side of her.

"Ooh, an eagle! Look!" The man pointed.

Sativa's eyes followed his finger. Sure enough, the enormous bird wheeled above the forest, too intent on its prey below to pay any attention to a ship sailing along the river. Or perhaps the regal bird simply did not care.

She envied the animal its graceful calm as it glided across the sky. She would never be so free. And yet, for the moment, she soared above the river, thanks to the ship that carried her to her destiny.

Twelve

Sativa spent most of her time atop the mast, where one of the men had nailed a little platform for her feet to rest on. She only descended when she had to – for mealtimes, and at night, when she ventured into the cabin she shared with Nekane so that she might sleep.

Nekane never noticed if she was there or not, and Sativa was hardly the person to comfort a grieving widow. If her plans came to pass, she would soon be happily married to a man she had no intention of losing to a dragon. If there were any such beasts left in the world. Sativa certainly hoped not.

Sativa was aloft when she heard the cry, "Captain! There's a ship in trouble ahead!"

The lookout on her left pointed.

Ahead of them, the river curved around a bend, and it appeared that a ship had taken that bend so fast, it had tipped over. Perhaps that was to be expected in such a strange boat, which looked very little like the broad-beamed river boat Sativa travelled on. The craft lay on its side, looking for all the world like a bowl a giant had sat on, squashing the usually flat base until it folded into a ridge at the bottom, and forcing the sides up like a sort of funnel. If it weren't for the pointy bits at either end, and the mast in the middle, Sativa would be hard pressed to recognise it as a boat at all.

It had ropes tied to it in several places, which stretched across the water and the shore, where dozens of people were trying to right the stricken vessel.

"We'll anchor here for the night," Captain Ziemo shouted, pointing. "Surely that little fishing village has a tavern, eh?"

The men cheered, and Sativa had never seen them work so fast. Even Sam, the cabin boy, seemed excited to be going ashore.

Sativa considered going with them. After all, when would she ever have another opportunity to visit a fishing village, or a tavern?

Almost as though the captain had read her mind, he turned to her. "Lady Melitta," he said gravely, "Would you be kind enough to watch over my vessel while we're gone? We will be under way in the morning, I promise you, as soon as the way is clear once more." He gestured at the stricken ship.

Sativa didn't know what to say. She wasn't sure if Melitta was familiar with ships, but after listening to the shoemaker's stories of her, there was little the woman could not do. Finally, she said, "I...I am not a particularly experienced mariner, Captain Ziemo. But if the ship should sink while you are gone, I will be certain to swim to shore, so that I might point to where your vessel lies."

Ziemo's eyes widened in surprise, before he let out a roar of laughter. "A good jest indeed, my lady. But my *Wydra* is sound as a drum. The only water in her bilges is the sweat of the men who work aboard her, I promise you."

"Men you promised some shore leave, Captain!" one of the men shouted as they lowered the boats over the side. Within moments, they'd climbed down the side of the ship and into the two boats, stranding Sativa on the ship with Nekane.

Rather than sit in the cabin with the endlessly weeping widow, Sativa climbed to her perch atop the mast and watched the men trying to save their ship.

It had run aground in the shallows, she saw now, and while the ship might look strange to her eyes, it did not appear to be damaged. She expected splintered planks or some part of it to be stove in, but instead it just lay there, like a toy boat some giant child had discarded, waiting for the boy to return for it so that he might make more mischief in the duck pond.

After plenty of pulling and shouting that achieved nothing, the men stretched out on the shore, opened a barrel of something, and started to drink. Someone lit a fire, and it soon had a stewpot suspended above it. Though she could not smell it, Sativa imaged the stew would smell delicious around about now.

She sighed. Their ship's cook had gone ashore with everyone else, so she would have to see to her own dinner for once. Descending to the deck, she helped herself to the ship's provisions. As she ate, she prayed that Reidar kept a good cook. More often than not, the meals aboard the ship were so bad, they had almost made her wish she was home in her father's hall. Almost, but not quite. So she choked down enough food to keep hunger at bay, and waited for the day when her ordeal would be over.

When the sun started to sink, one of the men on the other side of the river gave a shout. The others came to stand with him, staring at the grounded ship. Unable to hear what they were saying or see what captivated their attention, Sativa ascended the mast once more.

Waves lapped at the ship now, lifting it as all the assembled men had not managed to. Even as Sativa watched, it started to right itself. It was the tide coming in, she realised. She'd heard of such things, but never seen them until now.

She watched in fascination as the men worked with the tide to refloat their ship. Even she felt pride swell in her heart as the masts rose so high in the sky they were silhouetted against the rising moon. The ship was saved!

She felt the thump of booted feet on the deck below. The crew had returned early, perhaps to take advantage of the turning of the tide and the cleared channel. Best to stay aloft and out of their way as they readied the ship to sail, she decided. So Sativa watched the stars come out instead, some as faint as a whisper and others as bright as a trumpet blast in the sky. Movement caught her eye, and she watched in wonderment as a star shot across the sky like an arrow, then vanished.

What had her nurse said about such things? Were they a good omen, or bad? Sativa racked her brain until she found the answer. They were not omens at all, but wishes. The one who sees such a star must make a wish.

Quickly, she squeezed her eyes shut and wished with every spark in her soul that she would reach Reidar safely and soon.

"Please, oh please, leave me be!" a female voice begged.

Sativa glanced down at the deck. "Quiet, you," a rough male voice said, followed by the smack of skin against flesh.

Nekane cried out.

Sativa stiffened. What man would dare strike a lady? Not Captain Ziemo, certainly, or one of his crew. They were honourable men, or so she'd thought. She should do something. But what? She was no match for most of them, except maybe young Sam, the cabin boy. She might pretend to be Melitta, but Sativa was no warrior. She'd been taught to command men with her voice alone, for what more did a queen need?

She wet her lips, wondering what to say. What if the man was too drunk to listen, and turned on her instead?

It did not matter. No man should strike a lady.

"Leave her alone," Sativa said, or tried to. Her firm tone came out as more of a squeak.

"Who's there?" the man growled, lifting a lantern high. His other hand tightened around Nekane's arm, until the woman whimpered. "Show yourself, boy!"

Boy? Sativa seethed.

"What's the matter, Karl?" another voice asked.

Nekane's captor jerked his chin upward. "There's a boy atop the mast, Captain."

"Come down, boy, or we'll shoot you down!" the second voice boomed. It did not belong to Captain Ziemo.

Better to be obedient than dead, Sativa told herself as she descended. Her feet hadn't even touched the deck when a rough hand grabbed her arm and almost knocked her off her feet.

"What's your name, boy?" the hand's owner asked, bringing his hairy face so close to Sativa's that she could smell his breath. Not that she wanted to.

She coughed. "Sam," she said weakly.

"Want me to kill young Sam here, Captain?" Bad Breath asked. He shook Sativa until her teeth rattled.

The captain's hat cast a shadow over his face as his hulking shoulder loomed above Sativa. "Bring him along. We could do with a new cabin boy. Lost the last one, didn't we?"

The men laughed. Only now did Sativa realise there were more than three of them. There were at least a dozen – more than the crew of the *Wydra* – all carrying casks and chests from the ship's hold.

"You're pirates!" she cried, hating how her voice still squeaked with fear. No wonder they thought her a boy. "Stealing from Captain Ziemo – he won't stand for it!"

More laughter. "Your captain's drunk under a table, along with the rest of his crew. Strong brew they sell in the taverns hereabouts. Too strong for you. So what'll it be, boy? You can come with us or I'll cut your throat and throw you over the side. Plenty more boys who'd kill to be cabin boy on a pirate ship. More wealth than you'll ever see on a tub like this."

Pirates. So much for her wish for safety. Sativa swallowed. "I always wanted to be a pirate cabin boy," she whispered.

"Good choice. Now get them both to the boat, and see that they stay there." Someone gave Sativa a push, toward the side of the ship.

Peering over the gunwale, Sativa could just make out the boats lying in the *Wydra*'s shadow. Below her, a bulky shape swung away from the ship and landed in the boat. The man leaned forward and dropped a bundle on the bottom of the boat. The bundle yelped.

Nekane.

Sativa couldn't leave her alone with these pirates. Summoning what courage she had left, she swung her leg over the side and felt around for the rope ladder she knew had hung there in daylight. She'd never climbed down anything so frightening in her life. Slapping against the hull of the ship, splashed by waves, until hands grabbed her around the middle and hauled her aboard a boat. But not the boat that held Nekane – another one, full of chests that left her nowhere to sit but on top of one.

Sativa drew a deep, shaky breath. This would not end well.

Thirteen

Reidar paced the tower, unable to stay still. He could see several ships from the windows, but he knew none of them could be hers. Not yet. His envoy would have just arrived in Kasmirus, if he hadn't met with any delays. He probably hadn't even seen King Boreslas yet. So it was too much to hope that she might be aboard one of the vessels in view.

And yet...

Reidar sighed. He'd dreamed of her last

night. She'd had golden hair as a girl, the same colour as the straw that made her sneeze, so the beauty in his dreams had been blonde, too. She'd stood in the crow's nest atop the mast, her hair streaming behind her like a pennant in the breeze. As eager to glimpse him as he was to see her. Then she'd slid down that mast as lithely as any sailor, her curves hugging the wood like he wished they'd mould to him. And she'd run across the dock, her boots hammering on the timber as she flew toward him, her arms outspread like wings…

And then he'd woken up to realise that the hammering was not in his head, but outside, as some fisherman felt the need to mend his boat below Reidar's window.

By then, his dream bride was gone, for dreams were no more than moonbeams, and he was alone in his bed, longing for a lady he barely knew with no idea of what she even looked like now.

What would his men say, if they knew? They'd think him a fool, to be so besotted with a woman. A woman he hadn't seen in years.

Did she think of him at all, or had she forgotten him entirely? He wanted to believe she'd kept her promise, and the ring he'd given her, but his gift was likely lost among dozens of others from her many suitors, men who might be wooing her even now, while he was far away. Oh, they might be betrothed, but a woman's heart was far stronger than any childhood promise. Especially one she'd likely forgotten. If only he could stand before her and remind her.

Curse this war! Why couldn't his neighbours be content with their borders, and let him sit on his throne in peace for just a little while? A few summer raids were one thing, little more than fun and friendly rivalry between his men and theirs. But this…trying to claim his throne as their own, and his lands as well? These northerners had no idea who they were dealing with. They must think him some weak boy, easily set aside. If he was to join the war against him, they would soon learn he was as much a warrior as his father.

Reidar clapped his hands and laughed aloud. Were there anyone in earshot, they would think him mad, but he didn't care. He knew the cure for worrying about a woman. He would go to war, as his ancestors had. In the heat of battle, he'd have no cravings for a woman's warmth. Just a sword and a shield, waiting to sing a song of victory over his fallen foes. With an army at his back, of course. He might be a fool when it came to women, but not when it came to war.

Fourteen

The boat carrying Nekane arrived at the ship first – the very same vessel that had lain on its side for most of the day, if Sativa was not mistaken. It bobbed about in the waves as though it had taken no damage from its stranding, and now she was about to climb aboard it, Sativa certainly hoped it was as sound as Captain Ziemo's *Wydra*.

She glanced back, to see the *Wydra* still floating in its anchorage, though much higher in the water, thanks to the things the pirates had taken from her.

She'd heard that pirates sank ships, and killed all those aboard, after taking anything of value, of course. If they hadn't scuttled the *Wydra* and she and Nekane were still alive, perhaps these were not the sort of pirates she'd heard horrible tales about. Men of honour, maybe, who would take her to Reidar when she told them who she was.

"Take her to the captain's cabin," a voice said, carrying across the waves.

"No, no, please no…" Nekane pleaded as she was hoisted up onto the ship.

They were taking her to the best accommodations aboard, Sativa told herself. She would expect the same, once they knew she was a princess. Or even if she told them she was Lady Melitta.

"Up you go, boy," a man said, shoving her toward the ship.

Sativa stared up. This rope ladder stretched a lot higher than the one on the *Wydra*, but she would have to climb it, or be carried up like a sack of grain, as Nekane had. Judging by Nekane's protests, it wasn't a comfortable ride.

With one burly man above her on the ladder and another behind, at least she couldn't fall, Sativa told herself. Their weight kept the ladder from moving too much, too.

By the time Sativa hauled herself over the side of the ship and onto the deck, her arms were screaming a protest at having to work so hard. But none of the men complained, so she stayed silent.

Someone clapped her on the back so hard she nearly fell over.

Laughter erupted around her. "Boy's asleep on his feet. Wake up, boy. You'll get no rest until we get this cargo stowed."

Cargo? Oh, the things they'd stolen from the *Wydra*. Chests and casks she could not hope to lift. What had possessed her to tell them she'd be their cabin boy? Sativa should tell them the truth now.

"Captain's aboard!" The shout had all men

bowing their heads as the hulking shadow stepped over the gunwale and onto the deck.

"Where's the boy?" the shadow growled.

Sativa was shoved forward again. "Here, Captain Zydrunas," someone behind her said.

A lantern was thrust toward her face, so close she feared it might burn her. Sativa cringed away.

"You ever sailed before, boy?" Captain Zydrunas demanded.

"N-no," Sativa stammered. "This was my first time."

"Can you lift a cask?"

Sativa wanted to say no, but some darkness in his tone gave her pause. Instead, she knelt and tried to lift the nearest barrel. She managed to tip it a little toward her, before she overbalanced and went down with the cask on top of her.

The laughter was louder this time as the crew took their time rescuing her from the heavy barrel.

"Take him below decks, and show him

where he can sleep. Maybe he'll be more useful in the morning," Captain Zydrunas said.

Someone hustled Sativa down the steps below the deck, into a room that stretched from one side of the ship to the other. She had to duck her head to enter, and couldn't straighten once she was in, for the ceiling was too low. She bumped into something cold and hard, as high as her waist. Moonlight streamed through a gap in the wall, revealing the object to be a cannon, its mouth pointed through the hole. There was a whole row of cannons on each side, muzzles extended outward like gargoyles, or guard dogs ready to bite. Above them hung hammocks, stretched between the posts holding up the ceiling.

"That one's free, boy," a strange voice said. It sounded older than the others, and a whole lot friendlier. An arm extended from a hammock in the corner, pointing at the opposite corner. Sure enough, there was no sea chest below that one, like there were under the others.

"Thank you," she mumbled, picking her way carefully over the clutter of cannonballs, chests and other assorted things she never knew lurked below decks. It took her a few tries to get herself into the hammock, but when she finally managed it, she found the hanging bed surprisingly comfortable. Better than a straw pallet like the sailors on the *Wydra* slept on, too, for it didn't make her sneeze.

Sativa closed her eyes and settled herself for sleep.

"NOOOOOOOO!"

A piecing scream tore the air above her.

Sativa thrashed, floundered, and fell out of her hammock onto the floor. "What in heaven's name is that?" she cried.

But the building dread in her heart whispered an answer she didn't want to believe.

The old man in the corner piped up, "The captain's new bedwarmer, I expect. They all scream like that until he's broken them in. Sometimes, when he's done with her, he lets the crew have a woman for a while. You ever had a woman, boy?"

Nekane's screams seemed to reach inside Sativa and slice through her heart. Right above her, the captain was raping that poor widow. A lady. And when he was finished, he'd give her to the crew. So that they might do the same. Like she was some sort of whore.

Sativa shivered. Part of her wanted to try to save the woman, but she knew it was no use. She wasn't strong enough to lift a barrel, let alone fight the whole crew of a pirate ship. And if they found out she was a woman…then what? If she couldn't save Nekane, Sativa would be next.

No. If Sativa lay with another man before she married Reidar, even unwillingly, there would be no wedding. Bile rose in her throat at the thought of her own cowardice as Sativa huddled in her hammock, wishing the screaming would stop.

"A smart woman would take her own life before letting herself be taken aboard a pirate ship, eh, boy?" the old man cackled. "But most women aren't smart. Too soft to take a dagger to their breast. But their softness is the best bit."

The screaming continued long into the night, as Sativa cried silent tears, cursing her own stupidity for landing her in such a situation. Then her thoughts turned to Nekane, and what the other woman must be suffering, and Sativa got no sleep at all.

Fifteen

By morning, Sativa's horror-filled mind had only one goal: to be the best, most convincing cabin boy she could be until the ship approached shore…and then she would escape as fast as her feet could sprint. She soon learned that the old man who'd helped her the previous night was the ship's cook, and his culinary skills made the food she'd eaten on the *Wydra* seem like ambrosia.

After this journey was over, she swore, she'd

never take fruit or fresh-baked bread for granted again.

The best provisions the pirates had stolen from their victims belonged to the captain's table alone. Sativa thought of the horrible price Nekane had to pay to sup at that table, and shuddered. She could subsist on hardtack, dried fish and endless pickled cabbage for a little while, if it meant not having to share the captain's cabin.

After that first night, Nekane's screams had fallen silent, and Sativa hadn't heard her make a sound since. Not a sob, a complaint…nothing. The widow hadn't come out of the cabin, either, though she was certainly still there. In the absence of screaming, Sativa could hear the regular beat of the captain rutting in the bed above her hammock every night.

Some of the other men took this as a hint to pleasure themselves in their hammocks, a mentality that made Sativa feel even sicker. That one man could take pleasure in forcing an unwilling woman was one thing…but a whole crew who got excited at the mere idea of it? It was enough to keep her shuddering in her bunk for the rest of the voyage. Yet she could not stay below decks – as cabin boy, she had work to do.

Cook made her fetch and carry things up from the hold that he wanted. At first, it was just ordinary staples for the crew's meals, but then he started sending her down for the captain's special stores. Soon, she knew where everything was kept, and she began to plan. She set aside something each day – a skin of wine here, a dried sausage there – in a small cask behind the enormous tun of pickled cabbage.

As soon as they were within sight of shore, she'd wait until nightfall, load her supplies into a boat, and head for land. The one thing she hadn't found yet was coin – she'd need money to reach Reidar and she'd left all hers aboard the *Wydra*. Would it truly be stealing if she took coin from pirates who'd in all likelihood stolen hers when they took everything else?

Or perhaps she could call it fair payment. After all, cabin boys got paid, didn't they? She had no idea how much, but if she took more than she should, the pirates could come find her in Reidar's castle, and she would gladly pay her debt. Right after she saw Zydrunas punished for what he'd done to Nekane.

Nekane. She'd need to save her, if she could, too. Somehow smuggle her out of the captain's cabin and into the boat. Once they reached shore, if Nekane was too weak to travel, she would find someone willing to care for her until she could return. That would mean more coin, but Sativa didn't care. What Zydrunas owed Nekane was far more than money. No price was too high.

Sixteen

Another mug of ale, Reidar judged, and he'd have well and truly drowned out the pain in his arm. Today he'd met his first berserker, an experience he didn't want to repeat. The madman had run at him, screaming, then buried his axe so deep in Reidar's shield he'd cleaved the buckler in two, nearly breaking Reidar's arm in the process. Reidar's answering blow had sliced deep into the berserker's shoulder, at the base of his neck. The man had fallen to his knees, gurgling, before he died a noisy death at Reidar's feet. Reidar had only been dimly aware of it at the time, of course, because he'd had another foe to face, but now the battle was over, the man was once again on his mind.

The berserker had claimed to be the bastard son of either his father or his grandfather, Reidar wasn't sure, which he'd believed meant the throne Reidar occupied rightly belonged to him, and all of Viken's people would come to his way of thinking once Reidar was dead.

Except Reidar wasn't dead and the bastard's blood now fertilised the field, which didn't care whose son he was. Nor did Reidar care, not truly, for the man's claim died with him. What remained of his raiding party melted away across the border, either to join other armies or head home. Or to die of their injuries along the way, for his men had been particularly ruthless today. Perhaps it made a difference that instead of just fighting for their country, today they were also fighting for their king.

It was a heady thought. He'd fought alongside these men for weeks now, weeks he'd fought as fiercely as any of them, knowing that he fought for them as much as the land they stood upon, but this was the first time he'd understood what that meant.

They would die for him, just as he would fight for them. He was their king, and they were his men. He owned the hearts and souls and bodies of free, fighting men. Reidar only hoped that one day he would truly deserve the honour they did him. Until then, he would draw his sword alongside them, to defend what was theirs.

Now he understood how his father had died on a battlefield. It was the duty of a king to live and die for his people.

Reidar tipped up his cup, but it was empty. Sighing, he headed for the barrel to get some more ale.

"I must see the king!" an insistent voice shouted. A voice Reidar didn't recognise.

The man rode into their circle, reining his

horse in so close to the fire that its hooves kicked up sparks. He slid from his mount's back with practiced ease, then planted his feet before the fire like a man staking a claim.

Reidar edged closer, carrying his full cup. Most of the men present were deep in their cups, but they loosened swords and daggers in their sheaths, ready to take this new man down if their king commanded it.

"Where is the king?" the man demanded. "'Twas he who summoned me."

Reidar didn't remember summoning anyone. He squinted at the man. There was something familiar about him, but Reidar could not place him.

"Reidar!" the man cried, breaking into a smile. He strode across the trampled grass, heedless of the men who eyed him as he passed, and embraced Reidar. "Cousin, it is good to see you! Where is the king?"

Bursts of laughter exploded around the fire. Though Reidar still didn't recognise him, this could only be one man.

"Rudolf? I thought you'd sailed off the western edge of the world!"

Rudolf grinned even more widely. "One day, maybe I will. But those islands…I can see why our people love them so much. Their men fight just as fiercely, but so differently! We'll never conquer them as long as they live. And the women…my God, the women…"

"It's hardly fair to speak of women in a war camp where the only women are in our dreams," Reidar reproached him, forcing back the unbidden image of Sativa that had come to mind.

Rudolf clapped his hands together. "That's right! I'm not the only man who missed out on a marriage. I got summoned back here before I could ask for her, and yours got handed over as the price for a dragon's head."

"What?"

Rudolf waved his hand airily. "That foreign princess you were betrothed to. When I left Portnahaven, every man who could lift a sword was talking about the dragon of

Kasmirus, and how the king there had offered half his kingdom and one of his daughters as a bride to the man who could bring him the beast's head. Everyone thought I was leaving to do battle with the beast! They seemed quite disappointed when I said I was going home. Though after so long there, it feels like the Southern Isles are more a home to me than here. Has it always been this cold?"

Reidar's heart clenched in his chest at the thought of some other man marrying Sativa, but he banished that foolish notion. "Boreslas would not break off a betrothal with me without telling me so first. He has other daughters, I am sure. He would not break an agreement with the king of Viken. Even now, my envoy is at his court, to bring me my bride."

"King? So the rumours are true? Not just my father, but yours died, too?" Rudolf bowed his head. "I am sorry for your loss, cousin. Your father was a good king, and a wise one, too. Why else would he send me to the ends of the earth to learn warcraft from some foreign lord?" He laughed. "I can tell you tales of tactics their men use in battle that we would never think of. I would not have believed them, had I not seen it with my own eyes."

"Battle tactics? But Mother said – " Reidar clamped his mouth shut, but it was too late. Even he knew it was a sign of weakness for a king to rely so heavily on his mother.

"Is Aunt Regina still around? She will outlive us all, that battle axe will. I remember she caught me sitting on your father's throne once. She clouted me over the ear and gave me such a tongue lashing I couldn't open my mouth in her presence for a year. She said if she ever caught me sitting there again, she'd thrash my backside until I had nothing left to sit on!" Rudolf laughed as though it was all a joke to him.

It had been no joke to Regina, Reidar knew. For after Reidar himself, Rudolf had the best blood claim to the throne. Was Rudolf a danger to him?

Rudolf had been just a boy when he left, and now he was a man grown. A man Reidar did not know. But he needed to know him.

If Rudolf was loyal and no risk, Reidar could leave an army in his capable hands to harry the border raiders, and finally win this war. If he wanted the throne…giving him an army would be tantamount to handing him the country and Reidar's own head in the bargain.

"Tomorrow, we ride west, to where there are reports of a foreign force waiting to ambush us. In three days' time, we shall go into battle. Will you join us, cousin?" Reidar asked.

"The Southern Isles may have softened me, but beneath it beats a Viken heart still!" Rudolf declared. "I will fight at your side like we did as boys."

As boys, they had been closer than brothers. Reidar hoped that would still be the case, but it would be three days before he knew for sure.

"Ale for my cousin! We must toast his return!" Reidar said. A cup was fetched and filled, which Reidar then presented to Rudolf.

Rudolf took it, then managed to drop to one knee without spilling his ale. "Nay, a toast to my cousin, the new king of Viken. May his reign be long and filled with so many victories the bards forget to sing of anyone else!"

The other men shouted and joined Rudolf's toast, before proceeding to offer him food and a place at the fire.

Reidar hung back, observing all that passed. The only person in his thoughts was Rudolf, and whether he would prove to be his staunchest ally or his greatest enemy. Only time would tell.

Seventeen

Cook shoved a covered bowl into Sativa's hands. "Here. Take the captain his dinner."

Sativa almost dropped it in surprise. "The captain?"

Cook made an exasperated sound. "Yes, Captain Zydrunas, the man who commands this ship and crew. He doesn't come and fetch his food like the rest of the men — we must take it to him. And tonight, we means you. I'm far too busy to wait on him."

"Where do I take it?" Sativa asked. The captain was usually on deck, keeping his eye on everyone, but try as she might, Sativa could not remember ever seeing the man eat.

"His cabin, of course. Knock on the door, and if there is no answer, leave it outside the door. And be quick about it, for the captain prefers his food hot."

"Then if he does not answer, I should take it into his cabin, and leave it on the table," Sativa said thoughtfully. "For if he does not like his food cold, surely – "

"Do not enter the captain's cabin," Cook interrupted. "No matter what you hear, or what you think. Either he will open the door and take the food from you, or you leave it outside. You hear me?"

Sativa mumbled a resentful response. Even after weeks at sea, she still did not take orders gladly. Cook never seemed to care if she scowled, as long as she obeyed. The other men were not so happy about it, but the more she kept out of their way, the less they had to dislike.

So she carefully carried the bowl down the ladder, trying to ignore the rumbling of her belly as she inhaled the savoury smell of the captain's dinner. When she finally found her way ashore, she would spend the first week eating everything in sight, she was sure of it. She'd even settle for some of the stuff she'd eaten aboard the *Wydra*, for that was at least food, and not the swill Cook served to this crew.

But in the meantime, she made her way to the captain's cabin. This was where he kept Nekane. Perhaps she would answer the door and Sativa could tell her about her escape plan, so Nekane might be ready when the time came.

Cradling the bowl in her arms, Sativa knocked on the door, then waited. And waited.

Surely Nekane would come to the door. Where else could she be? Unless the captain had her pinned beneath him...Sativa swallowed. Last night she'd barely slept as the rhythmic pounding from the captain in this cabin above her hadn't stopped from dusk until dawn. Surely he couldn't be at it again now. Sativa might be a virgin, but even she knew men didn't last that long in bed. A man who could manage lovemaking for more than a few minutes was a miracle by most standards, and Captain Zydrunas did not seem the type to be blessed by angels. Sold his soul to the devil, more like.

She knocked again, louder this time. Perhaps the captain had not heard her over the noises he was making.

But she received no response this time, either.

Perhaps if she brought the man his dinner, he might leave Nekane alone for a little while, Sativa told herself. She could say she'd heard him tell her to enter.

She pushed against the door, but it didn't budge. She set her shoulder against it, and shoved harder. Still nothing. It wasn't until she looked down that she saw the bolt, fastening the door shut from the outside. Nekane couldn't answer the door because she couldn't get out, Sativa realised. No wonder she hadn't seen the other woman since they'd boarded the ship. She was a prisoner in the captain's cabin.

Sativa reached down to pull the bolt open.

"What in the devil's name are you doing, boy?" a voice roared.

Sativa jumped, barely managing to keep her grip on the bowl. "Bringing you your dinner, sir," she said, shrinking against the wall to put more space between her and the captain. In these close confines, he seemed bigger than ever.

He snatched the bowl out of her hands. "I'll take that. And you are never to enter my cabin, you understand? Never. It's forbidden."

"But what about the lady?" Sativa said before she could stop herself.

The captain's face loomed so close she could see the individual strands of his blue-black beard. "What about the lady, boy?" He spat the last word as though it was some sort of epithet.

Sativa swallowed. She had to say something. "Maybe she'd like a bit of company. It must be lonely in there by herself all day," she managed to say.

Captain Zydrunas snorted. "Never you mind about the lady, boy. She has all the company she'll ever need from me."

He unbolted the door, opened it just wide enough to let him through, and vanished into the cabin, slamming the door shut behind him.

Sativa craned her neck, straining to see, but there was nothing but darkness before the door closed the view off for good. But it also meant she was out of the captain's sight. She clenched her fists, swearing she would find a way off this ship. The captain could not always be near his cabin. One day, she'd find a way to sneak in and speak to Nekane. One day, they'd both be free.

Eighteen

Steel rang against steel as Reidar blocked another blow with his sword. And another, and another. Loath though he was to admit it, the slight man before him was too fast for him. His blows lacked Reidar's strength, or perhaps he was just holding back, hoping to tire Reidar enough to win. Reidar could not let that happen.

But not even a king is infallible, he realised as something stung his side. Reidar knew better than to look down to investigate the wound, for if it did not kill him, then the next blow would, if he did not block it. With a roared oath, he renewed his attack, praying his foe would fall before he did. The trickle of blood down his side told him time was of the essence now.

"Protect the king!" a voice bellowed.

Reidar lifted his shield to take the next blow, but the man's axe met steel instead. His eyes widened in surprise, meeting Reidar's gaze. So Reidar saw his eyes glaze over as the second sword withdrew from the man's throat, turning a live enemy into a dead one.

"Thank you," Reidar said shakily.

Rudolf lifted his bloody sword in salute. "Any time, my king." He turned away to fight another foe.

Hours or maybe minutes later, Reidar could not be sure, he called the end of the battle. There were few left alive from the raiding party, and his own men had wounds that needed tending.

The slice to his side had done little more than scrape the skin, Reidar was happy to discover, so once his wound was washed and bandaged, he had time to walk around their camp and speak to his men. Rudolf's steel helm had been so dented in the battle it took two men to pull it off his head, only to find his face covered in blood from a broken nose.

While one of the men cleaned up Rudolf's face, amid a lot of swearing from the patient, Reidar approached him. He dismissed the healer and tended Rudolf himself so that he might speak with the man privately.

"Why did you do that? Call the men to me during the battle?" Reidar asked.

Rudolf shrugged, then swore as the movement pained him. "Because it's a man's duty to protect his king. We're yours to command. There's no doubt in anyone's mind that you can fight as well as any man here, and none of us question your right to rule. But if you fall in battle, I'll have to sit on your seat, and Aunt Regina will never forgive me."

"What, you don't want a crown, cousin?" Reidar forced out a laugh to make the question sound more flippant than it was.

Rudolf smiled, or grimaced – it was hard to tell. "Right now, I want nothing on my head at all. My ears are still ringing from the blow to my helm. I would much rather a cup of ale than a crown."

Reidar wasn't sure if this was a jest or not. It certainly wasn't an answer. Nevertheless, he called for ale for his cousin.

Rudolf seized Reidar's arm and pulled him close so that no one might hear his words. "If you die without an heir, your crown falls to me anyway. We both know this. Go back to your castle, get yourself a bride, and put a boy in her belly. Several, if you can. Let me lead the army in your stead."

Reidar met Rudolf's blackened and bloodshot eyes. There was truth in them, he was sure of it. But something hidden, too. "To what end, cousin? You have a plan, I am sure of it."

"All men plan, but not all plans bear fruit. Rest assured, mine do not need you to die here on a battlefield like my father and yours. I want this kingdom secure as much as you do. These raiders and would-be usurpers must die!" Rudolf shook his fist in the direction the surviving raiders had retreated.

Something in Rudolf's voice urged Reidar to trust him. Maybe not completely, but for now. Reidar nodded slowly. "Very well. Will the men follow you?"

Rudolf laughed. "They did today. They're loyal men who serve their king. Why would they not?"

Reidar had to admit his cousin was right. And, if his count was correct, his envoy should have brought Sativa to Viken by now. At this very moment, she could be waiting for him in the very tower he'd built for her.

"Tonight we toast our victory, and tomorrow I shall return," Reidar said.

Rudolf winked. "Share a drink with your wife at your wedding feast, cousin, for I doubt this war will be over by then, and I wouldn't want you to delay on my account. We'll drink your health when we hear of it."

"I'll send a cask of ale from my cellars. The very best," Reidar promised. And he would. When he had Sativa safely in his arms, he would want the whole kingdom to celebrate.

Nineteen

Sativa hugged the mast as she did the one part of her job she actually liked – keeping watch. Captain Zydrunas' *Barbe* had a sort of man-sized bucket built at the top of the mast for the lookout, and Sativa would stay there all day, if she could.

It also meant she'd be the first to spot... "Land!" she cried, pointing. It looked like a just a shadow on the horizon, but it was growing larger, and she was sure...

"Check and see if the boy is right," Captain Zydrunas ordered.

Sativa's face grew hot. Last time she'd thought she'd spotted land, it had been a bank of storm clouds. They'd steered well away from them, but the waves had been big enough for her to realise why the lookout had what the crew called a crow's nest: when the ship canted from one side to the other, it was easy for a lookout to fall into the sea and be lost, like the last cabin boy. Sativa had hung on with all her strength and stayed aboard. But today, she was sure she was right. And if she was, it would soon be time to go.

One of the younger men, barely older than Sativa herself, scaled the mast and peered in the direction she'd pointed. "The boy's right!" he shouted.

She was nameless to them, and she'd resolved they'd remain nameless to her, too. Pirate scum such as these did not deserve to be remembered. The moment she arrived on land, she would do her best to forget everything about them.

"That's the coast of Viken. You can see the Sea Tower on the cliff!"

Sativa stared across the sea, hungry for a glimpse of it. Was this the tower Reidar had promised to build for her?

But no matter how long she looked, she couldn't see it. Perhaps when they got closer.

The captain gave orders to make for Viken, and Sativa was ready to dance for joy. Perhaps she wouldn't need to steal a boat at all. Instead, she could simply walk ashore once they docked and vanish into the town. Once she was in Reidar's kingdom, surely his people would help her find him.

By the time the sun sank beneath the western waves, they were no closer to the shadowy land Sativa couldn't wait to call home, and she sank into her hammock distinctly dissatisfied.

Morning brought a renewal of hope, as she started to discern the shapes of trees and then buildings upon the shore.

"Search for somewhere we can go ashore for water," the captain directed. "We're running low."

They weren't headed for a port after all, Sativa realised with a sinking heart. Then she would have to make a run for it when she found the opportunity. When they went ashore for water, perhaps, or at night, if no suitable stream was found.

All day they watched, sailing so close to shore Sativa could count the sheep and cows on the cliffs. Alas, the streams they did find were too hard to reach, and so they sailed on. More than once, she'd been tempted to dive from the bow and swim ashore, but she knew she would not succeed with everyone watching the shore so closely. So many men, bigger and stronger than she was, could surely swim faster, too, and they would haul her back to be punished.

She'd seen some of the punishments aboard the *Barbe* – men's backs whipped to jelly for drinking more than their share of ale, or stealing food from the captain's stores. If the captain knew how much she'd stashed away for her escape…Sativa shuddered. That was why she kept her supplies hidden, where no one could be certain who they belonged to.

Supplies she would need to retrieve tonight, before she left the ship forever.

When Cook sent her to the hold for dinner ingredients, she knew this would be her best chance to empty her cache. The dried sausages she stuck down her hose, where they'd be hidden under her tunic. She'd lost weight while working on the ship, so her tunic hung looser than it should. That would work in her favour tonight, though, for if she cinched her belt tight around her waist, she could tuck the wineskin down the front of her tunic and no one would be any the wiser. A small, cloth-wrapped cheese made up the rest of her supplies, which were already heavier than she was used to. Sativa was tempted to leave the wine, but unless she could replace it with coin, it might be the only thing of value she could trade when she got ashore. So, the wine stayed, curved against her belly as the leather warmed until it felt like part of her own skin.

She collected what Cook had asked for and lugged the lot up the ladder to the galley, where she could hear the captain roaring accusations at his crew.

He'd discovered the missing sausages, Sativa realised with a sinking heart. And he intended to keep haranguing them until the culprit came forward, when they'd all have to watch his punishment. Sativa muttered, "I shall be back. I think I dropped something," to Cook before she fled below decks.

Instinct told her to run and hide, but Sativa ignored it. She would run, yes, but not to somewhere aboard the *Barbe*. No, it was time to go, and now would be the best time to smuggle Nekane out of the captain's cabin, while he was busy.

Remembering the darkness last time, she took a lantern with her to the cabin. She set it on the floor as she worked the bolt open, then pushed open the door.

If the captain knew she was here…she didn't know what he would do. But by the time he found out, she and Nekane would be well away.

She stepped inside the room, holding her breath as she edged around the furnishings she could barely discern in the dim light filtering through the partially open door. "Nekane?" she whispered.

No answer.

What she really needed was the lantern that she'd left outside.

Swearing inwardly at her own stupidity, Sativa turned to retrieve it.

Just in time to see the door click shut, enveloping her in darkness.

Twenty

"Where is she? Spit it out, man!" Reidar said.

Sir Edwin ducked his head. "I cannot say, Your Majesty. Nor can King Boreslas, her father. I went to Kasmirus, as you commanded, and told him I was there to escort your bride home to you. For a week, he treated me as an honoured guest, holding feasts and hunting parties, while I waited for him to produce the girl. It wasn't he who told me, but some of his courtiers, that the girl was missing. She'd disappeared on the night of the huge celebration they held for the defeat of their dragon. The king sent men all over the kingdom, looking for her, but they've found nothing. She just disappeared." He looked like he wanted to continue, but closed his mouth.

Reidar was having none of it. "What are you not telling me, Edwin?"

Edwin seemed to struggle for a moment, before he relented. "There were tales, each more fantastical than the last. Some said they'd seen the princess marry the dragonslayer, some lord or other. But he's married to some lady from Queen Margareta's court, so that cannot be true. Others say her fairy godmother whisked her away, but no one has seen a fairy godmother in the city since the girl's christening. Some say she was kidnapped, but no one saw anything. The girl has lived all her life within the castle walls — sheltered, cared for, wanting for nothing. She had no reason to run away, and yet that is the excuse the king himself gave when he finally admitted she was gone. That or she was kidnapped."

The girl he'd known would not have run away from anything. Yet how could a girl be kidnapped from her own castle without anyone seeing it happen? "Someone must have seen something," Reidar growled. He leaped to his feet and prowled behind his seat, unable to sit still.

"Perhaps they did, Your Majesty, but you must understand…" Edwin coughed. "The whole city was drunk, sire. Celebrating. They had lived in terror of the dragon for years. It devoured all of the king's other daughters. Terrorised the countryside. And then a man brought the king the beast's head. Wine and ale ran like water that night. No one remembers what they did, let alone anyone else. They are not so different from us, truly. It was like one of our grandest victory feasts. The dragon could have come back to life and whisked away the princess, and no one would have noticed a thing!"

Reidar would like to think his men would

have lifted their swords to defend the girl, no matter how much ale they'd consumed. "Someone has seen her, and someone must know where she is," he said, slowing his pacing. "Offer a reward for information about her whereabouts. More if they can bring her here safely. Unharmed."

Edwin raised despairing eyes to meet Reidar's gaze. "Her father already has. He has heard nothing. He fears she may be dead, like her sisters."

No. Reidar would not believe it. His bride was alive, and she would be found. "Find her, Edwin," he said finally. "Take what ships you need, and scour the coast. Bring her to me alive, and I will shower you in riches. And if she is not..." He swallowed, not wanting to allow the thought into his head. "If she no longer lives, bring me what remains of her body. I will still reward you, but it will be with a heavy heart."

"And if I cannot? What if the girl's body lies in the depths of the sea, or in the belly of some beast? Or what if she does not wish to be found?"

Reidar sighed, suddenly tired. "Just find her, Edwin." What sort of madness had infected the man? Of course she wanted to be found.

Twenty-One

Sativa's breath caught in her throat. Perhaps someone had seen the door open, and simply pushed it shut. She would have heard if someone had come in, because if anyone found her…

Light burst upon her, an unshuttered lantern that to her dark-adjusted eyes appeared brighter than the sun.

"They say there is a hell made for the inquisitive, and they surely have a place for you, girl," a male voice said.

Sativa blinked away her blindness, then wished she hadn't. Captain Zydrunas stood before the closed door, holding her lantern high.

"The door was open, and I went to close it, but it smelled musty in here, so I thought I might tidy the place a little…" Sativa began, then trailed off. There was an unpleasant smell in the cabin. Not musty so much as rotten. Like decaying meat.

"What part of forbidden do you not understand?" the captain asked.

Sativa reddened. "I heard a woman call for help, sir, and my father told me an honourable man should help a lady in need."

The captain laughed. "You are a terrible liar, but it does not matter."

Sativa refused to back down. "I did hear a woman call for help." Not tonight, but before. Why was Nekane so silent now?

"You did not, but before this night is over, you will," the captain said, his teeth gleaming in the lamplight.

Sativa's thoughts raced. If she could get the captain away from the door, then perhaps she could get out, run up the ladder, and dive over the side into the water. She could swim to shore. She just had to make it to the water. And get the captain to move. "Then let her speak now."

Sativa hoped he would cross the room and reveal where he'd hidden Nekane. She must be gagged or unconscious, to be so silent. Sativa wouldn't be silent if there was even a slim chance of there being help at hand.

"You mean the lady from your ship? She will never speak again." The captain extended his arm and pointed.

Sativa glanced at the bunk. For a moment, she did not understand what she saw in the grey shadows. Then she realised what she saw was no shadow, lying upon the red coverlet, but a corpse. Naked and bloated, Nekane's skin had turned grey.

Sativa fought the bile rising up in her throat.

This was the source of the smell. She'd been dead for days. A week or more, surely. A week in which the captain had…had…

The bile won.

Twenty-Two

"Your mother still hates me," Rudolf announced as he strode into Reidar's solar.

Reidar set down his quill. "What are you doing here? Isn't there a war you're supposed to be fighting?"

Rudolf shrugged, then stretched out on the bench beneath the window, sitting in the only patch of sun. The cat whose seat he'd usurped hissed at him, then trotted off.

"It seems word has spread among your

neighbours that your throne is not worth the price they will pay to get it. That, or they are running out of men to send against us. The last two war bands we encountered took to their heels and ran away. Like rabbits!" He laughed.

"That still doesn't answer my question. Why are you here?"

"Your men can chase rabbits for a few days without me. I came to find out why you didn't send the ale you promised. Did the wedding guests drink it all, or did you just forget about us?" Rudolf sat up and peered into the corners of the room. "And where is your lovely bride? Or has she locked herself in her room, terrified after spending her wedding night with your mighty cock?"

Bawdy jokes about Sativa sat ill with Reidar. "She has not yet arrived."

Rudolf only laughed harder. "So she's heard tales about your cock and fled in fear before you can stick it in her?"

Reidar reddened. "I do not know what she's heard. I haven't seen her since she was a child.

Do not jest about my bride, cousin. I warn you." Doubt gnawed at him for the first time. Crudity aside, had she heard something about him that would make her not want the marriage any more? Not want him?

"Consider me warned. You used to like jokes, Reidar. Has kingship turned you so serious that you can no longer laugh?" Concern wrinkled Rudolf's brow, all traces of humour gone.

"Not about Sativa, no. She has disappeared from her father's court, and no one has seen her since. He's sent search parties. I've sent search parties. I've even offered a reward for her safe return. She has simply vanished, as though some foul sorcery is at work betwixt her kingdom and mine." Reidar released a weighty sigh. "And while I worry for her wellbeing, my mother reminds me hourly that I need an heir. I think she has paraded every highborn girl in the kingdom before me, and quite a few not so highborn, too. More than anything, she wants me to wed. The longer

Sativa is missing, the more I begin to think she might be right. Maybe I need an heir more than an alliance with Boreslas."

"Kings break betrothals every day, and alliances, too. What is so special about this girl that you cannot?"

Reidar eyed his cousin. Would the man think him weak if he confessed the truth? No one else knew. Time to test his cousin's loyalty. "In truth, I do not know. I made promises as a child, and so did she. I am loath to break my word, for what honour is there in that? I might not have seen her in years, but I have dreamed of her more nights than I can count. Not the child I knew then, but as though I watched her. She learned to ride like she was born to the saddle, and hunted with her father's court before she could lift a bow. She never made a kill, but she loved the chase. She would teach her sisters, teaching them to write so they might manage kingdoms of their own, when they were queens in their own right. And lately, I have dreamed of her flying through the air at a great height. Ships below her, or sometimes the sea. She's not an angel, but…it's like nothing I can explain. I know she lives, and she is coming to me. For weeks I have known this, and still she is not here!"

Rudolf nodded slowly. "There is some magic at work, then. A bond between you that perhaps only death can break. Tell me, what does this girl of yours look like?"

"As fair as the sun," Reidar replied. "No matter how many other girls my mother places before me, the only face I see is hers. A face I do not know!"

"You have it bad, cousin. I hope she is worth the wait. And, in a similar vein, I have a confession to make, too."

Reidar raised an eyebrow. "Oh?"

Rudolf's smile was rueful. "Will you ever release me to return to the Southern Isles?"

"You don't want to be king?" Reidar blurted out.

Rudolf laughed softly. "I never said that. I asked if you would let me go home."

Reidar wasn't sure what to say. "But you are my heir. Until I have a son, that is. And there is this war…"

"The war will never be over, but your neighbours will learn, and so will your own men. There are leaders among them, and they are loyal to you. There will come a time when you don't need me. You will choose a bride – whether your betrothed or some other girl – and there will be children to take your place. When that time comes, I ask you to let me return home."

There was no laughter in Rudolf's eyes now. Only pain.

"Why?" Reidar asked hoarsely.

"Like you, I dream of a girl. A woman, now. I made promises, which I intend to keep." Rudolf smiled sadly. "Oh, not like you. There is no betrothal between us. But yours is not the only war – and other kings have seen the richness of the Southern Isles, wishing to conquer them for their own. There are many lords of the islands, and some call themselves kings, but they recognise one man as their leader, and he has no sons. Only daughters."

Now Reidar understood. "You want to be king of the Southern Isles, and take one of the daughters for your queen." A king in his own right. "But the Southern Isles still belong to Viken."

"Not for long, if the other kings have their way. I mean to take a small force and together with the men of the isles, claim them for my own. I will still bend the knee to you, of course, but without someone to lead them, the isles will fall." Rudolf clenched his hands into fists. "I will not let that happen."

"What is there about these isles that inspires such passion?" Reidar asked.

Rudolf coughed. "My passion is not for the isles, but for the lady. The isles are her birthright."

Winning lands a world away for the love of a woman. Well. Reidar had never expected this.

"When my wife gives birth to a son, you are

free to return," Reidar said. "I'm sure you will find men here willing to flock to your cause, if only for the adventure of a trip to the Southern Isles. But do not take too many, for I will not lose the war here so you can have your woman!"

Rudolf bowed low. "As Your Majesty commands."

"Is she fair, this lady?" Reidar asked, unable to resist.

"Her skin is fair, but her hair reminds me of a bonfire blaze. Portia is like no lady I have ever met." It was Rudolf's turn to sigh, as his eyes turned to the south-west.

Reidar laughed. "What a pair we are, mooning after girls who are not yet our wives. But, God willing, they will be. What will we do while we wait for the time to be right?"

Rudolf shrugged. "What men always do, I suppose. Make war. Make merry. Make our mothers despair of us ever growing up."

Reidar clapped his cousin on the back. "Sounds like a fine plan. I have another. We have not celebrated your return yet, and Mother is always pestering me to hold another feast. She wants only to parade more maidens before me, of course, but what of it? It is many months since I have gone hunting, and the boars are fat this time of year. Let's put together a hunting party on the morrow, and on our return, there shall be a welcome feast in your honour."

"I have not tasted Viken boar since I left your shores, and the pigs in the Southern Isles cannot compare. Let us forget women and the worries of your kingdom for a few days, and enjoy the hunt!" Rudolf grinned. "Thank you, cousin. It is good to be back."

It was good to have him back, Reidar thought. Now all he needed was Sativa, and he could be happy.

Twenty-Three

Sativa wiped her mouth with the back of her hand. Her mother would despair if she knew, but Sativa had no handkerchief here.

"Why?" she whispered.

Captain Zydrunas shrugged. "Like most women, she was too noisy for her own good. Inquisitive. Complaining. And tears…ugh." He shuddered.

An arrow of remorse shot through Sativa's heart. She had disliked Nekane's constant tears and mourning, too, but she'd never wanted to kill her. She was a widow, and widows were allowed to weep.

"You are a monster," Sativa said. It was a calm statement of fact.

Why wouldn't he move away from the door? she raged inwardly.

"All men are monsters in their own way," he said loftily. He nodded at Nekane, and there was considerable pride in his voice as he added, "She said I was like a dragon."

"It was no compliment," Sativa shot back. "Dragons are mindless beasts, who don't know the difference between a sheep and a woman in wool. They burn and devour because they don't know any better. Men are more than that."

At least, the men in her father's court had been. Those aboard the *Wydra*. And Reidar.

"I would take a dragon over you any day," she added, more to bait him than anything else.

It worked. He moved away from the door, but only to approach her. "But you will take me, girl. She could not stop me, and nor will you."

He would kill her, and defile her dead body. Horror made her jaw drop, but some other instinct told her to draw her dagger. She did.

Zydrunas set the lantern on the table, and drew his own knife. Easily thrice as long as hers, the steel blade seemed to drink the light instead of reflecting it. He thrust across the table, and Sativa barely managed to dodge the wicked point. Her arm seemed to have a life of its own, driving down to slice his hand.

Zydrunas swore. "Little bitch. I was going to cut your throat, nice and easy, but you'll have no quick death from me now. You shall suffer."

Faster than Sativa believed possible, he whipped his blade to the side, slashing it across her belly. Warm liquid gushed out, soaking her tunic, but the wound came with no pain. Sativa pressed her hands to her belly, and they came away red. She turned horrified eyes on the captain as she backed away.

He made no move to follow her now. He knew as well as she did that she was as good as dead.

Instead, he crossed to the bed. He lifted Nekane's corpse in his arms, and she flopped like some obscene rag doll as he carried her over to the bench Sativa recognised as a privy. He kicked open the lid and forced the body in, feet first. He managed to get her halfway in, before she stuck, her torso sticking out of the privy like a giant glove puppet.

"She can watch you die, then," he said, forcing the corpse's eyes open. Gore dribbled down Nekane's bloated face — there was nothing recognisable about her eyes any more. The widow was with her husband, now.

Doubled over in the corner, one arm pressed to her belly, Sativa still pointed the knife at him, but for how long, she wasn't sure. "You deserve to die," she hissed.

He laughed. "Not today. Today, I get a new bride in my bed." He crossed to the door and yanked it open. "I will return when you are finished fighting, but still warm." And out he went, closing the door behind him. He drove the bolt home, a final nail in Sativa's coffin.

She collapsed on the floor, spent. What was there left to fight for, now? Not even she could fight death.

Twenty-Four

"There is a particularly fine beast I've seen in the southern woods, sire," one of the woodsmen said. "Powerful fierce, like he's possessed by some devilish spirit. We stay in the northern parts while he's about."

Reidar nodded. They couldn't have brought him better news. "Just the sort of challenge I'd like," he said, tossing a purse of coin at the man's feet. "Stay out of the forest for a few days, while we hunt. You will know when the beast is caught, for there will be a feast at the castle."

Both men bowed. "Thank you, sire. We will."

Reidar had given them enough money to feed two families for a week, or perhaps a little more. Surely that would be long enough. A week free of the cares of his kingdom, or worry for Sativa. Bliss, surely.

He called to his men, and the spearbearers, to follow him into the forest.

A quick fight, a bit of spilled blood, and victory to follow. Truly the sport of kings.

He kicked his horse into a gallop, and set off between the trees.

Twenty-Five

He'd left the lantern to taunt her, Sativa was sure of it. There was not even a window to look or squeeze out of – no exit but the bolted door. Her only escape was death, like poor Nekane.

Who was still stuck in the privy, poor woman.

Sativa's hands were sticky and red, and her tunic and hose were soaked. She hadn't known a body could lose this much blood and still live. And yet…still she felt no pain.

Did that mean she was near the end? The end where the devil of a captain would do things to her corpse?

Never.

There had to be a way out.

She glanced at Nekane. Perhaps the dead widow did hold the answer.

As Sativa approached her, the stench grew, until she had to haul her tunic over her nose to bear it. This was the smell of death, though, and not the privy beneath her. And if it was anything like the privy aboard the *Wydra*, it let out into the water.

Sativa swallowed, took hold of the corpse's shoulders, and shoved. No, the body was stuck. She studied it for a moment, then realised why. Gingerly, she pried the woman's arms out of the hole and lifted them. The body slid so fast it almost took her with it, but Sativa grabbed onto the lip of the privy in time to save herself.

Save herself from what? A watery death was

better than what waited for her here.

Something tumbled from her tunic, and she instinctively reached to catch it before it fell. Too late, she realised she could be grasping for her own innards, and drew her hand back.

To her surprise, a slashed wineskin dropped into the privy, landing in the darkness with a splash.

A slashed…but the wineskin had been full. Sativa fumbled at her soaked tunic, trying to undo her belt to see the skin underneath, and the wound that should be there. The one that would kill her. The wound that…

…wasn't there.

The stupid captain had stabbed the wineskin instead. But he'd soon be back, to do horrible things to her still-warm corpse. More than ever, she needed to get out.

She eyed the privy. It was the only way.

Sativa perched on the edge, uttering a prayer that she might reach shore safely. And not get stuck.

She took a deep breath, and let go.

Twenty-Six

The day ended without anyone sighting the boar, but Reidar was content. There'd been signs of the beast, and they were certainly in its territory now.

He shared a cup of ale with Rudolf by the fire as servants pitched his pavilion and prepared their meal.

"You should have seen your face. You were so certain you'd found the beast in the bushes, and that it would be your kill, when all the rest of us said we were too far north. Standing there like some ancient colossus…and out popped…a squirrel!" Reidar roared with laughter.

Rudolf didn't seem to find it as funny, though he did laugh. "You always were the better hunter. I left before I was old enough to join your father's hunting parties. It sounded big enough to be a boar!"

"Rudolph the great squirrel slayer!" Reidar howled. He laughed until his belly ached. He had not felt this free in years.

"Tomorrow will be better," Rudolf said. "You may take the beast, and when you miss, then I'll take my shot."

Reidar spat out his ale. "I do not miss!"

Rudolf smiled. "We shall see, cousin. We shall see."

The evening was a merry one, with plenty of ale and even a little singing around the fire, until someone reminded them all that singing would only drive the beast away, not bring it within range of their spears. They quietened after that.

When they retired for the night, Reidar felt an inexplicable chill. No one else seemed to notice, so he merely called for some extra furs and told himself that would be an end to it.

The cold seemed to have settled in his bones, and it took some time to dispel, but eventually he forgot he was in the forest and may as well have been in his chamber at home, he was so warm.

Rudolf was right. Tomorrow would be better. A sense of wellbeing washed over him, like he'd been engulfed by one of the waves he could hear crashing on the not-too-distant shore, and he drifted off into a dream where Sativa sat at his side instead of his cousin, and after they shared a cup of ale, they shared a kiss. The kiss lasted until he carried her to his bedroll and their night together was bliss. Oh, what a dream.

If only it were true.

Twenty-Seven

Sativa gasped as the freezing water engulfed her, her last breath before the sea closed over her head. She kicked off the side of the ship, heading for the wavering light at what she thought was the surface. She burst into cold air and wished she hadn't, as the breeze turned out to be colder than the water.

Dusk had fallen, but there was enough light to see the darkness that was the shore. Praying that no one aboard the ship saw her, she set out for land.

Her hose and boots drank seawater like a drowning man, weighing her down. Determined not to drown when she was so close to her destination, Sativa stripped off the offending items. Only modesty made her keep her tunic. That and the camouflage it offered her pale skin as the moon rose.

An eternity passed, as she stroked for shore. Kicking, pulling with her arms, taking breath after breath and spitting out salt water as the waves taunted her, but the beach drew ever closer.

Then a wave picked her up and her arms windmilled wildly as she tried to paddle out of it, but to no avail. The wave broke, plunging her beneath the water until she grazed the sandy seabed. Gasping, Sativa kicked off the bottom, only to find that her head broke the surface before her feet had left the seafloor. She staggered ashore, barely believing she'd made it. She wanted to lie on the sand and sleep for a week, but she couldn't. Not while she was still so close to the ship. Still visible to them, perhaps.

Her legs felt like they carried their own ballast, they were so heavy, as she dragged herself up the beach and into the trees. A breath of wind was enough to send her teeth chattering as her bones turned to solid ice. Still she trudged on. There would be no wind once she was deep enough into the forest.

A few steps in, then a few more. Soon, she could no longer see the beach, but she could hear the waves. Still she walked. She would continue until she couldn't any more, and then she would lie down and sleep.

Moonlight was dim between the trees, so she stumbled often, but Sativa refused to stop. It looked like it was growing lighter ahead. Light could only mean people, and civilisation. Someone who could help her.

A large fire sat in the clearing, sending up a prayer of smoke into the sky. Sativa thanked whoever had lit it, and approached as close as she dared, holding out her hands to warm them. She had nothing left to trade but the small cheese, wrapped in its now salt-stained cloth, but she would offer it gladly if it meant getting warm and dry again.

"You kept me waiting," a grumpy voice greeted her. Oh, the voice was old and scratchy, too, but the elderly woman wanted her irritation known.

"Please forgive me," Sativa said politely. She had heard that old women who lived too long sometimes lost their wits, and she had been taught to be polite to her elders.

A hunched figure stepped out of the shadows and straightened. "Your father taught you well, Princess."

Sativa squinted at the woman. "Do I know you?"

The woman cackled, then coughed. "Perhaps, perhaps not. I am too old to be your fairy godmother, in truth, but as my daughter is still learning to take my place, I wanted to see you one last time. I am Dalia."

Though the hem of her tunic was too short

to do it properly, Sativa attempted a respectful curtsey. "I am honoured, Godmother Dalia."

"Come, girl. My visions said you would be hungry, and in need of a fire's warmth. You are not out of the woods yet."

Sativa did as her godmother bade her. For the first time in she couldn't remember how long, she ate her fill, and the food was good. But the wine was too strong, and she began to wish that she had not drunk so much of it, for her eyes started to close of their own accord.

Sativa blinked back drowsiness, wanting to ask the question that burned in her mind before she surrendered to sleep. "Godmother Dalia, thank you for your hospitality. I am grateful but…I must know one thing."

Dalia grinned, her eyes seeming to glow in the firelight. "Yes?"

Sativa fought to find the words that wouldn't make her question sound like an accusation. "Why are you here now? Why not earlier, when I was kidnapped by pirates, or locked in that room, or earlier still, when my father tried to marry me to a shoemaker?"

Dalia nodded. "Do you know what my powers are?"

"You are a seer," Sativa said. "I do not know what else."

"I sometimes see the future, yes, as I foresaw your sisters would die because of a creature that came out of the darkness, as a different darkness would swallow you, too, in time. I have a talent for curses, or I did. It's been many years since I cast one."

"So you saw the pirates, and the shoemaker, and everything else?" Sativa asked impatiently.

Dalia nodded once more. "I saw the pirates, and much of your flight from your father's court. Yes. The shoemaker…ah, young George's fate has little to do with yours. He was always destined for Melitta. He's my daughter's godson, you know."

Sativa's head hurt. There was so much she didn't understand. "But why are you here?"

Dalia blinked. "Because you need me, of course! If I weren't here, you'd freeze your little titties off in the forest and never find your way to that handsome king of yours."

King? "Reidar is a prince, not a king."

"When his father died, your Prince Reidar became king. He's eager for a queen, though, so you mustn't delay. Tonight, you may rest, but in the morning, you must find him."

Sativa couldn't seem to stay upright any more. Too tired. Her head rested on the ground and it was too comfortable to resist. "Will you show me the way?" she mumbled.

"No, dear, I'm too old to be traipsing around the forest. My friend will show you the way. As long as you follow her, you won't get lost."

"Oh, good," Sativa tried to say but she wasn't sure if she managed to get the words out before she fell asleep.

Twenty-Eight

A shaft of sunlight tickled Sativa's eyelids as it passed. She pulled her blankets more closely about her, wondering why her chamber was so cold. The fire must have gone out in the night, or someone had left the shutters open. Probably her sister Stella, who liked to look up at the stars.

No, Stella was dead, devoured by a dragon, like the rest of her sisters. And Sativa could not be in her chambers, for she slept aboard a pirate ship, pretending to be a boy until the ship came close enough to shore to swim to safety.

Ugh. Swimming. Fighting the waves until they grew tired of her feeble flailing and flung her on the shore.

Now she remembered the night that had been. Or had it been a dream? Nekane, the crazy captain, and her future-seeing fairy godmother?

Sativa blinked her eyes open.

Last night's great bonfire had burned down to coals, and her one thin blanket did little to keep out the early morning chill.

"Mrow?"

Sativa stared in surprise at the source of the sound. A cat the colour of smoke sat beside the fire, licking at a package Sativa recognised – the cheese she'd stolen from the *Barbe*. The only food she had.

Sativa scrambled to her feet and attempted to shoo the animal away, but it only turned to hiss at her before returning to what was left of its meal. Precious little, she found, when she ventured close enough to see. No point in wasting her time for a bite or two of drowned cheese.

When the cat was finished eating, it sat to wash its fluffy fur, taking its time in a grooming ritual that could have satisfied a palace lap-cat, instead of this forest-born beast. When the beast's bath was done, it crossed the clearing and stopped to look back at Sativa. "Mrow?"

She shook her head at the expectant beast. "No. Dalia said to wait here for her friend, who would guide me."

"Mrow." Was it possible for a cat to look exasperated, or was Sativa simply imagining the expression on the cat's face?

She regarded the cat for a long moment. "I don't suppose you're a female cat? Dalia did say her friend was female, though surely she would have told me if she was feline, too."

"Mrow."

Sativa sighed. Try as she might, she'd never

understand the cat's meaning. Being able to talk to beasts would be a useful gift around about now. If she was wrong about this…

Reluctantly, she dropped her blanket on the ground, shaping it into an arrowhead that pointed in the cat's direction. The direction she would follow the beast, though it might be folly, and the way Dalia's friend would have to go in order to find her if the cat was not the promised guide.

Swearing roundly at all the sharp sticks on the forest floor and herself for losing her boots in the sea, Sativa set off behind the cat.

Twenty-Nine

Reidar sat by the rekindled fire, a crust of bread in one hand and a cup of ale in the other as he broke his fast, while the rest of the hunting party readied themselves for the day. His pavilion was already packed away, but others were not as used to travelling as he and several tents still stood in the clearing.

Einar strutted around without his tunic, pointing at the scars on his chest that were hard to see beneath all the white hair, and telling the tales of how he got them to any man who'd listen, and quite a few who didn't.

Dag had brought a hound that he swore could sniff out boars better than any beast alive, and he had a leash around its neck, letting it lead him around the clearing, sniffing for signs for their quarry. So far, it had found and frightened two squirrels, twice Rudolf's score from yesterday.

Rudolf emerged from the trees, straightening his tunic. Another man who had to piss away a lot of last night's ale.

Reidar nodded at Dag and his dog. "What do you say, cousin? Shall we let the beast lead the way today?"

Rudolf shrugged.

"He has a scent! Sire, we should follow it!" Dag shouted.

Others caught his excitement and headed for their horses.

Reidar rose. "Why not? Let's ride. I fancy roast pork for my dinner."

Rudolf was close behind him. "A wager,

cousin? That you will take home your heart's desire today?"

Reidar turned to stare at Rudolf. Such a strange thing to say. Almost as though the man knew what he'd dreamed last night. "There is no wager to make. I smell victory in the air today."

Behind him, Rudolf's voice said softly, in a tone so low Reidar suspected he wasn't supposed to hear: "We shall see. Stranger things have happened to kings while hunting. I suspect victory will not be yours on this day."

A chill closed around Reidar's heart, but he shook it off. Rudolf's words could be traitorous or prophetic, or mere nonsense he'd spouted to make mischief. Whatever the truth, it would out itself today, for one thing was certain – there was something different in the air. An expectation, a promise...of change. And he would embrace it.

Reidar leaped onto his horse's back. "Time for the hunt to begin!" he shouted.

And so it began.

Thirty

The damned cat was like water – endlessly running, while Sativa struggled to keep up. When Sativa stopped to rest or take a drink before crossing yet another stream, the animal would sit and stare at her, occasionally uttering that same, superior, "Mrow," that seemed to be all it could say.

Her feet hurt. No, all of her body hurt, and her belly added an extra growled protest at the absence of breakfast. In the tales she'd heard as a child, there were berries and all sorts of things to eat in the forest. So far, she'd seen nothing except her stolen cheese. The one the cat had eaten. Idly, she wondered if cats were edible.

As though the beast had heard her, the cat stopped, then scrambled up a tree.

Annoyed, Sativa stumbled to the trunk and peered up. "I can climb, too, you know."

Something exploded out of the underbrush behind her, setting the squirrels chittering away in fear.

Sativa risked a glance over her shoulder and almost screamed at the biggest tusked pig she'd ever seen, mere yards from her.

The beast hadn't noticed her yet, but if it did, one of those tusks could end her as surely as Captain Zydrunas' blade, and she had no skin of wine to save her now.

Sativa leaped, reaching for the nearest branch as her feet scrabbled for purchase on the tree trunk. Her muscles screamed as she climbed, but she knew she'd scream louder if the pig got to her.

Her bare feet slipped, leaving her hanging in the air a few inches from the ground.

The pig turned, and its small eyes seemed to glow red as it spied Sativa. The beast charged.

Her arms ached from trying to support her whole weight, but Sativa did her best to swing her body to the side in one last, desperate hope that she might gain a foothold on the slippery tree.

She managed to get out of the way of the pig's charge, but then it crashed into the tree. Hard. She lost her grip and came tumbling down on top of the animal's bristled back.

Instinctively, she hung on, but the rampaging pig was no tree. Still, she knew if she fell, it would trample her to death if it didn't gore her first. Yet she stayed on, and it took her a moment to realise why.

When the pig had hit the tree, its tusks had gotten stuck. It seemed more concerned at getting free of the tree than bucking her off.

She could climb off and run, but where

would she go? Could she climb a different tree before the beast fought itself free?

Hadn't the shoemaker told a tale of how he'd slayed a boar by getting it stuck in a tree?

Before she could answer her own questions, the cat intervened.

As nimble as any sailor, it ran down the tree trunk, jumped on the pig's head, then used it as a springboard to leap away into the forest.

And in so doing, freed the beast's tusks.

Summoning some vague memory from the shoemaker's tales, Sativa yanked out her knife and plunged it into the beast's throat. Once, twice, before the squealing animal threw her off.

Sativa landed heavily on her back, but she leaped to her feet, ready to run.

But the pig didn't seem to see her any more as it danced around in a frenzy, trying to dislodge the knife in its throat as its lifeblood flowed out onto the forest floor.

Finally, it collapsed in a heap, sides heaving, as it turned baleful eyes on Sativa once more.

Fury forced her to hold her ground. "After surviving pirates, I'm not about to surrender to a pig," she said.

The beast seemed to understand. It took one last breath, and then stilled.

Sativa waited for a long moment before she dared approach. She nudged the animal with her foot, but it didn't move. Only then did she lean down to retrieve her knife. The handle was slick with blood, and it took her a few tries to pull it out. She succeeded on the fourth attempt, only to have a gush of blood spatter her with gore.

Sativa glanced down. Between the wine stains and the blood, she didn't think Melitta would want her torn tunic back.

Her belly growled in agreement.

Sativa wanted to laugh. How she could still be hungry while looking at the bloody pig, she wasn't sure, but it was a pig. Pigs meant pork and bacon and ham and all sorts of things that would make a lovely breakfast. She'd have to butcher it first and work out how to cook it, but just the thought of roast pork made her willing to try.

Hooves thudded behind her. Lots of them.

Fearing the pig's herd had come to seek their revenge, Sativa whirled, knife in one hand, and murder in her eyes.

Thirty-One

"This way!" Dag cried, urging his horse after the dog.

Reidar had long since come to believe there was no pig at all, a thought some of the others had muttered aloud, but he was loath to call off a chase when he was enjoying himself. So he followed Dag and the others followed after.

The dog went mad, almost dragging the leash out of Dag's hand. Dag's horse reared back, and the man had a good deal of trouble getting both beasts under control. In the confusion, Rudolf moved ahead.

"What's the beast found this time?" Reidar asked. "Another squirrel, perhaps?"

The others laughed. All but Rudolf.

Rudolf was strangely silent for a long moment, before he said, "The hound has found a pig, all right, and more besides."

"What do you mean?" Reidar said.

Rudolf beckoned, riding forward.

Reidar followed.

Thirty-Two

Not pigs, but men on horseback. Lots of them, armed and dressed like the warriors they were. They crowded into the clearing, and yet they held back, keeping their horses away from the pig carcass.

The girl she had been would have dropped the dagger and begged for help, but Sativa had not journeyed across the sea for nothing. She'd bury the blade in her own breast before letting any of these men touch her. So she brandished her knife and held her ground.

"There's your pig, cousin," one man said. "It seems the victor on the field is a girl today."

Laughter bubbled up from the other men.

"I'll thank you to keep your covetous hands off my pig," Sativa snapped. Her fury blazed bigger than the bonfire last night.

"This is the king's forest, his private hunting preserve, and he alone owns everything in it. Including that pig," the first man said calmly.

Sativa thought for a moment. She'd heard similar things at home, but there was more to it than that. "The beast charged at me. Tried to kill me. I vanquished my foe, which makes everything he owns forfeit to me. The pig might only have meat, but the meat is mine!"

Laughter died as the men surveyed the scene. The blood, the pig, the dagger in her hand. Lust began to smoulder in their eyes.

One man pushed forward, while the rest hung back. He stared hungrily at her chest.

Sativa glanced down. Her tunic left little to the imagination, and her necklace had fallen out. Carefully, she tucked the amber ring out of sight and tried to hold the worst rip together.

This only seemed to inflame the man further. "Back away, all of you," he said softly. "She is mine."

Sativa swallowed. "The first man to touch me will die like that pig." She jerked her knife at the carcass. "I belong to no man. Not even your king. Who owes me a bite of that beast, once his cooks are done with it."

Thirty-Three

"Skadi," Rudolf breathed.

For a moment, Reidar saw what Rudolf did. The blood-spattered girl could have been a goddess from the old faith. Skadi, goddess of the hunt...but also the goddess of justice, vengeance and righteous anger.

"I belong to no man. Not even your king. Who owes me a bite of that beast, once his cooks are done with it."

Reidar laughed aloud at this girl's courage.

Armed with a knife before a dozen mounted knights, she showed no fear whatsoever. But a girl who could take on a full-grown boar with nothing more than a dagger was a force to be reckoned with. A huntress indeed.

And yet...she seemed familiar somehow. Something about the proud set of her head, as she dropped neither bow nor curtsey as she met his gaze. Almost as though she considered herself his equal.

And there was that glimpse of gold, now hidden beneath her shift, that made him wonder all the more.

He slid down from his horse. "We will make camp here for the night," he announced. Reidar waited until he and the girl were alone before he added, "I will offer you a meal and a bed for the night, and on the morrow I will take you to the castle where the king lives. You can bring the pig, too, and I'll see that the castle kitchens prepare it properly. You can't ask for fairer than that."

She stared at him for a moment, as though

reading his soul, then nodded. She crouched to wipe her blade on the grass before tucking it away. Only as she reached her full height once more did she fold her arms across her breasts, and Reidar realised that she must be freezing, wearing nothing but a shift.

He shrugged off his cloak and held it out. "Please take it. You must be cold."

Once again, she hesitated, before she accepted the cloak. "I thank you," she said.

He stood beside her in silence, though his curiosity burned fiercer than any fire. He had so many questions he wanted to ask that he wasn't sure which should be first.

When his servants seemed to take an inordinately long time setting up his pavilion, he decided to satisfy a tiny part of his curiosity.

"Show me what you wear around your neck," he said.

Her eyes seemed filled with fire. "What I wear around my neck is none of your business, sir."

So she did not know him, then. "What if I

were to tell you that I am the king of these lands, and everything and everyone within my borders is my business?"

She sized him up. Finally, her shoulders seemed to relax and she said, "If what you say is true, then perhaps it is your business, after all." She drew a leather thong from beneath her shift, and held it up. Suspended from the cord was a silver ring with a yellow-gold stone.

A ring that would not fit on even Reidar's smallest finger, now, but he recognised it like it was yesterday.

"How did you come to have this?"

She tucked the necklace beneath her borrowed cloak. "If you are truly the king of these lands, then you already know the answer."

Sativa. Hope welled in his breast, but Reidar forced it back down. He couldn't be certain. Not yet. "This ring was given to a girl to whom I made a promise. Only she and I knew of it, though there was one other witness to my vow."

Her eyebrows rose. "There was?"

He almost laughed, but he managed to control himself. "One who is not likely to speak of it. He was the fattest pony I had ever beheld."

She laughed. "I'd forgotten about Philip. I gave him to my sisters soon after that, who spoiled him far more than I ever did. If horses ever receive a divine reward, then I hope he is reunited with them in heaven."

There was no doubt in Reidar's mind now. He'd found her, and he had no intention of letting her out of his sight until they were married.

"Sire, your tent is ready for you," a servant said, bowing low.

Reidar bowed to Sativa. "After you."

The servant looked surprised, but Reidar caught many startled glances aimed at the girl as they headed for his tent. For a moment, he saw what they did – a bedraggled girl in a torn shift, whose only protection was the king's cloak. They would look at her very differently when he crowned her as his queen. Reidar grinned.

Only Rudolf dared to put his thoughts into words. He bowed extravagantly in his cousin's direction. "I wish you a pleasurable night, Your Majesty, with such pleasant company. Your little goddess might be a beautiful woman under all the dirt." He eyed Sativa appreciatively.

"Put your eyes back in your head, man," Reidar snapped. "Don't you have a wife waiting for you on some island somewhere? This one's mine." He put a proprietary arm around Sativa and pushed her into his pavilion.

"If you are sure, cousin," Rudolf said, turning away. "My best wishes for your health and happiness, then."

Happiness. Yes. Reidar's smile returned, and he stepped into his tent.

Only to meet the point of Sativa's blade, aimed between his eyes.

"If you think I will allow you to kill me and rape my corpse, you are mistaken," she said fiercely.

Reidar's mouth dropped open. It was a long

moment before he managed to say, "Honestly, neither of those things have ever crossed my mind. It sounds like you have endured quite an ordeal, Princess Sativa, since you left your father's castle. He's had men scouring the country for you, but it seems he underestimated you. Yet there is one thing I don't understand. Why are you here?"

"My father offered me as a prize to any man who could slay a dragon," Sativa said. "On the night he was to have me marry a shoemaker, I remembered a prior engagement."

Reidar laughed. "In that case, I offer you my protection, and my hospitality, for as long as you wish," Reidar replied. "Even my sword, to defend you against this shoemaker, should he come searching for you."

"He will not come searching for me. His heart lies elsewhere."

Reidar spread his arms wide. "Then what do you wish of me? If it is within my power, I will grant it, Princess."

For the second time, she tucked her knife away. Reidar hoped it would be the last, for this being threatened by women with weapons would take some getting used to.

"Years ago, you talked of a tower," she began cautiously.

Hope blossomed within him. "I promised a tower and a crown, to the woman who would become my queen," Reidar corrected.

For the first time, she smiled. "I'd settle for some water to wash with and a bed, then maybe a meal and something to wear that isn't covered in blood."

Reidar wanted to envelop her in his arms and swear to take care of her for the rest of her days. What had the girl been through to get here? Killing a boar with nothing but a knife. He couldn't have done it. Half foreign princess, half ancient goddess come to life, and every inch the woman of his dreams.

But her eyes were wary, as well they might be, for she did not know him yet.

"It will be as you command, Princess," he said.

She lifted her chin. "I do."

Thirty-Four

As Sativa settled into the king's bed – without the king, for Reidar slept outside the tent, as he insisted her honour demanded – she let out a sigh of contentment. She'd washed away weeks' worth of salt and dirt as best she could with just a cloth and basin of water. She'd eaten a meal worth tasting for the first time in weeks. And she now wore a tunic without holes, as fine as Melitta's had once been before time and trouble had worn it to rags.

She was safe. Whatever happened next was for Reidar to worry about, not her. No more pirates or perilous voyages or pea straw or pigs. Ever again.

She remembered the lust in his eyes, not unlike the look every man wore when he looked at a beautiful woman. What would it feel like to surrender to such a thing? Not the cruel hands of a man like Zydrunas, but the welcoming arms of Reidar. A king who could take what he wanted without asking, and yet he held back for honour's sake, or so he said.

He'd offered her his own cloak, his bed, his…everything. She'd crossed the seas to accept a man she barely knew, but she'd dreamed of for as long as she could remember. Could the dream match the reality?

His hands as he'd laid the cloak on her shoulders, wrapping its folds around her, still warm from his body. Strong and gentle, all at the same time. And reverent, too.

The look on his face as he'd brought her food. Not a servant – he'd carried the platter with his own hands, and shared it with her, for he'd brought enough for two. He'd pointed out the choicest morsels and insisted they were hers. The lust was gone, as though it had never been, replaced with tenderness. Did she imagine a little longing, too? Probably. But alone in her bed, nay, his bed, she let herself believe it. That Reidar longed for her the way she did for him.

Thoughts of him warmed her through the night, and in the cold morning, as well, as she mounted up behind Reidar for the ride back to the castle. At first, the heat of him between her thighs made her blush, but that was what she'd come for, hadn't she? To be his wife, to share his bed and his body and all that he could give her. So she held her head high, wrapped her arms around his hard torso, and hung on to the man who would be her husband.

All too soon, the forest gave way to farmland, and a castle appeared on the cliffs. Smaller than her father's, but above it loomed the most delightful sight of all — the Sea

Tower, Reidar's promise.

"Thank you," she whispered, pressing her lips to his neck. "Thank you."

He reached back and cradled her head in his hand, as though he wanted to prolong the kiss. "I am a man of my word, Princess. I promise you that."

Not a princess for much longer. She had promised to be his queen, and Sativa would keep her word, as he'd kept his.

When they rode through the gate of her king's castle, Sativa couldn't suppress a smile as she surveyed her new home.

Thirty-Five

The warm woman at his back set him on fire. The grin on Reidar's face didn't fade for the whole ride home. Some of the other men winked knowingly, thinking they knew what had passed between him and Sativa. He let them believe what they liked. It was no dishonour for a Viken woman to take a lover, unless she had a husband. Sativa could have chosen any one of them to spend the night with, and Reidar would have had no right to complain. It would have sat ill with him, of course, especially if she decided she liked another man more than him…

Reidar shook his head. But she had chosen him, and no other man. He'd even offered her a horse of her own to ride, but she'd refused and insisted on riding with him. He couldn't tell her how thankful he was for that – the reassuring weight of her behind him, reminding him that everything was right in the world, now that she'd been found. When she was ready and fully recovered from her ordeal, she would name a date for their wedding, and the wedding night that would follow.

Then he would do things to her he'd only dreamed of – all of last night, in fact – as he worshipped her like the goddess she'd resembled. So what if it was sacrilegious? She would be his wife, the woman he'd vowed to honour and cherish. What was worship but an elevated mixture of the two?

All too soon, their ride ended as his castle loomed into view, with her tower standing sentinel above it. Reidar wondered what she would think of a castle so much smaller than her father's. Cold, grey stone instead of warm brick, perched on a clifftop over a turbulent sea, instead of sitting comfortably on a hilltop overlooking vast fields of prosperous farmland.

"I offer you the hospitality of my home, humble though it is," Reidar said. He held his breath, praying she would accept.

Sativa's arms tightened around him as her soft lips kissed his neck. "Thank you. Thank you."

Every bit of him wanted to turn around, take her in her arms and kiss her breathless. Kiss her until he was breathless, too. Reidar realised he had his hand on her face, and he'd half turned to do what he was dreaming about. Not yet, he told himself, forcing his hand to take the reins again.

"The king has returned! The king has returned!" someone shouted from the gate, and then they all took up the cry.

It wasn't a cry of triumph. Something was wrong.

Hakon raced across the bailey and stopped, panting, as Reidar reined in his horse. "Raiders. A whole fleet of them, spotted from the Sea Tower this morning. Headed for the port. They should reach there soon after darkness, and if they do…"

Reidar understood. "With the army near the inland borders and our ships off helping King Boreslas with the search, they'll be defenceless. We'll go at once. Send any able bodied man you can spare after me."

"You're riding to war?" Sativa's voice asked near his ear.

Oh, by all that was holy, he'd forgotten her. But he didn't have time to explain.

"I must," he said, swinging her out of the saddle and onto the ground. "I will return when the battle is won, or the port is lost." He addressed Hakon. "Take her to the queen. Tell the queen to take care of her until my return." Reidar wheeled his horse around, ready to ride out of the gate.

Rudolf blocked his path. "You can't afford to lose the port," he said bluntly.

"I know that. I'm not a fool," Reidar snapped.

"The people of the Southern Isles have been defending against sea raids for centuries, sometimes successfully. They have an idea they came up with after watching some of our funerals," Rudolf said. He grinned. "Fire arrows. They set fire to the boats before the men can come ashore. Sometimes even ambush them where they know the boats will sink and the raiders will drown. You need fire arrows, and a narrow place they will be forced to sail through where they will be in range of our archers. How many archers can we have there in time?"

Hope blossomed in Reidar's breast. "More than we need. Every man and boy between here and the port can shoot a bow, because the lake is full of geese in the summertime, and any man who can shoot a bird may take it home for his table. Maybe we can save the port after all!"

He and Rudolf rode out, discussing likely ambush sites as they went.

Thirty-Six

Everything was wonderful…and then it wasn't, as Reidar dropped her on the ground like a sack of apples and rode off with his cousin to war, without even saying farewell. Not that she would have heard it if he had, for there was another word that burned in her brain with a ferocity she wasn't sure how to tame: queen.

As in: "Take her to the queen."

Wasn't she supposed to be his queen? His betrothed, his bride, the woman he would marry?

But if he already had a queen…it would explain why he hadn't even suggested sharing her bed. Why he hadn't mentioned marriage or their betrothal in the forest.

And why someone had seen the ships from the top of the tower – someone else already lived there.

Reidar's servant bade her to follow him and she did, but she paid little attention to her surroundings. For the first time, she wondered if she'd made a terrible mistake in coming here. If she wasn't wanted…

"Forgive me, Your Majesty, but the king said I must bring this girl to you." The look he shot Sativa was nothing short of a sneer.

Perhaps she deserved it – for how many girls would be as stupid as she had, to run away from her father's house across the sea to a man who no longer wanted her?

"What for?" a woman – presumably the queen – asked in annoyance

"I am not certain, Your Majesty, but he said

something about wanting her here when he returned. Perhaps he wants you to find her a place to stay."

"Find her a room befitting her station, then," said the queen, dismissing him.

The man waited until the door was closed before he swore and turned to Sativa. "Follow me, you," he said curtly, setting off at a fast clip.

Sativa itched for a glimpse of the queen, the woman with the commanding voice that Reidar preferred over her, but she would probably see the woman at dinner. More important that she find her room first.

The man led her down several passageways, the aroma of cooking increasing in strength the further they went. Rooms above the kitchen would not be so bad, Sativa decided. She'd never miss a meal, for she'd smell it cooking.

The man stopped, then pointed through a doorway that had no door. "You'll sleep in there."

Curiously, Sativa stepped inside. At first, the dimly lit room looked like another passageway, until her eyes adjusted and she saw that it was wider than that. Rows of straw pallets lined each side of the room, some with blankets or sacking coverlets, and others without. Pegs on the walls held an assortment of dresses and caps all made in a similar theme: practicality. If it weren't for the dresses, she'd have thought it a barracks hall, but the clothing marked it for what it was. The servants' quarters, where the castle maids slept.

On – Sativa sneezed – thrice-damned straw, the bane of her existence.

Sativa sneezed twice more before she turned on her heel and marched back the way she'd come. The man who'd guided her had disappeared, but no matter. Sativa would find her own way back to the queen's chamber, and confront the woman herself. She might be a queen, but Sativa was a princess, born with royal blood, and she would not endure such an insult.

After one wrong turning, she managed to return to the queen's chamber, and Sativa did not bother to knock. Instead, she burst into the room.

"What is the meaning of this?" Sativa demanded in the tone she knew carried to the farthest reaches of her father's court.

"Who in heaven's name are you?" the queen countered.

For the first time, Sativa saw her, and was startled to see she recognised the woman. Oh, she was older, certainly, her fair hair almost completely white, but Regina's haughty expression had not changed a bit. This was the queen? Not Reidar's wife, but his mother?

Relief flooded through her, giving her all the authority she needed to snap, "I am Princess Sativa, daughter of King Boreslas in Kasmirus, betrothed to King Reidar of Viken, and when he returns, I will be the queen of this place. What do you think Reidar will say when he discovers you sent me to sleep with the servants?"

Regina's eyebrows rose so high, they vanished into her hair. "Sativa? The dragon's prize girl? Impossible. She disappeared from her father's court months ago. The girl is dead."

"I am not a prize, and I am not dead," Sativa hissed through gritted teeth. "I will marry your son, and I demand the hospitality that was promised. With a bed befitting my station."

Regina managed to arrange her icy expression into a smile that held no warmth at all. "Very well, Princess. You may join me for dinner, by which time your bed will be prepared."

Sativa could afford to be gracious. "Thank you. I shall need some suitable clothing, too."

Regina eyed her tunic with the same distaste Sativa had once held for Melitta's clothing, once upon a time. "Yes, you will. My ladies will dress you."

Sativa was soon bundled into Regina's dressing room, a narrow chamber full of chests containing clothes from at least three generations of women, judging by the strange styles the ladies pulled out in their search for something suitable.

"This," one said, holding up a gown that glittered even in the dim light in the dressing room.

The gown was made of gold silk, and so richly embroidered it could probably stand up by itself. If that wasn't enough, someone had sewed dozens of jewels to it so that whoever wore it couldn't help but catch the light. It was a wedding dress, or one to be worn at a coronation. Not something for an ordinary dinner.

"It is too fine," Sativa said.

The second girl shook her head. "The queen said you must have the best. This is the richest gown in the wardrobe. If you don't wear it, the queen will punish us."

Visions of punishment aboard the *Barbe* flashed through Sativa's mind. Would Regina be so cruel as to have her ladies-in-waiting whipped? Sativa didn't want to find out.

She reached out to touch the silk. It had been so long since she'd worn anything half as pretty as this. She'd outshine everyone in the castle. Including Regina.

"Very well," Sativa said, and allowed the women to dress her.

When they were done, they guided her to the great hall, and left her with only Regina for company. Luckily, they were both at opposite ends of the great table, so she was spared the challenge of making conversation with a woman whose dislike could be felt from the other side of the room.

Sativa ate her fill of everything. It would take some time to replace the weight she'd lost aboard the *Barbe*, and she doubted Reidar wanted to introduce his people to a half-starved bride. She was a princess from a prosperous kingdom – she should look the part.

All too soon, she grew tired, and found she struggled to keep her eyes open. As Sativa tried to smother yet another yawn, Regina rose to her feet.

"My servants tell me your room is ready," Regina said. "Let me show you to your bed."

Sativa owned that it was a good idea, and followed the woman readily.

This time, the chamber wasn't far from the queen's own. A servant threw the door open and Regina peered inside. Her face lit with a genuine smile.

"Behold, Princess, a bed befitting your high station," Regina said, dropping a curtsey.

Finally. Sativa stepped into the room, expecting either another straw pallet or the sort of fine feather bed she had at home. Neither would have surprised her. What she did see made her jaw drop. It wasn't one fine feather bed, but at least a dozen, the mattresses stacked so high they nearly reached the ceiling. Sativa stopped to count them all. No, not a dozen. Twenty of the things, with a ladder beside them to help her climb to the top.

A calculated insult, or an over-the-top

honour. Sativa was certain it was meant as the former, but she smiled sweetly as though it were the latter. "Why, thank you," she simpered. "Just like the one I had at home."

Regina's composure failed, and her true hatred shone through. "Liar," she spat. "You are no more a princess than the maids in the kitchen. No one sleeps in a bed like that. You will never marry my son, for he's too good for the likes of you." She slammed the door shut and Sativa heard the key turn in the lock.

Sativa was tempted to shout something after the woman, but someone had to show their better breeding, and it had best be her.

Besides, climbing a ladder into a bed that looked softer than a cloud seemed like luxury after climbing the mast every day and sleeping in a hammock on the *Barbe*.

Sativa scaled the ladder and climbed carefully onto the stacked mattresses. She sank so deep she suspected getting out might prove a challenge, but one she would tackle after a good night's sleep on what had to be the softest bed she'd ever encountered. Silently, she thanked Reidar and his mother, for this felt like pure bliss. Yes, she would show Regina, and marry Reidar just like she'd promised. And maybe, just maybe, she'd ask him for a slightly less decadent version of this bed. One that didn't require a ladder. Because she could definitely get used to comfort like this.

Until a growing tickle in her nose could not be ignored, and she sneezed. Not once, but six times in succession. And then again.

There was straw in this room. In the mattresses, she suspected, though she had no way to tell.

"Damn you, bitch," Sativa said softly, as her eyes teared up from the straw dust in the air. That was what caused it, not emotion or self-pity or any such thing.

She only had to endure it until Reidar returned, and then everything would be rosy.

Sativa sneezed. And swore. And sneezed again.

Damned rose fever.

She hoped he came home soon.

Thirty-Seven

"What are you still doing here?"

Rudolf's words jarred Reidar out of what had been a deep sleep. In a stable, judging by the smell.

"Because I distinctly recall telling you last night that we'd take care of the damage those two boats wrought when they made it through our hail of arrows. And we did, thank you. We only lost the roof of one house to fire." Rudolf glared at Reidar. "Why aren't you home with your bride, getting ready for your wedding, like you said you would?"

Reidar's mind started to work. Now he remembered coming into the stable, calling for a groom to saddle his horse, but all the men were off defending the town, so he'd had to do the job himself. And then he'd closed his eyes for just a moment…

…and woken up here, in daylight. Reidar cursed.

"I fell asleep," he admitted.

Rudolf snorted. "I can see that. You're lucky no one's come in yet. I'm not sure what the townsfolk would do if they found a snoring king in their stable."

"I do not snore," Reidar grumbled.

"One day, I will ask your lovely wife to tell me the truth. Now, get you gone and marry the girl before someone else beats you to it!" Rudolf said.

"No one commands the king," Reidar muttered as he reached for his horse's bridle.

"As the king's cousin and heir, I think I

have the right to make strong suggestions that I think the king should follow, if he's not to turn into a complete fool," Rudolf replied. "Who else will, if I do not?"

Reidar had to admit the man was right. But he didn't have to admit it aloud, though. "Mind your manners, or I will not invite you to the wedding feast," he said as he climbed atop his horse. He set off before Rudolf could reply.

"You'll have to ask the girl to marry you first!" Rudolf shouted after him.

Curse the man, but he was right.

Sativa was in his thoughts for most of the ride home. He'd have to tread carefully, for she'd evidently endured some terrible trials between her father's castle and his. A wedding would have to wait until she was willing to let him touch her without pulling out a knife to defend herself.

He'd like to find whoever had frightened her and force them to endure whatever they'd put her through. That was a cheering thought. Perhaps he'd offer to let Sativa help, or at least observe. She would want to ensure justice was served.

But that would have to wait, too. First, he wanted to see her, to ask her what had happened, and whether she was still willing to marry him. At least he knew she was safe under his roof.

He handed the reins to a groom and vaulted off his horse in the bailey, wanting nothing more than to see Sativa again when he arrived home.

"Where is the girl I brought here yesterday?" he asked a passing serving girl, but she did not know. Nor did anyone else he asked, it seemed.

How dare they mislay their future queen?

Incensed, Reidar headed for his mother's chambers. She would know where to find Sativa. Perhaps she could also explain why the girl was being kept a secret from his own servants. They would be her servants soon enough.

"Where is she?" he demanded as he strode

into her apartment.

Regina set down her embroidery. "Where is who?"

"Princess Sativa." She would not hide her identity, he was certain of it. Not here.

Regina wet her lips. "You mean the girl pretending to be the dead princess."

Reidar fought to keep his temper. "No, I mean the very real, live princess I left in your care yesterday. The one who will soon be my wife." He prayed that this last part was true.

"You're a fool, my son, but most men are. Fooled by a pretty face and a tale of distress. That girl is no more highborn than any other maid in the castle. First, she had the gall to demand to wear the most valuable gown in the castle to dinner. Then she had the effrontery to demand the most outlandish bed, which she imagined was what a princess slept upon. I'll show you, if you like. Then you'll see she is playing you for a fool." Regina rose and swept out of the room.

No. His mother was wrong. Whatever she

thought, he knew he'd brought the real Sativa here yesterday. No one else could know what she did.

Regina stopped outside one of the guest apartments and turned the key in the lock.

"You locked her in, like a prisoner?" Reidar demanded. He didn't want to lose his temper, but his mother was pushing him much too far.

"I could not have her wandering around the castle. Who knows what she might steal?" Regina said, then threw open the door with a flourish.

Sativa stood on the threshold, her red eyes and nose streaming. "If this is the hospitality you show to guests, I hope the devil shows you better in hell," she said. "I scarcely slept in that travesty of a bed. It was impossible, with that bloody…that bloody…pea – aachoo!" She sneezed twice more, then glared at Regina.

"But that's not possible," Regina spluttered. "No one's so refined, so sensitive, she could sense something like that through so many mattresses. Not even royalty. How could she detect such a thing through twenty mattresses?"

Pea straw, the stuff that made her sneeze, Sativa had meant to say, Reidar was certain. He peered into the room behind her and saw a strange sight. A stack of mattresses, including the straw one his father had slept on every day of his life, insisting it was far better than feathers. The old pallet had burst under the weight of the ones above, strewing straw all over the floor. It had been better for his father, perhaps. But not for Sativa.

Who had suffered even more, and it was his fault.

Reidar fell to his knees. "Forgive me, Princess. I promised to protect you, and I failed. I'd planned to ask you to marry me, and name the day of our wedding, but I find I must beg your forgiveness first, and pay a heavy penance, before I'd dare ask anything of you."

Sativa stared down at him. Once again, sizing up his soul. Reidar prayed he would not be found wanting. "A handkerchief," she said.

He felt through his pockets, and produced one. "I'm sorry for the soot. We set fire to half a dozen ships last night."

"Thank you," she said, inclining her head. She wiped her eyes, then delicately blew her nose. "There. You asked for…things."

She swayed on her feet and Reidar caught her, rising to his feet when he realised she needed his support. She truly hadn't slept, and she was still weak from her ordeal.

"Tomorrow," she said. "Give me a bed without straw and a hot bath, and you shall have everything you ask for tomorrow."

Reidar didn't believe his ears. "What will I have tomorrow?"

Sativa slumped against him. Exhausted, poor girl. "Wedding. Forgiveness. Whatever. But I never want to see her again." She stabbed a finger at Regina.

"I will not stay here while she's polluting the place," Regina said hotly. "I shall go to live with one of your sisters until you come to your senses." She stormed off.

Reidar didn't intend to come to his senses any time soon. Sativa drove him wild, and he had to admit he rather liked it. Reidar lifted Sativa in his arms. "Whatever you wish, my queen," he said softly.

She smiled. "A bed," she said before her eyes closed. "And don't go away this time."

He carried her limp form up to the tower room she should have been shown last night, and set her in the middle of the bed. He pulled the covers over her, not sure what else to do.

All he could do was wait and watch over her until she woke.

Which was what she wanted, so he did.

Thirty-Eight

When Sativa woke, the sun was high in the sky, but she felt well rested.

Reidar stepped out of the shadows. "I brought you breakfast, but I fear it is cold now. I will send for some more. I didn't want to wake you."

He was as chivalrous as she'd always dreamed he'd be. But the time for chivalry was done. She would marry this man – this king – and she would pledge herself to him so irrevocably that he would truly know she meant what she said. Reidar was everything she wanted in a man, and despite what she'd said in the forest, in her heart, she belonged to him and him alone. It was time he knew that.

"Come here," Sativa said, her voice a little shaky. She'd never seduced a man before, and she was sure her inexperience showed. When Reidar turned to face her, she pulled her shift over her head and threw it on the floor, so she sat naked on the bed.

His eyes raked her body before returning to her face. "Princess…" Lust smouldered, just as it had in the forest.

She patted the bed. "Here, Reidar. My name is Sativa, not Princess. You will need to remember that, when I am your wife."

He took one tentative step closer, then another. His eyes held something akin to awe. Another step. He stopped beside the bed, as though something held him back. "Sativa." It sounded like a prayer.

"Take your clothes off, too," she said, her

voice shaking even more. "I wish to see the man who will be my husband."

To her delight, he shucked off his tunic. The hard muscles she'd held onto during their ride here were everything she'd imagined. Arms, chest, back…everything.

She rose up onto her knees, reaching out to touch.

He took a step back. "Don't," he begged. "If you touch me, I'm not sure I'll be able to restrain myself. I want you, the way a man wants his wife."

Looking down, Sativa saw that what he said was true. And she wanted him, too.

"Show me everything," she said, her voice breathless. "Take all your clothes off."

His eyes burned into hers as he did as she asked. Shoes, hose, until he stood as naked as she.

Then she rose from the bed, her steps as tentative as his had been before. She forced herself to stop when she was only a step away so she could gaze at his body before she said,

"What a glorious husband you will make." She swallowed, then added, "I want you the way a woman wants a lover."

Then she pressed her body against his, softness moulding around hardness, and lifted her lips for a kiss. His arm was firm at her back as his other hand cupped her cheek. No more words were necessary for his eyes said it all as he kissed her, tenderly at first then with an urgency that rivalled her own. Long and deep and so delicious he made her dizzy.

"I have dreamed of this," she gasped.

"So have I," he said. "Tomorrow, after we are wed – "

"No," she interrupted. "I don't want to wait. I want you now." She reached down and wrapped her hand around his manhood. So hard, and yet so soft. What would it feel like inside her?

Gently, he pried her hand loose. "Sativa." Another prayer, as her fingers stroked his length before she let go.

Her eyes met his. "Show me how you will

love your queen." Taking his hand, she led him to the bed, then lay down.

Something warred in his eyes. Sativa didn't care what, as long as she won.

"You said you would take me as your queen. So, take me."

He smiled. "As my queen commands." He climbed onto the bed beside her, his hands brushing lightly over her skin so that she shivered. His smile broadened, before he covered her body in kisses. She gasped and sighed under his caresses, until he said, "Sativa, have you ever taken a lover before?"

She sat up in surprise. "Of course not. I've been promised to you since I was six!"

He chuckled. "That never stopped the ladies of Viken from taking lovers if they liked. Marriage means being faithful to only the one. But if I am your first…then I must make sure you are prepared for me."

His caresses and kisses grew more fervent, making her gasp with delight as he drew pleasure from her body that she had not thought possible. After an eternity of foreplay, finally he declared that she was ready.

Sativa opened her mouth to say that she had been ready long before, but the sensation of him entering her took her breath away. She opened her legs wider, welcoming him inside. That first thrust seemed to take a glorious eternity, until she could take no more, for he had filled her completely.

She closed her eyes, relishing the pure pleasure she had never before imagined.

Reidar leaned forward, pushing deliciously deeper into her as he cupped her face in gentle hands. "Sativa, please tell me if I am too much for you. I will stop, I swear."

She opened her eyes, smiling in joy. "Don't stop, my king. Don't stop until we are both spent, and need to rest, before we can make love some more." At this, he moved within her and she moaned in pleasure. "Yes, more!"

Their bodies melded together in a union so perfect Sativa could not have dreamed it before this moment, and this moment was one she never wanted to end. A moment of unfathomable bliss between two shared souls. A promise joyfully fulfilled.

Much later, when the sunset light streamed through the window and kissed their naked bodies, lying side by side on the bed, Reidar turned to her and said, "Tomorrow is our wedding. After today, what will I have left to give you on our wedding night?"

Sativa laughed softly. "More of the same, I imagine, unless you have a different kind of lovemaking in mind. If we do this enough, we are sure to have a child. But until we do, give me the gift of your body, and your love, and I shall give you mine in return. Every day and every night, so that we may live happily ever after."

Blow:
Three Little Pigs Retold

DEMELZA CARLTON

A tale in the Romance a Medieval Fairy Tale series

# One

Midsummer festival fever had caught them all in her heathen coils. The higher born boys fought with practice swords in the yard, their bouts descending into pitched battle with no guard or master at arms to break it up. Rudolf found himself stunned in the dust, unnoticed by the others as they pursued longer held grudges against boys they knew, and he scrambled to his feet. Retreating from the yard seemed the most chivalrous thing to do, for he had more training than most of them, though not enough to stop the fight like his cousin Reidar might have.

Outside the walls, pine had been piled up for the bonfires, huge as haystacks, that would be set alight after dark to feed some ancient, beastly god. Now, the fresh, life-giving scent of the pine lay sharp over the bed of long-dead peat from the bogs, reminding him of the inevitability of death, even in the bright summer sun.

His thick furs itched in the unaccustomed heat that was so little like home, but he did not dare take them off. They marked him for what he was, a Viken prince among these Islanders, who wore linen and leather that was surely more suitable for summer.

Peat smoke spiralled in a dark prayer to heaven as it roasted pork to what he hoped would be perfection. The rich smell took him back home, to his farewell feast and the roasted beast that had been Reidar's first kill. Oh, now that had been a feast. Could these foreigners match it?

The crack of what sounded like a spitting cat forced his eyes open. No, it was just the beast's flesh spitting at the coals that roasted it, like its last act of courage before the old gods took it to Valhalla. Did pigs go to heaven, though, he wondered. The men of the new faith said no, but he didn't know enough about the old to be sure.

Hogs probably went up to the great feasting table in the sky, much like their bodies had here. Such was their fate, as this exile was his. At least he was not a pig, however much he roasted in his northern clothes.

He headed away from the clamour, toward the cliffs.

"Boy, boy!" an imperious, elderly voice called.

Rudolf turned. He'd learned the hard way not to ignore an old woman's commands. If he hadn't sat on that throne for a moment and

Queen Regina hadn't caught him, then he wouldn't be here, exiled at the other end of the world. Better alive than dead, though, and alive, he could train more so that one day, he could better serve his king. The man whose backside belonged on that cursed throne.

If the approaching woman was Queen Regina, Rudolf would have run. As it was, he forced himself to hold his ground.

The woman everyone called Nurse limped up to him. "Have you seen them? Wee devils, they are. Their father insists they must attend the feast dressed in their best, and I cannot find them anywhere!"

The Lord Angus's daughters were missing? Rudolf's heart turned to ice, as he remembered the day he'd lost his little sister to the ice on the fjords.

But there was no ice here, and little water, either, for the burns that had flowed only yesterday were little more than mud now after days without rain. It truly was a different world to Viken.

If he had a choice, today he would be in the swimming hole the other boys had spoken of. A pool they said never dried up.

A place deep enough for a little girl to drown.

Panic gave his feet wings as he crested the rise, following the dried up burn. If he could get there in time, perhaps he could save them. Perhaps…

A shrill scream stopped his heart, but not his feet. Still he ran. If a girl could scream, she could breathe, and he could still save her. By all the saints in heaven, please let him save her.

Low hanging branches sliced at his face, but still Rudolf ran on until he almost fell over the lip of the pool, or what had been the pool. Perhaps even this morning, it had still held water, but now…now it held three wriggling, shrieking girls as they played in liquid mud. Alive. Safe. All three. Portia, Lina and Arlie, so covered in mud he couldn't tell them apart — not that it was an easy matter anyway, given the girls looked identical.

Rudolf's heart dared to beat again and he took a deep breath. "Nurse!" he shouted. "I have found your three little pigs!"

Two

"You fought well today, and you have a knack for commanding men. I know several men owe you their lives after today, for it was your quick thinking in the heat of battle that saved them."

Rudolf's chest puffed at Angus's praise.

Angus continued, "You'll need new armour soon. You're not a boy any more, and your shoulders are too wide for that breastplate. Where there's gaps, an arrow will find them,"

Angus said, throwing the reins of his horse to a groom.

Rudolf did the same, but he lingered to stroke Hector's side as he was led off. He'd never owned a finer horse. Not back in Viken, or since he arrived here. How many years had it been now? At least six. Maybe seven.

"You like him, don't you? See, I told Lewis he couldn't sell him off the islands. Valuable breeding stock, he'll be, when you're not riding him."

Rudolf remembered his manners. "Thank you again, Lord Angus. He's a princely gift indeed."

Angus waved away his thanks. "No more than you deserve. My own father gave me my first warhorse when I reached manhood. My first ride, the bastard reared up and threw me on my arse. My brother laughed himself sick. You have a much better seat than did at your age. Better than Portia, though better not tell her I said that."

Rudolf laughed. "No, I won't, as long as you

know that's what I'll be thinking about when I'm staring at her bottom next time we go riding."

"Man your age should be looking for a wife. I know I was. Or will your father be sending one from Viken?"

Viken? Why would he send a girl after him? This was home. Rudolf would likely never see Viken again. "Viken girls choose their husbands, just like the ones here," Rudolf managed to say. "I left no sweetheart behind me, so no girl will be coming to find me."

An explosion of red blasted through the door to the longhouse. "There they are! I found them," Portia cried, tossing her hair off her face. She'd forgotten her shoes again, and with no Nurse to remind her any more, she'd probably been wearing holes in her stockings the whole time they'd been away.

"I brought you a gift," Rudolf said, pulling the feather from under his breastplate. He'd kept it in the pocket over his heart. "At the end of the battle, when those rank cowards were running away, a golden eagle circled the field and dropped it. Landed right at my feet. I thought you might like a new quill."

Portia dashed up to him and plucked the feather from his hand. Then she threw her arms around him and hugged him. Rudolf laughed as he returned her hug, conscious of Angus's thoughtful eyes on him.

Angus was planning something, to be sure.

"Can we go riding now?" Portia demanded. The woman-child had all the impatience of a child, while her body grew more and more into a woman's form.

Rudolf laughed again. "I have been riding all day, and Hector, too. I am starving. I hope you have a good dinner ordered."

Portia would not be put off. "Tomorrow, then? If we leave early, we might be able to make it up to Loch Findlugan, and search for its secret. While you were away, I went through Mother's things and found a scroll about the history of Isla. It said the standing stones – "

Angus interrupted, "Tomorrow, Rudolf needs to be measured for new armour. He's outgrown his."

Portia laughed. "Must be all the food he eats. And people call me and my sisters pigs!" This earned Rudolf a glare.

Rudolf hung his head. The tale of him finding the three little sisters, wallowing in the mud like pigs, had spread rapidly through the Southern Isles, as all good stories did. Even if seven years had passed since that day, Portia still had not forgiven him. She might never.

He glanced at Angus. "I'm sure I won't be needed all day for new armour. There will be time for a ride tomorrow. Perhaps not to Loch Findlugan, but we can take the horses for a ride on the beach."

Portia enveloped him in another hug, tighter and longer than the first. "I love you, Dolf!"

Rudolf patted her back awkwardly, his eyes offering an apology to Angus.

Angus nodded, unconcerned. "Enough talk of tomorrow. I'm famished. I fancy a fine leg of mutton for dinner, and I'm sure Rudolf does, too. Release your prisoner, Portia." He headed inside.

Portia let go, then tucked her hand into Rudolf's. "I'll release you on one condition. You must tell me all about the battle over dinner. How many men you killed, whether you were close enough to hear their last words...or did you shoot them with your bow?"

She was the same age as he'd been when he arrived on Isla, Rudolf realised, and just as bloodthirsty. "I did not use my bow this time. Angus had archers enough."

"I want my own bow. Viken women sometimes go to war with their men, you said. I could be one of the archers and kill those cowardly, thieving Albans before they could step ashore!"

Rudolf laughed. "Are you strong enough to draw a bow yet?"

Portia pouted. "No."

"When you are full grown, like me, you may

practice with mine. If you can hit the target, I promise you I will see that you have your own bow."

Her eyes lit with the fire that seemed to burn without cease within her. "Really?"

Rudolf could refuse her nothing. He prayed that Angus would agree. "Really."

Three

Portia reacted to the king's demands the way she always did when something vexed her: she went shooting.

Her bow was a comforting weight in her hand as she marched to the practice field. The smooth wood was exactly the right size for someone of her stature – as Rudolf must have known, for he'd given it to her on her last name day. Much easier to shoot with than his own monster bow, easily taller than he was. It had taken her years before she'd had the strength to fire anything from his bow, but when a lucky shot clipped the target, Rudolf had made good on his promise – a bow of her own, and archery lessons to keep her from shooting him instead of the target.

Not that she'd meant to do that. The arrow had accidentally gone through his boot, and she'd told him so. She wasn't sure he believed her, though. She sighed and took aim.

She emptied her quiver in record speed, wishing the plain wood target had a picture of the king's face painted on it. She did not even know what the bastard looked like. She imagined King Donald as old and fat with thinning hair, a petulant fool who demanded things that were not his like the spoiled child he'd once been.

She fitted an arrow to the bowstring.

How dare he try to claim her lands. Her father's lands, truly, but hers, too, for she was his firstborn.

She drew the arrow back.

How dare he insist they pay him tribute. A man who had no right to their lands, or the fruit from it.

She sighted along the arrow, blowing out her breath in a rush.

How dare he call their people foreigners. How dare he!

She released, and the arrow flew toward the target. It lodged in the side, so close to the edge that it only hung there for a moment before it fell to earth.

Earth that sorry excuse for a king had no claim on!

Portia stomped her foot for emphasis.

"Looking at the target, I wondered if Arlie had picked up a bow for her annual archery practice. But Arlie doesn't stamp her foot like that." Rudolf gestured at the target across the field. "Are you feeling sorry for the target, Portia? Trying not to hit it because hitting it would be cruel?"

Portia's face turned as red as her hair. Trust Rudolf to bring that up. No one else remembered something that happened ten years ago, except him. "I still think butchering pigs is cruel, but nothing I can say or do will stop it, for the rest of your will still eat it. So will I, and be properly thankful to the animal that gave its life so that we may eat its flesh." She sounded like the priest at last Sunday's mass, and she knew it. Before Rudolf could tease her for that, too, she continued, "It won't matter if I miss my target, anyway. Men all bunch up in an army, so if I miss one man, I'm bound to hit the one beside him."

He laughed. "Since when are you riding to war? Your father is not so short of men he'll need you to fight." His gaze travelled from her feet up to her face. "Unless you plan on wearing a man's garb. There's many a man on the island who's dreamed of seeing you without your gown, but I'm sure none of them imagined you'd be wearing armour."

Just as her blush faded, it flamed into life once more. Only Rudolf could say these things with such brutal honesty, without apology. Not for the first time, she wondered if he'd been one of those dreaming men. Men who would soon be off to war, with no time to dream of anyone, she told herself sternly. "I have no need to ride to war. Raiders come in boats when they see fit, and if the menfolk are not at home, then it falls to us women to defend our homes."

Rudolf inclined his head. "So it does. Here in the south, right up to Viken in the north. But your father will never leave you here unprotected, and you will always have me." He drew a dagger from his belt and sent it flying toward the target. He hit the centre. "I will defend you with my life, Portia."

That serious look in his eyes heated her all over again, but not just her face this time. There was something about Rudolf that lit a fire inside her. The kind of fire she liked, but could never stoke. "I'm sure my father will be very grateful for your service," she said sweetly.

He opened his mouth, but no words came

out. Then he shook his head, as if to rid it of ideas that had no place there, a feeling Portia understood well. Finally, he said, "But it would be lax of me to stop you from practising, when you so sorely need it."

"Why you – " Portia began, then stopped as Rudolf grinned. When he smiled, the man was charming enough to coax a honeycomb from an angry bear. Not even she was immune to him. Perhaps that's why she felt so hot inside. "Help me retrieve my arrows, then."

Rudolf pulled the lucky few from the target while she hunted through the grass for the rest. When the quiver was more than half full once more, she marched back to where she'd left her bow. Rudolf with his longer strides got there first, lifting the weapon in readiness, though he didn't hand it to her.

"First, I must check your stance, Portia," he said. "Show me how you stand."

Never one to like being ordered about, Portia set her hand on her hip and waved an arrow. "You'd better hope I don't decide to make you my target instead."

"You wouldn't do that," he said easily. "You like me."

No matter how much he irritated her and make her feel other unwelcome feelings she had to ruthlessly suppress, Portia had to admit she did. Not aloud, though. "I might also like to see you hopping around with an arrow in your foot again."

"You have your dreams and I have mine. I like mine better. Now, do you wish to practise, or no?"

Portia relented and stepped up to the bow, angling herself so that she faced Rudolf and not the target. She fitted her arrow to the string. "There. Good enough for you?"

Rudolf inspected her, even going as far as to march right the way around her, before he nudged her foot with his. "Your stance needs to be a little wider, pointed to where you wish the arrow to go." His arms came around her, lifting the bow so that the arrow no longer pointed at the ground.

Portia wanted to relax into his embrace, and surrender to the promise of protection he offered. It would be so easy, and yet it was something she could never do. Rudolf was a foreigner, a ward sent from Viken to learn to fight in her father's house. One day, he would be summoned home to fight for whatever Viken lord his family owed fealty to. Portia was her father's eldest daughter, and heir to Isla. The man she married would follow her father as Lord of Isla, the largest and most powerful of the Southern Isles. She could never marry a mere household knight. It would take a lord at least, or a lord's son, to hold Father's place in council. Rudolf knew this as well as she did, which was why he never took liberties, though he made it very clear he would like to. But that was an invitation she could never offer.

She straightened, paying more attention to the bow and arrow than the boy whose breath tickled the back of her neck. "Which foot do you like best, Dolf?" she asked.

"Your left one, because that's pointed at the target," he said, cupping her elbow in his hand. "Now draw, sight along the arrow..." His hand slammed into her gut, just below her breasts, forcing her to exhale. "Now I've made you breathless, you may shoot."

The arrow whistled across the field and thwacked into the target. Not in the centre, marked by the divot from Rudolf's knife, but nearer than any of her earlier attempts.

"There!"

Rudolf inclined his head. "Not bad. If you were aiming for a man's heart, you might have hit him in the throat. But we can improve on that."

With infinite patience Portia knew she would never possess, Rudolf helped her empty her quiver – all into the target this time. Then he headed across the field with her to retrieve the arrows again.

When the quiver was full, he held it out and asked, "Are you still angry, or have you done enough shooting for one day?"

Until she hit the centre of the target every time, it would not be enough. She sighed. A landless knight like Rudolf would not understand. "One more time," she said, reaching for the quiver.

Rudolf caught her hand in his. "You're bleeding. I say you have done enough. We should get you inside, so one of your sisters can bandage these fingers. You can practise more on the morrow, but first, I must get you some pigs' ears."

"Pigs' ears are no use to anyone, except the pig itself," Portia said, snatching her hand back. Her fingers tingled where he'd touched them, a hint of magic that called for more. She refused to yield. Isla would not yield.

Rudolf chuckled. "Get you to your sisters. I'll return your things to the armoury, and find you inside." He shouldered both her quiver and her bow and headed across the yard.

Portia sucked on her bleeding fingers as she headed inside. Arlie would exclaim over the blood, fanning herself in case she fainted. Lina would be the one to clean and bandage her, like Nurse had taught her to before age and infirmity had called the old woman from this life.

As it would one day call them all.

But not yet, if Portia had any say in it.

Four

The moment Arlie spotted Rudolf, she cried, "Dolf will go to war to save us! Won't you, Dolf?"

Portia hushed her. She might only be a few minutes older than her sisters, but sometimes the difference felt like years.

"If you ladies need saving, I would be honoured to be of service," Rudolf said as he approached. He met Portia's eyes without a hint of laughter and bowed low. "From what must I save you? Is there another spider?"

Lina laughed. "No, only Portia screams at spiders. This time, it's some pompous king, demanding tribute from all the island lords, which they will not pay."

"That's no way to talk about your liege," Rudolf said mildly. "I've never heard anyone call King Harald pompous before."

"That's because it's not him!" Arlie giggled. "It's some silly foreigner called Donald. He calls for tithes and men, to combat what he calls our foreign invaders, so that he might help us make the Southern Isles great again."

"Nay, he wants to make Alba great again, but he insists we are an important part of it," Lina corrected.

Portia frowned. "Important enough to attract his interest, because he thinks we might offer him men or money. No king has every offered us anything we didn't have to pay for. Not King Harald or this Donald. The lords of the isles know this, and they will refuse him, which will mean war."

"The lords are in the right of it. The isles are under Harald's protection, and they do not belong to some man called Donald. If he wants them, he will have to fight for them, and pay dearly," Rudolf declared.

Now Portia thought of it, he did sound like one of the lords. Somehow, over the years, Rudolf the boy had turned into a man, or at least something like one. A pity he would never be one of them. Because if he was…

"Perhaps this Donald should just ask to marry Portia. We all know no man on the islands is good enough for her, for she turns her nose up at all of them. Would a king suit you, Portia?" Arlie teased.

Rudolf's eyes were upon her, and Portia found she could not meet them. "Father knows as well as I do that I can only wed a man who can hold the islands. Hold them, and defend them, like he has. All this Donald has done is blow wind at us, and the isles have withstood greater gales than anything he's thrown at us thus far. I will wed when a strong enough man presents himself, and not before."

"See? Portia will never marry for love. Or she'd have picked Rudolf, long ago," Lina declared with a smile.

Arlie dissolved in a fit of giggles, falling back to kick her legs in the air.

Once again, Portia felt far too hot. She rose and marched out of the room, the sound of her sisters' laughter following her. And booted footsteps. Rudolf, of course.

"Portia," he began cautiously, as if wishing to warn her of his presence.

She turned and held up her hand to halt him before he said any more. "My sisters like to joke at my expense. And yours. I'm sorry if their levity sounds insulting to your ears. You are a strong and skilled warrior. Both my father and I know that. So do my sisters, I think. But when we hear whispered news of war…well, you see how we react. Lina will pick herbs to dry for every wound and ailment imaginable, and fill the cellars with all the food she can possibly preserve. Arlie…she will make light of everything, as she always does, for laughter is her way."

"And you shall shoot things, because even if every man on this island dies in battle, you will still defend it while you have breath left in your body," Rudolf finished for her. "Isla is your home, and the Southern Isles are your kingdom as much as Harald holds Viken, or Donald does Alba."

Now it was Portia's turn to laugh. "No one understands me the way you do, Dolf. I swear it is as though you have some magical power to see into my head. I'm glad I didn't shoot you."

Rudolf laughed with her. "I'm glad you didn't shoot me, either. If it comes to war, I hope I am never on the opposing side to you and your father. I meant it when I said I would protect you." He held out his hand. "Here."

Portia glanced down and recoiled. "What in heaven's name do you intend to do with those?"

"Give me your hand."

Reluctantly, she did as he asked. He wrapped the pig's ear around her middle finger, the leather surprisingly warm and soft from being in his pocket. Next, he threaded a thin leather thong through the holes edging the ear, until he'd laced it like one of her gowns. He pulled the whole thing taut, then tied it at the bottom. "Now the others." Soon he'd shrouded all three of her middle fingers in pigs' ears. The leather was paler than boot leather, as though the pigs' ears were tanned differently. In fact, the pigskin was so close to the shade of her own skin that it looked like she wasn't wearing the finger guards at all. "Next time, wear these when you need to shoot out your frustration. Your arms will tire long before you make your fingers bleed. Pigs' ears are tough."

"Thank you, Dolf!" Portia threw her arms around his neck. Too late, she realised as her body moulded to his that she shouldn't do such things any more. Though he cared for her as much as any brother, Rudolf was most certainly not one of her siblings. Awkwardly, she peeled herself away from him, only now realising that he held his arms stiffly at his sides. Stopping himself from returning her embrace, or pushing her away? Oh, she was so stupid.

"It's my pleasure, Portia," he said. With a slight bow, he left her.

Portia sighed, only now realising she held her well-wrapped fingers over her heart. If only she was as free as her sisters. But the world didn't work the way she wanted to, for life was nothing like a fairytale.

Five

When Angus, Lord of Isla, slumped into his seat at dinner, no one dared ask what made him so weary, for they all knew. Lina gestured imperiously for servants to fill her father's plate, while Portia poured wine for him. He would share what he knew after dinner, and not before.

It wasn't until Angus dismissed the servants that Rudolf began to worry about what he might say. If he wanted to share secrets with his family alone, then Rudolf should retire and save the man from doing him the dishonour of dismissing him.

Rudolf rose. "I took Hector for a long ride today, and it occurs to me that he was limping a little toward the end. I should go check on him before it gets too dark to see."

Angus lifted his hand. "Stay, Rudolf. What I have to say concerns you, too. The horse can wait until morning."

Rudolf sat down. He could feel Portia's curious gaze upon him, but he forced himself to keep his own eyes on Lord Angus. Hope flared in his breast, but he forced it back behind his ribs.

Angus drained his cup and set it down with finality. "As you all know, King Donald of Alba has laid claim to the islands, and a list of the tribute that he believes is his due. Tribute we have failed to pay in the past, he says, which must be paid, too. He sent these demands by way of a messenger, who was commanded to read Donald's missive aloud to me, and all the other lords, to make sure we understood. For, apparently, we are an illiterate lot on the Southern Isles, or so he says."

This time, it was Lina who leaped to her feet. "I suggest all the lords should pen him a message by their own hands, suggesting he shove his missive up his arse. No, that he instruct his messenger to do it for him, as he probably can't find his arse with both hands and a map." As quickly as she'd risen, she subsided again. Lina was both as calm and relentless as the sea. She'd make some man a good wife, one day, as long as he let her run his household without interfering.

Angus waved a hand in acknowledgement. "Our response to Donald is something all the lords of the isles will decide in council. I sent my own messenger with his, so they should start arriving soon, and I will be there to greet them when they do." He turned thoughtful eyes toward Rudolf. "I'd like you to come with me."

"So shall I!" Portia declared.

"No. You must stay here and protect your sisters," Angus said. "This may be a council of war, and no place for you. Your presence would complicate matters." He deliberately didn't look at her.

Portia looked ready to explode.

Rudolf placed a sympathetic hand on her wrist. "I would be honoured to attend a council. Then I will be able to carry a full account of the decisions back to the girls here if you are called away by other responsibilities."

Portia yanked her arm away. "You'd better," she said darkly.

She said little to him for the rest of the meal, and for the days before Rudolf departed with her father for Loch Findlugan. Her father received a fond farewell, but Rudolf merely earned a pointed look before she disappeared into the practice yard, where the thwack of arrows hitting the target could soon be heard.

He and Angus were barely out of sight along the road before the lord asked, "What do you think of her?"

"I think Portia is a lovely, strong-minded young woman," Rudolf said cautiously.

Angus laughed. "The stubbornest of my three little pigs, you mean. If it comes to war, as I fear it might, she would take up a sword to fight right alongside the rest of us. It would have been better for her if she'd been born a boy."

"I would not like her so much if she was," Rudolf said without thinking. He regretted the words the moment they left his lips, but it was too late to retrieve them.

Angus turned an appraising eye in his direction. "Yes, and she likes you, too. She doesn't think anyone notices, but sometimes she looks at you the way her mother used to regard me. She listens to you, too, though she won't listen to anyone else. Maybe you'll be able to control her."

Rudolf burst out laughing. "Control Portia? I pity the man who tries. She will huff and puff and blow his manhood away. She is your daughter, after all."

"And as my daughter, she is also my heir, as I'm sure you know." Angus paused, as if he wanted this to sink in. Finally, he continued, "The man who marries her will also inherit her claim to Isla, when I am gone, and perhaps even my place in council, if the other lords accept him. Birthright is not enough here on the Southern Isles, you understand. A man must also be a leader and a warrior worth following."

Rudolf nodded. His father had told him the same thing when he was a boy in Viken. Varg was the older brother, yet Harald had become king. "My people are much the same. This way, if a king dies while his sons are still young, another man may take the throne while the sons are brought up like any other highborn warriors. When the next king dies…his successor is chosen from among the men with suitable claims of birth, blood and marriage, but he must have the strength to lead the…I suppose you would call them chieftains, much like your lords."

"Here on the islands, every lord is a king within his borders, for an ocean separates him from the others. We have no kings."

This was less true than it appeared, as Rudolf well knew. "Ah, but there is King Harald, whose claim to these lands is responsible for the kind hospitality you have offered me for so many years. And this King Donald, a neighbour who covets what isn't his. And there is yourself, a lord among lords. If the islands had their own king, it would be you."

Angus nodded in satisfaction, as though this was the answer he'd hoped for. "You've fought with us, as one of us."

"We both serve the same king. Protecting these lands is as much my responsibility as it is yours, though I do not command any men." Yet, Rudolf added silently. He'd distinguished himself in the battles and raiding parties he had fought in, to the point where he easily assumed command when circumstances required it.

Lord Angus had taught him battle tactics and strategy were just as important as the strength of his army when battle was joined. But the men he commanded had always belonged to Lord Angus.

Unlike his father, who commanded all the armies of Viken, and the ships, too.

Lord Angus seemed to read his thoughts. "You fight well in the field, and the men follow you. That is no small thing in a land like this one. You understand battle tactics better than most, both on and off the field."

Rudolf was not accustomed to such high praise. "It is a while since I have had a worthy opponent. Perhaps you would agree to a chess match while we wait for the other lords to arrive?" He patted his saddle bag. "I brought mine."

Lord Angus shook his head. "I think your skills at that game surpassed mine a long time ago. But never let it be said that I turned down an offer for battle. We shall play on the shores of Loch Findlugan after the sun sets."

"I look forward to it."

They rode on in silence, lost in their own separate thoughts. As they always did, Rudolf's thoughts turned to Portia, and what she might be doing now without him.

Six

"You have a longer reach. You should be able to best him easily, Keith!" Lina called.

"Widald is so much stronger. Hit him harder, Widald, and you will surely win!" Arlie said.

Portia found her sisters watching a mock battle in the practice yard between two young men who were surprisingly evenly matched. She observed them for a few moments before she realised the men were not really battling at all. All that flexing of muscles, fighting without armour or even shirts, and blows that did not seem to land was a show to impress the two girls. A show that was working, judging by Arlie's gasps and Lina's white-knuckled hands as she clutched them to her chest.

"Your turn," Widald whispered. He hooked Keith's wooden practice sword out of his hand and sent it spinning across the yard, scattering chickens that squawked in protest.

"I yield," Keith said thickly. At some point, Widald must have landed a blow to Keith's nose, for it was still bleeding.

"You won!" Arlie dashed across the yard and wrapped her arms around Widald, who grinned at Keith over Arlie's head.

Lina beckoned to Keith. "Let me see to your wounds."

Keith winked back at Widald.

Portia pursed her lips and waited. When her sisters' ministrations culminated in an invitation to dinner that both men eagerly accepted, she knew the wait would soon be over. Sure enough, the men left the yard to put their weapons away.

"Does my father know you are trying to seduce my sisters?" Portia asked.

Keith and Widald exchanged glances, then bowed. "No, Lady Portia." Neither seemed to want to look at her.

"What do you think he will say when I tell him?" Portia said.

Widald lifted his head to meet her eyes. "When I ask for Lady Arlie, I would hope Lord Angus supports my suit."

"And mine for Lady Lina," added Keith.

Portia hesitated. They meant to marry her sisters, not simply seduce them? The girls were of an age for it, much like herself, but it had not occurred to her that they might marry so soon. Unlike the slavish daughters of other places, the women of Isla and the other Southern Isles were proud mistresses of their own destiny. They chose their own husbands, or at least most of them did. Even Portia's father could not force her to marry a man not of her choosing. Though the council might put pressure on him and hence her if they had a man in mind.

Perhaps that was why he had left her here –
he wanted to discuss possible husbands for her
with the council.

"We know how many suitors there are for
your hand, Lady Portia. Lina and Arlie might
not have the same claim as you, but they are
no less beautiful," Keith continued.

Of course they were. The three girls were
identical in appearance, if not disposition.
Little wonder that people had called them the
Three Little Pigs when they were children, for
most people couldn't tell them apart.

Her sisters deserved to be happy with men
who loved them. They could do much worse
than these two. Portia herself might do worse,
what with war coming and all. She would not
let her choice place Isla in danger.

"I wish you good fortune," Portia said
finally, "but not fertility. Not yet." With a
sharp look at them, she marched off.

But in the back of her mind, a tiny seed of
doubt took root: for the first time, she dreaded
her father's return.

Seven

Lord Lewis was the first guest to arrive at Loch Findlugan. His companion was a messenger from King Harald who had much to say to the council. Lord Angus glanced at Rudolf, then took the messenger for a walk around the lakeshore, so that they might discuss weighty matters in private.

Rudolf burned with curiosity as he watched them go, so he jumped when Lord Lewis's arm landed heavily on his shoulder.

"Let them go, boy. We'll find out what they have to say in council, soon enough. Who are you? I don't remember Angus having a son. You look older than those girls of his."

Rudolf gave Lord Lewis his full attention. "I'm Rudolf, Lord Angus's foster son. From Viken."

Lord Lewis clapped him on the back so hard it would have tipped a lesser man over. "Thought so! My mother came from Viken, and insisted on marrying an Islander, for she declared she wanted a man who wasn't a blonde behemoth. She was a shieldmaiden on one of your dragon ships, but she was fonder of the shield than the ship, and she liked my father more than fighting, so when her brothers departed, she stayed."

"Viken women are as fierce as the women here on the islands," Rudolf agreed. "They have the same strong spirit. I'm sure that's why she stayed."

Lord Lewis winked. "Spirited island girls, hmm? Methinks you have one in particular in mind."

For a moment, Rudolf thought he might blush as brightly as Portia. Except no one could outdo Portia at that. He fought to keep his voice light as he said, "I have no bride yet, Lord Lewis. While I am dependent on the kindness of Lord Angus, so far from my family, I have little to offer a lady."

"Hmm." Lord Lewis made a great show of clearing his throat. It was clear he didn't believe Rudolf.

Best to change the topic. "Did your mother ever teach you Viken war games?" Rudolf asked. "I have a chess set I brought from home. Lord Angus and I sometimes play in the evenings. I'd be happy to give you a lesson in how to play, if you like."

Lord Lewis laughed. "I haven't played that in years! Fetch your set, and we'll see who teaches a lesson to who."

Despite his claim of not having played in a long time, Lord Lewis proved a formidable opponent, and Rudolf lost more games than he won. By the time the other lords arrived to occupy Lord Lewis's attention, Rudolf was more than happy to beat a strategic retreat.

Lord Angus caught him packing his chess set deep in the bottom of his saddle bag. "Don't feel too bad. Lord Lewis has such a passion for the game, I have yet to see him lose. If you wish for a fairer match, where you have a chance to win, perhaps you and I can play after the council meets."

Lord Angus was rarely wrong, but this was one occasion Rudolf was happy to tell him so. "Actually, I won several games. Almost half." Rudolf couldn't keep the smugness out of his tone.

Lord Angus laughed. "Then I had best watch out, lest Lewis try to steal you from my household."

"Nothing he has to offer could entice me to agree to that," Rudolf replied. There was no place for him in any household that didn't hold Portia.

Lord Harris hailed Angus, who clapped

Rudolf on the shoulder with a vague, "Good man," before he headed off to join his newly arrived friend.

A fleet of fishing boats ferried the assembled lords across the lake to a tiny, bare island where two men were hastily erecting a sort of canopy to keep the rain off. Most of the lords' men had been left on shore with the servants, who busied themselves preparing food for the assembly. The firepit glowed to life and already a pig was turning on the spit, which would hopefully be ready by the time the council meeting was over.

Rudolf expected to be part of the shore party, but Angus had refused to board a boat until Rudolf was on it, so he sat in the bow, facing the green mound that didn't seem grand enough to be Council Island.

The grass grated under the fishing boat's hull. Automatically, Rudolf leaped out onto the waterlogged turf to help pull the craft further out of the water so that Lord Angus wouldn't get his feet wet. Of course, Angus didn't care, for he squelched down right beside Rudolf. "Good show," Angus whispered as he strode past to the top of the hill.

It took Rudolf a moment to realise what Angus meant. The other boats held off, waiting for Angus before they dared to set foot on the holy isle, which had been the place of council meetings for as long as anyone could remember. It was said that the druids and chieftains of a thousand years ago planned their campaigns against foreign armies on this spot.

And he'd been the first to step onto it, not Angus. Why hadn't Angus warned him? Unless he'd wanted Rudolf to precede him...

His suspicion grew stronger as each of the lords landed on the island and left their boats. Some merely glanced at him, while others openly stared. Lord Lewis grinned as though he was privy to Lord Angus's plans. Rudolf wished he'd thought to ask Angus to share his secret. Of course, he'd have had to know there was a secret...

"My friends, lords of the isles, honoured guest." A nod at Rudolf told him Angus meant him. "Welcome once again to Council Island. By now, you should have all received the message from King Donald of Alba…"

Muttering and grumblings erupted from the circle of men. No one liked King Donald, or his message.

Angus cleared his throat. "I, too, have heard it, and I share your discontent. However, for those who might not remember, he has asked for several things. First, that we recognise his claim to the Southern Isles, and acknowledge him as our king. Second, that we pay tribute to him – not just this year, but for every year of his reign. Third, that we provide him with men to fight the war he faces on his southern border."

The grumblings grew louder.

"In exchange, he offers us the opportunity to help him make Alba great again. He will send men to help us drive out the Viken people who have settled among us, and when they are all gone, the men will help us build walls to keep foreign invaders out." Angus held up his hand for silence. "And, he has offered one of his sons as husband for Lady Portia, who he insists must travel to Alba, where she will stay."

Rudolf jumped to his feet. "Portia will never agree to that!" he shouted.

But Angus never heard. Every lord was just as loud, so the cacophony of sound as the rulers vented their displeasure to the sky with shaken fists and colourful language drowned out individual voices. They were a rumble of thunder, heralding the storm to come.

But Angus was not the Lord of Isla for nothing. He waited patiently, letting the men rage until the volume subsided. Slowly, they sank back onto their benches.

All except for Lord Lewis, whose planted feet turned him into a mighty tree that would not be budged. "If you're going to throw out Vikens, then you may start with me," he roared.

Silence fell.

Most of the men looked shocked. Angus's expression never changed. They'd cooked this plan up between them, Angus and Lewis, Rudolf realised, impressed. This could only be the beginning. He settled down to watch what he knew would prove to be an intriguing show.

"My mother was a Viken."

"Mine, too."

"My grandfather came from Viken."

"My sister married one."

Around and around it went, until every man had declared his relationship to some Viken or other. Vikens had lived among the Southern Islanders for centuries, Rudolf knew, so over the last four hundred years, everyone on the islands had some Viken blood in them. It had been a long time since they'd been foreigners to him.

Angus broke the thoughtful silence. "This council made an agreement with the Viken king, an Erik who has long since gone to his heavenly reward. We would share the islands with his people, and they would defend us against invaders. We would stand together to defend our home." He stared around the circle, taking care to meet every set of eyes for a moment until he had them all. "King Harald sits on Erik's throne now, and we no longer share this soil with the council members who met on that fateful day. But we do stand with one of his descendants." Angus motioned for Rudolf to stand. "Prince Rudolf Vargssen is Harald's nephew. He came to my household as a boy, but he is now more than man enough to fight beside us as a member of my family, which he has. Often."

His interrogatory stare swept around the lords again. "King Harald is not here, but his nephew is. Prince Rudolf, what do you advise the council to do?"

He'd caught Rudolf unprepared, and Angus knew it. Rudolf wet his lips. "I would advise…the lords assembled here to honour your agreements. Oathbreakers are reviled on Viken as much as they are here. Is my uncle such a poor ruler that your oaths are worthless to you, and you will choose to buy another king of whom you know nothing? And not just with money and goods. You would buy him with the lives of your men, the virtue of your virgin daughters…for if he sets his sights on the Lady Portia, none of your daughters will be safe. What do we care for the greatness of our neighbours, who would drive a wedge between our combined peoples, and build walls for which there is no need? We do not need Donald or anything he has to offer, and I would advise you to tell him so."

Several men roared their agreement, but others remained silent. When the roars had died down, one man clambered to his feet, tugging his beard as though checking it was secured to his chin.

"You have something to say, Lord Calum?" Angus asked.

The bearded man nodded. "I do. It is clear the boy is Harald's man, however long he has lived under your roof, and of course his loyalty is to his king. To his family."

"I consider Lord Angus as much family as those I left behind in Viken," Rudolf said.

Angus waved him into silence. "Please continue, Lord Calum."

Calum nodded, then said, "I have no desire to be an oathbreaker, but I made no such oath to King Erik or Harald or whoever the Vikens have sitting on their throne. The council who made that long ago oath did so to ensure a lasting peace that we have known for generations. If a similar oath to King Donald now would bring a similar peace, while keeping to old agreements can only lead to war, should we not take the olive branch that is offered, and forge a new agreement?"

Another man rose.

"Lord Roe?" Angus prompted.

Lord Roe inclined his head in acknowledgement. "Donald isn't offering an olive branch. He's handing us a poisoned chalice. There's no promise of peace in his offer. He starts by wanting to make war on our own people, for Viken blood runs in all of our veins. Then he finishes with a demand for our men to fight his wars, which do not concern us. Donald is offering us war where we currently have peace. Harald does not ask for our daughters or our sons – he demands no hostages he can hold against us. I am with Lord Angus!" He sat down, smiling, as the other lords clapped.

All but Calum, whose expression had twisted into a sneer. "You're only kissing Angus's arse so he'll let your lackwit son marry his daughter!" He turned and lifted his tunic, baring his own hairy arse to emphasise his point.

It took several cries of, "Put it away!" and one "No one wants to kiss your hairy butt cheeks, you old walrus!" before Calum finally sat down.

Lord Harris, a giant of a man who didn't need to stand to be taller than the rest, cleared his throat. "Whether we choose Harald or Donald or declare some other poor fool king, I want one thing to be certain. Lady Portia must remain protected here on the Southern Isles, for as long as she lives."

Several men shouted their support, and a grateful Angus called for a vote. In the resulting hubbub, Lewis shuffled close enough to Rudolf to allow him to mutter, "Watch this well. Any man with an unmarried son will side with Angus. Those with none or too many daughters they wish to marry well will take Calum's side."

The lords divided and Lewis kept up his commentary: "Spinster daughter, daughters, doesn't like Vikens because his wife ran off with one, and Calum."

The other men argued loudly with one another, trying to persuade the others to cross to their side.

Rudolf lowered his voice. "Why does Calum hate Angus so much?"

Lewis glanced from one to the other. "Calum thinks he should be Lord of Isla, not his younger brother. But Catriona chose

Angus, then died early in their marriage after giving birth to three girls, and Calum has never forgiven him. If Angus supports something, Calum will oppose it."

Angus counted the men on each side. "The council votes to support Lord Harris's suggestion. My daughter will be protected here on the isles."

"How do you propose to do that?" Calum drawled. "Everyone knows the story of the Three Little Pigs. Locking that girl up is pointless, for she will only escape as soon as it suits her."

Rudolf had long regretted his flippant comment that had resulted in a nickname Portia and her sisters hated. Especially when the story that went with it was now being used so maliciously against her. By her own flesh and blood.

"Find the girl a husband! Then she'll be his responsibility."

Rudolf couldn't tell who had spoken, but he was soon drowned out by offers of sons, nephews, and, in the case of Lord Dand, the young lord himself. He wanted to shout at them all to be silent. Portia would have screamed it, and then delivered a scathing lecture on where they could stash their manhoods, if in fact they still had them when she was done.

Angus had been wise to leave her at home. Rudolf wished he didn't have to witness this.

Lord Lewis cupped his hands to his mouth. "Why not forge an alliance with Harald's family? The young prince here isn't married, so why not make him truly a member of Lord Angus's family by giving him to the girl?"

Rudolf had a sudden vision of himself wrapped in a giant red ribbon, being presented to Portia. At the very least, it would make her laugh.

Angus hushed them. "You have all offered many eligible bachelors for my daughter to consider. But the council has voted to protect her here in the isles, where a woman may choose her own husband. We should each choose our champion, to form a personal bodyguard for her, until that happens. In protecting Lady Portia, they will each have their chance to woo her, if that is their wish."

Now Rudolf wanted to laugh. Hard. Portia would not take the news well when she discovered she was to always be surrounded by a personal honour guard. He sobered when he realised he would be the one who'd have to tell her.

If there was a fate, she was the one laughing at him right now.

Eight

The council meeting dragged on in a series of
debates, which ranged from stories the lords
had heard about Donald to the difficulties of
tithing their own people. This continued until
the sun sank low on the horizon, and Rudolf
could smell roasting meat from the fire pit on
the shore. The fishing boats returned to ferry
them across the loch, and Rudolf found
himself in the same boat as Lord Ronin, one of
the men who had stood beside Calum in the

vote about Portia. At first, Rudolf wondered at the man's motive, but Ronin soon enlightened him. Just as Lewis had said, he was a man with many unmarried daughters, and an opportunity to sell them to an eligible bachelor like Rudolf was something Lord Ronin did not intend to miss.

Thankfully the boat trip was short, and Rudolf managed to avoid Ronin for the rest of the evening.

After talking all day, the lords still had plenty to say, though they spoke of more mundane matters. Daughters and wives, sons and servants, sheep and seals, cattle and crops. Rudolf had little to add to any of these subjects, so he simply listened.

Eventually, they all retired early, for they knew it would be another gruelling day on the morrow.

The second day started with less of a show than the first, for Rudolf knew to hang back and let Angus go first. The debate resumed, and Rudolf wished he hadn't come. Day after day, they droned on, seeming to get no closer to a plan of action than they were on the day they began. Yet there were useful suggestions amid the filibustering. Slowly but surely, each man realised what Portia had known instantly: that whatever action they took, it would lead to war.

Sometime on the fifth day, Rudolf was roused from his doze by an elbow administered to his ribs. He instantly regretted his late-night chess match with Lewis, whose sharp elbow was probably a dig at revenge for Rudolf's win last night. Feeling the entire council's eyes on him, Rudolf ventured, "Could you repeat that?"

Angus looked amused. "The council would like to know what kind of assistance King Harald will offer us in this matter. Can you tell us what kind of army he has at his disposal?"

Rudolf spread his arms wide and shrugged. "I have no idea. I was a boy when I left Viken, and I know more of your strengths than I do of my uncle's. Men have died in battle, old men who did not have retired. Boys have become men, and taken the places that belong to greybeards. To know my uncle's true strength, you would have to ask him."

Lord Harris said, "Never mind the numbers, then. Do you believe your uncle will offer men to help defend the isles against Donald?"

Angus stared at him hungrily, expectantly. Rudolf wished he knew what the man wanted him to say.

But he did not, so what Rudolf said was, "I would have to ask him."

Angus jumped in before any of the other lords could. "But a request from his nephew, his own blood, for warriors and weapons would be received far more favourably than anything from the rest of us. I propose that Rudolf make contact with his kinsman in order to enlist his support." Angus surveyed the circle. "Any man who doesn't agree, raise a hand."

Only Calum's hand waved like that of a drowning man for a moment before dropping limply into his lap, defeated. Angus produced a scroll and began to read from it. Amid all the waffling, Angus had paid attention to every word of their discussion. And from it, he had distilled a powerful liquor that would become their brave plan for the future.

Defences would be shored up, more weapons would be made, supplies of food and drink would be stored, and they would remain vigilant. There was no mention of Donald or even Harald.

In short, they would do nothing new. They would continue as they always had, preparing for an attack that might never come, but remaining in readiness for when it did.

The collected lords gave their assent to the plan, though Calum was predictably silent.

It was with considerable relief that Rudolf left the island for good, hoping never to return.

That night they feasted, celebrating their decision as much as the opportunity to see their friends again. For life held many uncertainties, especially with the threat of war, and who knew when they might share bread and meat again?

The ale flowed freely until Calum burst into a surprisingly familiar song. Even Rudolf joined in, though he did not know all the words. The song ended but the singing continued late into the night as all good feasts should. Rudolf grew brave enough to offer some songs from his homeland, though he found he had forgotten many of the words. By night's end, they all sang the same song, for at the bottom of a barrel of ale, all words sound the same anyway.

The next morning, Angus found Rudolf dunking his pounding head in the loch in the hope that the icy waters might wash away some of the cursed ale that still swam behind his eyes.

Rudolf rose and flicked the wet hair off his face. "Good morning, Lord Angus," he said. He glanced behind Angus to find a man he did not know. "And this is…?"

"Gustav Gustavssen, a messenger sent by the King of Viken. He came to summon you home." Angus looked as though the words pained him.

Rudolf did not believe it. "But I promised Portia…"

Angus sighed. "Portia will wait. More important is the help we seek from your uncle. I always knew this day would come, though Varg said it would not. Your King has need of you, and so do we. A message he might ignore, but you? He cannot. Tell him what we face. Tell him that we are loyal. Tell him everything that took place during your time here. Tell him we were honoured to host you, and that we would be happy to host you again for as long as you wish to stay. You and any Viken men you bring with you." Only now did the worry show in Angus's eyes. "Please, Rudolf. If you have any loyalty or affection for me or my family, I beg you to do this for us."

The lump in Rudolf's throat made it hard to speak. Yet speak he must. "I will," he vowed.

He squeezed his eyes shut, forcing out the words that cost him so much to say. "Protect Portia for me. That is all I ask. Protect Portia for me and I promise I will return with all the men I can muster."

Angus bowed his head. "I swear I will."

Rudolf said his farewells with the rest, smiling and nodding to hide the heavy heart within. By the time the sun was high in the sky, Rudolf was resigned. He would follow Gustav the stranger to his fate.

Nine

Portia met her father in the yard, barefoot and out of breath from running. "What happened? Will we be safe?" She peered around her father and her face fell. "Where is Dolf?"

"The council has decided to refuse Donald's demands. They have also sent a message to Harald, the Viken king, asking for reinforcements should Donald choose to invade." Angus sighed, a sound that sank beneath the weighty worries of all the world, or at least the Southern Isles. "Rudolf insisted on carrying the message to the king himself."

Portia didn't want to believe it. "He's gone to Viken? Why? And without saying goodbye?"

"Sailing takes time, and Donald could arrive at any moment. Or he might not arrive at all. Better to have King Harald's help sooner rather than later. Rudolf asked me to tell you goodbye, and to ask you to take care of his things until his return."

Her father might not know it, but his eyes wouldn't meet hers when he lied, just like now.

Portia took a deep, shuddering breath, forcing back the sobs that threatened to choke her.

Rudolf would not come back, and there would be war.

"What must we do to prepare Isla for the coming war?" Portia asked.

Father brightened. "During the council meeting, I made a list. Let's go through it together, shall we?"

He extracted a scroll from his saddlebag and

Portia steeled herself for the storm to come.

Ten

The bustling harbour of Portnahaven seemed like another world after the strange solemnity that shrouded Council Island and Loch Findlugan. Rudolf almost wanted to turn back, to see if he could capture the spirit of the place to carry with him across the ocean. For the first time in many years, he felt afraid of what was to come.

He had so much he wanted to do with his life, and none of it involved a return to Viken right now. He burned to know why Harald had summoned him. He'd lived on Isla for so long, he thought they might have forgotten about him.

Yet Gustav was proof that they had not.

People stared at Rudolf and Gustav, as though they had never seen a Viken before. Which couldn't be the case, for two Viken longboats lay in the harbour.

A skinny boy called out from the mast of a merchant vessel, "Are you going to fight the dragon for the princess?"

Rudolf laughed at the thought that even cabin boys believed in fairytales. "No, there are no dragons left in the world, boy. Heroes have slayed them all."

"Not this one! He devours sheep and maidens and the king has offered half his kingdom and a whole princess to the man who brings him the dragon's head!"

A likely tale, though one that was widespread, for even the men on the longboats had heard of it. The details differed widely, but three things remained – the dragon, the half kingdom, and the whole princess.

Word had reached Viken, too, before their arrival. All people could talk about was this dragon. No one seemed to know or care about a looming war for the Southern Isles.

Rudolf paid far too high a price for a horse to carry him to the castle gates, where he drew to a halt, not willing to enter in case it was still Regina's realm. He was not afraid of many women, but Harald's queen had wanted to kill him as a child.

He addressed one of the guards: "Is the king at home? I carry an urgent message from the Southern Isles."

The guard shook his head. "No, he's up in the borderlands, dealing with some Opplanders. He rides at the head of his army – he shouldn't be hard to find."

Harald leading the army? "What about Varg?" Rudolf asked eagerly. Wherever the army was, he would find its commander – his father.

"Varg fell in battle not long ago. That's why the king commands the army now."

Dead? Rudolf received the news like a punch to the gut. He wanted to double over and howl in pain, but he knew he could not. So he straightened, stiffened, and said, "Thank you."

He turned his horse away from the gate, and headed for the road to Oppland, and the borderlands in between. It wasn't until he was alone in the empty road that he felt the first tear fall.

He was all that was left of his family, and he would never see his father again. Never know if his father was proud of the man he'd become.

More than anything, he wished himself back on Isla, with Angus and Portia. Angus would know what to say to make him feel whole again, and Portia would be sure to hug him until the hole this loss left in his heart had healed over.

He would have settled for just Portia,

feeling her soft body against his as their embrace became more intimate, her soft sigh as she yielded to him as she'd yielded to no one else and…

Rudolf cursed. Now he had a raging hard-on, a hole where his heart used to be, a horse which didn't want to do anything he told it to, and a king to find. Who might kill him on sight, to please his queen.

Oh, fate would be rolling around on the floor, she must be laughing to hard at him now.

Grimly, Rudolf rode on.

Eleven

"I caught them showing off for the girls in the practice yard, so I warned them, but Keith and Widald would not listen. I caught Keith kissing Lina in the stillroom several times and I lost count of the number of times Arlie came to dinner with bits of grass or hay stuck to her underdress. Both men said they had honourable intentions and talked of marriage, but I'm afraid – "

Father cut Portia off. "Afraid your sisters

might be doing things only married women do? Well, you're all of an age for it. I shouldn't be so surprised. I like having you girls at home so much I admit I've waited longer than I should have to find husbands for you all, but perhaps I have waited long enough. Both Keith and Widald are worthy sons of loyal men. I take it your sisters are fond of them?"

Portia's mouth hung open. Her father wanted to reward them for seducing her sisters? "Y-yes," she stammered. "At least, I think so. Lina seemed happy about the kissing, but Arlie only blushed when I asked about the hay."

"Good, good," Father said. "I'll speak to the men myself. If your sisters agree, I will need your help planning the wedding. As soon as possible, I would imagine."

"Yes, Father." Portia struggled to moisten her dry mouth. "What about me? If I were to…find some man I liked kissing, would you be as happy for me to marry him as you are for Lina and Arlie?" She already knew the answer, but she prayed he might be more forthcoming about who he did want her to marry instead.

Angus sighed. "Portia. You know it is different for you. I would hope that you would stop at just kissing, and not let your feelings get in the way of what is best for you, and Isla. There is a lot riding on the man you choose to marry, and with war coming…we must wait and see. A marriage alliance to the right man at the right time might save us. You are too precious to waste. Instead, I must keep you safe. I have spoken to the other lords on the council, and they have agreed to send some of their best warriors to be your personal guard. They will arrive…"

Father kept talking, but Portia stopped listening.

Inwardly, she breathed a sigh of relief that she would not be asked to marry any man yet.

When the time came, she would do what was best for Isla and the rest of the Southern Isles, but was it too much to ask that she might be allowed to marry for love?

Twelve

Shouts and singing rang out across the valley, punctuated by calls for more ale. Rudolf was surely home, for that was the sound he remembered most. He'd had to sneak into the feasts he'd remembered, for he'd been too young to attend as a full man before he'd left Viken for the Southern Isles, but now he was a man he could take part in full measure.

Would they remember him? Accept him as the man he'd become, or think of him as the boy who'd been banished to the ends of the earth to keep him away from the throne that blood bound him to the same way it bound Reidar, his cousin, the man Regina insisted would be the king's heir?

They toasted the king's health and courage and long life, fearless roars echoing into the night. This was a victory feast, then, for they didn't fear an enemy hearing them.

A cheer rose up, then the bonfire flared as someone threw more fuel on top. Now he could see them – a band of men, mostly sitting, though some stood by, and a servant crouched beside a barrel to fill a cup of ale.

He'd not tasted Viken ale since he was a boy, and even those sips had been stolen, burning down his throat as he fought not to gag at the taste. Reidar had claimed to like it, but then he'd been older, bolder, closer to manhood.

Someone peered into the darkness, as though he knew someone watched them.

It was now or never.

He dug his knees into his horse's side, not wanting to be caught creeping. He was a Viken warrior as much as any of these men, growing up with the same songs they roared even now.

So why did this not feel like home?

He burst into their circle. "I must see the king!" he said, surveying the surprised faces, ale cups hanging halfway to gaping mouths.

He slid from his skittish horse. The foolish beast kicked up sparks with its hooves, frightening itself further. Not for the first time, Rudolf missed the palfrey Lord Angus had given him on Isla. Hector would have known how to make a proper entrance, though now he was in Portia's care, the horse would have no need to do so.

So Rudolf planted his feet as firmly as he'd tried to teach Portia, a memory that lent strength to his tone when he demanded, "Where is the king? 'Twas he who summoned me."

But King Harald was not here. These men were all strangers. Rudolf had been away too long. No sign of recognition on anyone's expression, as hands dropped to the dagger-hilts and axe handles. Then his eyes met the piercing gaze of the man by the ale barrel.

A man who stood straight and tall, no longer crouched like a servant fetching a drink.

"Reidar!" Rudolf cried in relief.

The boy had broadened, even aged a little, but there was no mistaking his cousin, or the way he lifted the cup of ale to his own lips. Reidar served no one; the heir to the throne had no need to kneel.

For a moment, Reidar could have been the Lord of Isla, pausing to take stock before delivering some weighty judgement. This was not the boy who'd hunted boar with careless courage so many years ago. This was a man who meant to be king.

And for the first time, Rudolf didn't care. Reidar could have his throne. Together with his horse, Rudolf had left his heart in Portia's safekeeping, on Isla. Though the girl did not know it yet.

"Cousin!" Rudolf cried, folding a resisting Reidar into his manly embrace. "It is good to see you. Where is the king?"

Loud laughter greeted him from all sides, and Rudolf realised his mistake. If Harald was not here and all those he'd spoken to swore the king rode at the head of this army, then the crown had passed to Reidar.

Uncertainty crossed Reidar's face for the first time — ah, there was a boy beneath the king still, though he tried to hide it. "Rudolf?" His grin of recognition was everything Rudolf could have hoped for. "I thought you'd sailed off the western edge of the world!"

The men around him relaxed, whispering to each other that he was Prince Varg's son, the other royal prince. Now the hostile eyes turned expectant.

Rudolf racked his brain for what they might expect of him. Gifts? Plunder? He had neither, for he hadn't gone raiding. It took him a moment to recollect that the people of Viken were no different to those of Isla when a traveller came to visit — they wanted to hear new tales.

So he kept his voice deliberately light as he spun a tale of paradise found at the Southern Isles. And the beauty of its women, though he didn't dare mention Portia by name.

Reidar's expression darkened at the mention of women.

Rudolf quickly changed topic to talk about the gossip in every port — the Kasmirus dragon that no man could slay.

Even that did not cheer Reidar.

Realising he was rapidly wearing out what little welcome Reidar offered, Rudolf bowed his head in memory of Harald. "I am sorry for your loss, cousin. Your father was a good king, and a wise one, too." After all, it had been King Harald's command that had sent him to the Southern Isles, even if he knew it had been his father's idea. Both men had seen how close the cousins were — like brothers, as far apart in age as Harald and Varg themselves. Yet Rudolf had faithfully promised his father that he would return to serve Reidar when his cousin became king.

Realisation dawned more suddenly than any sunrise. If Harald had died so recently, then he had been the one to summon Rudolf home, knowing Reidar would need him. Perhaps Harald had not had a chance to tell Reidar. With Regina pouring poison into Reidar's ear about Rudolf's desire for the throne, Reidar probably suspected Rudolf was here to make a claim for the kingship.

If Rudolf couldn't convince him of his loyalty to the crowned king, Reidar could have him killed before he could return to Portia and fulfil his promise to her. Rudolf knew himself to be a capable fighter, but he was no match for an army. He was here to fight alongside his countrymen, not against them. Did Reidar know that? Or was he little more than Regina's puppet…and Rudolf would be forced to claim the crown he did not want?

"Why else would he send me to the ends of the earth to learn warcraft from some foreign lord?" Rudolf forced out a laugh to hide his pain at speaking so ill of Lord Angus. But needs must, if he was to win Reidar's trust. "I can tell you tales of tactics their men use in battle that we would never think of. I would not have believed them, had I not seen it with my own eyes."

"Battle tactics? But Mother said – "

"Is Aunt Regina still around? She will outlive us all, that battle axe will. I remember she caught me sitting on your father's throne once. She clouted me over the ear and gave me such a tongue lashing I couldn't open my mouth in her presence for a year. She said if she ever caught me sitting there again, she'd thrash my backside until I had nothing left to sit on!" Rudolf laughed as though it was all a joke to him, though it had not been to Regina. No, the queen would never forgive the slight to her son.

So Regina still lived. Pity. Her son would stand stronger without her. Even Rudolf knew that. But if he could pry Reidar away from her, perhaps he might still be a good king. He and Reidar had been like brothers, and the boy he'd known was no lapdog. The man before him might still be a stranger.

A stranger who doubted him.

Rudolf met Reidar's gaze steadily. Perhaps sending him away had made Rudolf the stronger man after all. The true king could not walk away from this meeting as the loser, though he did not need to win.

Almost as though Reidar could read his mind, the king gave a slight nod. It was decided – whatever it was.

Reidar cleared his throat, raising his voice so the assembled men might hear. "Tomorrow, we ride west, to where there are reports of a foreign force waiting to ambush us. In three days' time, we shall go into battle. Will you join us, cousin?"

A challenge, and a fight. Reidar knew what he was about. Even if he'd wanted to, Rudolf couldn't refuse. "The Southern Isles may have softened me, but beneath it beats a Viken heart still!" Rudolf declared. "I will fight at your side like we did as boys."

"Ale for my cousin! We must toast his return!" Reidar roared.

Another man filled the cup – not Reidar this time – but it was Reidar the man handed it to, and Reidar who then presented it to Rudolf. A masterful piece of theatre.

But Rudolf was better versed in such things. Regina would never have allowed her precious son to play-act, but Portia and her sisters had pulled him into their playing as often as they could.

Rudolf took the offered cup with both hands as though it held the blood of the saviour himself. He held it aloft as he knelt before Reidar, praying he wouldn't spill any. It wouldn't do to splash the king's shoes. He raised his voice to a shout that matched Reidar's for volume. "Nay, a toast to my cousin, the new King of Viken. May his reign be long and filled with so many victories the bards forget to sing of anyone else!"

Silence reigned for a long moment as the other men waited to see their king's reaction. Rudolf barely caught the tiny nod, but it was there. Reidar might not be perfectly comfortable in the role yet, but he was definitely their king.

The men shouted, raising their own cups to second Rudolf's toast.

Only then did they offer him a place at the fire. And Rudolf took it, pleased to be accepted back into the land of his ancestors.

A land that was no longer home.

Thirteen

If there was one good thing about the threat of war, it was that Portia's archery skills improved. The finger guards Rudolf had given her clung like a second skin even as they protected her, while she loosed arrow after arrow at a target so full of holes it resembled cork instead of wood.

"Portia."

Portia lowered her bow. "Yes, Father?"

"I have some men you must meet."

Sighing, she unstrung her bow, knowing she would have no more time for practice if they had guests.

Sure enough, the hall seemed full of men — young, loud and dressed in their best armour. Lords' sons, she guessed. Now, more than ever, she ached with loss at Rudolf's leaving. He would have greeted the men and deflected their acquisitive stares. Without him, she had the distinct impression they regarded her like a succulent leg of lamb. That desire to devour.

Portia shivered, then straightened. She was the lady of this hall, and her welcome must honour the ancient laws of hospitality that bound them all. "Good day, and welcome to my father's hall," she said.

The men stumbled all over each other to bow.

"We thank you, Lady Portia," said a man with hair as red as her own. "I certainly think I will enjoy my stay here." He made no effort to hide his approval as he looked her up and down.

Like he was buying a lamb for slaughter, Portia thought uneasily.

Angus edged into the hall beside her. "The council agreed that you deserved a guard of your own to protect you, now Rudolf has returned to Viken. Each of the lords offered one of their best fighting men to be your protector. With the prospect of war, I thought it prudent to accept their offers. All of them."

Best fighting men? Portia gave a breathy snort as she surveyed the newly puffed-out chests and proudly lifted heads. Finest fighters indeed. These were men who did not realise guard duty was nothing to be proud of. Men their lords would not miss. They were certainly no true replacement for Rudolf.

"Welcome to my father's household, then," she said, fighting to hide her fury. She turned to her father. "May I return to the practice field, please?"

With her father's permission, she marched back outside and across the field to the target. She ripped the arrows out, not caring if they took chunks of wood with them. She'd ask for a new target when she'd shot this one to pieces – next week, at this rate.

Her arms filled with arrows, she turned and found the band of men watching her from the edge of the field. Had they never seen a girl shoot before?

She let the arrows clatter to the sod at her feet, then strung her bow. If they wanted to watch, so be it. She would give them a show.

Notch, draw, aim, breathe, loose. It was Rudolf's voice whispering the words in her head.

Loose.

Loose.

Loose.

Unbidden, a smile warmed her lips. It was almost like having him here beside her once more.

"Lady Portia?"

This whisper was not Rudolf.

"Lady Portia, I just wanted to say that you have no need to defend yourself now, for I would be delighted to do it for you. My sword is always ready."

Portia followed his gaze to his sword hilt, raising her eyebrows at the tent his other sword had pitched beneath his tunic. "So I see," she said drily, turning away. Her next arrow skimmed across the top of the target.

As she notched another arrow, an arm snaked around her waist. "Lady Portia, if you will permit me to assist you. I am a skilled archer, and I always hit my mark." His hand drifted higher, headed for her breast.

Portia stomped on the man's foot and twisted out of his embrace. "Not today, thank you." Not ever.

Her next arrow fell short of the target.

A heavy hand landed on her shoulder. "Lady Portia, if you but lift the bow a little higher – "

Portia whirled, drawing the bow back. The heavy handed one backed up so quickly he almost landed on his arse. She pointed her arrow at each man in turn, punctuating her words. "The next man who says my name or touches me is going to get an arrow through his manhood. And no matter how small that target might be, I will not miss."

When no one moved, she added, "Didn't your fathers warn you about me?"

Now they backed up a few steps. All but one man, who held his ground.

Portia aimed her arrow at the stubborn one.

He bowed deeply. "My father, Lord Lewis, did indeed warn me about you. He said that one day soon, we would all be forced to fight for our homes, as foreign kings battle over who owns us. And not just us. King Donald offered his son to be your husband, and King Harald will undoubtedly do the same. As the Lady of Isla, you are at the very heart of our people, of our home. When you marry, the council will crown your husband not as Lord of Isla, but as our king. None of us deserves that honour. Not yet. We are here to defend your honour, because to lose you is to lose all the Southern Isles." Now he straightened and lifted his chin, so that he might meet her eyes. "Lady Portia, I will defend you with my life. And any man here who thinks he has the right to seduce you against your will, a lady who is courted by kings, will have to get through me." He marched across the no man's land and planted his feet firmly in the middle ground between Portia and her would-be suitors. He drew his sword, then threw it on the ground, followed by his dagger. "Go on. If you think you're man enough to be king, fight me!"

His first opponent was the biggest of them, as broad and tall as Rudolf. He bunched one meaty fist and swung it at young Lewisson.

Lewisson dodged. His elbow swung behind him slightly before he jabbed his own fist into the giant's midsection. The man went down, with Lewisson on top of him.

They rolled on the ground, kicking and punching, until someone said thickly, "Yield!"

The two men broke apart. Only then could see Lewisson was the victor while the other man limped away, pressing a hand to his bleeding nose.

Lewisson's second opponent charged at him while his back was turned. Portia shouted a warning, but the stocky man bulled into Lewisson just as he turned to face him, too late to keep his balance. Lewisson grabbed him as he fell, so they both tumbled to the ground together. They wrestled for some time, each trying to break the other man's ribs as they rocked first one way, then the other.

"Enough!" Angus roared.

Lewisson rolled away from his opponent. He still had the presence of mind to place himself between the other men and Portia.

"You're here to protect the lady, not fight amongst yourselves. I have your oaths, boys. Break them, and I will send you home in disgrace."

Most of the men ducked the heads, shamefaced. Boys indeed.

All except Lewisson.

Portia held out her hand to help him up.

He laughed, waving away her offer of

assistance as he clambered to his feet. He wiped away a trickle of blood from his split lip. "My father forgot to warn me about how beautiful you are, Lady Portia. Now I see why a war will be fought for you."

Portia shook her head. Her voice was chilly as she said, "Not for me. For my home."

He inclined his head. "As you say. We all fight for something. I will fight for your honour and mine, Lady, but I have more at stake than most. I am the youngest son of Lord Lewis, to be sure, but I was fostered at Rum Isle with Lord Ronin and his daughters. Lady Rhona and I have…an understanding, I suppose you would call it. Her father had no men to send to serve you, so he sent me. If I serve you well, Rhona and I will be allowed to marry when I go home."

Portia's expression softened into a smile. "I'm sure you will. I pray that Lady Rhona will have you home soon."

His answering smile was bleak. "If my father is right, as he usually is, this war will be long and bitter. You will have need of every man among us to defend you. But at the end, I hope to invite you and your husband to my wedding."

"Thank you." Portia remembered her manners. "What is your name?"

His eyes widened, and he bowed low. "Forgive my rudeness. Lady Portia, I am Grieve Lewisson, foster son to Lord Ronin." He straightened. "I should probably let you get back to your archery practice. You set an example we should all follow." Grieve turned and cupped his hands to his mouth. "Oi, you lot. You can't expect Lady Portia to shoot all the invaders herself. Get your bows and show the lady you can do more than stand around looking pretty and staring at her arse!" He reddened. "Sorry, my lady. Your bottom, I meant."

Portia waved away both the swearing and the apology. Instead, she watched in wonder as the other men hurried to obey Grieve.

They soon had a row of targets, bristling

with arrows.

Grieve roared, "Cease fire!" He waited for the bows to lower before he pointed at the targets. "Right, retrieve!"

Portia marched across the field with the rest of them to refill her quiver. Out the corner of her eye, she watched Grieve as he walked the line of targets, offering advice to the others. Most of the men nodded in response.

So that was how you commanded men, she thought. Idly, she wondered if Rudolf would be as capable. He was no lord or lord's son, but there was something about him that made you want to follow him.

Grieve appeared at her side. "Do you need help with those, my lady?"

Too late, Portia realised she'd been so busy watching him, she'd forgotten about her arrows. Her face grew hot.

"No, but thank you," she said.

She might not have Rudolf, but Grieve might be a suitable substitute. At least for a while.

Fourteen

Rudolf had never liked the wait before a battle began. His armour hugged him like a protective parent, though he wished he'd forgone his helm for this battle. He wanted to see things clearly, and he was willing to risk his head to do so. Truth be told, he wanted to see how his cousin fought, and generalled the battle, but Reidar had placed him on one wing while the king himself stood in the other. Once the fighting began, he wouldn't be able to see across the Opplander army, for their men stood as tall as Vikens. Well, they must be kin, however distant, if they thought to claim Reidar's throne.

That, or fools who didn't care if they died.

Rudolf surveyed the Viken army. The Opplanders were fools indeed, no matter whose kin they were.

A roar rose up, commanding the Vikens to charge. As though they were one man, they did, Reidar with them.

Rudolf swore and took off at a run.

The king leading the charge? To hell with the Opplanders. Surely Reidar could not be such a fool as to believe he was like the great hero kings of old?

Rudolf blocked an attack that came in from the side, taking it on his shield as his sword slid below to gut the man before he could strike again. Rudolf pulled his sword free and kept running.

An axe came at him and he twisted away, but not before it took a chunk out of his shield. The man tried to raise his axe again for a better blow, but Rudolf was faster. The men of the Southern Isles sometimes fought barehanded, and when they did, they fought dirty. His boot caught the man in his midsection, folding him in half. He screamed as his axe bit into his own flesh, but Rudolf leaped over him and ran on.

Another axe clattered across his shield, badly thrown, followed by the arm of the unfortunate axeman. His corpse must be one of those littering the ground, a carpet of groaning, crawling dead, the like of which Rudolf had been told dwelled in hell. Something squashed and spurted beneath his foot, but Rudolf didn't care. His only care was his cousin, the king.

A giant of a man came at him, two hands clenched around his axe haft as he swung it in a deadly arc.

The blade took off the head of the Viken beside Rudolf, slowing for but a moment before coming to collect his.

Rudolf was faster. He ran at the giant and slashed upward with his dagger, aiming for the man's unprotected throat. Blood bubbled, but not before the axe finished its half-circle swing, for the weapon had a momentum of its own. Down went the giant, with Rudolf on top of him, pinned to the dying man by the axe handle across his back.

Rudolf stabbed again, determined to fight his way free. The giant screamed, gurgled, then stilled. Rudolf wiped the gelatinous globe that had once been the giant's eye off his blade before he rose.

He had a moment to see someone slice Reidar's side before another axe-wielding giant blocked his way. Rudolf hated giants.

"Protect the king!" Rudolf bellowed to the men around him as he lifted his sword to meet the down-swinging axe. Something squelched under his foot and a surprised Rudolf slid several feet before he stopped, now behind the giant who'd wanted to cleave him in two.

Now, there was nothing between him and

Reidar, except the king's opponent, whose axe blade was red with Reidar's blood.

Rudolf broke into a run, lifting his sword to run the man through. Perhaps he should have slowed, for his blade went straight through the man's throat as he turned to avoid a sword wielded by another of the king's men. It mattered not. The king was alive, and his opponent was dead.

Reidar eyes were wide with a panic Rudolf shared. Yes, he had almost died. "Thank you," Reidar said.

Rudolf longed to tell him to leave the battlefield to his more than capable men, but Reidar would not welcome a command from his cousin, however well meant. So all he said was, "Any time, my king," before he turned away to take on another Opplander.

Out of the corner of his eye, Rudolf saw Reidar leave the field of his own volition, not as a coward, but as a general walking among his troops. The battle was almost won, anyway — only a few Opplanders remained.

Including one last giant, who charged up to Rudolf as though he was a human battering ram. "You killed my brothers!" he shouted.

Rudolf didn't see the man's axe strapped to his back until it came up in a deadly arc he was too slow to dodge, though he knew it would cleave through his head, helm and all. So he grabbed the giant's arm instead, and hung on with all his weight.

Then the axe blow landed, and the world went black.

Fifteen

Father threw the scroll down on the table with a sigh. "Portia, do we have everything we need to put on a lavish feast? The sort we'd do for an important guest?"

Portia's heart leaped within her. "A guest?"

With her sisters married and gone to live with their husbands, that left just her and Father in the huge longhouse, and sometimes not even him, when another council meeting was called. Oh, she had her men, as Father called them, but they slept in the barracks across the yard. A barracks they'd built, to protect her honour, they said, though she suspected she had Grieve to thank for that.

He had this habit of asking her, oh so politely, every morning how she'd slept. After one particularly noisy night, she'd confessed that the men's snoring had kept her awake, and they'd started building the barracks that very afternoon.

They had settled down to do what they'd been sent here for - protecting her. Protecting her from what, Portia wasn't sure. Herself, maybe. Not that they had much to protect her from. The most dangerous thing to occur in all their time guarding her had happened yesterday, when her bowstring had snapped and sliced her arm. Rudolf would have seen the thinning string and told her to replace it long ago, she was sure of it, but he was still in Viken, and she was here with...her men.

Unless he was the guest.

Father sighed. He did far too much of that

lately, and his smiles were more rare than summer snow. "Donald keeps sending more messages, and the council refuses to respond. In the last one, he said he would send envoys that we could not ignore. According to this missive, his envoy has arrived at Isla, and he invokes the ancient laws of hospitality for us to welcome the man."

Laws the Islanders obeyed, but would the foreigners? Portia wondered. Sharing bread and meat with someone under your roof gave them guest right, the right to your protection for as long as they stayed. Accepting this hospitality then gave the guest an obligation to honour the host. Neither could take up arms against one another while they dwelled under the same roof. Twenty years had passed, but people still spoke about the day Calum had struck her father at a feast. Portia had only been a baby at the time, and her father still grieving her mother's death, but she knew the details as though she'd been there.

Calum had arrived late, when everyone else

was seated. He'd marched into her father's hall, and levelled him with one blow before accusing him of murdering Portia's mother. He'd remained in the hall only long enough to seize the remains of a ham which he swung by his side as he marched out, never to return.

When Nurse had told it, she'd added some fanciful embellishments of her own. Calum's eyes had glistened with tears, and his usually cleanshaven face had been shadowed with stubble. He'd never shaved since, Nurse said. Or that he'd called down a curse on Angus as he departed, swearing he would lose everyone he loved, a fitting fate for Catriona's killer. Then he'd choked on the ham and she'd had to save him.

Given how many times she'd had to save Arlie from choking on whatever food she tried to swallow whole in her eagerness to eat, Portia had believed it.

"Portia?"

Portia shook her head. "Mm?"

"I said he will be here by nightfall. Do we

have sufficient supplies for a feast, or will we need to send for more?" Angus asked with a bite of impatience in his tone.

It was Portia's turn to sigh. Lina would know, if she were here. She would have enough on hand to feed every man on Isla. "I will ask the cook." She turned to go.

Father caught her arm, his grip gentle but firm. "Keep your men near all the time now. I fear you will have need of them."

Her father was rarely wrong, and there was no point in arguing. "Yes, Father." At least she wouldn't be lonely.

She buried herself in preparations for the impromptu celebration that she had no heart for, so deeply that when she heard the clop of hooves on the road, she was surprised to find the sky fading into dusk.

It sat ill with her to set a place for Donald's man at her father's right hand, for that was Rudolf's place, though it had been years since he'd last sat there.

Would he ever return?

"My lady, are you well?" Grieve's voice cut through her grief.

Portia nodded and wiped her eyes. "Of course. A mote of dust in my eye, is all. Blown up from the road, as our guests approach. We should take our places in the hall before the dust in the yard gets worse with so many men and horses." She lifted her chin turned her gaze on the open doors to the hall.

Donald's envoy shuffled inside like a seal walking on its tail flukes. A wide, grey column of a man, tapering only at his feet. A gold medallion suspended from a thick, gold chain was his only badge of office, distinguishing him from the other members of his small party.

When the envoy reached the dais that held the lord's table, Father rose, spreading his arms to offer a traditional welcome.

"You call this a hall?" the seal man complained. "I wouldn't keep pigs in this." He sniffed. "And where is the girl?"

Father hesitated for only a moment, but it

was long enough for Portia to feel his anger build. Not that he let it show in his voice. "Sir, I welcome you to our humble home, where you will be offered every hospitality. I am Lord Angus of Isla, and this is the Lady Portia, of whose famed beauty I'm sure you have heard much."

And woe betide him if he hadn't, Portia added silently.

"That plain, freckled lass looks nothing like a lady, or a beauty. Prince Malcolm will be most disappointed. He'll have to bed her in the dark with his eyes closed. If she's the best you have, your women must all be uglier than this hall. I'm surprised King Donald thinks you are worthy allies at all. Savages like you people don't deserve to own land."

Portia rose, her blood heated to boiling within her. "And I am surprised you are fool enough to insult a man in his own hall, when his men outnumber you so. King Donald must be even more of a fool to send you as an envoy, unless he dislikes you so much he wants you to die."

The envoy paled, tugging at his collar as he licked his lips. "Tame your sow, Angus, and teach her to be silent, or Prince Malcolm will cut out her tongue."

"My lady," Grieve whispered. "Might I recommend – "

"No, you may not," Portia hissed. Only two men could tell her what to do. Rudolf, who was not here, and –

"Portia, please," Angus said.

Portia sat down, glaring at the envoy.

Angus continued, "Will you accept our offer of hospitality…ah, I do not believe I caught your name, sir."

"You may call me Lord Mason, for if a hall such as this makes you a lord, then I am surely one twice over, for I have a castle and my cousin is a captain in the king's guard," the pale-faced seal said with shaky grandeur.

A nobody, then, and Portia had guessed right. Donald did not care if this man lived or died.

Yet her father sat the nobody beside him in the place of honour and served him first.

Mason's complaints continued:

"This lamb is too tough."

"We only give such food to pigs."

"Why have you no music in this hall?"

Portia choked at the third one. Men sang when they were merry, and deep in their cups. Not when they waited for a word from their lord to avenge the insult done to him by his ungrateful guest.

Mason clapped his pudgy hands. The sound was moist, tasting of fear. "My men shall provide music for us."

The small band of men who'd followed him into the hall now clustered in front of the closed doors and pulled out various pipes and drums. To Portia's fascination, they began to play.

What came out couldn't be called music. No, it sounded like two tomcats fighting over a she-cat screaming in heat.

She wanted to laugh, or cover her ears as

many of her father's men were doing, but she could not. No, she sat like the lady Mason said she was not, and presided over the meal with the composure of a queen. Pretending the caterwauling was as pleasant to her ears as it apparently was to Mason.

Food came and went from the kitchen, and Portia began to grow drowsy. Too much wine, she suspected, but it was too late to do anything about that now.

Mason rose to his unsteady feet. "Now, where is this bed you promised me? Little more than a straw pallet, I suspect, but King Donald will change all that in time!"

King Donald would change nothing at the islands, Portia swore, then rejoiced as the pipers finally finished. The silence was…heavenly.

Except that it wasn't silent. There was the clink of metal, the thump of boots, the…

Someone threw the doors open. "My lord!" the man gasped.

"What is it, man?" Angus asked.

"A…an army! Albans, by the look of them. The yard is full of them. Men and horses!"

Mason seemed smug. "You offered King Donald's envoy your hospitality, Angus. You didn't think I'd be fool enough to come alone, did you? The rest of the envoy waited for their horses to be brought ashore. Some of them may have to sleep in the fields, for now, until we can build barracks for them."

"Get into the barracks with your men. Now!" Angus hissed before he rose and forced a smile. "Of course, Lord Mason. I wish I had known how many guests you'd brought. I fear our paltry feast tonight will not feed so many."

Portia let Grieve hustle her through the kitchens to the barracks, her men falling in behind them. "You, get her things. You, clear mine out and find me a bed in the barracks hall. You and you, you're to stand watch until I tell you otherwise. No one enters the barracks unseen, you hear me?"

His men murmured their assent and divided to do Grieve's bidding.

Portia stared at the barracks hall, a smaller version of the longhouse with beds lined up along the walls. Fires at either end failed to keep away the chill tonight as Portia shivered.

"You will have your cloak soon, my lady," Grieve said. "You shall sleep in the loft, and pull the ladder up after you. Your men will sleep below to keep you from harm."

Portia couldn't seem to form words. Chaos swirled in her head, and she thought she might faint. She drew in a steadying breath, followed by another. "Grieve, tell me true. Is there an Alban army outside, one that outnumbers my father's men?"

Grieve looked into her eyes for a long moment. He had served her for long enough to know not to lie to her. "Are you sure you want to know?" he said finally.

"You could have just said yes," she grumbled. "I want to see them."

"Ascend to the loft. You will see all you need to, my lady."

She hauled her body up the ladder, and

soon saw what Grieve meant. The roof that looked so solid from the outside had peepholes along its length, large enough to see through. Or shoot an arrow through, she thought idly.

Men milled around in the yard, and in the fields beyond. Small fires burned on all sides, silhouetting men like monsters from a nightmare.

King Donald had invaded, and she did not know if any of them would survive until morning.

Sixteen

Day dawned, and no one was dead. Except the dozen sheep they'd slaughtered to feed the Albans.

Portia dressed and made her way down the ladder.

"Wait, my lady. We must go with you."

Portia remembered just how many Albans were outside, and decided to do as Grieve said. Cowal and Damhan blocked the doors to the kitchen and outside, anyway. Or they did, until a nod from Grieve had them leading the way out into the yard.

Swallowing, Portia followed.

There were no horses here now, but that meant room for more men. Men who stared with longing and awe.

"That's the girl?"

"Prince Malcolm's bride?"

"Wish I had a wife so pretty."

"Beautiful, isn't she?"

"Wonder why the king doesn't want her himself."

Portia allowed herself a tiny smile at their admiration. It almost soothed away the sting of Mason's insults from last night. He might think her ugly, but he stood alone.

"Make way for milady!" Cowal bellowed, his hand on his sword.

He wasn't the only one. All of them were poised to draw their weapons in her defence. Portia prayed it would not be necessary.

As though they'd heard her silent prayer, the tide of yellow tunics parted, bowing with respect that did not appear feigned. She straightened her spine and marched proudly to the hall. When she reached the warmth it offered, she wanted to relax, but she knew she could not. Men crowded in here, too, as thickly as the yard.

"Good morning, Portia," Father said gravely.

"Good morning, Father," she said as she took her accustomed seat. A servant brought her bread and meat and fruit, and she thanked the girl profusely. When Mason curled his lip and made a disgusted sound, Portia turned to him and said, "Good morning, Lord Mason. I trust you slept well."

His response was a wordless glare.

"I wonder how long you will be willing to endure our humble hospitality?" Portia bit into her bread, not expecting an answer.

"Until something more suitable is built," Mason said. "I have sent men scouting for suitable locations already. I don't suppose there's a quarry on this island. Wood and straw, everywhere I look." He eyed the thatched roof as though it had insulted him.

Portia wouldn't have been surprised if it had. Mason definitely deserved it.

"I hope you find what you're looking for soon," she said sweetly.

"The sooner I have a house befitting my station, the sooner I can keep the prince's bride safe, where she will not be a distraction to my men. Angus, is there somewhere you can keep her in the meantime where she will stay out of trouble?" Mason asked.

Portia wanted to tell him that he was the one who'd brought trouble to her island, but her father's quelling glance kept her quiet. Mason wasn't worth wasting her breath.

"Portia, it might be best if you took your meals in your chambers from now on," Father said.

Her chambers? Or did he mean the loft in the barracks?

Grieve seized her plate. "Let me carry that for you, my lady." He motioned for Damhan to take her cup. With Dermot following close behind her, Portia found herself herded through the kitchen and back to the barracks.

By the time the door closed behind Dermot, Portia was so mad she could spit. "Do you mean to hold me prisoner here? Me?"

"Lady Portia, those are Albans out there. Our people honour you as you deserve but those men would carry you off whether you will or no. When they fight battles on their own soil, they expect their wives to follow after them, and collect the valuables off the corpses of those they've slain. If one of those men tries to take you…" Grieve trailed off.

He didn't need to continue. If someone tried to take her, her men would defend her. That would violate the tenuous truce between guests and host, and there would be war. Her men would die. Her father would die. And Portia herself…she swallowed. Whatever happened, she wouldn't like it.

Hiding in a loft was a small price to pay for her freedom, and her life. Even if her freedom was restricted to a smoky loft above a room where ten men slept and snored and occasionally forgot there was a lady listening.

"I will bring you anything you ask for, as long as you stay safe, my lady," Grieve pleaded. "As long as we have you, Donald cannot conquer Isla."

If only he could bring her Rudolf. She could endure anything, if he were here.

"If you swear to bring me news of everything that goes on outside these walls…" When she saw Grieve nod, Portia bowed her head. "Then I surrender myself to your care, Grieve."

Seventeen

Rudolf woke to someone trying to yank his head off.

"One, two, three, pull!"

No, make that two someones.

"Stop, you hellspawn whoresons! You'll pull my head clean off my shoulders!" he roared.

"Will you listen to that? He's not dead, after all. The king will be pleased."

Rudolf couldn't see through his helm any more, so he reached up to take it off. The steel wouldn't budge. A careful examination revealed a sizeable dent that ran from his eye to his mouth. If he hadn't worn a helm the blow would have killed him.

"Right, let's try this again. You pull, and I'll try to manoeuvre it so that it actually comes off without taking my head off, too," Rudolf said.

An eternity of tugging, face-pulling and swearing later, a third man joined in the fray, shoving down Rudolf's shoulders as the other two men pulled the helm up.

"Fucking…whoresons…rot in hell!" Rudolf shouted as the steel ripped off his nose, or at least that's what it felt like. When he dared to feel his face, he found his nose still attached, but badly broken. "Thank you. I hope you get your hats stuck on some day so that I might return the favour."

They all laughed, including Rudolf. Because that's what you did if you survived a battle against the odds.

Then a healer came over with a cloth he

pressed to Rudolf's already tortured nose. "Fuck off!" Rudolf mumbled through the cloth, but the healer took no notice.

Reidar's wound was tended to, Rudolf noticed with satisfaction as the king sat down beside him. Reidar still looked like something troubled him, though – something that made him send the healer away.

That got Rudolf's attention.

Reidar dropped his voice so low that only Rudolf would hear the words. "Why did you do that? Call the men to me during the battle?"

Because he needed the help and he was busy, Rudolf wanted to say, but that made Reidar sound weak. Angus would not have questioned it. Harald had been a fool for not teaching his son the most basic things about kingship. "By Lucifer's leathery balls, man! Because it's a man's duty to protect his king. We're yours to command. There's no doubt in anyone's mind that you can fight as well as any man here, and none of us question your right to rule." He tried to smile to lighten his words.

"But if you fall in battle, I'll have to sit on your seat, and Aunt Regina will never forgive me."

"What, you don't want a crown, cousin?"

Rudolf's head throbbed at the thought. "Right now, I want nothing on my head at all. My ears are still ringing from the blow to my helm. I would much rather a cup of ale than a crown." And Portia's hands carrying the cup.

Reidar's face clouded, then he turned away from Rudolf as he called for ale.

It took a moment for Rudolf to realise what caused the cloud – suspicion. Regina's poison had truly taken hold in Reidar, and he would never be the king he needed to be while he clung to the lacings of his mother's gown. Reidar belonged on his fucking throne while Rudolf dealt with the borderlands, and it was time the man saw that. To damnation with suspicion and jealousy and playing politics. They spoke plain in the Southern Isles and Rudolf refused to dance around the truth any longer.

Rudolf seized Reidar's arm and pulled him

close so that no one might hear his words. "If you die without an heir, your crown falls to me anyway. We both know this. Go back to your castle, get yourself a bride, and put a boy in her belly. Several, if you can. Let me lead the army in your stead."

Reidar raised hopeful eyes to meet Rudolf's. "To what end, cousin? You have a plan, I am sure of it."

Harald had needed Varg, as much as Reidar needed Rudolf now. Rudolf cursed inwardly. Portia would have to wait. "All men plan, but not all plans bear fruit. Rest assured, mine do not need you to die here on a battlefield like my father and yours. I want this kingdom secure as much as you do. These raiders and would-be usurpers must die!" Rudolf raised a fist and shook it, as much at the Opplanders as at the Albans keeping him from Portia.

Reidar regarded him for a long moment before he nodded slowly. "Very well. Will the men follow you?"

Rudolf laughed. "They did today. They're

loyal men who serve their king. Why would they not?" Angus would not have doubted him. But then Angus knew him, as Reidar did not. The sooner Reidar left, the sooner he could take command of this army and scour the borders of men who thought the King of Viken was weak. The sooner he was victorious, the sooner he could ask to return to Isla with an army to drive Donald from her shores forever.

Eighteen

News trickled in slower than the rain leaked in through the thatch above Portia's bed. Oh, she'd moved the bed and set a pot beneath the leak, but it hadn't helped speed up the messengers bringing word to Angus about what had befallen the rest of the Southern Isles.

Befallen was the right word, all right. Most of the isles had fallen, much as Isla had. Islanders were hospitable folk, after all. There were exceptions, of course. Lord Calum had taken umbrage at his envoy's demand to hand over his daughter to be the man's bedwarmer, and slain the man on the spot. Dermot had lost two brothers in the ensuing brawl, but Lord Calum still lived, albeit under the heel of an Alban boot. They'd heard no word about his sister, Bedelia, except that she was being held hostage to Calum's good behaviour.

Much like Mason held her here, Portia thought but did not say. Her men knew better than to mention her captivity, and Dermot hastened to continue his report.

"Lord Lewis alone holds out against the invaders," he announced, with a nod to Grieve. "A contrary sea delayed the invaders' ship, so the rider Lord Harris sent from Orken Isle reached him in time to warn him of the treachery of Donald's envoy. Mahon met them with a storm of fire arrows, as though they were the Viken raiders they hate so much. Some still made it ashore, though, and now it is war on Myroy Isle. Lord Lewis has disappeared, leaving Mahon in his stead, intent on killing as many Albans as he can."

Mahon was promised to Bedelia, Portia remembered. She hadn't realised it was a love match until now, but there was naught she could do about it. War parted too many. Grieve and Rhona, Bedelia and Mahon, her and Rudolf...

"Is there any word from the Viken king?" she blurted out.

Surely Rudolf would return if there was.

"None, my lady. Or none that we have heard, anyway," Grieve said. "Mason has been absent much these last few months, though I hear he is still on Isla. Building somewhere suitable to keep a princess, or so he says. Any man with experience in working stone has been called to help with this edifice the man insists on building. He'd been bringing men from the other islands, too, which is why we have so much news to share now."

"Any news of Rum Isle?" Portia ventured.

Her men exchanged uneasy glances. There

was news, but it was not good, Portia guessed.

Yet Grieve grinned. "Lord Ronin's longhouse was burned to the ground with no survivors, 'tis said, and the Albans have left the isle entirely, for there is little left on the barren rock." When the others stared at him, he added, "My Rhona is a witch, gifted with fire. Nothing burns on that isle that is not under her power. A blaze that could destroy her father's turf longhouse has to be her doing. My lady lives."

Portia wished she had his confidence about Rudolf. At least they had something to celebrate. "Fetch some wine, then. We shall toast the health and courage of Lady Rhona, Lord Lewis and all who still fight."

Wine was brought and poured. Portia raised a cup with the rest, not having to feign her smile, for any good news was worth celebrating.

"What good tidings have you heard that I have not?"

Her men scrambled to their feet, wine spilling as they remembered to bow to Lord

Angus.

"We drink to the courage of Lords Ronin, Calum and Lewis, and their families," Portia said, her eyes daring him to object as she drained her cup.

Angus sighed. "Leave us, please. But do not go far."

Grieve did not hesitate. "Heber, Brian, Dermot – stand guard. The rest of you, archery practice."

"What does the winner get this time?" Berrach asked.

"The chance of victory against Lady Portia in a game of chess this evening." Grieve waited for Portia's nod before continuing, "And remember she can see you from the loft. Let's show her we can defend her even when she cannot practise with us!"

Portia gritted her teeth in what she hoped was an encouraging smile as the men left. Sometimes they set up a target for her in the barracks hall, but it wasn't the same as testing the breeze to see if it would speed or hinder an arrow toward its target. She couldn't remember the last time she'd felt rain on her face. Too long.

"You know if Mason hears you, there will be trouble," Angus began. "It is not politic to wish a guest's enemies well, while he still dwells under your roof."

"Turf him out, then, and tell him that he and his army are no longer welcome here," Portia challenged.

He sighed again. "You know I cannot."

That she did, though neither of them liked it.

"Portia, I must leave you for a little while. King Donald has commanded me to provide men to fight the Normans on his southern border, and I must obey." Angus's eyes refused to meet hers.

"Why, Father? What right has he to command you in anything? You are the High Lord of the Southern Isles!"

"If I do not, Mason will take you to Alba."

Portia began, "My men will not allow him to
— "

"Your men will be slaughtered. He has an

army, Portia, while you have only ten good men. Men who will die to protect you, and Mason will still win. To preserve their lives and yours, I must go."

Portia fought back the building tears. "But what will stop him from doing that if you are gone?"

"He has sworn an oath that he will hold you safe on Isla until my return. I have seen the fortress he is building, and if any edifice can be considered impregnable, it is that place. Please, Portia. Give him no reason to go back on his word. I know you do not like him – nor do I – but if you cross him, it is not just your life at stake. You hold all of Isla in your hands, and it is time you protect her as your mother did. A day may come when a man will rise to claim the isles as their king, and it will be up to you to judge if he is worthy. While the Albans are here, the council cannot convene, but you can make a choice. Whatever happens, you must survive, for while you live, your claim lives with you."

Tears streamed down Portia's face. She was

helpless to stop them, or the tide of fate that washed over her with them. "What if I choose wrong?"

Angus's eyes were hard. "If you marry the wrong man, then your dagger must correct your mistake."

Portia swallowed. "You wish me to take my own life?"

"Heavens, no! Did I not just tell you that you must survive? Portia, if you take a husband who is not worthy of you or Isla, then you must bury the dagger in his breast, before he can do any more harm. That is why you must choose wisely, when the time comes." He bowed his head. "Even if I am not here, I trust you will make the right choice."

If she knew the answer to that, would she not have made a choice already? No such man existed, except her own father, and he still lived. For now. "Father..."

"You are the heart of Isla, my lady. Your father is right. When the time comes, you must have courage." Grieve stepped into the barracks. He bowed to Father. "Until then, I will protect her with my life, my lord."

Angus inclined his head. "I would expect no less of you. Your father would be proud, son. I hope you have the chance to tell him one day." He wrapped his arms around Portia and kissed the top of her head. "Farewell, Portia, and you keep that heart safe, you hear me?"

All too soon, the Lord of Isla was gone, and Portia fell to her knees, weeping as she had never done before.

"My lady," Grieve said hoarsely.

She wanted to throw her arms around someone, anyone, just so she wouldn't feel alone. But there was no one left here who could fill that emptiness inside. Rudolf, her father, even her sisters…all gone.

"Leave me," she choked out.

And then she was truly alone, with an unceasing downpour of tears mirrored by the sympathetic sky above. For Isla's heart was broken, and the pieces might never be whole again.

Nineteen

"We agreed on this. I told you war was coming."

Reidar didn't say anything, but he glared plenty.

"There's no excuse now," Rudolf continued. "Let me return home, with the men you promised. You have your heir. Two, even. And a queen who will no doubt give you more if you ask her."

It was the mention of Queen Sativa that did

it. "You have a perverse obsession with my queen!" Reidar snapped.

"Send me away, then, as far from her as you can." Rudolf had told him many times he didn't care for Reidar's wife, but since that one flippant comment the day he met her, Reidar wouldn't believe him. Jealous fool.

"That's what she says, too."

This was new.

"Sativa says we must not concede territory we might need to divide among our sons. Even the islands at the edge of the world."

"She's quite astute, your queen. Did she tell you how many men to send with me, too?" Rudolf fought not to sound mocking, but he wasn't sure he succeeded.

"A large raiding party. Three ships."

Rudolf's eyebrows rose. He'd hoped for one. Three was…unexpected bounty. "Thank you."

"But you may only take volunteers. I won't order any man to die so far from home."

"You don't seem all that concerned about

me dying," Rudolf said.

"I'm not ordering you anywhere. If you weren't such a stubborn bastard, I'd order you back to the borderlands, but you want to be a hero, to save these islands." Reidar eyed him. "If you can't, I order you to sail right back here so I can tell you I told you so."

"I will not fail," Rudolf said coldly. "I've fought more giants than I can count, protecting your borders. Albans will seem like mere children in comparison."

Reidar grinned. "If the Albans are so soft and tiny, there would be no need for you to go back, then, would there? The Southern Islanders would have defeated them already."

That was what worried Rudolf most. They should have. Unless the Albans had tried some trickery that the Islanders hadn't seen until it was too late. Surely Angus or Lewis…

"You did not see them. Like men who have been at sea too long, their arms and legs like sticks. Driven away from their own land. They weren't fighting men, Reidar. These were

Vikens who'd settled on Isla to farm it. Fishermen, farmers, wives, children. Slaughtered, and their village burned to the ground. Those who made it to the boats and arrived here may as well have been ghosts." Rudolf shook his head, but the images would not leave him. "A foreign king has laid claim to our land, and killed our people. I will not endure it on our northern borders, and I will fight it in the southern reaches, too!"

"Like Sativa when we found her." Reidar bowed his head.

Only now did Rudolf realise why the king had refused to see the refugees, though he had not refused them anything else. Sativa had been captured by pirates on her way to marry Reidar, and Rudolf had seen her the day she arrived in Viken. With her torn, bloodied clothes barely covering her emaciated body, Sativa could have been one of the refugees on that fishing boat.

Rudolf had spoken to them all — every man, woman and child. In between slurps of stew from the king's own table, they'd told him what they knew of the situation on the Southern Isles.

The Albans had conquered them. How, they did not know. It seemed the lords had come to some sort of agreement with them almost overnight. Even Angus, though Rudolf did not want to believe it. Angus could not have known about the attack on their village, they'd said, for he was off fighting some foreign war on Alban soil.

"And Lady Portia?" he'd asked, not wanting to know the answer.

Vanished, he was told. No one had seen her since the Albans arrived. She'd last been seen at her father's longhouse, with the young lordlings who were never far from her. They were still at the longhouse – they hadn't gone to war with Angus, which was strange. They did archery training in the mornings, for all to see, Alban army or no. But there was no woman among them.

"Portia is still there on Isla. I know it,"

Rudolf said, more to himself than his king. "If it were Sativa, would you rest before you had rescued her?"

"I sent our ships out to find her. East, west, north, south…I searched everywhere. And if she had not come to me, I would be searching still," Reidar said. He seemed to see Rudolf clearly for the first time. "Will three ships be enough?"

"I do not know, and I will not until we get there. Some said the Albans had conquered all of the islands, while others said some still held out. Myroy, Rum…I would have thought Isla, too, and if there is still fighting there, that is where I will go first. If the Islanders know I am there to help, that I come in your name, surely they will join with me to drive out the invaders." Rudolf could not allow himself to believe otherwise. Angus and Lewis were honourable men. They would not have sent him to Viken to beg for help from Harald and now Reidar if they'd meant to ally themselves with Alba.

"I still owe you a barrel of ale I promised you from my wedding," Reidar mused. "I'll send it for your wedding instead. Do you love the girl, Rudolf?"

Rudolf didn't hesitate. "Yes. I've thought of nothing else since I left. Every other woman I've seen only makes me think of her. Even the queen."

Reidar seemed to have forgotten his earlier jealousy. "Do they look so alike?"

Rudolf laughed. "Your queen is like a statue made of gold and ivory, a goddess our ancestors might have worshipped in the old faith. Portia…is a mighty blaze wrapped in lambs' wool. All that passion and power, trapped in a person as soft as goose down. If she were a man, she would be a warrior so mighty even I would fear her. But she is a woman, and all I want to do is stoke that blaze, feed it and protect it until she's willing to engulf me with that roaring passion."

Reidar looked faintly nauseated. "What you dream about in your bed at night is not the sort of thing you tell your king."

Rudolf shrugged. "You asked, my king." He rose. "May I go and recruit some volunteers? I have three ships to fill, and the sooner it is done, the sooner I can be back in my bed, dreaming about the girl I plan to marry."

"Away with you, then!" Reidar sounded stern, but his smile betrayed him. "And don't sail off the edge of the world with those ships, either. I want them back!" he called after Rudolf.

Rudolf made a rude hand gesture and kept going. Not even Reidar would stop him now.

Twenty

When Isla rose out of the mist, Rudolf let out a warcry from the bow of the *Sea Wolf*. His men took it up, echoed by those on the *Sea Dragon* and the *Sea Lion*. The sound had one purpose: to strike fear into the hearts of Viken's enemies. His enemies.

They veered around the cliffs, headed for Portnahaven, the harbour nearest Lord Angus's seat. Nearest Portia, Rudolf promised himself.

He waved at the watch tower on the headland, but no one waved back. He could feel the eyes on him, though. Angus was not fool enough to leave that tower empty.

The pale, rocky sand stretched out on either side, offering him a true Isla embrace to welcome him home.

This was home.

A strange glow appeared in the fog. A glow that spread along the beach like a trail of witchlights in the mist. But witchlights were white.

"Fire arrows!" Rudolf bellowed, but the warning came too late.

The first flaming missile took Sture in the chest, toppling him overboard. Yrian let out an impressive string of expletives, and his men started rowing the *Sea Lion* away from Isla instead of toward it.

A volley of arrows peppered the *Sea Dragon's* sail, scorching the wool that was fortunately too wet to burn.

Frey ordered the *Sea Wolf* to retreat, for

Rudolf was too shocked to say anything. The men of Isla knew his warcry. They'd fought beside him often enough in the past. Had they all forgotten him? He hadn't been away that long.

When he'd managed to recollect his wits, Rudolf ordered his men to sail to two other landing spots on the island, but the fog had lifted by the time they reached Macherie, revealing the row of archers waiting for them to come into range. The third landing place was at Kildalton, where the Viken refugees had come from.

Where a thriving town had once stood, now there was nothing but scorched ground, surrounding the stone church and cross that the invaders hadn't been able to burn.

But behind the blackness was a sea of tents. An army camped here, and a shout from their man on watch soon had them lining up archers, ready to shoot Rudolf and his men.

Despair descended on Rudolf as it never had before. To be so close to Portia, and not even be able to land on Isla? Fate was a cruel bitch.

"My prince, what about Myroy?" Frey asked. "There were no archers there when we passed."

The man was right. Lord Lewis ruled Myroy, or he had, and he had been a friend to Rudolf for the little time he'd known him. He might have news about Portia, and what awaited them on the other islands.

"Set a course for Myroy Isle," Rudolf said.

He'd return to Isla, and next time, he wouldn't leave until the whole island was his, Rudolf swore.

Twenty-One

While his men stayed offshore, Rudolf rowed a fishing boat he'd borrowed into Uig. Lord Lewis had waxed lyrical about the mead in the Uig tavern, and it seemed like the most logical place to ask for information on Myroy Isle.

No archers arrived to greet him. He'd changed from Viken furs to Isla wool, so no one gave him a second glance as he strode up the beach into the town. The tavern was right where Lewis had said it would be, though nowhere near as full. Only something terrible could keep men from drinking. And Rudolf was here to learn what.

He ordered a jug of mead, and paid with coin he hadn't used since he'd left Isla. For a moment, he wished Lewis was here to share the drink like he'd promised he one day would. One day would come, when the war was over, Rudolf swore.

"Is it always so quiet here?" Rudolf asked the tavern keeper.

The man jerked his chin at the jug. "Once you've tasted that, you'll be singing soon enough."

Rudolf hastened to pour himself a drink and compliment the man on it, though Rudolf never tasted a drop. "I mean, I heard word in port that something terrible had happened in the Southern Isles. Some said there was war."

"When there's war, things get burned and men die. Do you see any dying men here?" The tavern keeper peered into Rudolf's face. "I didn't catch your name."

"Rudolf," he offered, pouring a second cup of mead. "Lately come from – "

"Wulf, you're finally here! I thought you'd never come, and I'd die waiting!" an elderly voice cackled, as a heavy hand with the weight of the world behind it thumped down on Rudolf's shoulder. "Get my friend Wulf another jug, for he's promised me a battle!" The smell of strong spirits engulfed Rudolf as the oldtimer gave his cheek a sloppy kiss.

The man kept up a monologue that sounded more nonsense than words, never letting go of Rudolf, until he had the second jug of mead in his hand. His grip turned to steel as his words became clear. "Come, Wulf, I have your oath!" Surprisingly strong fingers dug into Rudolf's shoulder as he was all but dragged outside by the oldtimer.

"This way, Wulf!"

Back to the beach, then along the shore until the fishing boats retreated behind a tumble of rocks. Still the oldtimer led him on.

"Did you bring your chess set, Wulf?" Blue

eyes seemed to see into his soul.

How did this oldtimer know? "I did," Rudolf admitted, extracting the board from the bag of belongings he'd brought along. A couple of spare tunics, and his chess set.

The oldtimer's hands set up the pieces with an easy familiarity Rudolf recognised.

"Now, shall we play, boy?" the man demanded.

"Lord Lewis – " Rudolf began, not daring to believe he was right until the man confirmed it.

"Hush, Wulf. You're here to play, not tell tales about better men than you or me! The birds in the trees have ears, you know." He tried to tap his nose and missed. On purpose, Rudolf suspected.

Rudolf lost three games in quick succession before Lewis held his hand up. "They're gone, I think," he said. "And you have been wasting time in Viken, instead of practising strategy. I'm disappointed in you, Rudolf."

"I was busy fighting real battles for my king, instead of pretend ones where nobody dies,

Lord Lewis."

Lewis shrugged. "Harald did fine without you for all these years. Why did he have such need of you now? Did you not tell him about the Albans?" He made the first move.

Rudolf shoved his own pawn forward. "Harald has need of no one any more. His son, my cousin, sits on the throne now, to the annoyance of all his neighbours, who feel his lands and crown belong to them instead." He studied Lewis's second move, and captured his pawn, setting the piece upon the rock beside the chessboard.

"So you have been practising, after all." Lewis regarded the board, and made his move. "Why are you here?"

"To play games with you, it would seem," Rudolf said bitterly, watching Lewis capture his first piece.

"Nay, the game is but the beginning. If you want to capture the queen, you must be ready not just to serve your king, but to become one." Lewis moved his queen into the middle of the board, a move which to an inexperienced eye looked reckless, but Rudolf knew it was anything but.

"Does she still live, Lewis?" He moved his knight to where he might tempt the queen.

"Angus believes so, or he would be home by now. Much like my son, who is one of the young men assigned as Portia's personal guard. If she's still on Isla, as I believe her to be, you'll need an army to free her. Do you have an army yet, son?"

Rudolf's knight claimed another pawn. "I have three ships full of men, but it is not enough," he admitted. "I need more than men, or ships."

"Aye, you're right. You need allies. Powerful ones." Lewis gleefully captured the knight. "Your king's in danger, son."

A rabbit exploded out of the underbrush, flew along the beach and scrambled under a rock, where it sat, quivering.

"Let's go for a walk, Wulf," Lewis said loudly, seizing Rudolf's arm with one hand and the full mead jug with the other. "My old legs get tired, sitting for so long."

Their listeners had returned, Rudolf guessed.

He feigned drunkenness alongside the suddenly unsteady old man, as they made their way along the water's edge. Lewis let out a few scraps of song, slurring the words, before changing to another tune that he murdered as well.

"Which is your boat?" Lewis whispered.

Rudolf led the way, and Lewis leaped aboard. He shoved the boat into the water and was well out of bowshot before anyone could reach them.

"I hope you weren't lying about that ship, son," Lewis said. "You'll have allies aplenty if you can free them of the Alban curse. The Albans have guest right, and most of our lords are still honour bound to defend them."

So that's how they'd done it. Taking over the islands in a night would have required a lot of coordination. Perhaps Donald was not as stupid as they'd thought.

"Is there anyone I can ask?" Rudolf said.

"Well, there's me, but all I can give you are men, and supplies. If you want to win, what you need is a witch."

"I thought all the witches on the islands had died out," Rudolf said. From what he'd heard, it had been no loss. Some of them had enjoyed the evil they wrought.

Lewis laid a finger beside his nose. No missing it this time. "That's just what they want you to think."

The ships came into view, and Lewis's smile widened. "Oh, you've done well. This new king must like you. When I was a boy, I'd have said three Viken longships could conquer the world. When this is all over, I hope to be able to say it again."

Twenty-Two

The tiny rock island Rudolf rowed up to looked like nobody lived on it – let alone some powerful witch.

"Are you sure this is the place?" Rudolf grumbled, forcing his frustration into each stroke of his oars.

"Absolutely," Lewis replied, settling contentedly in his seat. Of course he was content. He didn't have to row.

"How do you intend to find your witch?"

"No need, son. She will find us. Unless I miss my guess, she already knows we are here. The real challenge will be persuading her not to set fire to our boots. Or the boat." Lewis eyed the gunwales. "I hope you can swim."

Cursing Lewis for a fool, nevertheless Rudolf brought the boat up to shore and beached it. He waited for Lewis to climb out before dragging the coracle up beyond the high tide line. This time, his wet boots might work to his benefit, if the witch was as volatile as Lewis said.

Lewis led the way up the rocks and onto a rise. He cupped his hands to his mouth. "Lady Rhona, I have a proposition for you!" he shouted, turning to repeat his offer to the other three corners of the island.

"I'm already betrothed, and not to that beast of a man." The sharp female voice came from behind them.

Rudolf whirled. The diminutive girl stood on the sand with her hands on her hips.

Lewis gestured for Rudolf to say something.

"I am no beast, lady," Rudolf said gravely. "I am Rudolf Vargssen, Prince of Viken. I have come from my cousin, King Reidar, to cast the Albans out of the Southern Isles."

She sniffed. "Just you and old Lewis here? You have no chance, Prince of Viken. Not without an army that can match the Albans."

"I have three ships." Rudolf pointed.

"Is this the wolf we are waiting for?" Rhona demanded.

Lewis inclined his head. "He is."

She marched around Rudolf, looking him up and down. "What is your stake, Prince of Viken? What do you get out of saving the Southern Isles?"

Rudolf had never feared anyone so much as he did this dark-eyed imp right now. He opened his mouth, but no sound came out of his inexplicably parched throat.

"He wants Lady Portia," Lewis supplied.

Rhona's eyes narrowed. "Lady Portia is no prize, like the women of other lands. She is the Lady of Isla, and if she does not like you, may heaven help you, for no one else will."

Rudolf laughed. "Portia liked me well enough before I left. If she likes me still…well, I guess we shall see. As long as the lady is safe, I will be satisfied."

"She is safe enough. My betrothed guards her with his life."

"My son has sent word?" Lewis asked eagerly.

Rhona eyed Rudolf, then answered, "When he can. His letters are carried in secret and left in a place only he and I know. The lady lives, and so does he."

"How goes the hiding, Lady Rhona? Are your sisters sick of fish yet?"

Rhona turned her glare on Lewis. "They complain constantly. The sooner this war ends, the better."

"Would you like to help with the war, Lady Rhona?" Rudolf ventured.

She pursed her lips. "My father will not approve."

Lewis laughed. "Old fool. He thinks my son

should save you, for what man would follow a hero who got himself saved by a maiden?"

"Something of that sort."

Lewis jerked his head at Rudolf. "We can blame the victory on the Viken. I'm sure he won't mind."

Rudolf stiffened. "I prefer to fight my own battles, but I am not such a fool as to refuse the help of an ally. There are shieldmaidens among my people, Lord Lewis's late mother among them, who fight alongside their men. If you can assist my army…"

"Ha!" Rhona bit her lip, and the bush behind Lewis burst into flame.

He yelped and ran down to the water, but the fire followed him, blistering the very sands to glass until the sea steamed around him. "I told you! This witch can burn anything! With her on your side, you can't help but win!"

Rudolf fell to his knees. "Lady Rhona, I beg you to help me free the Southern Isles from the invaders. I will give you anything you ask."

She tilted her chin downward so that she might regard him. "I want all I've ever wanted.

My husband. Free him from his oath to Portia, so that he can come home and marry me." With a wave of her hand, she extinguished the fire and a breeze came out of nowhere to blow away the smoke as though it had never been. "What would you have me burn first?" The fire burned in her eyes now, and it was a terrifying thing.

"Myroy Isle, and every other island where Albans seek to hide," Lewis said, splashing out of the sea. He shrugged off Rudolf's and Rhona's stares. "What? I'm the Lord of Myroy. I can burn it if I want to." He fumbled around under his cloak and pulled out the jug of mead Rudolf thought he'd left on the shore at Myroy. Lewis uncorked the jug and lifted it in a toast: "To winning this damned war!" He drank deeply.

Rudolf held out his hand to Lady Rhona. "Do we have an accord?"

Her hand seemed so small in his, but the heat in her fingers reminded Rudolf that power came in many forms. "We do, Wolf Prince."

Twenty-Three

Rudolf rowed ashore under cover of darkness. Lewis snorted awake mid-snore as Lady Rhona leaped into the water to help Rudolf drag the boat beyond the waves.

"My lady…" Rudolf began.

"Shut it, Wolf," she snapped. "Your lady's not here. Lewis?"

"We check the houses. See if there's anyone left. Then I alert the tavern." Lewis smiled evilly.

The only lights in Uig were in the tavern, but Rudolf checked anyway. House after house was empty – people and their possessions gone. He met up with Lewis on the road to the beach. "No one left," Rudolf said.

"I found a few hiding, but they only came for supplies. They'll return to the caves tonight." Lewis squared his shoulders. "Are your men ready, do you think?"

Rudolf smiled. "Light the lamp, and you shall see."

Lewis unshuttered his lamp, and an answering light flared to life in the bay.

The sounds of a Viken drinking song floated across the water.

"Hey, I know that one," Lewis said. He seized Rudolf's hand and broke into a run.

"Vikens! In the bay! In ships!" he shouted, repeating his frantic call to arms all the way up the road to the tavern. He staggered through the door, breathlessly announcing, "Vikens in the harbour!" before he collapsed spectacularly on the floor.

Rudolf had to step over Lewis to enter the tavern. "I saw them too," he said. "Invaders!" He didn't need to pretend. Albans were enough to bring a genuine snarl to his face.

The men he'd taken for Islanders earlier in the day rose from their seats and headed outside with grim purpose.

"Vikens! To arms!" The shout from outside issued from more than one mouth.

The barman set out two cups and filled them, then pushed them toward Lewis. Lewis took one, and gestured for Rudolf to take the other.

"Fill one for yourself, man," Lewis commanded, and the barman obeyed. All three men lifted their cups before Lewis continued, "To victory!"

The barman drained his cup, then wiped his mouth on his sleeve. "So it is time, then?"

"Time to fight!" Lewis slammed his empty cup on the counter. "Come on, son. Drink up, or you'll miss it!"

Rudolf did not need to be told twice. Down

went the mead, and it was with the memory of sweetness on his tongue that he said, "Leave town now, if you want no part in the battle."

The barman slapped a greatsword on the bar, followed by a bow and a clacking quiver of arrows. "I'm no coward. Lead the way, my lord."

Rudolf returned to the now deserted street. The Alban drinkers had run off for reinforcements and the unmistakeable march of booted feet in the distance heralded their arrival.

Rudolf cupped his hands round his mouth and let out his loudest warcry. A faint answer came from the boat in the bay. The rest of his men were in place, then.

The booted feet quickened their pace and for the first time, Rudolf saw them. As though every Alban he'd ever killed in his boyhood had come back to life, carrying torches as they raced to take their revenge. But not tonight. No, tonight they passed him by, headed for the beach.

The Albans formed up along the shore, lifting bows and nocking arrows. Runners made haste along the lines, carrying buckets of oil and torches to set the fire arrows alight.

In the bay, the *Sea Wolf*'s sodden crew struck up a tune again, louder this time. They paddled parallel to the shore, still singing.

"Fire!" someone shouted, and the arrows flew. Arcing across the water to shoot the waves, sending up puffs of steam before they sank.

"Again!"

More arrows flew, but the boat was out of range.

Frey rose from his seat and bellowed, "The shore's that way, you fools! Turn this boat around!"

The singing men proceeded to row the boat in a circle, following the curve of the bay. Arrows rose and fell, but didn't hit their mark.

"Cease fire!" The Alban commander had seen sense. "Wait until they are in range!"

But Frey was not as drunk as he seemed,

and every man aboard the *Sea Wolf* knew to keep their distance, however loudly they sang.

While Frey kept the Albans distracted, the rest of the Vikens crept out of the dunes. All of the raiders were veterans who'd fought the Opplanders under Rudolf's command – the enemy would not know they were there until they wanted them to. And then, it would be too late.

Rudolf silently signalled where he wanted his men. When they were in place, he let out another warcry.

"Vikens in the town!" came the shout from the beach.

Arrows rained down on the houses, setting fire to roofs and walls alike. Vikens poured from the houses and into the street, running from the town as though fleeing from the fire.

The Albans gave chase, only to find the way blocked by a hay wagon that hadn't been there on their march in.

Rhona freed the horse from the wagon, gave it a slap on the rump to send it away, and stared at the wagon. The hay blazed into life.

The Alban soldiers turned to go back the way they'd come.

Only to find the way blocked by another wagon, driven by Lewis. Rhona cast some spell and set that alight, too.

Panicked soldiers turned to the houses, only to be met by a hail of arrows from both sides.

Rudolf climbed atop the tavern's roof – the only one not burning, for fire arrows didn't work on sod – and set his own bow to work. Beside him, the tavern keeper proved to be a surprisingly good shot.

In the flickering orange light, Rudolf glimpsed hell – dead and dying men, crawling and crying for help that would not come. Albans, all, as his men abandoned the burning houses to climb on the roof beside him.

Men still milled around on the beach – Albans who hadn't managed to get into the town before it went up in flames. Rudolf lifted his bow to finish the job.

A hand shot out and grabbed his bow.

"Nay, let them run," Lewis said softly. "Rhona can speed them on their way. They have a tale to tell."

Ribbons of flame snaked across the sand, biting at the boots of the Albans who remained on the beach. "Run, ye cowards!" she screamed. "The Wolf Prince is coming for you, and all your kind! The Wolf Prince will burn out every Alban until the Southern Isles are free of you!"

The men swarmed over the fishing boats, launching a frightened flotilla into the bay as the *Sea Wolf* beached itself on shore.

"Shall we go after them, sir?" Frey shouted.

Rudolf shook his head. He watched the boats drift away, reminding himself that each battle brought him closer to Portia. To home.

"The war has begun," Rudolf said.

Lewis slapped him on the back. "And we'll need more mead before it's done. Padraig, get our Viken brothers a drink!"

"Yes, my lord," Padraig the barman said.

Twenty-Four

Portia watched the Albans pack their things onto their horses and head for Portnahaven, casting frightened looks around them as they went.

"Where are they going?" she asked.

"Some say to fight the Normans back in Alba, while others say they're being sent to fight the Wolf." Grieve shrugged and rubbed at a stubborn spot on his armour. "The lot of them pray that they might be sent home, for they've found a cold welcome here."

"I hope they're being sent to the Wolf, and he kills the lot of them," Portia said.

Tales of the Viken prince had reached her even here, for with Mason gone, her men shared meals and news with the Albans. News they were only too happy to bring back to her.

"They are fighting men, no different from us, truly," Dermot piped up. "And I wouldn't wish the Wolf on any man. They say he moves like a ghost, taking a town before anyone knows he is there. And he burns places to the ground, with all the people inside, too. 'Tis a terrible death, to be burned alive."

Portia paled. "Towns? You mean the Viken prince can't tell the difference between our people and Albans?"

"Perhaps. It's not like the Wolf has lived among us, my lady," Grieve said. "Or mayhap he does not care. Our people gave the Albans shelter, invited them onto land the Viken king claims. While they dwell in our halls, we must defend them, too. If he sees us as Alban allies against him, you cannot blame a man for calling us all his enemies."

"I have not taken up arms against him! Neither have you." Portia smoothed her skirt to hide her consternation. "Surely he will not consider us his enemies."

"But we will take up arms against him, my lady. We are all honour bound to defend you. We swore an oath."

She remembered. How could she not? But the thought that these men, her only friends, would be forced to die for her, was one she was not willing to face.

"Why do they call him the Wolf?" she asked. "Surely the prince has a name."

"He has many names, lady," said Damhan. "The Wolf, or the Wolf Prince. Lately, the one I hear most from the Albans is the Big, Bad Wolf." He laughed. "He sounds like a villain from a children's tale, but he frightens grown men as well as children."

"Why?" Portia persisted.

"He's a Viken giant, as big as they come,"

Brian said. "Any man who burns whole villages cannot be good. They say he torched the port at Myroy when he first landed, and every town he's touched since. And he is as crafty as a wolf. The Albans who fled Myroy said they would see one Viken and hurry to attack, only to find themselves surrounded and outnumbered. He has a mighty army, all giants like him, and he will not stop until the Southern Isles are his."

A man so mighty, even the Albans fled from him. And all Portia had to protect her were ten good men. She shivered. "What does he do to the women he captures?"

"He's a Viken, so 'tis not hard to guess," Brian said. "Rapes 'em, takes the pretty ones to his ship to be whores back in Viken, and kills the rest."

"Brian!" Grieve roared. "Have you forgotten who you're speaking to?"

Brian shrugged his meaty shoulders. "Sorry if I offended, Lady Portia, but you did ask."

She had, though she wished she hadn't. Her

people had allied with the Vikens to stop them from such things, but it was all for naught if this Big, Bad Wolf saw fit to ignore that and enslave them all instead.

"Set up my target for me. I wish to practise archery again, so that when I see this Wolf, I can shoot him," Portia said.

Cowal grinned and rose. "I shall do it, my lady. If you shoot the Wolf, I want to watch."

Twenty-Five

Isla rose from the ocean, naked in the sun. Waiting for him. Rudolf's heart swelled within his chest.

No archers stood on the shore this time, and his three ships led a veritable flight of dragon boats from every inhabited island in the Southern Isles. They were filled with men from all the isles, too, not just those from Viken. Isla was ever the heart of the isles, and they would not be free of the Albans until they had been driven from Isla's shores.

Rudolf saluted the watch tower as they passed, wondering if they had sent a runner with word to wherever the remaining Alban army lurked. It mattered not. He and his men knew every landing spot on Isla, and they would not be driven off this time. They would land, and they would fight, until they won. Isla would be his.

The sand crunched beneath his boots, and Rudolf almost wept. Home. He was home. Movement in the watch tower above caught his eye, and he turned to squint at the cliffs. A flash of red or orange, maybe, on the heights? If he looked closely at the window just beneath the thick straw thatch, he could almost see it.

He grabbed Frey, whose eyes were better than his. "Look at the watch tower, and tell me what you see," Rudolf commanded.

Frey shaded his eyes. "I see…an archer. Maybe more than one. Would you like me to take some men to flush them out, sir?"

Portia. His mind flew to her, though he

knew it could not be. Portia would not be atop some tower, waiting to shoot men coming ashore. She would be with her men, who would protect her.

Unless this eyrie was the best place to keep her safe. Two archers could hold the cliff path for a long time.

"Pick two, and follow me," Rudolf said, setting off up that very path. He huffed and puffed a little, for it was steeper than he remembered. He knew when he was within bowshot, for he'd manned the tower himself for Lord Angus. Only then did he tug his helm down over his head and take his shield off his back. The familiar weight on his arm reminded him of the borderlands – the last place he'd needed it. He'd fought no open battles since he left Viken. On Isla, though, that would change. Everyone said this was where the Alban leader lived, and where else would his army have retreated to?

Peering over his shield, Rudolf definitely saw something orange at the top of the tower.

Orange, and moving. He took a deep breath, followed by another, but there was no smoke in the air. Not fire, then.

Three strides up the path, he heard the whistle of an arrow. Up came his shield, but the missile fell short, slicing into the turf several yards ahead. He darted forward to retrieve it, then skipped back out of range before he dared to examine the arrow. An arrow from Isla, not Alba — he'd recognise the feathers in the fletching anywhere.

More arrows flew, bouncing off rocks and the path ahead.

"You'll not have Isla while I live and breathe, oathbreaker!" a female voice shrieked as a fist shook out of a window, high above.

Rudolf laughed.

"What would you have us do, sir?" Frey asked, bringing Alf and Erik up the path with him.

Rudolf blew out an exasperated breath and pointed at the tiny fist. "Fetch her down, and anyone hiding up there with her. Tell her if she doesn't come, I will bring the whole tower down around her."

Alf grinned. "Gladly, sir."

Rudolf held up his hands. "Without hurting her. She's to be brought to me, unharmed."

His men dashed inside. He waited, knowing they'd reached the top when shrieked curses cascaded down. He wasn't sure who was the whoreson or the walrus's…tail-warmer, but he filed the insults away for a later date. They would keep.

Slowly, the shrieking descended. The men let out cries of pain as the valiant lady fought back, and Rudolf almost regretted not allowing them to defend themselves. It was their own fault for not going into battle with full armour, he decided, feeling a smile lift his lips as the lady's boots came into view. Boots, and the most enormous belly he'd ever seen.

It took both Alf and Erik to hold her arms while Frey brought up the rear, keeping her upright so as not to damage the baby she carried.

Rudolf couldn't seem to close his mouth. Portia, heavily pregnant? To who?

"If you've torn my dress, you whoresons, I'll see you sew it back together yourselves!" she threatened. Her blazing eyes turned to Rudolf, who was glad his helm protected him from her wrath. "And you! A misbegotten wolf who has broken every oath the Vikens have sworn to us! Conquering your allies – your friends! You are no friend of mine, you…you…dog!" She even tried to spit at him, but Angus's daughters were too well-bred to manage such a feat.

Not Portia. He should have known from her poor aim. Arlie couldn't shoot a target a yard in front of her. Portia would have pinned the toes of his boots to the path before turning him into a pincushion.

Rudolf swallowed back his disappointment. Arlie would know where Portia was. Though not Portia herself, her sister was the next best thing. "Take her to Rhona," he said.

Not all of his men could be trusted around a pretty woman, even a pregnant one, but they kept a goodly distance from Rhona, and rightly so. She'd burned a few boots before they'd learned.

Erik and Alf left with the girl, but Frey remained.

"Was there anyone else?" Rudolf asked.

Frey shook his head. "Just her, and this." He held up the bow and quiver. A half-full quiver and a man's bow. What Arlie had been thinking, climbing to the top of the tower in such a state to shoot a bow she hadn't the strength to use, he did not know. But he could ask her that, too.

"Once the men have landed, find somewhere to make camp. Send out scouts, and have them report to me before sundown. Based on their information, we move out in the morning," Rudolf said.

"Yes, sir."

He supervised camp construction, breaking up more than a dozen fights that erupted before the men were settled. They might all oppose the same enemy, but they were an independent lot with grievances going back generations that none of them would forget. The men of Vatersay could not abide to be beside the men of Langroy, and the men of Eriska and Grimsay brawled if they so much as spoke to one another. Add those to the general complaints that one man had a better campsite than another, be it bog or rock or soft grass, and the men from Islay would defend their island with fists or weapons, if need be.

When evening fell, he was more exhausted than he'd believed possible. His shoulder ached from intercepting a punch meant for one of the Myroy men, delivered by an Eriskan with fists like hams. But as enticing scents started to waft from well-established cookfires, he knew his day was not over yet. He liberated a small pot of stew, three bowls and some bread, and headed for Rhona's tent. Where he would have to interrogate the prisoner.

Rhona met him outside, as if she knew he was coming. Magic, most like, but it still unnerved him. He'd seen the things she could do and he had to admit she terrified him just as much as she did his men, but he hoped he hid it better.

"I hope you know what you're doing," she greeted him. Rhona jerked her head at the tent. "My business is magic, not midwifery. If she births the babe in there, you'll be the one catching it, not me."

Arlie was in labour, and Rudolf would have to deliver the babe? He couldn't hide his horror. "I'll send someone for a midwife directly," he said, turning to find someone, anyone, he could ask.

Rhona laughed. "She doesn't need one yet. Some months to go, I understand." She eyed the food in his arms. "Did you bring any wine? Ah, no matter. I heard the Eriskans brought plenty. I shall go and find some, for maybe that will loosen the lady's tongue. She had little to say to me that is not about the babe in her belly." She set off, and the men parted to allow her to pass.

Whoever her betrothed was, he was a lucky

man. She paid the other men no heed, unless they became impertinent. Then the smell of burning leather boots would waft across the camp and a healer would be summoned to put salve on the burns.

Rudolf cleared his throat as he poked his hand through the tent flaps. "Are you in a fit state for visitors, my lady?"

Arlie's voice was just as he'd remembered it. "If you're looking for the witch woman, she's gone for dinner. If you're her lover, I suggest you find somewhere else to spend the night. I will not share a tiny tent with some rutting fool she will forget as soon as her true husband returns."

Rudolf stepped inside. "I'm not Lady Rhona's lover, I promise you, Arlie. I came to talk to you."

Arlie's eyes lit up. "Rudolf!" She tried to rise, but instead she just seemed to rock back and forth. "Damn this belly, I feel like a whale. You must come here and give me a kiss!" She held out her arms.

Rudolf kissed her cheek and sat beside her. "I brought dinner. It's not roast pork from your father's kitchens, but it's the best we have."

She took the offered food and ate with the appetite of a woman starving. Rudolf wordlessly handed her his portion as well, and began to worry there would be none left for Rhona.

"Maybe later," Arlie said, setting Rudolf's bowl down. "I am so hungry all the time, and yet if I eat too much, this baby of mine is like to kick a hole right through me. Very defensive of his territory, he is."

"Who is his father?" Rudolf asked. If some Alban had taken liberties with Lord Angus's daughter, he'd kill the man himself.

"Widald the whale hunter," Arlie said, her fond smile telling the tale of her love for her Islander husband. "He spotted a likely bull in the water yesterday, and left with promises to bring me back a whalebone cradle. How could I refuse such a man?"

"But why were you in the watch tower? And why was no one with you?" Rudolf pressed.

Arlie shrugged. "It is the best place to watch for whales, and for whale hunters coming home. The girls from the village come to visit every day, bringing food and word of what is happening. None have visited today, but when I saw this army sailing in, I sat at the window with Widald's old bow to defend my home, as any good Islander wife would when raiders come. The things this Wolf Prince has done..." She shook her head and muttered something about walruses under her breath. "What are you doing with this man and his rabble, Rudolf?"

Rudolf didn't know what to say. Telling her he was the leader of what she called rabble didn't seem like the best idea. Evidently she hadn't recognised him as the man she'd shot at, now he'd taken his armour off. Finally, he said, "They may seem disorganised, but they are united in a common purpose. Viken men and men of the Southern Isles fighting the Albans together, as our longstanding alliance says we will do."

She pursed her lips. "Not just fighting the Albans. I've heard the stories, even here. I bet Portia has, too. Whole villages burned, and everyone killed. How could you, Rudolf?" Tears sprang to her eyes. "Women. Children! How could you kill children?"

"I've never killed a child!" Rudolf protested, but he had hazy memories of Opplander boys wielding axes they could scarcely lift. Boys old enough to be at war, who were trying to kill him, however clumsily. He'd been the same age when he first went into battle, and he hadn't shied away from anyone who tried to kill him. As for women…like Vikens, Opplander women fought as fiercely as their men. He had several scars from wounds inflicted by women warriors. "This army has only fought Albans. Well, mostly Albans," he amended, thinking of the brawl he'd broken up only an hour before when a Viken had mistaken a Myroy man's drinking cup for his own. "They are good men, Arlie, I swear to you. They are here not to conquer Isla, but to free it."

"And this Wolf Prince? What sort of man is he?" she challenged. "Why do you follow him, Rudolf?"

She truly did not know he and the Wolf were one and the same, and Rudolf did not want to be the one to enlighten her. If he did, then he would have to tell her the truth – he hadn't come to free Isla, but to free Portia. What manner of man went to war over one woman? It sounded like madness, even to him. Madness that a whole army followed.

"I do not know," he muttered, rising to his feet. Before she could say another word, he'd left the tent to walk the camp perimeter with only his own dark thoughts for company.

Twenty-Six

When day dawned, Rudolf was resolute. He'd managed a second interview with Arlie, where she'd told him the last she'd heard, Portia was still in her father's house. No one had seen her for months, but her personal guard were there, and her men did not hide, so where they were, she would be, too.

It was strange to think of Portia as having multiple men, like she kept a harem of sorts. What did one call a stable of men? A barracks, or a company, perhaps — for they were a military unit, sworn to protect her, and not her lovers.

It took the men half the day to break camp, to Rudolf's bewilderment. If they did not move faster, it would take them three days to reach Angus's house, when it was less than a day's ride. But determination drove him — determination to free Portia and her lands from the enemy, and he needed the army at his back to ensure he did, this time.

Their slow progress gave him time to send out plenty of scouts, and mull thoughtfully on their reports. None of his men had seen a single Alban. In fact, they'd seen few men at all, though the villages on Isla were far from deserted. Women and children eyed the army warily as they passed, some unsheathing daggers they tried to hold in the folds of their skirts, ready to defend what was theirs.

His men knew better than to attack a village without an express command from Rudolf. These were their own people, not their enemies. He made sure to pay for any livestock they took, and the sight of coins loosened tongues that hadn't been free to speak for some time.

The Alban camp had been around Angus's house, though there were rumours of a second to the north, where Mason, the Alban commander, had a castle, or so it was said. Everyone seemed to know someone who had worked on the edifice, but none had seen it, or knew where it was. Somewhere hard to reach, they all agreed, before telling him it was on a clifftop, an island, or in the middle of a lake.

Rudolf found himself imagining an underwater castle, where basking sharks sat on thrones while mermaids serenaded them. Or would it be the other way around? He'd heard tales of a mermaid who married a king, and she now presided over his court, her long gowns hiding her tail and scales from all those who might know her for what she was.

"Sir, the men from Vatersay and Longroy are fighting again. It seems the only land left for them to pitch camp is a bog barely big enough for one of their groups, let alone both, and with no distance between them."

Rudolf swore. They were like brawling children. A pity he could not spank them all. "Send for Lady Rhona," he instructed. "Ask her to dry out the bog. Once she is done, I am sure there will be room for everyone. They will be bedfellows in the bog, or they may sail home."

Yrian grinned. "Yes, sir."

He liked the young witch, Rudolf was certain of it. He didn't seem to fear her as much as the rest, though he kept a healthy distance from her, too. If Rhona's betrothed died before she could marry the man, Rudolf had no doubt Yrian would offer himself in the man's stead.

Rudolf crested the rise and his breath caught in his throat. He knew they'd set up camp on the same site the Albans had deserted, but the sight of Angus's longhouse sent a wave of longing through his body that he wished would carry him to the door and happier times.

His scouts said the place was deserted, but Rudolf knew better. Even if Angus and the Albans had left, someone remained. The house and outbuildings had a watchfulness to them that Rudolf had learned not to ignore.

He wore a breastplate, but not his helm, and he carried his bow and his quiver on his back. His sword bumped against his side with each step, but he would not need his shield today. Not for this.

The cookfire in the kitchen had burned down to coals, but there was no mistaking the fact that it had been used to prepare a meal today. A basket of apples lay on the table, their leaves not yet withered, as though they'd been picked only hours before. Someone was here. Someone who cooked, and took care to harvest the orchard.

A shrill scream that sounded like a distressed horse came from outside.

Rudolf picked up an apple and went outside

to investigate.

The mare, a skittish beast that lifted her tail, threw back her ears and eyed him with menace before letting out a squeal, trotted away from him to rub herself against the fence. She stared him a while longer, as though daring him to try and ride her so that she might buck him off, before heading to the feeding trough to finish off her oats.

The second scream didn't come from her — it came from the stables. Rudolf hurried to help.

The stables were as empty as the kitchen, except for the screaming horse, doing his best to kick down the door of his stall.

"Hector!" Rudolf lifted the bar to let the stallion out, then held out the apple. Would his horse still recognise him after all this time?

Hector ignored the apple and stepped on Rudolf's foot as he shoved past him to leave the stable.

Rudolf followed him, not willing to lose the beast.

Hector took off at a gallop, soaring over the fence, before landing in the mare's field. He moved purposefully toward her feeding trough.

Rudolf halted. The perverse beast had put himself where Rudolf would have taken him. Perhaps he knew better, and Rudolf should return to the buildings. Reuniting properly with his horse could wait.

He returned to the yard between the longhouse, the kitchen and the stables. Only now did he see the new building, its fresh cut timber splintering his memories of this place. The barracks hall had not been here when he left, and its newness meant it could only have been built by Albans, for who else would construct a wooden barracks where a sod-roofed longhouse would do? The only Islanders who preferred timber were the men of Myroy, who didn't have enough sod for roofs, though they had plenty of trees.

The barracks did not belong, and they would burn, he huffed to himself.

Rudolf reached for his quiver. He stabbed his arrow point into a block of the soft, white, waxy substance that made it burn whatever it touched. He marched into the kitchen and thrust the arrow into the ashes, but the stuff didn't catch. Swearing, he found some pine needles in the box of tinder and threw them among the coals.

A wisp of smoke rose up. Throwing his arrow on the flagstones behind him, Rudolf dropped to his knees and blew the tiniest puff of air at the smoking needles. He held his breath for a moment, watching, praying…and then they caught, flames licking up them as if they wanted to swallow the needles whole.

Again he stuck the arrow in the heart, and this time, the flames gratefully accepted his offering. Rudolf hurried out side with his blazing arrow, knowing he needed to fire the thing before the stuff melted and set fire to the kitchen.

Outside, the sun blinded him for a moment. He turned, glared at the barracks, and let his arrow fly. No need to aim when his target was as big as a house. His arrow arced up and hit the roof, then disappeared, as if by magic. Rudolf's mouth dropped open. What in heaven's name had happened to his arrow?

Smoke curled out of a hole he hadn't seen before. Several holes, actually – arrow slits in the roof, he realised.

"What do you think you're doing, you stupid beast?" a female voice yelled behind him.

Rudolf whirled in time to see a redheaded woman sprint past him, carrying a broom. He followed her around the stable to the field where Hector had…ah.

"Get off her, you randy bastard!" she shouted at Hector, who was too busy servicing the mare to care.

"You're too late, he's probably already got her with foal by now," Rudolf called, more to protect his horse than anything else. He would not want to be interrupted while making love to a lady, though he'd have chosen a more private place than Hector had.

"Did you let that menace out?" The woman rounded on him.

"He would have kicked the door down if I did not," Rudolf said.

She snorted. "You try telling Portia that. Mache is her mare."

"Lina?" he ventured.

"Of course, you fool. Portia would've whacked you with the broom, not the bloody horse. First for being away so long, and then for letting the horse out. Then I think she might've burst into tears." Lina smiled. "What kept you, Rudolf? She's missed you so much."

"I serve at my king's command," he said simply. What more could he say? "Where is she, Lina?"

"If you were here sooner, I could say the loft." Lina pointed at the barracks building. Her eyes widened. "Why is there smoke?" She hurried toward it.

Rudolf grabbed her to pull her back. "Because it's on fire."

Lina wrenched out of his grasp. "Well, aren't

you everybody's hero, then? First you let the horse out, and then you set fire to the barracks. What else have you done? If you bring the army down on this house, I will hit you with this broom."

Rudolf stared down at her eyes, as fierce as Portia's could be. He swallowed. "What if I told you the army is here to free Isla from the Albans?"

"So Keith was right." At Rudolf's blank look, Lina explained, "My husband. He's Father's steward, sending supplies to where he's fighting the Normans. He's seeing to a shipment of salt mutton, or he'd be here. Are you here to free Portia, too?"

From husbands to mutton to Portia, Rudolf wasn't sure if he could keep up. Especially with the barracks definitely on fire now — flames licked at the roof through holes that didn't seem so tiny any more.

"Where is Portia?" Rudolf asked again.

"He's taken her."

"Who?"

Lina sighed. "You've been away too long, Rudolf. Lord Mason, the Alban bastard who tricked Father and the other lords into hosting Donald's armies. He's an arrogant prick who pisses off anyone who hears him, but he works well with stone. He built himself a castle in the north, the sort of thing even the Normans would envy, or so 'tis said. You'll need an army to get in, and maybe not even then. That's where he's taken her."

"Where?"

Lina shrugged. "Some holy spot in the north, where the lords meet and drink so many barrels of ale they empty half our cellars."

"Council Island, on Loch Findlugan?" Rudolf asked, horrified. He didn't want to believe it. The Albans had built on the holiest site in the Southern Isles?

"That's the spot!" The fire crackled loudly behind her, seizing Lina's attention for the first time. "So you really are burning down Portia's barracks, are you? You're lucky she likes you. Her men built that, and kept her safe in the loft while the army was here. They won't take kindly to you when they see you've destroyed all their hard work."

"Are they with her?" If he could not be with her, at least someone kept her safe until he could be.

"Of course. They are her sworn men. She – " Lina stared. "Who in heaven's name is that ruffian?"

A man staggered up the street, dressed in stained rags. He looked like he'd been buried in a bog and clawed his way out again. "You have to help me!" he shouted. He fell to his knees at Lina's feet. "Don't let the Vikens get me. Don't!" He caught sight of Rudolf and crumpled into a sobbing heap on the ground. He pawed at Lina's boots. "You must do as I say, you ugly whore!" His words ended in a scream as his clothes started to smoke.

Rudolf dragged Lina back from the flames a second time as the man turned into a human torch. Only one person could have done this.

"Rhona!" he shouted.

Rhona strode up the street, looking supremely unconcerned. "He grabbed me, said some things that were not very complimentary, and tried to order me about. I set fire to his boots, and he ran off, so I thought that was the end of it. So when he did the same to this lady here, I figured he hadn't learned his lesson." She leaned over and spat on his smoking skeleton. "He was Alban, anyway. No loss. Oh, and he dropped this." She held up a large gold medallion, attached to a thick gold chain. "Probably stolen. Albans rob the dead on the battlefield. Keep it as a war trophy."

Rudolf wanted to say something, anything, but he couldn't seem to find the words. He'd killed many a man, but Rhona's cold-blooded slaughter seemed different, somehow. Despite the blaze behind him, he shivered.

Rhona regarded the burning building. "Ah, I'm not the only one who's been setting fires. Nice work, Rudolf. Perhaps you don't need me any more."

"I do," he blurted out. "The Albans have

taken Portia to their castle in the north. On Loch Findlugan. The very heart of the isles. I need all the help I can get to free her from them."

Rhona gave him a long look. "I'll honour our agreement, if you'll do the same."

Rudolf bowed his head. "You know you have my word."

Twenty-Seven

Loud hammering startled Portia out of sleep. "What is it?" she mumbled sleepily.

"Stay aloft, my lady," came Grieve's quiet response from below.

She heard the scrape and thunk of someone unbarring the door. "What's amiss?" Berrach rumbled.

"Tis the Wolf. He's landed on Isla, and she must be moved."

Fear trickled down Portia's spine. The Viken

prince was here. The man who killed and burned everything in his way. Who would kill her men, burn this building like the woodpile it was, and when he got hold of her…Portia swallowed. Would he care about her claim, or see her as just another woman to rape?

"Seems to me there's more danger on the road than here," Grieve said.

"Perhaps, which is why we must move quickly, and under the cover of darkness. If we reach the castle by dawn, no one will be able to reach her. She will be safe behind my walls, I swear."

Mason. Their visitor was Mason, who sounded as frightened as Portia felt. Good. She hoped the Wolf raped him first, or at least ran him through so she could watch.

"My sister will be here tomorrow. We must wait for her. I cannot leave her for the Wolf," Portia called down.

Grieve tried to hush her, but Portia would not be silenced tonight. She shoved the ladder through the trapdoor and began to climb down. "You hush yourself, Lewisson. If I do not agree to go – "

"Then I will tie you to my saddle and carry you myself," Grieve finished for her. "I'm sorry, my lady, but your safety is more important than your wishes. Or your sister. We shall leave your things in the longhouse with a note for her to send them on. Pack only what you can carry, for if the Wolf is on Isla, then he is within a day's ride of here. We cannot defend you here with so few, but what I've heard of Mason's castle is such that it might be defended by ten men, for it is a formidable place. Dermot will wake the kitchen maids and the cook – they will come, too, for there will be no other women to keep you company otherwise."

Portia wanted to argue, but she knew he was right. So she glared at Grieve instead.

"You've been complaining for months about being a prisoner here, and how you never get to go riding. Don't you want to ride Mache?" Grieve coaxed.

"She's in heat. She'd bite anyone who tries to saddle her. I must leave a note for my sister, telling her not to let Mache get near any of the other horses until she settles. If she hurts Hector, Rudolf will never forgive me."

Grieve's shoulders relaxed. "Thank you, my lady. It would try me sorely to have to tie you to the saddle like a prisoner."

She smiled grimly. "Sore is right. I'd bite or stab anything I could reach. I'll not be thrown over any man's saddle without a fight."

"Aye, I know."

"Have the men prepare the horses. All but Hector and Mache. They must stay." For a moment, she hesitated. What if the Wolf hurt Hector? If he did, she would tell Rudolf what his countryman had done.

"You pack your things. I will take care of all else," Grieve said.

Back up the ladder Portia went. She bundled up some spare clothes and pulled on some boots. Everything else she owned went into the chest of her mother's that her men had brought from the longhouse for her. She lifted her bow and quiver. "What will happen to the things I leave?" she called down.

"A groom will take the wagon, and follow behind us. Whatever you want him to bring should arrive late on the morrow," Grieve said.

She shouldn't need to shoot anyone between now and then. She'd be inside the castle before it was light enough to see her target, surely. She dropped the bow and quiver in the chest and slammed the lid shut. "I'm coming down. 'Twill just take a moment to pen a note for my sister, and I will be ready." She dropped her cloak and bundle on the barracks floor and launched herself after them.

"My lady!" Grieve lunged forward to catch her.

Portia landed neatly on her feet without falling over. She grinned, proud of herself. "I'm not a flagon of mead. I don't break that easily. Do you think I'll be able to run in this castle you're taking me to, or is there a special dungeon prepared for me that's smaller than this one?" She'd never seen a castle, but envisioned it as a sort of stone version of her father's longhouse. Or his hall, maybe. She could run the length of the hall, at least.

Heber laughed. "Lady Portia, this is a castle. It's huge. There's a practice yard inside the walls, or so my cousin says."

His cousin had helped build it, so Heber should know.

"So there'll be space where I can practice shooting outside?" she asked hopefully.

"You shall see when you get there, my lady. Are you finished with your letter yet?" Grieve said.

Portia laid down her quill. "I am." She sent up a silent prayer for Lina's safety, and rose. "Let us go."

She fastened her cloak and took up her bundle as though this were an ordinary day, or night, but she couldn't stop the thrill she felt inside. She should be more frightened, but she was giddy at the thought of freedom.

In the harsh light of day, she could worry

about the Wolf again and what he would do to her and Isla. Tonight, she intended to relish her first ride in longer than she liked to remember.

Her horse, a beast she did not know, sensed her excitement and pranced about like the animal had been locked up for too long, too.

"My lady, we must make haste!" Grieve said.

She grinned. "Haste, you say?" She squeezed the mare between her thighs and whispered a command, letting the horse have her head. The mare flew.

Startled shouts came from behind her as her men urged their horses to match her speed.

Portia laughed merrily. "I have not forgotten how to ride, boys. Have you? Let's see who reaches the castle first!"

Loch Findlugan was too far for a true race, but she held her own until she felt her horse growing tired and allowed her to slow. Her men caught up, muttering curses they normally would not voice. At least not around her.

"My lady…" Grieve began.

Portia turned innocent eyes on Grieve. "You did say we needed haste."

"That I did, but that's not something I need to remind you any more, I think. I wanted to show you that." Grieve seized her bridle and pointed.

From this height, she could see clear to Portnahaven...and what lay between. A sea of campfires, showing the sheer size of the Wolf's army. Thousands of men, surely. More than she'd ever seen, anywhere. Who could stand against an army like that?

"We do not stand a chance, do we? They will take what they want, and no one will stop them." Tears formed and fell. Tears for Isla, the precious island they would conquer.

They were already lost.

"Of course we do. We are the Southern Islanders, my lady. They may burn our homes, our harvest, our whole damn island, but our people will survive and rebuild. You will survive to lead them. I swear it." The same darkness that hid her tears concealed Grieve's expression, but Portia didn't need to see it to know.

"I don't want you to die for me, Grieve. Not you, not any of you."

His teeth glinted in the moonlight as he grinned. "Then you'd best pray the Wolf is a reasonable man who is willing to negotiate. After a week against Mason's walls, maybe he will be." He moved ahead to order their party into what he called a more defensible formation, before returning to her side.

The joy of the night-time ride began to pall sooner than Portia expected, but she did not complain. Anything to be out of her loft prison.

The sky was lightening as they approached the loch. Portia had not been here since she was a child, and she'd read and reread her mother's scroll on the history of this place so many times in captivity that she knew every word by heart. Here was the seat of the original lords of this land. Her ancestors, through her mother's line. Her mother's people had carved those standing stones, weeping sweat and tears as they dragged them into place to honour deities long dead.

Or perhaps not, for there was a holiness to this place that hung over it like fog. Maybe the old gods had made their last stand here, and were buried in the mounds that ringed the loch round. Here, she and her men would make their last stand, too, before she was forced to surrender Isla and likely her maidenhead.

But not yet. The Wolf would have to breach other walls first, and mighty walls they were, too. Her breath caught in her throat as she took in the enormity of what Mason had built. The castle covered Council Island, so the waters of the loch lapped at the walls. Not all the way around, but then it had not rained for days. The water level would soon rise, and hide the island again.

She began to believe that maybe, just maybe, there was some hope left.

Two boats waited to take them to their island home, and Portia surrendered her horse to a man she didn't know, who swore he'd take care of the mare before sending her home. She glanced at Grieve, who was doing the same with his horse. Time to trust his judgement, she decided, for she was too tired to think any more.

Her boat drifted under a stone arch topped by a spiky metal gate. It was open to allow her entrance now, but the heavy chains holding it in place spoke of how quickly it could be lowered to keep the world out.

Dermot helped her out, and Portia found she needed his assistance, for her legs ached after the unaccustomed ride.

"Guard her," Grieve said, directing the rest of his men to search the place.

Dermot and Cowal stood by her side, staring up at the high walls as avidly as Portia did.

"It's huge," Cowal breathed. "You'd need a dragon to get into this place."

Dermot laughed. "Didn't you hear? That dragon in Kasmirus is dead. Some knight slew it, and won himself a bride."

"As long as the Wolf doesn't have it. No one's sure how he manages to burn whole villages when it's pouring with rain. A dragon might do that."

"Someone would notice a honking great dragon in the isles by now!" Dermot scoffed. "If the Albans didn't see such a beast, then he doesn't have one. Maybe this Wolf is beast enough on his own."

Dermot and Cowal debated about how to beat wolves and dragons while Portia fought to stay awake.

"It's empty."

Portia blinked her eyes open. Damn, she'd fallen asleep on her feet. "Mm?"

"It's empty," Grieve repeated. "No one here but us. Now the servants are here, I shall shut the gate and you'll be safe, Lady Portia."

"Can I sleep?" she mumbled.

He laughed. "Yes, my lady. The men are preparing a pallet for you in the tower room. Tonight, I'll have a bed brought up, but now you may rest."

"Where's the tower?" she slurred, looking around.

"With your permission, my lady."

Portia had her legs swept out from under her as Grieve lifted her in his arms. If she'd had the strength, she'd have shouted at him to put her down. But she did not, so she settled back and told herself she'd tell him off in the morning.

Behind her, the gates clanged shut, and darkness descended.

"You must let me in! You must!"

Shouted words woke her, and Portia struggled to rise. How long had she slept? It looked near noon, but it was hard to tell with so many clouds in the sky.

Loud clanging as someone rang the gates like they were a bell. "Let me in, damn you!"

Portia stuck her head out of the tower window.

Mason sat in a boat outside the gates, whacking at them with his oar. He shook his fist at her. "Let me in or I shall take a stick to you, like your father should have, you ugly whore!"

"Insulting my lady will not let you in, you great blubbery fool," Grieve shouted back from the walls above the gate. "In fact, I am honour bound to keep you out, for you threatened her, and I must keep her safe. Go back to your homeland, for you're not welcome here, or anywhere else on the Southern Isles."

"But there's an army on the way! An army of Vikens! The only safe place is inside those walls!" Mason insisted.

"Then I thank you for building them, as they will protect my lady. 'Tis a fitting parting gift you give her, after trespassing on her hospitality so long. Get you gone before they get here, man. For if they catch you outside the gates, they will squash you like the cockroach you are."

"What about your laws of hospitality?" Mason demanded.

"'Tis not my roof you lived under, nor my lady's. You may ask her father for shelter if you wish, but I've seen you shit upon guest right for too long to be stupid enough to offer it to the likes of you. Perhaps you should not have sent Lord Angus to fight so far away. Maybe if you hurry, you may reach his house before the Wolf's army do. Maybe he'll give you shelter if you offer to build him a castle such as this."

"I hope he gives that ugly whore you serve to his men, so that they may rape the bitch to death. She deserves no better," Mason shouted as he rowed back to shore.

Portia wanted to shout back in kind, but the barb in his words had hit home. Perhaps the man was right, and that would be her fate. She would rather take a dagger to her own breast first.

She slid down the wall to sit on the cold flagstone floor. Would she end her days in this prison?

"My lady, I will not let that happen." Grieve stepped into the tower room and closed the door behind him. He moved to the window and pulled the shutters closed, too, filling the room with shadows. "There is a reason why I chose this room for you instead of the lord's chamber, though the other is warmer. We have taken the room below you as our barracks, so anyone attacking the castle must fight their way through us before they can reach you. And if they do, then you must escape." He slid his fingers down the window frame, and pulled a section away from the wall. A dark void beckoned – a space within the walls Portia would never have guessed existed. "You must climb down, then follow the passage to the hidden door. There is a boat down there, so that you may row ashore. If the castle walls are breached, we will give you the time you need to get away." His eyes met hers, saying the words that he did not.

"I won't let you die for me, Grieve. None of you," Portia said.

He smiled faintly. "Lady Portia, you are the second most powerful lady I know, and not even you have the power to prevent that. I stand by my oath."

"And what of Lady Rhona?" Portia demanded.

"If nothing else, Rhona will avenge me. She has a temper that matches yours, my lady." He bowed. "Now, get some sleep, while it is still quiet. Or you'll wish you had, for there will be an end to peace once that army arrives."

She had to laugh at that. It was either that or cry.

Crying could wait until she had to make use of that secret passage, she promised herself. For if she descended into the darkness, all would be lost.

Twenty-Eight

That blocky stone structure rising out of Loch Findlugan where Council Island should be was an abomination. The gods of the old faith would have struck it down with lightning, thunder and whatever else they had in their arsenal. He wished the new ones would do it instead, but he didn't think saints dealt in lightning. Pity. He'd happily hail it as a miracle if they did.

At least his army were getting better at

setting up camp, though he had to admit the failing light hurried them along better than he could. No one wanted to be caught out in the rain without their tent up. Not when they'd marched in it all day.

Perhaps they were too tired to start any fights tonight, was all. Or awed by the place where they stood – for Loch Findlugan was the home of Council Island, a holy place where no Islander was allowed make war on another.

And he'd brought war to it.

Lord Angus would never forgive him for this. 'Twas a good thing he wasn't here to see it.

Rudolf would not have done this if it was an Islander who held Portia prisoner. No, he'd have called the man out and the battle would have been between just the two of them, as was proper. But the Albans had brought in their army and fortified Council Island itself. He had no choice. Better that it was a Viken leading this army and not an Islander, then, even if Islanders outnumbered the Vikens in his army.

He'd been considering possible attack strategies since the castle came into view, and he still had nothing. How did one attack a rock? Not even Rhona could burn stone. In all his years of fighting, ambushing and being ambushed in Viken and on the Southern Isles, he'd never come up against something like this. You couldn't climb those smooth walls the way you scaled a cliff. And the damn thing was in the middle of a lake, with no sign of the boat fleet that had carried him to the island last time. A tiny coracle was the only craft he could see — a one-man craft that might take two or even three, if they were slight and didn't mind the closeness. Children, maybe, or two women...

He would not need to attack if he offered them something they wanted. More than anything, he wanted an end to this war. If Portia was safe, he would be willing to trade almost anything.

Portia was the politician, as astute as her

father, or Lord Lewis. Rudolf was a warrior and a strategist. She would know what to offer, when all he wanted was her.

A trade, perhaps. If he offered the Albans her sisters as hostages, perhaps they'd be willing to negotiate. Maybe even open the gates…

Lina settled Arlie in the boat, shoving a cushion between her sister's back and the gunwale. "If anything happens to her or the babe because of you, Wolf, I and my kin will hunt you to the ends of the earth to exact our vengeance."

Rudolf nodded. Coward that he was, he couldn't look her in the eye, so he'd worn his helm for this. Full battle dress, in fact, as he paced along the shore, letting those in the castle get a good look at him.

A young Eriskan lad had volunteered to row the ladies across the lake. He looked no bigger than Rudolf himself had been the day he arrived at the Southern Isles, but he had the same courage. And so Rudolf had agreed, letting the most vulnerable members of his army assault the castle. For they had a better chance of gaining entry than he.

His men lined the shore, and theirs lined the battlements, watching the coracle's progress as it rippled between them. Could two armies hold their breath? For it seemed the only sound he could hear was the plash of oars as the two flame-haired girls retreated from him.

A third flash of orange at the tower's top window stopped his heart. Portia!

He wanted to fly across the water and take her in his arms, but she was as far out of reach as heaven itself right now. Even her face was out of view – hidden by her hair as she faced the oncoming boat, not him. She'd seen her sisters, all right.

She turned her head further still, meeting the eyes of…was it one of the men on the battlements? She gestured imperiously, her meaning clear. She wanted them to let her sisters in.

One of the armoured men on the

battlements let out a shout, waving his arms with as much energy as Portia.

Was he commanding his men to open the gates, or fire on the defenceless boat? Surely no man of honour would open fire. They couldn't…

The gate at the waterline began to rise.

Lina shouted and pointed, and the Eriskan boy headed for the opening gate.

The boat slid into the darkness before the gate clanged shut once more. His army began to disperse, heading for their tents or whatever they wanted to do while they waited. Polish their armour, perhaps.

But Rudolf was rooted to the shore, his eyes fixed on the tower window that no longer held the flaming beauty who'd haunted his dreams for so long.

Gods help him, from the old faith and the new. He'd sacrificed a boy, two women and an unborn babe just for the hope of seeing her again.

He hoped Portia would forgive him if he

failed.

Twenty-Nine

Despite all her talk of wanting to run and shoot and do all the things she hadn't done in the barracks hall, Portia found herself peering out the window just like she had when she lived in the loft. She could sit in the tower windows, if she'd wanted to, but the stone was too cold, so she hung back, not wanting to touch it. There was plenty to see.

The army came in an orderly column, creeping into the valley like ants until they grew into men and settled on the shore where her own men had left their horses. The beasts were gone now, back to her father's stables with a groom, for there were no stables here to house them. Most of the army marched on foot, with a few hooded or armoured figures on horseback.

The Wolf Prince could be no one other than the proud peacock who led them, probably insisting no one else could ride before him lest they kick up dust or mud that might foul the highly polished sheen of his armour. His poor horse had to bear the weight of not just him, but all his weapons, too, for the man had sword, shield, axe, bow…he carried an armoury on his back, as though he expected an attack at any time. And so he should. A Viken who attacked the Southern Isles was an oathbreaker of the worst kind, breaking an alliance that had stood for centuries.

She wanted to take up her bow and shoot him then and there, but she knew he was out of range. Even from this height, she was too far from shore to shoot anything not on the lake's surface. If he could be persuaded to board a boat, though…

The tiny coracle Mason had left in the mud wouldn't stand up to more than a few well-placed arrows before the holes in the hide let in enough water to sink it. Wearing so much armour, the Wolf was sure to sink, and good riddance.

His army set up camp with alarming efficiency, which surprised her when she realised only the first few ranks of troops were Viken. The lines marching over the hill now were unmistakeably Islanders – so many men! She hadn't known there were that many men on all the Southern Isles, yet here they were.

Why?

Why would her own people follow a man who burned their homes and killed their families? No man of the Isles would throw away his own honour in such a way. He'd kill the Wolf with his own hands, for sure.

For the first time, she began to doubt the

tales she'd heard. That the Albans feared him, she'd known. But her own people…they weren't stupid. They wouldn't stand by and watch their own people die.

Did they believe the Wolf was their ally? Big and vulpine, perhaps, but not so bad?

The vast army made themselves at home on the valley floor, while the Wolf paced the camp. He was a big man, bigger than most, and he'd pitched his own tent in the centre of the camp, bigger than the rest, of course. The cloaked riders favoured the second largest tent, on the far edge of camp, away from the water. Three of them. One waddled like he was as fat as Mason, but there was something about the way the figure walked that made her certain it wasn't him. Besides, an Alban among this army would be in chains, or tied to a stake. Not free to walk about the camp.

"Have you never seen an army before?"

Portia looked up to meet Grieve's raised eyebrows. "Not like this one."

"Me, neither. Now I know what Lord

Angus faces in Alba. 'Tis a fearsome sight." He held out the covered bowl he'd carried up the stairs. "I brought your dinner. Seeing as you didn't come to the dining hall with the rest of us..."

She took the bowl. "Thank you. I suppose I have spent so long alone, I am not accustomed to...to..."

"Freedom?" Grieve supplied. "This is all new to me, too, my lady. There is what I know, and then there is...this." He waved at the view.

"What are they doing?" Portia leaned out of the window, to get a better look. "They're sending someone out in the boat."

Two of the cloaked figures. Witches? Priests? She couldn't be sure. They were accompanied by an Islander boy who rowed the boat like he'd been born to it. A fisherman's son, probably. But the cloaked riders...

The Wolf stood on shore, speaking to the riders. Together, they reached up and lowered their hoods.

Portia let out a shriek. "It's Lina and Arlie! My sisters! And Arlie…Arlie's pregnant!" She pointed at the girl's belly. "I'm going to be an aunt!"

Grieve swore and bolted down the stairs.

"If you don't let them in, I'll open the gates myself!" she called after him.

Soon after, he appeared on the battlements, gesticulating wildly as he argued with Brian. More than once, he stabbed a finger in her direction. Finally, Brian headed down to the gates.

Portia watched the boat sail beneath the castle, before it was her turn to race down the stairs. She was breathless by the time she reached the bottom, but she didn't slow. It had been too long since she'd seen her sisters.

They clambered up the steps, looking just as tired as she'd been when she first arrived. Of course, they'd been riding all day.

Portia issued orders for a feast to be prepared, and for water to be brought up to her room so that they might wash, for where else would they sleep? The enormous bed was more than big enough for three of them.

She wasn't sure who to hug first. Arlie, lest her baby decide to arrive this very moment, or Lina, who she'd only just missed?

Grieve stood beside them with a grave look on his face. "Tell them what you told me."

Arlie's face crumpled as she burst into tears, leaving Lina to say the words: "We are here as the Wolf's envoys. He offers everyone in the castle safe passage off Isla, if they open the gates and lay down their weapons."

Portia's mouth was dry. It was too easy. It must be a trick of some kind. Or..."What does the Wolf ask in return?"

"That King Donald gives up all claim to the Southern Isles and its people..."

Portia had expected that, and she would happily support it.

"...and that you surrender Portia to the Wolf."

Even Lina leaked a few tears as she said it, though she quickly wiped them away. "I'm sorry, Portia. That's what he wants."

"What does he want of me?" she asked.

"It doesn't matter. He shall not have her!" Grieve said.

The men on the walls rumbled their agreement.

"How long do I have?" Portia whispered.

"It does not matter. He will have to tear down the walls and kill every man among us before he can touch you!"

"He wants your answer by noon tomorrow," Lina said.

Portia nodded. She blinked back tears. Tomorrow, it would be time to end this.

"Then tonight we shall have a feast, to remind us of happier times, and tomorrow, he will have his answer," Portia said.

"His answer lies at the point of my sword!"

Portia linked arms with Arlie and Lina. "Come, I'll take you to my chamber where we may wash while the men make plans for the morrow."

It took some time to help Arlie up the stairs,

and even longer to catch her breath. Being cooped up in that loft had not done her any good. She hoped the Wolf would let her see the sun a little, at least. What there was of it.

While Arlie collapsed on the bed, complaining about how her back hurt, Lina pulled Portia aside. "There's something else. I didn't want to say it in front of all those angry men out there, for they are beyond reason right now."

"What is it?"

"It's Rudolf."

Portia's mouth was dry once more, and she feared it might be a desert until the day she died now. "What news of Rudolf?"

Lina wet her lips. "He's down there. He rides with them, Portia. This is the help he brought, at our father's command. Most of the men are our people, fighting to be free of the Albans. They fight with the Wolf, not against him."

"And Rudolf?"

"He has the Wolf's favour, I am certain of

it. Because he was the one who took us prisoner, and it was nothing like I had heard. He has treated us as well as any of the men in that vast horde. Food, a place to sleep, a tent to keep the rain off…horses to ride, while the men march. None of the Vikens has laid a finger on us, and no man among them has even hinted at it. They fear the Wolf's wrath." Lina gripped her shoulder. "Portia, make your men see sense. When they surrender, you'll get to see Rudolf again. Isn't that worth it?"

She wanted to say that it was. A week ago, she might have given anything to see Rudolf again. But to see the man she'd loved for as long as she could remember as she surrendered herself to another man? A man who owned his allegiance, as he would own her, too?

Darkness lay on her heart, as never before. This morning, she thought she could bear whatever the Wolf would do to her. But if Rudolf had to watch? It would break her heart.

She forced a smile for her sisters. "No more talk of war, or the morrow. Tonight we feast, and talk of the past. For I have missed much, it seems. I know Arlie was always a greedy guts, but when did she learn to eat melons whole?"

The talk turned to lighter things, but the darkness within remained. Later, she would surrender to it. Now…she had her last supper to enjoy.

Thirty

Portia waited until her sisters had fallen asleep before she crept over to the window. Despite their protestations about receiving kind treatment from the Wolf, their journey from their burned homes to here could not have been an easy one. They would sleep for some hours yet — so soundly, perhaps, that they wouldn't notice her absence at all.

Night air puffed through the window, chilling her bare arms. It was colder out here on the loch and the stone walls seemed to drink the chill, making the castle colder still.

Portia dressed quickly, trusting her long skirt and cloak to protect her from the biting breeze. Stockings and shoes would only slow her down tonight.

Her bow and quiver might come in useful, though. She slipped her finger into the quiver, questing until she found what she sought. She stashed the pouch in the pocket of her cloak before slinging the bow and quiver over her shoulder, leaving her hands free.

Placing both hands on the wintry stone, she climbed onto the windowsill. It was wide enough for her and her sisters to have used it for a bed, or for her to stand there while she opened the hinged section of the timber window frame to reveal the secret passage.

A whiff of the fish oil that she'd used to silence the hinges reached her nostrils, but it was better than a loud squeak rousing sound sleepers. She would endure far more discomfort before this evening was through.

A ladder led down into the darkness between the castle's inner and outer walls. A passage to freedom or, in this case, answers.

Portia twisted, trying to step from the sill to the ladder, but something caught on the window frame, holding her back. Cursing quietly, she backed up. It was the bloody bow, of all things. Which wouldn't be much use if she ran into trouble — she was better at shooting enemies from a distance. Stabbing someone with an arrow was silly, especially when she already had a dagger. Portia considered for another moment, then unhooked the offending thing from her shoulder and dropped it on the floor. The quiver clattered down atop it, and Portia winced, wishing she hadn't been so loud.

Her gaze darted to the bed, where her sisters slept on.

She allowed herself to breathe again.

The ladder rungs were rough under her feet, making her wish she'd brought her boots, but she refused to return for them now. Instead, she pulled the window panel closed to hide her descent.

Darkness cloaked her, settling like a layer of wet wool. Or was that her dread at what waited for her? Not in the darkness, but across the loch.

If dread weighed her down, at least it gave her the push she needed to keep climbing down until her feet sank into sucking mud. Trying not to think of corpses sucking at her toes each time she took a step, corpses of the men who would die tomorrow if she failed, Portia made her way along the secret passage to its hidden entrance, or exit, in her case.

She stumbled over the boat Grieve had told her would be there, but she didn't take it. Not yet. She'd memorised her mother's scroll, and if it was correct, there was another, more ancient way across the loch that didn't require rowing.

She continued down the passage until she found what she sought.

A timber half door, covered in a thin layer

of stone to conceal its true nature from the outside world, yielded to her touch. Its hinges were not so silent, but there was no one about to hear their squeaky protest.

Moonlight turned the loch into a mirror, for there was no breeze down here. No need, for the air was positively frigid. Portia scanned the shore, looking for the standing stones she knew had to be there. Stones that had seen the passage of so many people, yet they would still stand after this battle, sentinels of time.

One…and then she found the second, a finger pointing at the sky as if to remind her that she could only hide in darkness, so she only had until dawn to find her answers.

She edged around the castle walls, knowing she had to line the stones up properly to be certain she stood in the right place. Her ancestors had done this from time immemorial, or so her mother's history scroll had said. There was no need to be frightened of following in their footsteps.

But her ancestors had not faced a legend, a

man who'd had so many stories spun about him that he seemed the very devil himself. And yet…her sisters' safety spoke of someone who understood chivalry and honour, who might save what others sought to destroy.

She wasn't sure what to believe any more. She dreaded, and yet she hoped.

Which was why she would face him alone.

Portia paused to squint at the stones again. Now she could only see one – perfectly aligned. She took a deep breath, and stepped into the loch.

Icy water swirled around her feet, and her breath huffed out in a startled cloud of condensation. Her boots would not save her from the loch, but she wished she'd worn them anyway, if only for an extra moment's warmth before they grew sodden and slowed her down.

She held her hem high to keep it from getting wet, until she realised that the water didn't even reach her ankles. She let the fabric fall, lifting her gaze to the stones to keep her on her course. The ancient causeway lay hidden beneath the surface of the loch and one wrong step would result in a ducking. Her nearly numb feet already found it hard to feel the stones, so she must maintain her vigilance.

The shore came closer and closer, and Portia dared to hope she might reach it before the numbness spread to her knees.

She was only a few yards away when a male voice demanded, "Halt!"

She blew out a breath she hadn't known she'd been holding.

Hope sank to the bottom of the loch, threatening to drown her courage with it.

Thirty-One

"I told you ghosts don't take orders!" one voice insisted.

"They might. She might have been a really obedient wife in life. How many spirits have you seen?" a second voice reasoned.

"It doesn't matter. She's walking on water. That makes her a ghost, or a witch."

"It's angels that walk on water, you fool! The devil's servants sink!"

"I heard a sailor at Beacon Isle tell the story

of a woman who walked on water. She was a witch. She could see into men's souls to decide whether to sink your ship or save you, they said."

"There are good men and bad in every bunch, or on every ship. How'd she know which ships to sink if there were both kinds of men aboard?"

"I don't know – do I look like a witch?"

"You look like the idiot who just ordered a ghost to halt."

"Well, she did, didn't she? She even gave you a gift."

Rudolf listened to the exchange with amusement, but his curiosity got the better of him. This was his army camp, and no one got in or out without his knowledge. Not even a ghost.

"The gift's not for me. It's for the commander, she said. If she is a witch, maybe she's trying to curse him."

Rudolf poked his head out of his tent. "What is this cursed gift?"

The two men stopped, looking sideways at each other until one of them said, "It's like this, sir. There's a lady out on the lake who walks on water, who asked me to give you this." He set the small pouch on Rudolf's outstretched palm.

He weighed it for a moment, wondering if it was empty.

"I have heard of a woman who can walk on water. A witch so powerful that water obeys her. She used to live at Beacon Isle, but now she wears a crown. Queen Margareta, her name is, and her kingdom is not too far north of here," Rudolf said.

"Begging your pardon, sir, but what would a queen be doing out on yon lake so late at night?" the gift-bearer asked.

Rudolf emptied the pouch into his hand. "Handing out gifts, or so it would seem."

Both men recoiled and crossed themselves. "Dead virgins' fingers! That must be a powerful curse, sir. Throw them away before the magic takes hold!"

Rudolf prodded one of the pale fingers. It was hollow, as were its companions. When he turned them over, he found the lacings holding them together. The finger guards were so well-worn they still held the shape of their mistress's fingers. Portia would not abandon these on the eve of battle.

Unless she intended to stop the battle from taking place.

Rudolf tucked the finger guards safely back in their pouch. "Take me to this woman. I must see her for myself."

The two men hesitated, before the one who hadn't spoken yet ventured, "Sir, is that you issuing orders, or are you under the influence of the witch's curse?"

"Make me ask again, and you'll be on latrine duty until next year. Both of you," Rudolf stressed.

"Yes, sir!"

They trotted off, hunting hounds eagerly leading the way to his quarry.

Or so Rudolf hoped. If the lady had gone…

Yet as he reached the lake's edge, his breath caught in his throat. There was someone standing in the water, though she appeared to be floating on its surface. Now he understood why his men had mistaken her for a ghost.

Rudolf extended his hand. "Why don't you come ashore, my lady?" he asked.

She turned so that the hood's shadow hiding her face pointed toward him. "Would you step ashore, knowing the land is occupied by an enemy's army?"

Rudolf pulled the finger guards from their pouch. "The lady who owns these will never be my enemy. I promised to protect her, and my promise still stands."

She lifted her hands to her hood, ready to lower it. "What can you tell me of the man they call the Wolf Prince?"

"A highborn Viken, cousin to the king, commander of this army and conqueror of the Southern Isles." It sounded quite impressive, laid out like that. Maybe it would impress her enough to make her forget how long he'd been away.

"Not this isle. Not yet," she said fiercely.

No, it was not enough to impress Portia.

Rudolf spread his arms wide. "Look again, Lady. This army has already taken Isla. The only holdout is that tiny fort on the lake, and it will not hold out for much longer."

"A week," she said softly, as though it pained her.

"You think it will take that long?" He wanted to say that he could take it in a day, if she needed him to do so. For if this was truly Portia, he would scale the walls alone to save her. Yet here she stood, hardly a prisoner.

"We only have enough food for a week. I know the state of the castle store rooms, and how much we eat. Lina would not have made the same mistake, but I was not prepared for a siege with so many mouths to feed. I do not wish my people to die. I want to sue for peace."

"Name your terms."

Her head darted to the left and right. "First,

take me to the Wolf's tent, where we might discuss this in private. Can you give me that?"

"Of course."

She nodded. "Do you swear to grant me safe passage into your camp?"

Into it, but not out. Interesting. "I do so solemnly swear."

"Then take me there, Dolf."

He held his hand out once more, more out of courtesy than any expectation that Portia would need it, until she stumbled. Courtesy be damned. He dived forward to catch her.

"Release me." It was a command.

He set her on her feet on the grass before he did as she asked.

She tugged her hood down. "Lead the way, Dolf."

It took all his willpower not to glance back over his shoulder as he took her to his tent. Now, he wished he'd accepted the hospitality of one of the nearby crofters so that he could offer her something better than this. Portia deserved better than this.

He straightened the coverlet on his pallet, as though he hadn't been roused from sleep by her arrival. The ancient laws of hospitality demanded that he offer her something to eat and drink, but he had nothing here. His tent was a place to sleep. Nothing more.

Rudolf stepped out of his tent and hailed the first man he saw. "Bring me a jug of mead," he said.

The jug was brought. Too late, Rudolf realised he should have asked for cups to go with it.

He re-entered his tent, and there she stood.

Her red hair glowed in the firelight of his brazier, haloing her like the saint who had given Loch Findlugan its name.

"Portia," he breathed. It came out like a prayer to heaven. A prayer that after all he'd endured, this angel might become his.

"Dolf?" she asked uncertainly. "I have watched the Wolf striding around the camp in that armour all day. This is his tent. Tell me the truth now, for I must know. Who is he?"

Thirty-Two

Rudolf set the jug on the ground and bowed. "Prince Rudolf Vargssen, cousin to Reidar Haraldssen, King of Viken. Reidar's father and mine were brothers."

Oh, how she didn't want to believe it. But how could she not believe him? "So you are the Wolf. The man who has killed, raped and plundered his way across the Southern Isles to take my home from me."

Rudolf shook his head. "I swear to you, I

am the Wolf, but I have done none of those things. I have never raped a woman, nor killed one since I set foot on the Southern Isles. Not even my aunt, who would not have been so kind to me. I have killed men, it is true, though they tried equally hard to kill me. As for plunder..." He waved at the unadorned interior of his tent. "Do you see anything of worth here? I have taken nothing from the islands that was not given to me freely. The lords of the isles are with me. All but your father, who I'd hoped to find here with you. As for your home..." He ducked his head. "I may have set fire to it. Just a little," he admitted.

"But Mason and his men said..."

"Is Mason your husband?" Rudolf demanded.

Portia had never seen such pain in his eyes. "Mason is Donald's man, sent here to secure the islands for Alba. And build high walls to keep people both out and in." Her gaze arrowed in the direction of the castle on

Council Island.

"Is he your husband?"

Portia laughed bitterly. "Mason who thinks so much of himself? No. He believes I am beneath his notice. The fat pig of a man desires one of Donald's daughters, and he thinks subduing us will earn him that honour. He holds me safe from Viken raiders and other unscrupulous men, who might want to marry me for their own ends. More likely, he thinks to marry me off to whoever Donald sends to replace him. One of Donald's sons, he said."

"If you are a prisoner, how did you get out?"

She shook her head. "I cannot tell you that. The Dolf I once knew would not ask me to betray my sisters by letting the leader of an enemy army into the chamber where they sleep."

If anything, her words had hurt him even more.

"I have never been, and will never be your enemy, Portia."

For a long moment, she stared at him. Heaven help her, but she believed him.

All the fear and frustration and years of missing him and dreading the future bubbled up. She swallowed back a sob. She couldn't cry now. She had a peace agreement to broker with the Wolf, who was not the Dolf she'd known before the war. This man was harder, commanding armies and conquering islands. Conquering her island.

"What terms will you offer us, then, so that my people and yours are not enemies?" Portia said. Oh, but it hurt to call the other Islanders his people. This man was a foreigner to her, while she'd considered them friends. Once considered him a friend.

Rudolf shook his head. "That's not how it works. I have given the castellan my terms. I will let everyone in the castle go, unharmed, if they lay down their arms and release you."

"He cannot. Grieve swore an oath to my father, he and all his men, that they would protect me."

"But he does not have you now. I do. What will he do if you do not return?" Triumph glittered in Rudolf's eyes, something else she'd never seen there before.

Something died inside Portia. "Then Grieve and his men will come in search of me, even if it means attacking the camp. We both know they would die. Grieve is a good man, and so are those who serve under him. Good men, loyal to my father, and loyal to me. They don't deserve to die. Not yet."

"And what do I deserve? I have fought for years for this. For these islands. For your home."

She closed her eyes to stop the tears from falling. She should have sent Lina to negotiate on her behalf. Lina's knees would not have weakened at the longing in Rudolf's tone.

"You can have the islands. All of them. And my home. As long as you promise to spare them, too."

Rudolf shook his head. "They must lay down their arms, yet you say they will not. I once vowed to protect you, too, and I would fight as long as I had the breath left to shout a battle cry. If these men are as loyal as you say, they will fight to the death – theirs or ours."

"Or mine." It came out as a whisper, but Portia couldn't stop it.

"Never," Rudolf swore. He seized her shoulders. "There must be another way, Portia. I let go of you once, and I will not lose you now. Not to Donald or Mason or any man who dares to lay claim to you and your birthright." He dropped to his knees. "I will give you everything I've fought for. Every island, every rock, every fishing boat. For you."

Her breath caught in her throat. He couldn't mean…

"What would you ask in return?" she asked faintly, pressing her hand to her breast to hide her hammering heart.

"You. Other men may desire your dowry, but all I've ever wanted is you." He held out his hands in supplication. "Marry me, Portia."

All her adult life she'd wanted to hear those

words, dreading the day she'd have to refuse him. Tonight, she'd come to offer herself to the Wolf, knowing it would cut her off from Rudolf forever. But now…

"If Grieve came in search of me, he could not break a marriage bond," Portia said thoughtfully. "My claim would pass to you, my husband. If I stand at your side as your wife, Grieve would open the castle gates to you."

She'd said something wrong. The shining love in Rudolf's eyes had gone. Had she imagined it?

Rudolf rose. "Of course. You think of your men. This Grieve must mean much to you." He sounded bitter.

"Until my father returns home, they are the last of his men. Just as they swore to protect me, I have a responsibility to them," Portia said. She had little choice, and it lightened her heart enough to see her way clearly for the first time. "Yes." Her father would understand. Rudolf had been her heart's choice, long ago, when she could not have him. As the Wolf

Prince, she could. Hope blossomed. "But it must be tonight, before anyone notices I am gone. Or someone will die."

He eyed her. "A marriage is not valid without vows to be faithful, followed by a consummation. We must do that tonight, too."

She swallowed. Consummating a marriage was the hardest part. She'd never forget Lina's or Arlie's cries of pain on their wedding nights. Dolf might protect her, but he could not save her from himself. It was but a small price to pay to end a war. "It shall be as you say. We must wake the priest who serves Saint Findlugan's church, and ask him to marry us."

Thirty-Three

"I wish you both well. You may…you may use my house for the consummation. I shall return in the morning," Father Fintan said, ducking out the door and into the rain before Rudolf could stop him.

Rudolf and Portia stared at each other for a moment. His heart sank at the fear in her expression. He'd dreamed of this night for half his life, but never had he imagined his first night with her would be in a tiny, cold cottage with a straw pallet so thin and narrow they may as well be making love on the floor like animals. He'd imagined a roaring fire, a room so warm she'd want to take her clothes off, and a big, carved bed like the one he'd slept in in Viken.

"We don't have to do this if you do not wish to," Rudolf said.

She tossed her head. "We do. My father, Mason and this bloody king of his will dissolve a marriage that hasn't been consummated as quickly as salt in a stew pot." She hoisted her skirts up to her waist. "Where would you have me, husband?"

Husband. The word sounded so good on her lips, and yet…there was no love in the way she said it. Like his firebrand of a wife had died inside by marrying him.

Rudolf dismissed the priest's pallet, but that left him little more to choose from. He wanted to hold her close, to kiss her, to make her comfortable when he made love to her for the first time.

Reidar had made his bride scream for joy on their wedding night. They'd known each other for barely two days, and the whole castle had known just how much the queen loved her king. Rudolf had loved Portia for half his life, and he vowed he would show her that tonight.

Women enjoyed lovemaking more when they were on top, he'd heard, so Portia must mount him. That mean…"There," he said, pointing at a bench by the wall. He sat down on the broad seat, and patted his knees. "Sit here, my lady."

With some difficulty, owing to her bundled up skirts, Portia climbed into his lap. Gently, Rudolf guided her around to face him, so she straddled him.

"This is not how my sisters did it," she protested. "Their husbands made them lie down and…" She paled and didn't finish.

"When we have a bed worthy of you, I shall lay you down upon it, and show you every pleasure a man can give a woman," Rudolf promised. "But tonight, it is here or the floor,

I'm afraid."

He could feel the heat of her, now, burning through his tunic. With her skirts so high, she was naked to the waist, and he longed to stroke her lovely legs right until he reached the apex where they met and then…

She squirmed in his lap. "Why are you so hard?"

His cock only hardened further in response. He freed it from the folds of his clothes and laid it beside her leg. "Because you are so beautiful," he said.

She didn't seem to hear him. Her alarmed gaze was fixed on his cock. "You're going to stick that huge thing into me?"

He wanted to laugh, but he feared that wouldn't help. He'd never seen his fearless Portia look so frightened. "Actually, the way we're sitting, you'll be in control of that. I'll just position it right, and all you have to do is sink down on it, as slowly as you like."

"Very well."

She rose. If she hadn't been wearing her

clothes, Rudolf could have kissed her breasts. Next time they made love, he vowed, they'd be naked and he'd kiss them for twice as long to make up for it. Maybe even suck on her nipples a bit, too, if she liked that.

His cock was rock hard now, jutting toward her so eagerly it took all his willpower not to grab her hips and slam her down upon it. They had all night, he reminded himself. All night to take this as slowly as she needed.

Portia set her hands on his shoulders and glanced down. "It looks even bigger now. Are you sure it will fit?"

"Of course," he soothed, cupping one hand around her bottom to bring her closer. He wrapped his other hand around his shaft, positioning the head of his cock right against her sweet spot. One small push and the irresistible heat of her engulfed the tip. He sucked in a breath, fighting down the urge to thrust hard and deep into her. "Now, just sink down and I'll slide right in."

He closed his eyes, savouring the feel of her.

Her nails dug into his shoulders as her molten heat embraced him, inch by inch, so tight he wanted to moan in bliss. He had to let her control this. He had to. Because if he did…in two or three thrusts he'd be done, she felt so incredibly good.

He cupped her bottom in both hands now, squeezing her soft flesh to stop himself from pushing her all the way down in one mighty shove.

And then, in one delicious eternity, she'd sheathed him completely, clenched down so hard on him that Rudolf feared his cock would blow then and there. He didn't dare move, she felt so exquisite. "God, Portia, that feels amazing."

She let out a sound that sounded like a sob.

Rudolf's eyes flew open.

Tears streamed down Portia's cheeks. "Please, finish this quickly, Dolf. It hurts so!"

He shifted and she cried out – definitely not in pleasure.

"Please," she begged.

He ripped his cock out of her as if he'd burned it, as well he might have. He tucked himself away, swearing at himself for being such a fool. Portia stumbled back, away from him, clutching her skirts to her face as she sobbed into them.

A thin trickle of blood ran down her thigh. Maiden's blood, for Portia was a maiden no more. He'd seen to that, and pretty damn clumsily, too.

Rudolf rose and sat Portia down on his seat. He found a bucket of water and a cloth, cleaning off the blood before she could see it. She cried out as he touched the cloth to her lower lips and Rudolf stopped. He'd dealt with most of the mess.

He dropped the cloth in the bucket and smoothed down Portia's skirts before he took her in his arms. "Shh, it's all right. It's over, it's over. Everything's put away, so you just hold onto me and cry as much as you need to."

God, she felt good in his arms, too. Not quite as good as she did with his cock buried balls deep in her, but nearly. Nearly. Maybe another night, when –

"Please don't make me do that again, Dolf. It hurt so much!" Portia begged.

Maybe never. Rudolf sighed. Who'd have thought he'd have such a clumsy cock? So much for giving his bride a blissful wedding night, or any night, for that matter.

"I'll never do anything to hurt you, Portia. I swear it." He swallowed. "And there's no need for more. The marriage is consummated. You did it. You and everyone on your island are safe. No one can dissolve our marriage now."

He held her as she cried herself out, murmuring endearments aloud even as he silently cursed himself. He had what he wanted – the wife of his dreams, and all the Southern Isles. So why did victory feel as cold and miserable as stroking his own cock in the rain?

Because that's what he'd be doing, as soon as Portia fell asleep, he told himself, so he wouldn't frighten her with the sight of him again. But in the meantime, he could hold her close and love her, in whatever way she wanted. Because one thing was certain — Rudolf loved his wife, and he'd do anything for her.

Thirty-Four

Portia awoke cold and stiff, like she'd slept on the stone. And with ache between her legs that reminded her…

Rudolf. He'd returned, and she'd married him last night. She'd known he was too big, but she'd done it anyway. And now he was…

Not here.

But it couldn't have been a dream!

She wouldn't have dreamed such a terrible wedding night. Not with Rudolf. Heaven help her, she'd cried herself to sleep in his arms.

No wonder he was gone.

"Good morning, my lady. Do you wish to break your fast?"

Portia sat up. The middle aged priest who'd married them last night stood by the table with his head bowed, as if not daring to look at her.

"Or perhaps you would like to wash?"

Memories of Rudolf's hands on her thighs as he cleaned the most intimate parts of her made her blush. What must he think of her?

She turned suspicious eyes on the priest. "Do you know who I am?"

He smiled. "Of course, Lady Portia. Prince Rudolf was most adamant that I take good care of you until he returns to collect you. He even sent a man with breakfast, so that you might not go hungry. This is more than a poor priest usually sees unless he is invited to a feast." He waved at the table. "I look forward to the feast when they make him High Lord of the Isles, as is his due."

"What?" Her father was High Lord of the

Isles, not Rudolf. Rudolf didn't hold lands here. He was a Viken prince. He probably owned an ice floe somewhere in Viken.

"I remember the first council meeting Lord Angus brought him to. He was the first man ashore, at Lord Angus's behest. I knew it then, but it is even more clear now. Prince Rudolf will rule us well."

Rule? Rudolf? She'd married him, but…

The priest coughed. "Sorry, my lady. I forget that you are a new bride and perhaps have other things on your mind. Many new brides see their husband differently in the light of day after their wedding night. I often have to remind them that if they lay with their husband often enough, he will never stray, and may soon bless her with strong sons or beautiful daughters. I counsel – "

"Where is Rudolf now?" Portia interrupted. She had no need for a lecture on her marital duties from a man who knew little about them.

"I imagine he is with his army, preparing for battle."

"No!"

"I am sure he will return when it is all over. He asked that I keep you safe."

"To blazes with safe. There should be no battle. Good men will die if he continues with this stupidity." She smoothed her dress, retying her laces though she did not need to. "Do you possess a comb?" Heaven help her, but she would not turn up at an army camp with straw in her hair.

"Of course, my lady. No mirror, though, but sometimes I find the collection plate is shiny enough to see myself." He held up the bronze dish, and Portia peered at her reflection.

She cursed as she saw the straw in her hair. Combing the mess would be more painful than coupling with Rudolf last night, but she must. She made short work of it, then thanked the priest for his help.

"Eat, my lady." The priest pushed the bread toward her.

She did not have time, yet she must. Portia seized a piece of bread in one hand and a chunk of cheese in the other. She could eat on the way.

The priest helped her fasten her cloak, and she burst outside into the late morning sun. Nearly noon. She broke into a run.

Thirty-Five

Just before noon, the gate opened to let out a boat bigger than the coracle Rudolf had sent across the loch yesterday. With three armoured men aboard, it was no surprise. Two red heads watched from the tower window, but he knew neither belonged to Portia. No, she was safe with Father Fintan.

He'd ordered his men back from the lake shore, but they still stood to watch. Few wore weapons or armour as he did – this was supposed to be a peace negotiation. Yet the men in the boat looked ready for war.

As the three stepped ashore, one emerged as a definite leader. The castellan who'd ordered the gates open yesterday, Rudolf guessed. Was this Portia's man, Grieve, or someone else?

Rudolf removed his helm so that he might see them better. The men waited until they reached him before they did the same.

"Wolf," the castellan said, with the slightest nod. No, Rudolf did not know this man.

"Rudolf?" one of his companions said, nudging the third man. "We thought you'd buggered off back to Viken!"

"Damhan, Dermot," Rudolf greeted them after a moment's thought. "As you can see, I have returned."

Dermot grinned. "You never were one to run from a fight. I remember the day you arrived, I knocked you down once, but none of the other boys could touch you. You just got up and brushed it off. That's the day you found the Three Little Pigs!" His glee faded as quickly as it had come. "It seems we need your help again."

The castellan hushed him with a glare. "We are not here to ask for help. We are here to negotiate better terms than the ones you offered yesterday." He planted his feet firmly. "We will not hand over Lady Portia."

Won't, or can't? Rudolf wondered. Did they know she was missing?

"Did you ask Lady Portia?" he asked.

The three exchanged glances. Yes, they did, and yet they'd come to negotiate with him, knowing they had nothing he wanted. That took courage.

"What the lady wants is of no consequence. We have sworn an oath to protect her, and we will."

Rudolf snorted. He couldn't help it. "Have you even met Portia?"

This could not be Grieve. No man she spoke of so highly would try to peddle such nonsense.

He toyed with the idea of telling the man he

was her husband. Then he'd have his answer, for no man who loved her could hide his pain at hearing that.

The castellan drew his sword. "Have you?"

A collective gasp rose from the men behind him. This was no way to conduct a peace negotiation.

"Sheath that thing, you bloody fool!"

The castellan's eyes widened and he nearly dropped his sword. "Rhona?"

"You lay one finger on this man, Wolf Prince, and our alliance is over!" Rhona said, striding to the man's side.

It seemed the alliance was over already.

Rudolf narrowed his eyes. "Who are you?"

The castellan opened his mouth, but it was Rhona who answered, "He's Grieve Lewisson, my betrothed, and the head of Lady Portia's personal guard." She turned on the man. "Why have the Albans sent you to negotiate?"

Damhan and Dermot burst out laughing. "What Albans? They've all fled, like the cowards they are. Even Mason, when we shut him out. Council Island and the castle belong to Lady Portia."

"No. It belongs to my husband." Portia's voice rang out over the water as she strode along the shore. She wore no shoes and her gown was muddied to the knees, but she walked like a queen. No sign of last night's downpour of tears. Now, she was the storm.

"Lady Portia! Thank the heavens!" Only now did Grieve sheathe his sword. "What happened to you? We thought…my lady, your boots!"

If his men hadn't noticed before, they did now.

But that's what he loved about Portia. Thousands of armed men watching, holding their collective breath, and she merely tossed her head and said, "I'm sure my husband will buy me new ones when he is done here." She laid a possessive hand on his arm, lining up beside him against Rhona and Grieve. She lifted her burning gaze to Rhona, something even Rudolf would have hesitated to do.

Should he warn her? he wondered, but there was no time.

"Lady Rhona," Portia said, offering the woman her cheek. "It is a pleasure. I have heard so much about you."

The two women kissed. A little stiffly, to be sure, for they were strangers, but the power play between them was palpable. The witch who terrified his men capitulated to Portia.

"I look forward to your wedding. You must sit beside me at the feast to celebrate mine," Portia said. She shot a pointed look at Rudolf. "Of course, you and Grieve must sit with us at the high table. I insist."

"My lady," Grieve said weakly, looking from one woman to the other.

"I hope you mean Rhona, for I'm not yours any more. Protecting me is Prince Rudolf's job now." Her fingers squeezed his arm. "Isla is ours!"

Rudolf's men took up the cry until it echoed around the valley. He wanted to weep, but knew he could not.

The war was over, and Portia was safe. His to protect.

"But what will your father say?" Grieve asked.

Portia didn't flinch. "We will find out when he returns home. In the meantime, my husband will take his place in council."

And not a man among them dared argue. The Lady of Isla had spoken.

Thirty-Six

She smiled through her wedding feast and said all that needed to be said, but inside Portia felt empty. Rudolf would scarcely look at her, and every time she tried to get his attention, she'd find some lord or other already occupying it. He never even noticed when she bade him good night and headed up to her tower room, where she slept alone.

Her days were as dull as when she'd lived in the loft, for she saw so little of him, it was like she had no husband at all. At night, he did not come to her room, or summon her to his, as was his right. Why, she did not even know where he slept, or if he did. The lords never left him alone, and rumours circled, each wilder than the last.

Her men were hers no longer – they'd been pressed into doing things for their lordly fathers. Grieve had been sent to fetch Lord Lewis from Myroy, and there was talk of her father returning. Talk was all it was, until she saw the party riding over the ridge.

The men on lookout saw him, too. "Lord Angus! The banners of Isla!"

Preparations were made to turn the great hall into a council chamber, for there were important matters to be decided. Matters that could only be discussed here on Council Island.

Matters that she had no business being part of. So Portia sat alone in her tower, hoping her father might visit her when the meeting was over.

"There you are!" Lord Angus had other ideas, evidently. He'd aged, and he was now missing part of his ear. "Why are you not at Rudolf's side, in the thick of things, like you used to be?"

Portia managed a small smile. "Every time I see him, he has a lord on each arm, and a line of more men waiting to speak to him. He has no time for me. And there is talk of crowning him as King of the Southern Isles, an office we have never had. They wanted to do it right away, but Lord Lewis insisted we had to wait. For you, he said."

Angus nodded. "Aye, I've heard. It's been a long time coming, but it's for the best. Lord Lewis knew I would not want to miss the coronation of our first king."

"But you're the High Lord of the Isles! I thought he was your friend — why would he want you to answer such an insult in person?"

Angus laughed. "'Tis not an insult. He is a better man than me, and younger, too. I put him forward years ago, before Donald's army came to Isla. Rudolf will make a good king. Do you not think so?" He peered at her. "You chose the man, so surely you must."

"He will make an excellent king," Portia said warmly. She'd seen enough over the last few days to know that, if she did not already.

"But?"

She swallowed. "I thought he had feelings for me, instead of marrying me for my claim, like the others might have. But…"

Angus laughed so hard he nearly fell off the windowsill. "No feelings for you? Rudolf? That man's been in love with you since the day you donned a woman's gown. And I've seen the way you look at him, too. Why else do you think you got a personal guard while he was gone? It was not that he has the strength of ten men, though he is a mighty warrior. Nay, it was because I promised to keep you safe for him until he returned. He would never have left for Viken otherwise."

Portia couldn't seem to close my mouth. "But he has been so distant since we married.

He hasn't..." She felt a blush burn her cheeks. "He hasn't summoned me to his chambers at all since our wedding night."

"Ah, he knows you too well, is all. Rudolf knows you are not the sort of woman he can order about. You'd punch him in the nose, or some more tender place, I'd wager, and he knows it. 'Tis up to you to come to him, I'm sure." It was his turn to blush. "Your mother came to me before we were married, and would not take no for an answer. She'd taken some fertility potion a witch had given her, and she wouldn't give herself to any man but me. I think we made you girls that night." He continued, too lost in reflection to realise that Portia had stopped listening.

Rudolf wanted her. Maybe even loved her. If her father could see it...

"Tonight," she said, so softly she didn't think her father heard. "Tonight, I shall bed the king.

Thirty-Seven

Rudolf stepped into the lord's chambers and slammed the door shut. Why in heaven's name had he agreed to be their king?

"Congratulations, my king." Portia stepped out of the shadows. The laces across her breasts had come untied, and her gown was in danger of slipping off her shoulders.

Rudolf's fingers itched to help, though whether to help her out of her gown or touch her breasts as he retied the laces for her, he wasn't sure. He knew now why he'd accepted the questionable honour of a crown. "I did it for you," he said simply. "As long as the Southern Isles are your home, this is where I shall be."

She frowned. "What will the Viken king say?"

"We will find out soon enough. His men sail home on the morrow, and they will tell him all." He waved away her worries. "I have no doubt Reidar wants to see me bend the knee with a crown on my head, so that he may laugh at me. But if he sees you, he will understand." Rudolf seized the crown and dropped it on top of a nearby chest. "Now I know how heavy the thing is, I remember why I never wanted one."

A tear slipped down Portia's cheek. "I don't understand."

Rudolf reached out to wipe it away. He never wanted to see her cry, much less make her do so. "My cousin, King Reidar, gave me leave to take a force across the sea to free the Southern Isles from Donald and his minions because I begged him to. I came for you, Portia. I took the Isles because they are your birthright, and your home, and I will not see anyone take them from you. Everything I have ever done is for you."

More tears fell, but this time Portia wiped them away herself. "Truly?"

"Truly."

She took a deep breath. "Then it is only fitting that I should do something for you, too. You must have an heir, and though it pains me to do it, I must give you one." Off slid the gown, with no help from Rudolf, puddling on the stones at her feet. She stepped out of it like a nymph out of a lake, lifting the hem of her shift.

Rudolf's breath caught in his throat as the filmy linen rose over her head before descending to join its fellow on the floor. "God, you're beautiful," he said hoarsely.

She toed off her stockings as she made her way to the bed. Naked as the day she was born, Portia spread her body across the covers, the greatest gift any woman ever gave a man.

"Please make haste, Dolf. It's cold, and I would prefer to get the painful part over with as quickly as possible." She shuddered, her nipples hardening until Rudolf could look at nothing else. "The pain was hard enough to bear the first time we did this."

Rudolf's brow furrowed. "But I thought it only hurt for a girl's first time. After that, there shouldn't be any pain." He'd never asked a girl about it, but he would never forget that first night Reidar spent with his queen. Her screams hadn't sounded pained.

"Are you sure? My sisters said their first few nights with their husbands were just as painful. It took them a full week before the act became bearable."

Rudolf had no idea – he had no experience with virgins. "You bled that first night. It takes time for a wound to heal, and perhaps that's why it took your sisters a week. It has been a week since we…since I…"

Portia wet her lips. "Can you check for a

wound?" She parted her thighs wider.

Rudolf swallowed. He wanted nothing more to be inside her, loving her like Reidar did his queen. But if it meant hurting her… "Of course, I will check." He climbed onto the bed and knelt between her legs. He lifted his gaze to caress the soft skin of her inner thighs, remembering how glorious it had felt to plunge between them. Sliding between those wet lips, gleaming so tantalisingly before him now. Perfect, unbroken skin, with no wound to be seen. He wanted to reach out and stroke her, but he restrained himself. "You look perfect to me."

Portia rose onto her elbows, still frowning. "Did you check inside? It wasn't until you were inside me that I started hurting."

He lifted her legs over his shoulders, parting her lower lips with his fingers. Silky soft and so wet…his manhood grew rigid, but Rudolf fought to ignore it. Still he could not see anything but perfection. "I can't see inside you," he admitted. "But perhaps I can feel for it." He pushed a finger inside her slowly, stroking her inner walls.

She shuddered and clenched around his finger. "Dolf!"

"Did I hurt you?" He repeated the motion, more slowly this time.

She gasped. "No. You didn't hurt me. That feels…delightful."

The more he stroked, the hotter and wetter she became, until she cried out and clenched down hard on his finger as though she would keep it inside her forever.

"More," she sighed.

More…what? Rudolf slid a second finger into her, and started stroking harder. Watching her face this time, as her breathing grew shallow and her eyes closed, he sent her to her climax faster this time. God, what he would give to join her in reaching such a pleasurable peak together, he thought as she arched her back up off the bed and cried his name.

More than anything, he wanted to put more than his fingers inside her.

It would be different this time, he promised himself as he shucked off his clothes. At the slightest sign that he was hurting her, he'd stop, but he needed to be inside her. Now.

He lifted his manhood, poised to thrust deep into her.

"What are you doing?" she asked, fear darkening her eyes.

God help him, he couldn't. Couldn't hurt her again. It would kill him to see her cry and know he'd caused it.

Rudolf rolled onto his back so he lay on the bed beside her. He ached to impale her. Soon, he promised himself.

"Just like the night we were wed," he said breathlessly. "You sit on top of me, so you can control how deep I go. There is no wound I can feel, inside or out. I won't hurt you, Portia, and this will feel better than my fingers, I promise." He prayed that this last part wouldn't be a lie. He'd never forgive himself.

"If you are sure…" Portia rose up onto her knees and shuffled until she straddled him, one leg on either side of his. "I'm afraid," she admitted.

"Don't be," he said, grabbing his cock in one hand as he rested his other hand on her hip. Gently, he guided the tip of his cock inside her, holding firmly to her hip when she reflexively flinched away. "Now, move down, Portia."

She bit her lip, nodded once, then lowered herself onto him. Inch by inch, he glided into her molten core. God, this woman was heaven. This time, he kept his eyes firmly on her face, alert for any sign of pain. He would not hurt her again while he was lost in his own pleasure.

Her mouth dropped open and her eyes widened, but still she descended, engulfing him so completely that her well-rounded backside rested against his balls.

"It doesn't hurt," she breathed. With agonising slowness, she rose up, and then down his length again. "That feels...good." She raised herself again.

If he left this all up to Portia, her next

climax would take all night, so Rudolf took control. He fastened both hands around her hips and met her downward slide with a hard thrust.

She gasped, surprised, but then she smiled. "Again."

With Rudolf's help, she soon rode him in a rocking rhythm that felt every bit as good as he'd imagined it would. And when he felt her clenching around him in her third climax, Rudolf shouted her name as he found his own release.

"I love you, Portia," he gasped out, staring up at her.

Her breasts heaved as she fought to catch her breath, huffing and puffing as though she intended to blow the very castle down around them, but her brilliant smile was telling enough until she managed to say, "I love you, too, Dolf. Can we do that again?"

"Every night," Rudolf promised. "A good husband keeps his wife happy, and I intend to see you happy ever after."

She smiled mischieviously. "The tomorrow you shall take me for a ride, just the two of us, and when we reach a good place to stop, we shall make love all over again."

He stroked her leg, feeling his spirits rising once more. Portia was the only woman for him, now and forever. "Who said we must wait until tomorrow?"

Her eyes widened with alarm, before her expression softened to surprise, and she did some stroking of her own. "Don't make me wait, Dolf."

"Never again," he vowed, and when they came together again, it seemed the very air sang for joy.

Return:
Hansel and Gretel Retold

DEMELZA CARLTON

A tale in the Romance a Medieval Fairy Tale series

One

"What about that plant? Can you tell me its properties?" Mother asked, pointing.

Rhona eyed the yellow flowers. "Tansy. Useful to combat gout or help a woman lose an unwanted child. We use it in tansy cakes and to scent the rushes on the floor on feast days."

"It can also be used to dye cloth in shades

of yellow and green," Mother said.

Rhona sighed. "I will never remember them all."

Mother turned and smiled. "Of course you will. One day. It takes practice, is all. There are books at home full of this, but your head needs to be full of it, too, for you won't have the book in the woods with you." She pointed at a plant with downy leaves. "What of that one?"

Rhona glared at the plant. "A stinging nettle. The young plants can be boiled and eaten, and the older ones can be soaked and the fibres woven into cloth. Best to wear gloves when you pick it, though." She had made that mistake once, and had no intention of doing so again. Nettles hurt.

"And that – " Mother gave a cry as her horse stumbled, and she tumbled from the saddle.

"Mother!"

Rhona slid from her horse and dashed to Mother. She lay face down, with a spreading pool of blood beneath her.

Rhona shook Mother's shoulder, and she'd never been so relieved to hear a groan in her life. "What should I do, Mother?" Rhona asked urgently.

"Use your magic, and get me home," Mother whispered.

"But you said…" Rhona snapped her mouth shut. She was old enough to know that her mother changed her mind when circumstances required it. "Very well."

Rhona took a deep breath, then bit her lip. The breeze came the instant she summoned it, plucking her clothing as it passed, but saving most of its power for Mother. She let the air currents lift Mother back onto her horse, but the animal shied as soon as it smelled blood. The frightened horse bolted, and Mother fell a second time.

This time, she didn't move.

Rhona sent another gust of wind, stronger this time, to pick Mother up and bring her to Rhona's own horse. Rhona's gelding was an old warhorse who shied at nothing, even as he was made to carry two women instead of one.

"Mother, should I go slowly, so I don't hurt you more, or should I hurry, to get you home faster?" Rhona asked.

No response.

That meant Mother wouldn't feel the jolting if they galloped, and they would arrive sooner. Rhona kneed her horse into flight, and the gelding willingly obeyed.

It was both the longest and the shortest ride of her life. Rhona shouted for help as she arrived at her father's house. Her arms ached from holding tight to her mother, but she refused to let go until Mother was in better hands than hers. Healer's hands, hopefully. Someone who knew how to stop the bleeding, for all Rhona's knowledge of herbs had fled when her mother fell.

"Rhona needs a healer, too!" someone shouted. Her oldest sister, Nuala.

Rhona shook her head irritably. "I'm fine. It's Mother who needs help."

"Why are you all covered in blood, then?" Nuala demanded with all the force of a twelve-year-old demanding to be considered a capable adult.

Rhona glanced down. The front of her dress was stained red. "Mother," she choked out, and ran for Mother's bedchamber. Nuala was hot on her heels.

Mother's eyes fluttered open. "Go get the other children, and your father," she said.

Rhona moved to obey, but Mother caught her sleeve. "No. Nuala, not you."

"I am sorry, mistress, but there is nothing more I can do. We can only wait," the healer said.

Mother nodded and waved the man out.

"I'm sorry. I should have gotten you here faster. I should have – " Rhona began.

Mother hushed her. "I do not have much time, he says. I lost too much blood. No one could save me, not even you. To think I'd hoped to give your father a son...but now I never will, and the babe will die with me. Just like my sister."

"Aunt Brigid – "

"Was no aunt to you, though she was my sister. She protected me as only she could, and so when she died, I swore to protect you. Now…it is your turn." Mother winced, then went on, "You must protect your sisters from whatever comes, but especially from Alban invaders. But you cannot use your powers, or they will know."

Rhona almost didn't want to ask, but she had to know. "Know what?"

"That I am not your mother. Brigid was."

"And my father…?"

"Is still your father. When the Albans attacked our home, I was already betrothed to him, his virgin bride, but the Albans…they…" Mother swallowed. "Brigid found me, too late to stop them. She swore she would protect me after that, but when it came to my own husband…the man I loved, I could not stand to have a man touch me. So she…pretended to be me, in the dark. We hid her pregnancy from your father and I told him you were mine. He does not know, and if he were ever to find out…I fear it would break his heart. He can never know you are a witch like Brigid. Never. But you must protect your sisters, like I protected you. Promise me!"

"Mother, I – "

"Promise me!"

Rhona fought to hold back her tears. "I swear on my father's life that I will protect my sisters."

Mother – no, Aunt Blanid – subsided. "Thank you."

Then Sive, Maeve and Father arrived with Nuala, and all Blanid had time for were whispered words of love and farewell for her family before she left this world.

Then Rhona wept with her half-sisters, for they had all lost a mother that day, and life would never be the same again.

Two

"Tell us a story!" Sive demanded.

Nuala rolled her eyes at her youngest sister, but Rhona fought back tears. Blanid would have told her daughters a story to help them sleep, and Rhona had promised to take care of them.

Rhona moistened her lips. "How about the tale of the Three Little Pigs?"

Nuala gave the smallest nod, but Rhona caught it. This had always been Nuala's favourite.

"Once upon a time, there were three girls," Rhona began. "As alike as piglets, all born together, and none could tell them apart. Their mother had died when they were but babies, so a nurse cared for them. One day, when their father and all his household were busy preparing for a feast, the three sisters escaped into the woods, unseen. The nurse searched high and low, but could not find them anywhere. The girls had found a pond, hidden deep in the woods, where they began to play, not hearing the calls of their nurse or the other searchers. But it was a hot day, and a young wolf, separated from his pack, was thirsty, so he, too, was drawn to the pond to drink. And he found the three girls, playing in the mud. He snapped at one of them, but she was so covered in mud, she slipped free of his grasp, pulling her sisters deeper into the water where the wolf could not go. So the wolf, hungry and angry that his dinner had run away to where he could not reach it, set up such a howling that soon all those around heard it. Including the nurse, up at their father's house. When she heard that terrible sound, so close to the house, she thought of the girls. She took up a branch from one of the bonfires, and set off into the woods. She reached the pond, and when she saw the wolf on the edge, she beat him until she drove him off. Then she called the girls out of the water, but the frightened children wouldn't come. Finally, their father came, and the girls were dragged from the mud, looking more like pigs than human children, and forever after, they were known as the Three Little Pigs. Their father made them promise never to run away again, and the younger two agreed, but to this very day, the eldest has refused to give him her promise, and 'tis said that one day she will succeed her father as Lord of the Isles."

Maeve snorted. "That's not true. Girls can't be lords. She'll be a lady, and her husband will be the lord."

"She's already a lady. She doesn't need a

husband for that," Nuala said, her eyes shining. This was why she loved the story so much, Rhona thought. Nuala had the true heart of a woman of the Isles, who would never be her husband's inferior. If she chose to marry at all.

"All girls must have husbands, Mother says. To protect them," Sive said. Then her lip wobbled and her eyes filled with tears. "Mother!"

All three girls took up the wail, for they would never forget. Tonight the loss was fresh in their minds, and no story could soften that loss.

As Rhona's much longer arms wrapped around her sisters, she thought again of the Three Little Pigs. Three sisters, like the girls in her arms. Which made her the nurse with the stick, in accordance with Aunt Blanid's dying wish.

Rhona swore she would wield a mighty stick indeed, should any wolf seek to hurt her family. A blazing brand to set his fur on fire.

Three

The moment Grieve saw her, he knew he was in love.

Bedelia, Lord Calum's only daughter, a dark-haired girl ripe with curves in the all the right places. She blushed rosily as she offered a curtsey to Grieve and his older brother, Mahon.

Lord Lewis, their father, talked of marriage alliances and taking the girl on a tour of the island. Both brothers had heartily agreed to take Bedelia on the tour, and so it was settled.

Yet they had scarcely set out before a rider came galloping up to speak to Mahon on an urgent matter that simply would not wait. With a curse and an apology to Bedelia, Mahon turned his horse around and headed to where he was needed most. One day, he would succeed Lord Lewis as the lord of Myroy Isle, and he shouldered many of his father's duties in the meantime.

But that left Bedelia to Grieve, who thanked fate profusely, as he proceeded to show the girl the beauties of the northernmost of the Southern Isles. None of the views he presented to her compared to his own view, though — of the rosy cheeked maiden smiling at all she surveyed.

She spoke of her brothers, and how different life was at Langroy Isle, far to the south, so close to Alba you could see it across the water on a clear day. If Grieve sometimes lost track of her words, he blamed the lovely lilt of her voice, that turned his mind into a blissful fog of possibilities.

If he could persuade this girl to fall in love with him as readily as he'd fallen for her, the marriage alliance Father had spoken of would be more than just talk.

And he would have all those lovely curves in his bed…

Grieve daydreamed until dusk, when they returned home again, for the welcome feast Father had promised Bedelia.

She had the place of honour at Father's side, displacing Mahon, who sat between Bedelia and Grieve.

Grieve comforted himself with the thought that the next day, he would have her all to himself again, as they toured the western shores of Myroy, for Mahon would surely be called away for more important things again, leaving Bedelia and Grieve alone for love to blossom.

Father must have planned it this way, Grieve was certain of it.

Mahon was at least five years her senior,

while Grieve was only a few months younger than Bedelia. Young for marriage, but not too young.

And Bedelia liked him, while she scarcely said a word to Mahon. Why, she could not even look at him for more than a moment. Whereas she'd shared plenty of smiles with Grieve while they rode together.

Yes, Grieve thought as he looked at her. Bedelia was his happily ever after, and nothing fate could do would change that.

Four

"Girls, I'd like you to meet my new wife and your new stepmother, Doireann. She has sworn to be a good mother to you girls, after your own was so cruelly taken from us." Father pushed the diminutive dark-haired woman forward. "Say hello."

Nuala, Sive and Maeve chorused their greetings, but Rhona merely nodded. She and her father had discussed the woman before he'd agreed to marry her. Doireann was a widow from Scitis Isle, whose husband had died defending their holding from Alban raiders. A fitting stepmother for her sisters, Father had said and Rhona had agreed, but Rhona had not realised she would be so young. Why, Doireann was only a few years older than Rhona herself.

Perhaps Father hoped to sire a son on the girl. As though she would want another child to care for while she was still busy with Nuala, Maeve and Sive. Sive was scarcely out of swaddling clothes, or so it seemed to Rhona.

"Perhaps you can all go berry picking in the woods tomorrow," Father suggested.

"They aren't ripe enough yet. In a week, would be better," Rhona said.

Father nodded sagely. "In a week, then. Doireann will be settled then, won't you?"

Doireann nodded obediently.

Overwhelmed by so much at once, Rhona guessed. She would be the same, if she married a lord who already had children.

Hope blossomed. Perhaps that was what

Father had in mind. Giving the girls a stepmother, so that he might free Rhona herself for marriage. Not that she'd met a man she wanted yet, and Father would not press her into a marriage she did not want. No matter who her mother had been, Rhona was still a woman of the Southern Isles, a woman who chose her own fate and who she might marry.

Doireann was given chambers adjacent to the one Sive and Maeve shared. Not Blanid's room beside Father. She raised no complaint, and meekly did as she was bid. In fact, she said little or nothing, hardly daring to raise her eyes from the floor.

Maybe she was in mourning as much as Father was.

Rhona left her stepmother to her own devices and returned to her embroidery. She hated sewing with a passion, but someone had to teach Maeve, and Nuala would not. Nuala had claimed the dairy as her domain, for churning butter and cheesemaking were her favourite chores. Blanid had approved, and Rhona saw no need to interfere. She liked fresh butter and cheese as much as the next girl, though perhaps not as much as Sive liked drinking fresh cream. A habit Rhona had not yet managed to cure her of, though her stepmother might have more success.

"You may go," Doireann said grandly to Ciara and Siobhan.

The two maids looked at each other, then Rhona.

"Return to your duties at the house, but leave the pony and the baskets," Doireann continued, growing impatient.

Berry picking was something the whole household did, from the lowest servant to the highest lady, or it had been for as long as

Rhona could remember. They all ate their fill while filling their baskets, for berries were a summer treat that didn't last for long.

Remembering her father's admonition to make her stepmother feel welcome, Rhona forced a reassuring smile for the two girls. "I'll leave some for you to pick on the morrow, I promise. We shall manage. The girls are much bigger now, so they can carry a basket each." It would have to be a very small basket for Sive, or a very empty one, Rhona thought as she watched Maeve take Sive's hand to show her which berries to pick.

Nuala headed off on her own, swinging a large basket by her side as she selected the best looking bush.

Ciara and Siobhan mumbled something and headed home. Only then did Doireann take up a basket of her own. Ignoring the others, she proceeded to strip a bush on the far side of the clearing.

Rhona sighed and followed suit, only to find Doireann deliberately moving away from her, deeper into the forest, leaving her bushes half-picked. A quick glance told Rhona that her sisters were doing fine without her, so she followed Doireann. Deeper and deeper, until they were surrounded by trees and there wasn't a berry bush in sight.

"The berries are all back there," Rhona said, pointing.

Doireann waved away her words. "Let the children pick berries. I must find the holy spring. I know it's here. They say it was blessed by Saint Columba himself, and sprang up at his touch, and one cup will make any woman fertile, no matter how barren she may be. I heard Lady Catriona of Isla drank the miraculous waters of it on her wedding night, and that was the reason she gave birth to triplets."

Rhona shook her head. "I've never heard of such a spring. And Saint Columba didn't like women, so it does not seem likely he would work that sort of miracle. Especially not here. He feared the witch women of Nimbanmore."

Doireann scoffed, "There are no witches left in the world, least of all here. The faithful wiped such wicked creatures out centuries ago!"

Rhona wondered what the woman would say if she told her stepmother that magic was alive and well, coursing through her blood in readiness for when it was wanted, but she held her tongue. Blanid had told her to hide it, and hide it she would. No one must ever know.

"But the miraculous spring is real. It must be. I shall find it, and drink from it, so that I might bear Lord Ronin a son!" Doireann ducked between two trees, then trotted down a slope.

Rhona glanced back at her sisters. They were already out of sight. If she followed her stepmother, the girls would not know where they had gone. "Doireann, wait. The girls…"

"Go back to the children! I will find this spring on my own. It's not like you need it. You have no husband yet! Wait for me in the clearing. I shall not be long," Doireann called back before she disappeared from sight.

Rhona was torn. If something happened to her stepmother, her father would never forgive her. But if anything happened to her sisters…alone in the woods…Rhona would not forgive herself, and nor would Blanid. Wishing she didn't have to, Rhona said, "Very well. We shall wait."

Her dread-filled heart weighed more than her empty berry basket as Rhona returned to her sisters.

"Where is she?" Nuala asked, popping berries into her already stained mouth.

"Doireann has gone for a walk in the woods by herself. She wants us to wait here for her," Rhona said.

"More berries for us!" Sive cheered. Her hands and face were so covered in berry juice, she looked like she'd slaughtered a pig. Or a piglet, perhaps.

Rhona managed a smile for her sisters. "Let's see who can pick the most before she comes back."

Six

Twilight came, with no sign of Doireann. Rhona had spread a blanket upon the ground, and Sive lay on it, snoring softly. Maeve looked like she wanted to join her, and even Rhona longed for her bed. Nuala was determined to pick berries until the last of the light was gone, but that time was fast approaching.

Finally, Nuala plopped herself down beside Sive. "I wish I'd brought a cloak. I'm cold," she announced.

"I'd prefer a fire," Maeve said. "Much warmer."

Rhona could not magic a cloak into being, but she could build a fire. The warm day meant there was some tinder and a few sticks, but not much. A fallen tree held plenty of timber to burn in its broken branches, but Rhona had not thought to bring anything with which to light the fire.

Nevertheless, she piled up a collection of fuel, then crouched over it so she hid it from her sisters' sight. Only then did she dare bite her lip and unleash the most powerful part of her magic.

The log blazed to life, as though Rhona had added it to a roaring fireplace and not a cold nest of sticks.

Maeve clapped her hands. "Thank you, Rhona!" She stretched out her fingers to the blaze.

Darkness descended, leaving the four of them alone in the woods. Luckily the biggest beasts on Rum Isle were its cows — they would not have wolves to worry about, or bears. "We should probably huddle up together with the blanket by the fire to keep warm, while we wait for Doireann to return," she said. "I'm sure she'll see the light of it, if she is lost, and come back soon." This last was a lie, but her sisters did not need to know this. It was just another burden she would carry alone.

On the morrow, they would return home, and tell Father his wife was missing. He would send men out to search, and they would find her. Rum Isle was too small to hide her for long.

Rhona set several logs beside the campfire, so that she might add fuel through the night if she needed to, before joining her sisters in their blanket bower.

Nuala's eyes drooped, and she soon added her snores to Sive's. Maeve was still awake, though, and her watchful eyes regarded Rhona.

"Is she coming back?" Maeve whispered.

Rhona wet her lips. She didn't want to lie, but... "I hope so. Father would be heartbroken to lose another wife so soon after Mother's death."

An owl screeched in the distance, and Maeve squeaked like she'd been the owl's prey. "What is THAT?"

"Just an owl. You are too big for it to carry, so it is nothing to worry about. It is catching mice."

Maeve shuffled closer to Rhona. "There are mice in the woods?" Her eyes were wide with terror.

Rhona smiled in the dark. She would never understand her sister's fear of the small creatures. "Not while the owls are out hunting. They are running to hide – probably in our barn."

"Good. Then the cat will get them. She has six kittens, you know." Maeve snuggled closer to Rhona. "Mother said you will protect us. It's true, isn't it? You will keep us safe?"

"As long as I draw breath, I will let nothing and no one hurt you, or any of my sisters," Rhona promised her, and every word rang with truth.

Using any means necessary, Rhona added in her head, as she threw another log on the fire. Even magical ones. No one hurt her family.

Seven

"The pony's gone!" Maeve cried.

Rhona winced at the rude awakening, wishing she could sleep a little longer in some place more comfortable. But she had to put on a brave face for her sisters. "I'm sure he's just gone to find some breakfast," she soothed. But there was plenty of grass in the clearing – grass he'd eagerly devoured yesterday. "Or he was thirsty."

That made more sense. "We should go

down to the river for a wash and a drink, too, before we head home. Perhaps we shall find him there, and Doireann, too," Rhona continued, clambering to her feet.

The pony was indeed nowhere to be seen, along with the panniers of berries he'd been carrying. True to her word, Rhona had left some berries on the bushes, so there was enough for breakfast.

She helped Sive wash her breakfast berry juice from her face and hands, but when they still found no sign of the pony or Doireann, she had to admit defeat. "Fill your pockets with berries for on the way. Time to go home," Rhona said.

Eight

Rhona staggered up to the house, her arms aching from carrying Sive. What she wouldn't give to have the pony who'd carried Sive into the forest, but they'd seen no sign of the creature since last night. She tucked Sive into her bed, figuring the girl could wash when she woke in the morning. Maeve and Nuala had washed in the water butt outside, and were no doubt raiding the kitchen for dinner.

Rhona debated whether to join her sisters

and grab a bite to eat, or head straight to bed and break her fast in the morning. Her stomach had churned with worry too much to allow her to eat today, and even now she wasn't sure if she could keep any food down. Not without knowing if Doireann was all right. Her father would never forgive her for losing his wife.

Though the hour was late, she should probably wake him to tell him the ill news. She padded softly to her father's chamber, and raised her fist to knock.

A distressed cry came from Sive's chamber. "Mama?"

Rhona's heart broke anew, and she turned to go to her sister.

"Rhona?"

Her father stood in the open doorway, looking distinctly displeased.

"I must see to Sive," Rhona said.

Father seized her arm. "Let Doireann do it."

To Rhona's surprise and relief, her stepmother emerged from her father's chamber, squeezed past them, and headed for Sive's room.

"So she made it back?" Rhona choked out.

Her father's brows lowered further. "No thanks to you. What possessed you to take off like that, and with your sisters?"

Rhona was lost for words for a moment. Finally, she said, "I thought it would be safer…"

"Then you are a fool. A foolish child, who I thought was past such things. Really, Rhona? A miraculous spring blessed by Saint Columba himself? Where did you hear such nonsense?"

Rhona glanced at Sive's chamber, but Doireann had closed the door.

She did not want to make trouble for Doireann. "I do not remember, but I thought it strange that such a spring should exist so close to home, when I had not heard of it."

"Keeping your sisters out all night in search of this nonsense! What were you thinking?" Father demanded.

She hung her head. "I am sorry, Father. I

lost track of the time. We should have returned before dark, but Sive was tired, and – "

"Enough! You are too young to take care of your sisters, no matter how mature your mother thought you might be. They are Doireann's responsibility, not yours. She told me she tried to dissuade you from finding this imaginary spring, especially when your sisters insisted upon following you, but you refused to listen and left without another word. What if one of you had been hurt, hmm? Doireann arrived after dark last night, quite distraught that you had not returned, though you had promised to be but a moment. You were gone hours, leaving her alone in woods she did not know!"

Rhona struggled to make sense of her father's words. No, it was Doireann who had set off to find the spring, who had told HER to wait, not the other way around. And her sisters had never left the clearing, except to wash by the river, and that was hardly but a step away from where they'd camped in the clearing.

"But, Father, I – " she began, not sure how to continue.

"I do not want to hear excuses, for nothing will excuse such reckless behaviour. Do you think any man will want a wife who puts the children under her care in danger, just to satisfy her own curiosity? Go to bed. On the morrow, you will beg your stepmother's forgiveness, and you will submit to whatever punishment she gives you. She is the lady of this house, and whatever she asks you to do, you will obey. Is that understood?"

Rhona swallowed back her fury. "Yes, Father," she lied.

"Good. We will not speak of this again, and hopefully the matter will be forgotten before rumours can spread outside our household. If Lord Lewis were to hear…but he shall not. Both Doireann and I will watch your behaviour carefully from now on, Rhona. So soon after losing your mother…I will not lose you girls as well!"

Seething, she made her way to her chamber and closed the door. She had not been sent to bed without dinner since before Nuala was born, and certainly never before when she had nothing wrong!

How had her father gotten the idea that she had gone searching for the stupid saint's spring? Rhona had not heard a whisper of the place until Doireann mentioned it.

Realisation dawned. Of course, Doireann had reached home before her. Perhaps Doireann had expected them to have arrived already, and she'd been shocked to find the girls missing. Had she spun a story for her father, painting herself in a good light and placing the blame on Rhona?

Maeve might have made up such a story, but Rhona would never. Father had called Rhona childish, when it was his wife he should have been looking at. Why, the woman was not much older than Rhona, and if her father asked for the marriage to be annulled...perhaps the widow had nothing left, after the Alban raiders had taken everything from her.

Rhona's fury eased the tiniest bit. If she was faced with such a future, perhaps Rhona might lie. Perhaps. But that did not excuse Doireann. On the morrow, Rhona would not apologise to her stepmother. Instead, she would make sure the woman understood she knew what her stepmother was doing, and while she would forgive her the once, if Doireann ever blamed Rhona for her own faults again, Rhona would not be so lenient.

With that firm resolution uppermost in her mind, Rhona prepared for bed. It wasn't until she was tucked up in her blankets that her belly reminded her that she'd barely eaten all day. She rolled over onto her side, hoping to silence the grumbling sounds. She could eat her fill on the morrow, and every day thereafter. Rum Isle might not be the wealthiest of the isles, but they would never run short of food. Not while her father ruled the island.

Nine

After a week spent cleaning every inch of Blanid's former chamber twice, as Rhona's first effort hadn't met with her stepmother's approval, Rhona was ready to stuff the scrubbing brush down Doireann's throat and drown her with the bucket of dirty water.

One good thing had come of all this cleaning. Rhona had moved all of Blanid's things into her own chamber, though the haphazard jumble of chests made it difficult to reach her bed at the end of each exhausting day. Rhona promised herself she would go through everything and keep it safe for her sisters, but for now, she had to drag the mattress back to the bed from where she'd left it airing by the window.

Her arms ached as she made up the bed again, but Rhona had to admit a certain satisfaction at a job well done. The room was no longer Blanid's – if her spirit had lingered, it would not stay here. Even Blanid's favourite candlestick now sat on the table beside Rhona's bed – Doireann would not have it. But she would surely want some light, so Rhona headed down to the kitchen to see if a spare one could be found that was suitable for the new lady of the house.

It took some rummaging until she found a brass one so tarnished she barely recognised it for what it was, but when she carried it to the kitchen table, the cook exclaimed, "Why, I have not seen that since your grandmother died! 'Twas her favourite. Well I remember her coming down here when young Ronin could not sleep. She would sit the candle on that very table, cradle the boy in her arms, and sing him to sleep in that very chair. More often than not, I'd find her still there in the morning, fast asleep, when I came to light the morning fires. I was in my first year of service then."

Rhona blinked, trying to imagine Belen as a young maid, perhaps the same age as Nuala, and not the woman she'd known all her life. "I was looking for something suitable for Doireann." The old candleholder would not do for her stepmother, Rhona knew. Doireann would want the best, shiniest one in the house.

"And it will be, once it's had a polish," Belen said. "I'll get one of the girls to do it. Ciara!"

Ciara looked up from peeling the carrots. "Yes?"

"Polish that, will you? It's for her ladyship upstairs." Belen rolled her eyes heavenward.

Ciara didn't make the mistake of thinking that meant Rhona. "At least I can spit on that."

Rhona laughed. "I should probably clean

that, too. She said I was to prepare the room myself, with no help from anyone else."

"You've done the work of two maids this week, and given both Ciara and Siobhan quite the holiday. 'Tis only fitting that she do this for you now, as is proper. The lady of the house should not rub her hands raw polishing some old brass." Belen gestured toward the chair where she'd said her father had fallen asleep in his mother's arms. "Rest a little, Lady Rhona."

Rhona smiled at the title. "I am no lady. Just my father's daughter on a good day, or a drudge on a bad one, like today."

"Not to us. Not to any of us. That slip of a girl might have married your father, but she is not Lady Blanid, or your lovely self. Lady Blanid ran this house, and indeed the whole isle, as smooth as the sea on a summer's day. She never came into the kitchen without a kind word for what was cooking, and a helping hand where it was needed. She never needed no titles to command respect. She was a lady, and so are you. That Doireann…she's as common as muck, and meddlesome besides. Why, she finds fault with every dish that comes out of this kitchen, though 'tis exactly what she ordered. She asks for less salt, so I spare the salt, and she complains 'tis too bland. I add more, and she complains 'tis inedible and sends the whole mess back to the kitchen. Well, let me tell you, that stew most certainly was not inedible. I had two helpings myself!" Belen grinned.

Resting while everyone else worked was not in Rhona's nature, so she picked up Ciara's knife and set to work on the carrots.

"You should hear her hold forth about the only way to chop carrots!" Belen continued.

Rhona faltered. "What way is that?"

"Never mind. I'm sure whatever you do will be good enough for everyone else, and more than good enough for her."

Rhona resumed peeling. Working with a knife was calming, much like preparing herbs in the stillroom, for the repetitive task allowed her mind to wander. But never far. Her thoughts turned to Blanid, or Brigid, or Doireann, and none of them were comforting right now.

Rhona said, "Belen, would you tell me a story, please? One of the folktales where the wicked are properly punished, and the ending is happy."

Belen tapped the spoon on the side of the stewpot. "My lady wishes for a tale? Lady Blanid was one for tales. We could swap them for hours – she knew more than me, for her family collected tales along with the plants they grew. Let me see…she used to tell this chilling tale of a brother and sister, lost in the woods.

"Once upon a time, there was a poor woodcutter and his wife who had two children, a boy and a girl, but they did not have the wherewithal to feed them. So one day, the father took the children into the woods with all the food they had, and left them there, hoping someone might take pity on the mites…"

Parents too poor to feed their children. That was something Rhona would never allow to happen on Rum Isle, she reflected, as she listened to the tale. Poor Hansel and Gretel would not have needed to take shelter with a wicked witch here.

By the time Belen's tale ended, the carrots were cut and Ciara stood beside Rhona, with her mouth open and the polished candlestick in her hand.

"Her ladyship will want the best beeswax candle for that. No tallow for her," Belen said, fitting a candle into the stick before handing it to Rhona. "When you're finished taking that up to her room, come back. I have a treat for you, and your sisters, if you choose to share it. One of the beekeepers brought some honey today, and he was so thankful for the poultice you made for his knee — which is quite healed, by the way — he brought you some honeycomb."

Now it was Rhona's turn to grin. "I will fly up those stairs, and back. You'll see!"

Up she went, but she slowed her steps as she heard voices. Specifically, her father's and

Doireann's.

"I said no!" Her father sounded weary.

"But I need you in my bed, for 'tis not a proper marriage if it not consummated. You do want me, don't you, Ronin?" Doireann wheedled.

"I need you to take care of my daughters. My poor motherless girls."

"I could give you sons, if you but lie with me. Much better than girls."

"Watch your words, woman. I love my daughters, and if it were not for them, I would have left you to the charity of Scitis Isle. They need a mother, a woman to take care of them. Rhona is too young, no matter what she may think. Besides, she will one day leave us to have her own children, and then what? Nay, take care of the children you have, woman, and leave me alone!" Father threw the door of Doireann's chamber open and stormed out.

Rhona ducked into the shadows, where no one would see her.

"But anything could happen to them. Like

my family, taken from me in a single raid, and you will go from four girls to none. If you had more children, at least some would survive..." Doireann continued, reaching for Father. "Lie with me, Ronin. I promise I will bring you pleasure, and perhaps one day a son..."

"Lie with yourself!" He shook her off and shut the door to his chamber. Shutting her out.

Rhona felt a perverse pleasure at seeing her stepmother humiliated so, but if Doireann knew she had overheard...

"Anything could happen to them, Ronin. And when it does, then you will come to me. I swear it." Doireann's eyes glittered.

Rhona shivered, hugging the shadows even more fervently. If Doireann meant her and her sisters ill, then she would protect them any way she could. Doireann would not harm them. This Rhona swore, hoping the fire in her soul would hold her oath stronger than her stepmother's. For only one of them could win, and Rhona could not lose her sisters. Not now, not ever. And as for marriage? There was no way she'd leave her sisters at the mercy of her stepmother for some man.

Ten

Lord Lewis rose and the hall fell silent. "It is with great pleasure that I announce the betrothal of Lord Calum's daughter, the Lady Bedelia, to my son, Mahon."

What? Grieve tried to shout the word, but somehow before it left his throat his voice died.

Bedelia was to marry his brother? How?

The hall erupted in cheers and calls for more ale, so that they might drink to the health of the happy couple. Grieve drained his own wine cup, but his voice wasn't at the bottom of the cup, either.

He forced a smile as the toasts went on and on, until he finally found a chance to escape from the hell that the hall had become.

The moment he reached the yard outside, Grieve leaned against the wall, ready to throw up every bite he'd eaten. She was marrying Mahon? Why?

"Grieve!"

He thought he'd imagined her voice calling his name, but when he raised his head, there she was, haloed in the golden light spilling out of the hall. No, not a halo – hellfire, for that's what she was to him. Terrible temptation that would damn him forever.

He turned away.

"Why are you not happy for us? As my only friend here, I thought you would be the first to congratulate us, and wish us well."

Grieve moistened his lips. He prayed his voice had returned. "I thought we were friends, and maybe even more. But I was mistaken. We spent every day together, talking, laughing, as I showed you Myroy Isle, while my brother was too busy to spare even a moment for you. Yet you choose him, the brother you barely know, over me."

She drew herself up, dark eyes flashing. "I know he is the man I love, and the man I shall marry."

Grieve couldn't believe what he was hearing. "How can you love him? You've barely spent more than a moment in his company. It is those fairy stories you told me about – you have read too many of those, where a pair meet and fall in love in less than a moment. Such stories are not real!"

"I knew it the moment he kissed me," Bedelia insisted. "There was magic in his kiss. I felt it from my lips right down to the tips of my toes."

"You haven't been alone long enough with him for a kiss!" Grieve protested. "You've been with me every day! If I'd been forward enough…forgotten common courtesy…and stolen a kiss, would you have chosen me instead?"

He'd considered it, many times, but he'd always stopped himself. Now he regretted it more than ever.

"On my first night here, he asked if he might kiss me good night, to apologise for being absent from my side all day. His lips touched mine and…my heart was his." She stamped her foot. "He stole nothing I did not freely give. Not that first kiss, or anything after." A rosy blush coloured her cheeks.

Realisation dawned. Last night, Grieve thought he'd heard a woman's voice in Mahon's chambers. A maid or one of the girls from the village, he'd thought, and dismissed it. But it had been no maid. His brother had bedded the wanton Bedelia.

Grieve wasn't sure what came over him. Anger and bitterness and longing all collided and he couldn't think any more. He seized Bedelia's shoulders and pressed his lips to hers, desperate to show her how much he loved her.

She shoved him away, swiping a hand across her mouth.

"Your brother has more honour than you'll ever know," she snapped.

"Honour? What honour is there in taking you to his bed before you are married, treating you like a whore?"

Her hand landed on his cheek, a sharp sting from such a small hand. "I came to his chamber, to give him my answer to his proposal. I asked him to prove that he would be a good husband to me. This is still the Southern Isles, not Alba. A woman is free to choose, and I have. I chose well." She spat at his feet and stormed off.

"Bedelia, wait – "

Bedelia strode past a man whose face was in shadow. A man Grieve could not afford to ignore.

"Good night, Father," he said as he attempted to follow her.

Father caught his arm. "No, leave the girl.

She will be your brother's wife soon enough, and you'll only make trouble for them. It seems you leave me no choice but to take you to the Council meeting with me, for I cannot leave you here."

Grieve hung his head. "She played me for a fool, Father."

The grip on Grieve's arm tightened. "No, you made a fool of yourself, son. Better men than you have made fools of themselves over women, and I'm sure you will not be the last. Better to learn wisdom, and not follow those who do not want you. Perhaps one day, a woman will invite you to her bed as readily as Bedelia did your brother. But until that day comes, stay away from your brother and his wife. Or I've no doubt she'll bruise your other cheek to match the one you'll have in the morning." Father laughed. "Pack your things. We leave on the morrow. Better to be early to this meeting, for I fear the Albans are preparing for war, and we must be ready when they come."

"I'll take war over women any day," Grieve muttered. Maybe he wouldn't need to marry at all. Not with Mahon and Bedelia rutting like rabbits. Why, they'd have a litter of heirs in no time.

Father only laughed. "Spoken like a man who knows little of either. But that will change."

Eleven

Father frowned over the message a breathless courier had just delivered. He'd run all the way from the harbour. "I must leave now – the Council meeting has been called early. The Alban king is looking at the Southern Isles again, and the raids are getting more and more brazen. Lord Angus and Lord Lewis believe it means war, which we must plan for." He seized Rhona's shoulders. "If you see boats coming, take Doireann and your sisters and hide. The caves will be well stocked, so you may hide there until my return."

Doireann hurried up. "What is this? What are you hiding?" She addressed Rhona, not Father, but it was Father who answered.

"Doireann, I must go to a Council meeting. If Alban raiders come as Lord Lewis says they will, you all must hide. Rhona knows the way." Father turned to go.

Doireann dug her claws into his arm. "You cannot leave me here with raiders on the way!" she screeched. "They will kill us all! I demand you take me to this hiding place at once!"

With difficulty, Father pried her off. "I do not have time. I must sail with the tide. Rhona will take you there, if it becomes necessary." He headed upstairs to pack.

Doireann followed him, her loud protests and pleadings audible to everyone in the household. Rhona pitied the woman, who had every right to fear a raid, for she had lost everything in one before. But Scitis was a barren rock, nothing like Rum Isle. Rum Isle protected its own.

Finally, Father departed, riding off at a gallop before Doireann got the idea in her head to go after him.

Doireann fumed for a moment, before she turned her fury on Rhona. "Take me to this safe place. Now!" She dug her fingers into Rhona's arm, much like she'd done with Father.

Rhona looked deep into the crazed woman's eyes, and saw something other than fear. Desperation, perhaps? She did not know. But she would not stand for being manhandled by this woman. Fury burned deep within her, and it was almost like Doireann felt it, for she released Rhona with a hiss of pain.

"If you insist, I will take you to Sanctuary in the morning. It is a day's journey, for we can only ride so far, before we must proceed on foot. But we will never find it in the dark." Rhona turned and headed back to the stillroom.

To her relief, Doireann did not follow.

Twelve

Grieve stayed on the shore of Loch Findlugan among the other lords' sons and retainers. Servants busied themselves with preparing tents and food for their lords, but like the other sons, Grieve had little to do.

Not for the first time, he wondered why his father had bothered to bring him to the meeting, if there was nothing for him to do. Only the lords of the isles were allowed on Council Island.

Father should have left him at home. Bedelia had been sent back to her father's house to prepare dresses and such things for her wedding to Mahon, so it wasn't like Grieve would have been in the way at home. Maybe Grieve shouldn't have mentioned his desire to challenge Mahon for Bedelia. But what else did a man do when his brother had stolen the affections of the woman he loved?

The familiar thwack of metal finding its mark roused Grieve from his dark thoughts. He'd always enjoyed archery – so much so that his father had allowed him to train some of the other local men to hit a target. If the Albans invaded, it would be by sea, and every arrow that found its mark before the Albans reached shore meant one less man to fight.

Laughter greeted Grieve as he joined the men assembled in front of the target. He soon saw why.

"Has a witch cast a spell on the target so that no one can hit it?" he asked.

More laughter. Someone handed the bow to

Grieve. "Let's see if you can do better."

They backed up, allowing him space to line up his shot. An unfamiliar bow, when he'd been too busy riding with Bedelia or sailing to practice…Grieve would be lucky to hit the target at all. Yet he refused to back down from the challenge. Notch, draw, breathe…release.

His arrow thwacked into the target, slightly left of the centre.

A smattering of applause broke out.

"Who's next?" Grieve asked, holding out the bow.

Someone snatched it from his hand, muttering that they could do better.

The man beside Grieve stuck out his hand. "I'm Damhan. Lord Roe's son."

Grieve shook his hand. "Grieve. I'm Lord Lewis's."

"Are you the one Bedelia's going to marry? She's fallen hard for you. Singing and hugging herself and talking of nothing but going home to Myroy," another man said, eyeing Grieve with interest. "I'm Dermot. Lord Calum's my father."

Grieve hung his head. "No, she's to marry my older brother."

Dermot grinned. "Lucky escape for you, then. She's Father's little princess, leading him around like he had a ring through his nose. She'll do the same for your poor brother, I've no doubt. You're better off finding a girl more biddable, or one who has no brothers, and a claim to an island that'll come to you when you marry. They say one of Lord Angus's three daughters will inherit Isla."

"You mean the Three Little Pigs?" Grieve blurted out. Everyone had heard the tales of the girls, who must be homely as hell to have kept such a terrible name.

Damhan waved his hand, as if dispelling an unwelcome odour. "Ah, they only got called that for the day they played in the mud. Comely girls, all three of them, with their mother's red hair. Though with a dowry like Isla, none of them need to be more than tolerable. I'd court any of them, if they looked my way."

"My father says Isla had best be held by a Viken after Angus, and he's keeping the oldest girl for an alliance with the Viken king."

The bow had come back to Grieve, and he took his turn. His second shot was better than the first — and much better than any of the others.

"She's still a woman of the Southern Isles, or she will be, if she's too young to be a woman yet. No Viken will have Lord Angus' daughter against her will while a single Islander draws breath. If she falls in love with an Islander, she'll marry where she pleases. Much like her mother did, to my father's endless sorrow," Dermot said, drawing back the bow. His shot landed in the dirt three feet in front of the target.

"Try again," Grieve urged him. "Only this time, aim a yard higher. The arrow will naturally fall to earth, so you need to let it soar more first."

Dermot nodded, and did as Grieve

suggested. A moment later, his arrow thwacked solidly into the centre circle of the target.

More applause and a couple of cheers.

"Who's next?" Dermot asked, lifting the bow up in invitation.

"Me," said a boy. "But only if Grieve here can offer me some coaching. So that next time I shoot an Alban, I hit him right between the eyes instead of between the legs."

Laughter erupted, and cries of, "There's nothing to hit between an Alban's legs, anyway!"

Grieve grinned. Maybe Father had been right to bring him along after all.

Thirteen

Rhona did not sleep well, so she slipped into the stillroom for some willow bark to ease her headache on her way to breakfast. Dealing with Doireann and a headache was more than any saint could be expected to endure, and Rhona was certainly no saint.

Yet as she entered, she had the distinct feeling that something was wrong. The drawers were not all closed properly, and she made a particular point of shutting her jars away from all light so that the herbs might keep for longer. The books were out of order, too — Blanid's carefully drawn herbals, listing every plant she'd ever heard of, and quite a few that Rhona knew would never grow on Rum Isle. Rhona knew them by heart, of course, but occasionally she still checked some of the more exotic ones before administering them to anyone. She didn't know how her grandparents had procured some of the plants they possessed, but they'd made sure Blanid's stillroom held everything their own garden could supply.

"Lady Rhona, her ladyship demands to know when you are ready," Ciara said.

After Belen took up the title, they'd all started doing it, and Rhona could not bring herself to tell them to stop. They didn't look at her differently, nor curtsey at her like she was some princess, but now they came to her as they must have once come to Blanid. The message was clear — the staff saw Rhona as the lady of the house, not Doireann. It earned her more of Doireann's dark looks, even as it lessened the weight of her father's disappointment, just a little, but not enough to make her feel safe in her own home again.

And now someone had been through her herbs – since she'd left the stillroom last night.

"Ciara, did you or any of the others come in here last night, or this morning? Perhaps to get some willow bark, or herbs for cooking?"

Ciara shook her head. "Not me, mistress. I wouldn't know one herb from the other."

"But the herbs are all in my books, and I was still abed. You or one of the others might have opened one of the herbals to read…" Rhona stopped when she realised Ciara has trying to smother a laugh. "What is it?"

"You forget, Lady Rhona, that the only ladies who can read in the house are you and your sisters. Unless it was a matter of life or death, we would all let you sleep, and ask you for what was needed when you woke."

Of course. No wonder the girl laughed. Her sisters would wake her if they wanted something, knowing they would have it faster from her than from a lot of tiresome reading. "What of Doireann?" Rhona asked urgently.

Ciara shrugged. "I do not know. But surely she would summon you if she wanted something…"

Unless Doireann wanted something she did not want Rhona to know about. Medicines could be poisons if used in the wrong dosage, as Rhona knew well.

"Have my sisters come down for breakfast?" Rhona asked.

"Yes. Her ladyship insisted. Then she asked for some small cups so that they could all drink a special cordial…"

Rhona swore. Whether by design or mistake, Doireann might have poisoned the girls already. "Tell her I'm coming." She rummaged through the bottles, but she couldn't be sure which one Doireann had taken. Unlike the cupboards, the bottles appeared untouched. Everything seemed to be there, unless Doireann had poured the contents of one into a bottle of her own. And Rhona wouldn't know which bottle to check — it wasn't like she kept track of how much was in each one. Blanid might have known, but she wasn't here now.

Rhona paused to grab a cloak before heading outside, where Doireann sat on the box seat of a cart. A cart full of chests and casks, which were occupied by her bleary-eyed sisters. Sleepy from being woken too early, or because they'd been drugged?

Please, don't let it be the second, Rhona prayed silently as she approached the cart. "It will take longer by cart," Rhona said.

"I am not leaving my things here to be stolen by raiders. Show me to the place where we will be safe!" Doireann insisted.

Reluctantly, Rhona climbed onto the cart beside her sisters and they set off down the road, or what passed for one on Rum Isle.

"Which way?" Doireann demanded every time they reached a fork where the cart tracks went more than one way.

Rhona would respond with right or left or to continue straight, until she felt as drowsy as her sisters in the summer heat. She'd brought a cloak, but perhaps she should have thought to bring a hat.

"I'm thirsty," Sive announced.

Before Rhona could stop her, Maeve uncorked a flask and held it to her sister's lips. Sive gulped the liquid down, her eyelids drooping, before she slid off her box and lay down on the bottom of the cart, sound asleep. Beside Nuala, Rhona realised in horror. Then Maeve picked up the flask and drained the contents. She toppled to the floor, too.

Rhona snatched the flask from Maeve's slack fingers. "What did you give them?" She inhaled deeply at the lip of the bottle, trying to discern the contents. Strong spirits burned the inside of her nostrils, softened by the scent of lavender. That couldn't be all she'd given them. Some poisons had no odour, but one could taste them...

"Just a draught to put them to sleep, so that

they will stay quiet. Now, tell me where Rum Isle hides its riches, and nothing worse will happen to them," Doireann said, her eyes flashing.

"Rum Isle's secrets are known only to its own. You may have married my father, but you will never be one of us," Rhona spat. She tipped up the flask and let a drop of the treacherous liquor fall onto her tongue. Spirit burn and lavender sweetness, without the one thing Rhona dreaded – the bitter gall of opium from the Holy Land. Perhaps Doireann had not found it yet. As it was, the liquor was a strong sleeping potion, no more, that would leave the user with a hangover and headache when they awoke, at worst. She let the flask slip from her fingers.

Just in time to see something dark blot out the sun before it collided with her head, and all the lights went out.

Fourteen

It seemed almost no time at all before the final feast was over and the Council dispersed to go home. Grieve rode with Dermot, Damhan and the boy whose name was Brian, while his father lagged behind, discussing serious matters with Lord Ronin. At least, they looked serious – Father could be discussing a chess match with the man, for all Grieve knew.

Ships lined up in the harbour, waiting for the tide to take them all home.

Grieve made to follow Father to their vessel, but Father shook his head. "You're to go with Lord Ronin. He needs an archery instructor for his men, as he has no sons of his own. Albans will strike at Rum Isle before they make it to Myroy, you may be sure, so it behoves the lords of the inner isles to keep up their defences to give the rest of us warning in the event they send more than a raiding party."

Lord Ronin inclined his head. "Your father tells me you have the makings of a good master-at-arms, young Grieve, and some skills with a bow."

Grieve lifted his chin proudly. "I have trained my father's men since I came to manhood, Lord Ronin, and I was easily the best archer among the boys on shore today. But with practice, they might be able to match my skill."

Father laughed. "He'll never be good at chess, like I told you. Too forthright for playing at politics. But I hope he will be just the man you need, Ronin." He gave the command for his crew to raise the sail and was soon out in the bay, out of earshot.

No word of farewell, or when Grieve might be allowed to come home. Maybe never.

Lord Ronin eyed Grieve. "We shall see. Come, boy. You're too old to be a proper page or fosterling, but still young enough that I can call you my squire. Master-at-arms and other such offices can wait until you've had time to prove yourself."

"Yes, my lord. And I will," Grieve swore.

Lord Ronin smiled. "Good man. Climb aboard." He gestured toward his boat.

For a moment, Grieve was lost. An unproven boy, a new squire, a good man…what was he really? He had no home, and no family around him any more.

Time to choose his own fate. Grieve strode aboard the ship bound for Rum Isle, vowing to show Lord Ronin, his father and any other man with eyes to see that he would prove he was every bit as good as his brother. Better, maybe. And Bedelia? She could be miserable with Mahon, for Grieve would not give the girl another thought.

Fifteen

The bright summer's day had given way to miserable weather, but the rain pattering on the ground was nothing to the drumming inside Rhona's head. Rhona groaned, sat up, then groaned again.

"Where are we?" Nuala asked.

Rhona blinked. Her sisters huddled together under a pine tree. Of course, they hadn't thought to drag her under shelter, too. Then again, if they'd drunk enough strong spirits to send them to sleep, they wouldn't feel much better than she did right now. In no shape to be dragging anyone's body.

"Not at home, where we should be," Rhona grumbled. She shuffled under the tree with her sisters. Only now did she realise fog had crept over the island, as it did on days like this. They could be spitting distance from home, and she would not be able to see it.

Rhona bit her lip, hoping to stir up a breeze to improve visibility.

"I'm cold!" Sive moaned, climbing into Nuala's lap.

Rhona let the breeze swirl away into the woods. Yes, the fog lifted just enough to show the tree trunks before it was all whiteness once more. They could not be far from the edge, if Doireann had dumped them from the cart. She would not have had the strength to drag Rhona far from the road, unless she'd had help.

But who on Rum Isle would help Doireann against Lord Ronin's children? No one Rhona knew. And as the mistress of Blanid's stillroom, she knew everyone on the island.

"We must wait for the fog to clear, and then we will find shelter from the rain. I'm sure there is a cottage or croft quite close, but we might miss it in the mist. Once we know where we are, we can go home," Rhona promised.

"Can you tell us a story to pass the time?" Maeve asked.

"The Three Little Pigs?"

Maeve shook her head. "Something else. Something new. We have heard that tale too many times."

And there would be no nurse come to save them today, Rhona knew. It would be up to her and her sisters to find their way home. She thought of the tale Belen had told her, the first night she'd called her Lady Rhona. That might do. "Have you heard the tale of Hansel and Gretel?"

The girls shook their heads.

Rhona drew in a deep breath. "Once upon a time…"

Sixteen

Grieve eyed the huddle of buildings on the clifftop as they approached Rum Island. "You'll need better fortifications than that," he observed. "Plus a barracks hall or two to accommodate your people if you are invaded. Father had me build a new hall at the beginning of this year, so we'd be able to house the women and children, not just the menfolk."

Lord Ronin laughed. "Rum Isle may be

closer to Alba, but we are not as numerous as the people of Myroy or Isla. I think you'll find we have shelter enough for all of us, but the fortifications are not a bad idea. When we get the island men assembled, we can discuss it then." He nodded at the house. "First, I must greet my family, for they'll have missed me."

Butterflies rioted in Grieve's belly. Lord Ronin had spoken affectionately of his wife and daughters, but meeting them was another thing entirely. What if they did not like him? He managed with strange men and boys just fine, but girls? Bedelia was the only one he'd shared a house with since his mother had died, and he didn't want to remember how badly that had gone.

"This is Doireann, my wife," Lord Ronin said, wrapping an arm around a woman who resembled Bedelia. Well, small and dark, at least — she was thinner, without the luscious curves that had attracted him to Bedelia. And Doireann did not smile.

"Where are the girls?" Lord Ronin asked

her.

Doireann's frown deepened. "I must speak to you about them. The oldest one, she turns the others against me. Not three days ago, they disappeared, and I could find no trace of them. I have not seen…"

"Father!" The same word cried by three different voices, as three girls raced along the path to embrace Lord Ronin.

The three girls looked like they'd been playing in the woods, judging by their muddied clothing and the twigs and leaves that clung to them.

Their mother looked like she was building up to give them a good scolding. One Grieve did not intend to witness.

"I'll go see about some timber to start those fortifications, shall I?" he said to no one in particular, and headed off in search of an axe.

Seventeen

They'd seen Father's ship arrive in the harbour, and hurried to get to the house before he did. Alas, they'd been too slow.

Doireann and Father stood outside the house, at a distance where no one could stand close enough to overhear them without being seen.

At least, no one who did not have magical means of hearing.

Rhona bit her lip, letting a little of her magic

out to create a breeze that brought back the sound of Father's conversation with Doireann. As she suspected, the woman was telling lies again.

"You girls run ahead. Father is home," she said to her sisters.

Nuala and Maeve seized Sive's hands and took off up the hill, shouting Father's name.

Rhona longed to run with them, but it was more important to make sure Candace arrived safely. The old woman had grown an alarming shade of pink as she huffed and puffed her way up the hill. Still, she waved away Rhona's offer of assistance.

"If I cannot walk up this hill under my own power, how will I ever run around after those three little fillies? Nay, if you are as spry when you are my age, girl, then you will thank the heavens yourself." Candace grinned and continued ambling, ever upward.

"You must not let them eat or drink anything she has touched. Nor let her touch them, either," Rhona said. "She tried to poison us once. There is no knowing what else that witch will try next."

"It's been a long time since there's been a witch at Rum Isle, or any of the Southern Isles," Candace said, shooting a sideways glance at Rhona. "Not since your aunt, Brigid, died. But she was a good witch, always willing to help. Perhaps this one is not as experienced, and gave the children the wrong dose or the wrong herb. She is young, you said, not much older than you."

Rhona tossed her head. "I would not make such a mistake. Mother taught me better than that." No, Aunt Blanid, she corrected in her head.

When they reached the house, Doireann had left, and Father stood alone.

"Widow Candace," Father greeted her, before offering Rhona a kiss. "It is a long walk from your cottage. What brings you here?"

"Doireann poisoned us, then left us in the woods," Rhona snapped. "I managed to get the girls to Candace's cottage, but Maeve took a chill, so we stayed a little until she recovered enough to walk home. Candace has agreed to come and help take care of the girls, as their nurse."

Father blinked. "I'm sure it is all a mistake. She's such a sweet girl, she would never…" He shook his head. "I apologise, Widow Candace, for the stories my daughter has been filling your head with. I shall send you home on horseback, with gifts from my cellar to repay you for your time."

"My cottage is cold now my daughters are all married. Seems I could be useful here, if your daughters are giving you trouble," Candace said.

Rhona opened her mouth to protest, but a hard look from Candace silenced her.

"Your new wife is just finding her feet, after all. I'm sure I shall be a great help to her. I am used to work, and the lady of Rum Isle has enough cares resting on her shoulders." Candace moved toward the house. "I shall start by seeing those girls wash up. They look a fright, after walking in the woods. You'll see. I'll take good care of them." This last earned Rhona another look from Candace before she vanished inside.

Whatever Candace believed, at least she would watch over her sisters. Rhona couldn't ask for much more than that.

"I must speak to Doireann," Father said. When Rhona stepped forward to follow him, he held up his hand. "Alone, Rhona. I will speak to you later."

Damn right, he would. And she'd have just as much to say. In the meantime, Candace would keep an eye on the girls, while Rhona changed out of her soiled gown. Something brighter and cleaner was needed, as befitted a dinner that would double as her father's welcome home after the Council meeting. Ugh, and a clean shift. One that didn't have leaves in it, or mudstains in places where no mud should be.

Rhona marched toward her chamber, intent on making herself presentable once more.

There was still some water in the jug, so she stripped off and washed. The fresh shift clung to her still-damp skin, letting off a faint whiff of lavender. The shift had not lain in the chest long, then – those in the bottom would smell much stronger.

She reached for the blue gown she'd worn at the last feast day, when Mother – Blanid – had presided over the feast with all the joy of a woman who'd had no idea it would be her last celebration. Blanid had clucked over the gown that day, telling Rhona she needed to wear more womanly things, for the hem of the gown that had been suitable for the girl Rhona had been was far too high for the woman she had now become.

The dress fell from Rhona's nerveless fingers back into the chest. She should give it to Nuala, but then what would Rhona wear? Blanid had promised to make her new gowns that fit her better, but she'd died before she could even cut the cloth, and Rhona was no seamstress.

The only womanly gowns Blanid had left had been her own. Gowns that would be wasted on Doireann, who had no right to wear them, either, Rhona fumed.

For the first time since Blanid had died, Rhona knelt beside the chests she'd moved from Blanid's chamber to her own. She opened the first, and breathed in the rose scent that Blanid had made wholly her own. Not least because her precious roses, which were carefully tended in the sheltered southern herb garden, had come with her to the island when she'd married Father. Other women had dowries of cloth and jewels, lands and houses, but Blanid and Brigid's parents had been renowned for their glorious garden, modelled on the one where Rhona's grandmother had grown up. So it was no surprise that Blanid had arrived with as many medicinal plants as her parents could provide.

Or had that been Brigid's doing?

Rhona would never know, now, for the two women who might have told her were now dead, silenced forever.

But with them both gone, she had a responsibility to remind her father who ruled here. And it wasn't Doireann, the conniving widow from Scitis.

Rhona dug through the dresses, looking for the sky-blue gown Blanid had worn which matched her own. Instead, she found one of yellow-gold silk, so soft to the touch she'd lifted it out of the chest before she knew what she was doing. It was lined with cream lambswool, as soft inside as out. Rhona had never seen Blanid wear this gown, yet when Rhona pressed her face to the fabric, she smelled an unfamiliar scent – sharp and fresh, tingling her nostrils as though it was something she should remember, but had forgotten. Citron, was that was this was called? No, the word was lemon. A kind of fruit that grew in warmer climes than here.

In her grandparents' garden, most likely.

Rhona slipped the gown over her head, letting the lambswool embrace her like it had been made for her. Only her waist was narrower, so she tightened the laces a little before tying them again. Blanid's bronze mirror stood in the corner, polished to a high sheen so that Rhona might see how well she looked. Or how well she might look, if she picked the bird's nest remnants out of her hair.

Swearing, Rhona unbound her hair and found a comb. It would take some time to get all the twigs and leaves out, but she would need to if she wanted to remind Father that she was a woman grown, and every bit as worthy as Doireann of being believed.

When she had finally freed her hair of snarls, tangles and twigs, she had to decide whether to pin it up, or leave it loose. Loose would attract more leaves the moment she ventured into the woods again, but that's how Blanid had worn hers at every feast day. A few pins, or a headband fashioned from a pair of narrow braids, were all that restrained the golden mane Blanid had proudly worn loose as she presided over the people of Rum Island.

The thwack of an axe hitting wood reached Rhona's ears. She peered out the window, wondering why anyone would be chopping wood so late in the day. They had cut turf enough to feed the house fires well into next month – no one should be cutting precious timber.

But there was no one at the chopping block, and besides, the sound was coming from down by the river. The only timber by the river was the willow trees, bred from the one that had been part of Blanid's dowry. The only source of willow bark on the island. If anyone was cutting into those trees, they'd have her to answer to. Especially if they wasted any of that precious bark.

Rhona slid a pair of boots onto her feet and marched out for confrontation.

Eighteen

"What in heaven's name are you doing?"

The voice was feminine, but authoritative. Accustomed to being obeyed. It could only belong to Lord Ronin's wife, Lady Doireann. Grieve let the axe hang by his side, no threat to the lady. "My lady, Lord Ronin wishes to build better fortifications to protect your house and all those who live there." He lifted the axe for another swing.

"Touch that tree again, and I promise you

shall regret it. Even more so when I refused to give you any willow bark for the pain."

Grieve whirled, shocked. Lady Doireann had looked so small and docile – not the sort of woman who would threaten him with pain for touching a tree, of all things. "M-my lady?" he stammered.

He glimpsed the tall figure coming toward him, before the sun chose its own moment to enter the fray. The rays blinded him, and appeared to set fire to her. One moment a woman, the next a golden pillar of flame, heading inexorably for him. The axe dropped from his nerveless fingers. Grieve wanted to run, but at the same time, he didn't dare take his eyes off the terrifying spectre before him.

"What is wrong with you, boy?" she demanded.

As if to make his mortification complete, the sun hid its face behind a cloud once more. The fiery goddess transformed into a woman. A woman who didn't look a bit like Lady Doireann. Wheat coloured curls hung to her waist. The breeze played with some of the outer tendrils, the movement reminiscent of tongues of fire. Add that to the butter-coloured dress she wore, and it was easy to see how his overactive imagination had turned a girl into a goddess, with just a bit of sunlight.

He laughed shakily. "For a moment, I thought you were on fire," he admitted. He traced the shape of her body in the air. "Sunlight in your hair and in your dress. It looked like you were wreathed in flames. I thought I was going to die, and that you were going to burn me to death, without the flames touching you at all."

She backed up a step, her eyes widening in horror. She almost tripped over the hem of her gown, which was a little long for her, he'd only just noticed. She cast her eyes down. "My mother told me many times not to play with fire."

Grieve managed a smile. "My mother told me the same thing," he said. "But I did not listen. I once burned down a whole hay shed.

My brother told me the cat had had a litter of kittens and that I could see them in the morning, but I was impatient, and took a candle in there at night..." Now it was Grieve's turn to bow his head. "I earned a sound thrashing from my father for that, and as a punishment he made me rebuild the hay shed. After that, I preferred to build with wood, not set fire to it."

Her eyes was still wide. "And what of the kittens?" Her voice trembled. She might look like a woman but she could not be much older than Grieve himself.

Now Grieve grinned. "They were never in the hay shed. The cat had her kittens in the barn, where the dairy cows slept." He held out a tentative hand for her to shake. "I am Grieve Lewisson, from Myroy Isle. I am to be Lord Ronin's squire."

She eyed his hand suspiciously for a moment, then took it in her own. "Rhona." Her eyes dared him to ask for more than just her name.

All Grieve's instincts screamed that this would be a trap, though what sort, he did not know. "It is a pleasure to meet you, Lady Rhona, guardian of this tree. I have heard tales of naiads, but this is my first time meeting one." He closed his mouth, giving her a challenge of his own.

Her narrowed eyes made him worry that he'd made a mistake. Perhaps he should have just complimented her on her name the way he had when he'd met Bedelia. Then again, look how well that had turned out.

Then Rhona gave a tiny smile. "I think you mean a dryad, not a naiad. Dryads live in trees. Naiads are river spirits. But both are myths. They don't exist. At least, not outside of stories. And we are both too old for such things."

Grieve recognise the regret in her tone, for he shared it. Life was much simpler as a child, believing all his mother's tales to be true. "Then why protect this tree so passionately?"

"Because it belonged to my mother," she

said. "She brought the trees, and many other medicinal plants, when she came to… When she came to live with my father."

"And your father is…?"

She gave him a look of deep disgust. "Not stupid enough to build a fortification out of willows, or anything that burns so easily. Here on Rum Isle, timber is too precious. We build with sod and stone, so our kittens are safe from boys who like to play with fire, and our people sleep safer in their beds, knowing that when Alban raiders come, and they will, they will not be burned alive, for it would take powerful magic indeed to burn down a sod house." A girl she might be, but the hard look at her eyes said she knew as much about war as Grieve himself, or perhaps more. For a moment, she looked like his own father, telling Mahon how to prepare for war. She seized his arm, her touch searing through the cloth as though the flames Grieve had seen earlier were not as imaginary as he thought. "Come. We shall both go to see my father together, and if his witch of a wife is behind this… I will make her rue the day she was born."

Grieve let the girl pulled him into Lord Ronin's house, all the while musing that if one of the two women he'd met today was a witch he would place his wager on Lady Rhona and not the mousey Doireann. But he kept this thought to himself, lest Rhona turn her fury on him again.

Nineteen

"Brigid," Father breathed, his eyes wide.

Rhona glanced down. Had this gown belonged to her mother – her birth mother, not Blanid? That would explain why she'd never seen Blanid wear it. She rubbed her fingers down the silk. She'd treasure it now she knew.

But now she had more important matters to attend to. "Father, why was this boy cutting down trees by the river?"

"Ah, you've met Grieve, your new foster brother," Father said. "He is Lord Lewis' son, and to be treated with every courtesy. As you are not needed here, will you show him around the island and introduce him to everyone? Lord Lewis sent him to help with our defences, so show him everything."

He meant Sanctuary, Rhona knew. Strange that he did not mention its name before Doireann. Did he not trust her either? Rhona could only hope. She moistened her lips. "Yes, Father." She headed upstairs to pack some things to take. A horseback tour of the island could be done in a day, but if she was to show this stranger Sanctuary…she wanted to take her time, to find out if he could be trusted. Unlike Doireann.

Three days, she decided, if they left this afternoon.

She would need riding clothes, not this beautiful gown. The only thing she had left from her mother. Not to mention another cloak, for hers was still covered in mud from when Doireann left her in the woods. Candace had offered to clean it, but Rhona had wanted to show it to her father as proof of his new wife's perfidy. But it could wait until she returned.

As long as Candace took care of the girls.

Rhona headed for her sisters' room, where she could hear giggling.

Candace sat with the three of them, reciting a rhyme that named each of Sive's toes before tickling the small girl.

"Did you tell Father what she did?" Nuala demanded.

Rhona hung her head. "I tried, but he still does not believe me. Mistress Candace, I swear to you that every word I spoke to you and my father is the truth. She has drugged my sisters once, and next time, she might give them more than a simple sleeping potion. She said as much to me before she knocked me out." She rubbed the lump on the back of her head, still tender after almost a week. Who would have thought Doireann could muster so much power in a single blow? "Please, whatever you do, do not let the girls eat or drink anything that Doireann has touched. I trust the staff, for they are all loyal to my father, but they still must obey her. They will tell you if she touches anything in the kitchen, though she hardly goes in there. But if she does – "

"Hush, girl. I will keep them safe. Your mother nursed my girls through a winter fever when I thought I would lose them. Lady Blanid should have sent word when she was taken ill. I would have been here directly to help." Candace smiled.

"But I must go away for a few days. Will you..."

Candace bowed her head. "I will care for the Lady Blanid's girls like they were my own. By the time you return, Lord Ronin will have accepted me into his household as a nurse again. You may not remember your wet nurse, but Lord Ronin remembers me well. I will make sure of it, if he tries to forget."

Did that mean Candace knew who Rhona's

real mother was? Rhona opened her mouth to ask.

"Where are you going?" Maeve demanded.

Her sisters could never know. "Father has a new squire, and he wishes me to show him the island. When we return, I will introduce him to you."

"Will he have new stories?" Sive asked, her eyes shining.

Always, it was stories. If only fairytales were true, and some handsome prince or knight in shining armour would come to save them from Doireann and this war with the Albans.

Rhona managed a smile. "I shall ask him while we ride, and let you know the answer when we return." She made a private wager with herself that the answer would be yes — Grieve had seemed to like telling stories. Perhaps he would have some even she had not heard yet, that he could tell to amuse her on their journey.

Smiling to herself, Rhona headed for her room.

Off came the beautiful golden gown, to be carefully placed in the chest with Blanid's things. She would need a thicker shift – wool instead of linen. She loosened the laces and let the shift slip to the floor.

A male voice swore.

Rhona whirled in panic, and met the eyes of a red-faced Grieve, who turned around as though his life depended on it.

"What are you doing in my chamber?" she demanded, clutching her shift to her chest.

"I'm not in your chamber, just on the threshold," he said. "Your father told me to follow you, so I did. I waited for you to speak to your sisters, before following you here. How was I to know you intended to undress?"

It sounded reasonable enough. It wasn't like he'd tried to hide.

But…

"Why didn't you say something when I took off my gown? Before I removed my shift?" Rhona demanded. She tugged the woollen shift over her head, so she wouldn't feel so exposed.

"Because I was mesmerised, my lady. It wasn't until I regained my senses that I realised what I should have done. I froze. I could not help myself. I've never seen…" He swallowed, seemingly unable to continue.

"A naked woman before?" she finished for him, feeling her fury build. Oh, if only she could use her magic to blast him out the window. She'd never felt so humiliated in her life.

He managed a watery smile. "Oh, no, I've seen one of those. A few, actually. Just…never one as beautiful as you. One glimpse and…I lost my mind, my lady. I could no longer think or speak. I could only stare." He ducked his head. "Please accept my forgiveness. I did not mean to offend you. I swear it will not happen again."

Beautiful. He'd called her beautiful. No one ever said that. Well, except her father, and he didn't count. Maybe she would forgive him. After all, she'd never seen a naked man before.

She'd probably stare, too.

Instead of the brown overdress she'd intended to wear, Rhona chose the rose-coloured one Blanid had once favoured for festival days, until Maeve was born and her waist thickened too much to tie the laces. Blanid's wine-coloured riding cloak went perfectly with it. Oh, but her hair...

Rhona pulled out the pins and set to work, braiding it in earnest. When she had her hair as firmly under control as the blush that had briefly coloured her cheeks, she turned and said, "Shall we go, Grieve Lewisson?"

Twenty

If he'd known she was about to undress, he would have turned his back on her. That would have been the honourable thing to do. But his breath had caught in his throat as the gown came off, and then her shift…

Yes, he'd seen naked women before. But none of them had such perfect breasts. And nipples as pink as…well, the dress she now wore to hide them. As if anything could hide the swell of her breasts now he'd seen them —

they were permanently burned into his brain. He would dream of them for the rest of his days, Grieve was certain of it.

Still he waited for her to slap him like Bedelia had, but she did not.

Then she stood before him, only a breath away, her eyes level with his. Gazing at him expectantly.

"What did you say?" he asked, feeling even more stupid.

She gave him a mischievous smile, as though she'd plucked the thought from his mind and it amused her. "I said, shall we go, Grieve Lewisson?"

He'd never heard his own name sound so…seductive. "Anything you wish, my lady," he managed to say.

"We will not return for a couple of nights, so bring whatever you'll need," she said, bundling a few things together. She tucked the bundle under her arm.

Grieve held out his hand. "Allow me to carry that for you." He might have forgotten his courtesies earlier, but that meant all the more reason to remember them now.

Rhona laughed. "You've seen quite enough of my underthings, Lewisson. You see to your own. I shall meet you in the kitchen."

Feeling his cheeks grow hot all over again — she'd been the one caught naked and unaware, so why was he so much more embarrassed? — he headed for the room he'd been told would be his. A comb, some spare clothes, his cloak…what else did he need? His mind refused to work properly. All he could see was her pale skin, curves he ached to touch…and those breasts!

He gritted his teeth and forced the image out of his head as he descended the stairs two at a time to where his nose told him the kitchen lay.

"I do not know what your father is thinking, Lady Rhona, truly I don't. First her ladyship and now young Lewisson…but you may rest assured that Candace and I will keep an eye on them for you. We are old friends, us two, though the friendship soured a little when she married. We both wanted young Paddy, you see, but he had eyes only for her..."

Grieve stepped inside the room, inhaling the scent of roasting meat and fresh baked bread. He wanted to eat it all.

"He looks like the younger one, not Lewis's heir at all," the woman continued. The cook, Grieve assumed. "Your father and Lewis can't be serious about this."

"Lord Angus himself was a younger son, and now he's Lord of Isla and High Lord of us all. Stranger things have happened in tales as well as in truth. Who can say what will come to pass?" Rhona said. She bit into a crust of bread.

"Who indeed?" Grieve said, reaching for the loaf.

The women's eyes widened – evidently they had not seen him enter.

He tore off a chunk and chewed with relish. No matter what this cook thought of him, at least she would feed him well. "This is the best bread I've tasted in weeks." He swallowed and continued, "I am my father's second surviving son. My brother Mahon will be lord after Father. He will also marry Lord Calum's daughter. Father has not told me about his plans for me, though he sent me here. What do you know that I do not?"

"He expects you to marry one of Father's daughters and succeed him as Lord of Rum Isle. As I'm the only one old enough, it seems Father has set his sights on giving me to you. Hence this farce about defence and a tour of the island."

Lady Rhona? His? Desire burned deep within him at the thought. If only. But the look in her eyes dispelled that idea as quickly as it had come. Lady Rhona would never accept him as a husband, especially not if her father pushed her to do so.

"Defence against Alban raiders is never a farce. They are a very real threat to us..." Grieve began.

"The boy's right about that. Lewis always

was a strategist, and his son must be the same. It can't hurt to have his help defending the place. I will give you as many provisions as the horses can carry, just in case." The cook pulled two loaves from the oven, wrapped them well, then handed them to a maid who carried them outside.

"Come, Lewisson. We may still manage a few miles before dark," Rhona said, leading the way outside.

Two horses stood in the yard, saddled and ready to go. The bread-bearing maid fastened the nearest one's saddlebags. "Safe journey, Lady Rhona," she said with a respectful bow of her head. She glanced at Grieve, but said nothing as she went past.

Bemused, Grieve stared after her. First the cook, now the maids. At home, all would have at least bobbed a curtsey to him, though they'd known him since childhood. Here, things were very different indeed, if the servants had little respect for their betters.

"Wipe that look off your face, Lewisson,"

Rhona advised him from her perch atop a horse. "Siobhan is betrothed to the first mate on Father's ship. She's not for you."

"No, but you are," he said without thinking. He swung up onto his horse, only to find himself face to face with the furious girl.

"I belong to no man. Not my father, not you, and definitely no one who even thinks a woman can be owned. No self-respecting Islander woman would allow such a thing. I choose to take you on a tour of Rum Isle because my knowledge of the island is second only to my father's, and you might be able to help us defend our home against all enemies."

Now it was Grieve's turn to bow his head. "I am your servant, as I am your father's squire, Lady Rhona. I am indebted to you for your kindness, I'm sure. All enemies of such a lovely lady are, of course, my enemies as well."

She almost smiled at that, but when he looked again, the smile was gone as though he'd imagined it. "Pretty words, Lewisson. You'll need more than words if it comes to war." She set off at a fast trot, and it took Grieve a moment before he could persuade his horse to follow, by which time she was several lengths ahead of him.

He feared she always would be, but that didn't stop him from striving to catch up. Lady Rhona was a woman he wanted to catch, but only if she allowed it.

Twenty-One

Rhona headed for the eastern watchtower, reasoning that it was the only suitable place to take him that was an easy ride before dark. Sanctuary could be reached just as easily, for they didn't have a cart, but she wasn't sure she was ready to show that to him yet. Better to take him on a full tour of the island and see what kind of man he truly was before revealing any secrets. Lord Lewis was no fool – if he'd sent his son to help Father, then Grieve could help. But if he was a strategist like his father...he might use Rum Isle as a pawn in a much larger game with higher stakes than Rhona could see. Rum Isle might not be important to Lord Lewis and his son, but it was everything to those who lived there.

"Are you planning on pitching me off a cliff, my lady?" Grieve asked after some time.

Rhona smiled. To someone who didn't know what to look for, the clifftop watchtowers looked like ordinary crags. "Maybe later. You have not yet vexed me enough for that. Perhaps on the third offence I will not be as forgiving."

She dismounted, and glanced over her shoulder to see what Grieve had made of her half-joking response.

"I shall endeavour not to cut down any trees, or look at you, without your permission. Is there anything else you'd care to warn me about, so I do not offend you again?" He lifted his hand. "Wait, I already know I must be kind to kittens."

"It is always wise to be kind to kittens," Rhona said. She headed for the standing stone that marked the entrance, then slipped into the rock crevice behind it. It was a tight squeeze, but grown men used this passage every day, so she knew she would fit. When she was through, she extended a hand. "Come, Lewisson, if you wish to see Rum Isle's first line of defence against invaders."

He grumbled as he squeezed through the gap, then stood beside her. "A cave." He did not sound impressed.

Rhona laughed. "Rum Isle is full of caves, some on the land, and some on the cliffs, and some you can only reach at high or low tide, for the ocean hides a veritable army of rocks to keep Rum Isle safe. The ancient peoples of the isles found this one, and improved upon it." She led him deeper into the shadows to the steps. Twisted and winding, worn by the tread of generations of boots, the steps led up into the tower, or at least that's what they called the top of the crag. The roof of the top cavern had caved in, leaving it open to the elements, but with a clear view all the way to Alba on a clear day. Today, like most days, it was hidden in mist, but she could still see for miles. As could tonight's watchman.

"Good evening, Lady Rhona," he said.

"Good evening indeed, Ximeno," she said. "This is Grieve Lewisson, my father's new squire from Myroy Isle. My father wants him to see all our defences. Where is Nuno?"

"He said he would go get our dinner from Mother. Did you not see him?" When Rhona shook her head, Ximeno continued, "Then he must have met a pretty girl, who distracted him."

Grieve burst out laughing, then stopped when he realised he was the only one.

"What's funny?" Rhona asked coolly.

Grieve was still grinning. "Why, doesn't he mean you? But we saw no one on the way here…"

"Nuno is sweet on Ciara, though I am not sure if she is as sweet on him. He makes frequent visits to his mother, though, hoping to see her, so Belen encourages him, even if Ciara gives him no hope." Rhona sniffed. If she wanted a man, she would not toy with his affections like Ciara. Though it seemed to drive Nuno wild, so perhaps she knew her man better than Rhona thought. Still… "Ximeno, can you tell him how we run things here? I'll unsaddle the horses for the night."

Without another word, she hurried down the steps and away from the only man on Rum Isle who thought she was worth looking at.

Twenty-Two

Grieve watched her go, too bewildered to ask why. Ximeno just shrugged, then began to point out the features of their clifftop eyrie, including what Grieve had taken for an eagle's nest but was actually a watchfire which could be seen from the other three towers when it was lit. He stroked the smooth stone, shaped into a natural tower with only a little help from men. The other towers Ximeno pointed out looked almost identical to this one — natural formations that no one would look twice at, approaching the island for the first time. Unlike the wooden watchtowers at Isla and Myroy, which stood out for what they were.

When Ximeno's spiel seemed to wind down, the man took Grieve's arm and looked around before dropping to a whisper. "A word of advice, if I may. Lady Rhona might not be the prettiest girl on the island, but it is cruel to mock her for it. She is the best healer on Rum Isle, perhaps in all of the Southern Isles, and it does not matter if a man must look upon her face instead of his sweetheart's when the lady's help is needed. And she's still the Lady of the Isle – when she marries, her husband will be Lord Ronin's successor, for his claim will go to her. If you intend to stay here, it is not wise to offend Lady Rhona."

"She's already talked about throwing me off a cliff," Grieve admitted, but his thoughts were more on Ximeno's words than his own. Not the prettiest girl on the island? Had Ximeno even looked at the girl? Even clothed, she was lovely. Tall and fair as a Viken, perhaps taller than any other woman he'd seen on Rum Isle, but far from ugly.

"Then you had best guard your tongue most carefully. You must have offered Lady Rhona a grievous insult to offend her so," Ximeno said. "She will be a true lady when her father passes, much like her mother was. Nothing like the new one. They say she throws screeching tantrums if her whims are not acted upon, and never does a thing for anyone. Why, we found her with a cart bogged in the mud the other day, partway home. She beat Nuno with a stick when he didn't get the cart wheel free fast enough. If you ask me, Lord Ronin should get that one pregnant as quickly as possible, and hope the childbed fever takes her like it did his first wife. Poor Lady Blanid. Lady Rhona must be heartbroken even her healing arts could not save her."

"I...thank you," Grieve said. "I should probably help Lady Rhona with...the horses." He stumbled down the uneven steps, wondering how the watchman managed not to break his neck each time he had to race down them to report a raiding party.

"So, do you still think we're defenceless?" Rhona greeted him.

"There's a saying on Myroy that as long as a man still has his wits, he will never be defenceless," Grieve said, stretching his frozen fingers out toward the fire. "I never said Rum Isle was without defences, just that it would benefit from stronger ones." He drew in a deep breath, hoping to inhale courage with the air. Something to stop his knees from shaking, as he added, "And when your watchman spoke of a pretty girl, of course I thought he meant it as a compliment to you. Why would he not? Why, just look at you."

"I believe you already did that, this afternoon," Rhona said dryly.

As if on command, Grieve's cheeks reddened. "I said I was sorry for staring, but I'll never be sorry for seeing what I saw. A vision of loveliness no man would want to forget. And I'll challenge any man who dares say otherwise."

She shook her head, but there was a smile on her lips. "Pretty words, Lewisson, no more. I am not so vain as to wish I were the most beautiful girl in the Southern Isles – I know my own reflection, and I am content. I'm sure your flattery is well meant, though unnecessary. I've already set out our bedrolls, and you may share my bed tonight." She gestured at a stone alcove, where Grieve saw his things beside hers.

His mouth dropped open, but he couldn't think of a word to say. He stared, yet he could detect no hint of laughter in her expression. She expected him to share her bed?

"I…I thought it was customary to start with a kiss," he said.

Uncertainty flared in her eyes. For all her forwardness, she was as nervous as he was.

Grieve grew bolder, stepping forward so that he could embrace her. He lifted a tentative hand to her cheek, which was as soft as he'd imagined it to be. "So beautiful," he murmured.

Her lips parted, but no sound came out.

Gently, oh so carefully, he touched his lips to hers. Her slight gasp dared him to do more, as her fingers tangled in his hair, holding him close. Only then did he dare to tease her tongue with his, and the taste of her, the softness of the woman in his arms, was enough for him to lose his mind. Once he'd started, he could not stop kissing her – no, not even to draw a breath that had not caressed her breast first with its airy fingers.

By the time Rhona pushed him away, her eyes blazed with the same desire coursing through his veins. With trembling hands, he unfastened his cloak and dropped it on the stone floor. Then he seized the hem of his tunic…

Her hand covered his, pulling the hem down. "Keep your clothes on, Myroy boy. I said you may lie with me – to keep warm, for 'tis cold in this cave, even with the fire going.

If I want you to be my lover, I'll tell you so, but not tonight. Though that was a fine kiss. If I do choose you for a lover, I'd hope for many more such kisses."

He stepped away and straightened his tunic. "My apologies, my lady. Your beauty bewitched me again. If you desire another kiss, you have only to ask."

She laid a hand on his chest. "Rhona. You are a lord's son, and I am a lord's daughter. After sharing a kiss like that…we should at least be friends."

"Only if you call me Grieve, the name my mother gave me. And accept that when I say you are beautiful, I mean every word. If other men cannot see it, then they are fools."

She took a deep breath, looking as enervated by the exchange as he felt. "Very well, though it is strange to think every man I have ever known is a fool. Doesn't it seem more likely that the one man who sees things differently is more foolish than the rest? Grieve?"

It was strange yet lovely to her his name on her lips once more. He wanted to hear her gasp it, moan it, maybe even scream it for joy. One day, he promised himself.

"If I am a fool, then I do not know it. How would I know? Ah, I have heard some kings keep fools in their courts, who amuse them by telling tales. Shall I share some of the stories I know, and see if they amuse you?"

Rhona sat beside the fire and broke a loaf in two, before handing him half. "Tell all the tales you want. If you tell me one I have not heard, then I will open a bottle of my father's best wine. Belen slipped one into the saddlebags."

A challenge, the likes of which no Myroy man could refuse. Grieve took the bread and began, "Once upon a time…"

Twenty-Three

Shuffling footsteps woke Grieve. A man tiptoed through the cave, taking exaggerated care to make as little noise as possible as he ascended the steps. Nuno, he assumed, for the man looked like last night's watchman, his brother.

Grieve took a deep breath, and inhaled an unfamiliar floral scent. He glanced down. He'd shared Rhona's bed, just as she'd promised, but he had not expected to share tales with her half the night until he'd fallen asleep with her warm weight in his arms. Now, the fully clothed girl was pressed against his side, one arm flung across his belly as if to claim him. Her hand was dangerously close to where he dreamed she'd caressed him. Where he wished she'd touch him now, for he stood to attention for her in anticipation of a more intimate embrace than the one they were in now.

If his father and Lord Ronin sought to matchmake him with Rhona, then he would embrace their plan with all his strength.

"Marry me, Rhona," he whispered into her hair.

He snorted softly. He'd known the woman for a day, but he knew he'd never get her out of his head.

Rhona shifted, and her hand drifted lower, then fastened around him. By all that was holy, how could he feel the heat of her touch through his tunic? Whatever she touched, she burned.

"Well, you're a big one, aren't you?

Dreaming about some girl back home?" she asked, giving him an agonisingly good squeeze before letting go.

Grieve swallowed. "Thinking about the girl in my arms right now," he said. "The beautiful Lady Rhona."

She shifted away from him and sat up. "No good morning kisses for you, then. You go take care of that, for we have a long ride ahead of us. I must show you the rest of the island, and tonight, we'll sleep in Sanctuary. The island's biggest secret of all."

Already his arms felt empty without her, but Grieve did as she said. Riding with a raging hard-on for the woman beside him would make for a hell of a day.

Twenty-Four

Perhaps it had been the wine, or all those well-told tales, but as she'd cuddled up to Grieve's warm body in her bedroll that night, Rhona knew she'd made her decision. She would show him Sanctuary. But not because her father had ordered it. No, she'd show him because she wanted him to stay and become one of them.

She'd known him for a day, and yet it felt like she'd known him forever. An easy familiarity had sprung between them last night, like they were a long-lost brother and sister. Yet that kiss…no, that had not been brotherly at all. While her lips were locked with his, she'd seriously considered taking things further, perhaps even letting him make love to her. She'd never thought much about marriage, but she did know one thing – she'd not go to her marriage bed as some virgin maiden who'd never known a man's touch. No, when she took a husband, she'd already know he was a skilled lover.

If Grieve could set her body aflame with a single kiss, imagine what he could do with the rest of his body…and hers…

She dreamed he'd asked her to marry him, but before she could answer, she awoke. Perhaps that was for the best, for she'd found him pitching a tent in his tunic with a look of panic on his face lest she notice. She'd have to be blind indeed not to notice he carried a mighty sword beneath his belt as well as the one that hung from it.

Idly, she wondered what it would feel like to have that length of hot, hard flesh slide inside her, as his hands caressed her and he told her over and over again how beautiful she was.

Rhona almost laughed aloud. A daydream, that's what it was, conjured out of the silly stories they'd told last night. Knights and princess, genies and sultans, courtesans and princesses…all living happily ever after, with no thoughts of war or what might happen in the future. If only life were like the stories.

If it were, then she and Grieve could lie abed, making love to each other so that every moment was happy ever after. But not today, for Nuno had returned, and that meant Ximeno would want their cave to sleep in after standing watch all night. So she freshened up and broke her fast, while Grieve readied himself for the ride along the western side of the island, before they headed to Sanctuary.

The prettier side of the island, some said, because it was the side furthest from Alba. But it was also the least sheltered part of the island, for there was nothing to stop the waves from rolling in and smashing against the cliffs. The spray flew so high Rhona tasted salt on her lips more than once.

If she were to kiss Grieve again, would his lips be salty, too? Her eyes met his and a smile lifted her lips almost of its own volition. Her heart raced as though she'd galloped along the clifftop, instead of keeping to the slow pace such uneven terrain demanded. Grieve was several yards away, yet he'd stolen her breath somehow.

Perhaps…

"What do you think of the plot between my father and yours?" she asked him.

"Which one?"

"The one to make us marry."

Grieve reined his horse to a stop, and Rhona's mount almost collided with his. Close enough to touch, and he did, capturing her hand in his own. "I know nothing of any plot, for the gossip in your kitchen was the first I had heard of it. But the more I think on it, every moment I spend with you, the less I care whether there is a plot at all." He pressed his lips to her hand, a chaste kiss compared to the one they'd shared last night. "I would like to kiss you again, Lady Rhona, and with you in my thoughts, there is no space for anyone else." For a moment, his eyes were dark and full of feeling, before he turned away to gaze toward the horizon. "But you must show me all of Rum Isle's defences. I must make sure…the island…is protected."

The love that had blossomed in her breast as she anticipated another delightful kiss shrivelled in the summer sun as Grieve put more distance between them.

Rhona sighed. She dreamed too much, she knew, for there were too many stories in her head. Grieve was right to be practical about these things, for love could not stop a war.

Twenty-Five

Grieve cursed his clumsiness with words, and with women. For a moment there, it seemed they'd shared the same thoughts, and then it had all gone wrong. Was he supposed to say he heartily approved of their fathers' plot? That couldn't be right – she had made it very clear that she would follow her own heart, not her father's plans.

He scarcely paid attention as she showed him the other three watchtowers and the harbour, introducing him to everyone they met. He smiled and nodded and shook hands, accepting more cups of ale than was good for him.

More than once, he'd had to take a trip into the bushes, to Rhona's amusement.

On the third such detour, she'd waited until he'd climbed back onto his horse before she said, "At least you gave me a show of your own this time. 'Tis a fine arse you have, Lewisson. A mite pale, but I don't suppose it sees much sun."

She'd been watching him piss? Grieve's face grew so hot he feared his skin would crisp off. And then…he smiled, at the knowledge that she'd been watching him. Maybe she was not as cold to him as he'd thought.

He hurried to catch up to her. "Are there any other parts of me you consider fine?" he called.

She tossed her head. "I'm sure I'd have to see more of such parts before I could make a judgement like that."

He drew even with her. "And what parts of me would you like to see more of, my lady?"

She darted a glance at him, then looked away. "I'm sure I don't know. But you have seen all of me, so it seems only fitting that I should see all of you. And I thought we agreed to use first names, not…anything else."

"So we did. And if my lady wishes to see all of me, she has only to ask."

She closed her eyes. "Grieve…"

"Yes, Rhona?"

"Stop. We have arrived."

Grieve looked around. "This is no sanctuary. A sheltered depression, out of the wind, with the river running alongside, but it is too open. The enemy would only need to follow your trail here, and there would be no escape. You'd be slaughtered."

"And yet no enemy has ever taken Rum Isle," Rhona said softly. "You see that waterfall?"

Grieve's gazed followed her pointing finger. "It's pretty," he said cautiously.

Rhona laughed. She slid down and began to unfasten her saddle. She gave her horse a slap on the rump in dismissal and carried her things toward the waterfall.

Grieve hurried to do the same. But the buckles refused to unfasten, so by the time he'd freed his horse, Rhona was nowhere to be seen.

"Rhona?" he called, feeling like a fool. He set off for the waterfall, wondering if he would see her from there.

The waterfall turned pink, before she emerged from behind it, brushing water droplets from her cloak. "Are you coming, or are you waiting for an enemy army to appear?"

It was another natural watchtower, Grieve guessed, as he scrambled up the damp rocks to where Rhona stood.

"Come and see," she said, turning to lead the way.

He was surprised to find the entrance was big enough to walk through without ducking his head or turning sideways — unlike the watchtowers she'd shown him. The passage beyond narrowed as it led upward, and he left his saddle beside hers, shouldering his bags so they wouldn't catch on the walls. The combination of slippery stone and the sharp incline made it a challenge to keep his footing, but Grieve managed to follow Rhona without actually falling, though he slipped twice. He noticed several passages that led to the left and right, but Rhona did not turn, and he had no choice but to follow where she led.

Then she stopped so suddenly that he slammed into her, wrapping his arms around her to keep from knocking her over.

"Welcome to Sanctuary," she said, glancing over her shoulder at him. "And if that's your saddlebags I can feel digging into my shoulder, I think you've just squashed the bread."

Grieve realised he still held her, and reluctantly relinquished the woman he only wanted to pull closer. He mumbled an apology.

"This is Rum Island's stronghold. None

have ever taken it, and none shall while Islanders hold it," Rhona said.

Grieve could see why. The place was like one of the legendary ancient fortresses – in fact, it probably was one. The cavern was huge – his father's great hall would fit in here twice over, with space to spare. Why, you could fit most of Myroy Island's people in here. A stream ran along one side of the cavern, presumably an offshoot of the river that fed the waterfall at the door.

In the light of the flames of the firepit, which was already lit, though Rhona could not have been here long enough to light such a fire, Grieve could just discern steps at the opposite end of the cavern, spiralling upwards.

"Is there a watchtower atop here, too?" he asked.

She nodded. "Two, actually, though they are not so much towers as higher caverns through which the river used to flow. The island is riddled with caves, but these are the highest and the biggest. From the east spire, you can see clear to the sea, and with men in both east and west, two men can keep watch over the whole island, while our people live comfortably in the cavern below. There are smaller caverns, branching off. Some are store rooms, while others belong to particular families who have lived on Rum Isle for generations. There used to be a cavern where we kept our horses, but the roof collapsed and no one has yet shifted the rubble. The main cavern is a meeting place, an underground village square, where the cook fire is kept burning while anyone resides here."

"Ah, so that's why the fire is lit! Here I thought you must have some magical means of making a blaze so quickly, but the watchmen here must keep the fire burning instead." Grieve grinned at his own joke.

Rhona didn't seem to find it funny. Instead, she seemed lost for words.

"Are you going to introduce me to the watchmen of Sanctuary? Which spire first, east or west?" he prompted.

"There is no one here but us. The

watchmen of the cliff towers retreat to Sanctuary when their families are here, but in summer it is empty but for the harvest, stored for when we need it in winter." She blinked, then seemed to regain a little of her earlier enthusiasm. "Would you like to see my family's cavern? It's called the Lady's Chamber, because it's usually the Lady of Rum Isle who leads her people here, while the lord and his men defend the island long enough for their families to reach safety."

She led the way along the stream, then crossed a set of stepping stones to the far bank. Behind a rock pillar was a third set of steps Grieve hadn't seen before, and light glimmered at the top.

"Do the men of the isles make it to Sanctuary, or is it a fight to the death?" Grieve asked. Not that any Islander would run from a fight – they were not cowards. But Alba had many more men than the Islanders could muster, and anything Grieve could do to make sure the Islanders lived to fight another day, he must.

"Sometimes," Rhona said. "The cliffs are a natural defence, and every man on Rum Isle must keep a bow with a number of arrows. They are supposed to practice archery every day, too, but I fear they have been lax of late. It has been a long time since Albans last raided our shores. Most of the heroic tales of this place are about the courage of ladies, not men, though. And some include commanding the army of archers, when our men are away."

She reached the top of the steps, and edged to the side so that Grieve might enter the cavern beside her.

Light streaked down from a hole in the roof, sparkling through the waterfall that splashed down into a pool which overflowed into a second cascade that undoubtedly fed the stream below.

Grieve laughed. "Are you sure it's not called the Lady's Chamber because it has a bath in it?"

Rhona smiled. "It's not a bath I'd enter by choice. The water is icy cold, so it's better to take a bucket of it and set it by the fire to warm before you wash." She cupped some in her hands and drank. "Freezing, but as pure as anything you'll find on Rum Isle. Taste it yourself."

Grieve knelt beside the pool and cupped his hands.

Rhona made a sound between a squeak and a scream.

Grieve jumped to his feet, his hand flying to the hilt of his sword.

But there was no enemy to fight, or at least none that would take damage from a sword.

Rhona stood in the middle of a puddle of water that must have come from the roof, which had soaked her to the skin on its way down. "Can you get me some dry clothes, please?" she asked.

"Of course." Grieve hurried down to the main cavern, grabbed her saddle bags and raced back up the steps.

When he reached the chamber, the bags dropped from his hands and he lost the ability to speak.

Twenty-Six

The moment Grieve left, Rhona stripped off her wet clothes and used the dry parts to mop the water from her skin. After the long day's ride, she needed a wash, though this wasn't how she'd imagined it.

What was taking Grieve so long? Could he not find her bags? Rhona scanned the cavern, looking for the chests her family kept here. The clothes and blankets would certainly be in need of an airing, but a musty tunic was better than nothing.

Ah, there they were – stacked by the sleeping alcoves. She pried open the catch on the topmost one and lifted out blanket after blanket, looking for the clothing she knew had to be here somewhere. It wasn't until she reached the bottom of the chest that she encountered what felt like a sleeping fur, but when she pulled it out, it turned out to be a winter cloak made of sealskin. She rubbed the velvety fur against her cheek, remembering when this cloak had belonged to her grandmother and she used to bury her face in it.

Something fell to the floor behind her.

Rhona swung the cloak around her shoulders, holding it closed with one hand as she whirled to face the intruder.

"By all that's holy..." She marched up to Grieve. "You're making a habit of catching me with my clothes off. A vainer lady than I might think you like what you see so much, you wish to see it again."

"I do." The words had no sooner left his lips than he turned as pale as mist. "I mean – "

Rhona held her cloak open. "There, then. Look your fill, and may your eyes burn out of your head after the devil is done with you, for – "

"My God, you're beautiful."

Now Rhona was the one lost for words. Grieve stepped forward and kissed her, drawing her body against his warmth, and cocooning the rest of her in the cloak. This man could kiss her forever, if he wished, but Rhona became increasingly aware of something hard pressed against her hip. She glanced down, and forced herself to break that irresistible kiss.

"Stop poking me with your sword," she said.

Grieve turned red as he glanced down, too. "I'm sorry, my lady, but like I said, you're beautiful..."

"No, not that sword. Take it off!" Before she could think the idea through, she unbuckled his belt and let it drop to the floor, sword and all. "Better. Now, kiss me again."

"I think it would be best if I obeyed your earlier order, my lady. The one where you asked me to get your clothes. Because if I kiss you again, while you are like this..." Grieve gestured at her body, the longing clear in his eyes as he looked at her. "I fear I will forget all thoughts of chivalry and honour, as though the devil himself sat on my shoulder, whispering in my ear. I will already pay a painful penance for the thoughts in my head right now."

But Rhona's blood was afire, and so was his. She was certain of it. "It is me you owe penance to, staring at my body so. It seems only right that I should get to do the same." She reached for the hem of his tunic, and tugged it up over his head.

"Lady Rhona, I think if I were naked, too, it would only make things all the harder."

Her breathing came fast now. "Then you should take off your hose, so we can do something about that."

Despite his half-hearted protests, Grieve

soon stood naked before her, wearing nothing but his cloak. Now it was Rhona's turn to look her fill, at the lean, muscled man before her. Yes, oh yes. He was everything she could want in a man. In a lover.

She threw herself at him, twining her arms around his neck as she kissed him deeply. As her breasts met his hard chest, her body seemed to flame to life, just as she knew it should. She reached around to cup his butt cheeks, which were every bit as firm as they'd looked. But that only pressed other parts of him harder, more insistently into her belly, demanding more.

More that she wanted to give.

Rhona drew him down to the pile of blankets, letting out a contented sigh as his weight settled atop her. Then his lips descended to her breasts, kissing, sucking, setting off currents deep inside.

"Yes, oh yes…" She scarcely recognised her own voice, so breathless with need.

She wrapped her legs around his hips,

wanting to feel him everywhere. She reached down to stroke him, guiding him to where she wanted him.

She cried out as she felt something hot slide inside of her, but it was too small to be what she wanted. His fingers, she realised. "I want you, Grieve. All of you."

"I'm your first. I can feel it. I don't want to hurt you."

Yet his fingers stroked her, driving her mad with desire for what she really wanted. Taunting, tempting, tantalising…tipping her over a cliff she'd never seen, into bliss. For the first time in her life, she soared in a man's hands. This was better than her dreams.

"Grieve, I need you. Please." It came out as a joyful sob in a voice Rhona still didn't recognise as her own.

His eyes darkened with desire as he lifted his head to meet her eyes. "Rhona, are you sure?"

She'd never been so sure of anything in her life. "Make love to me, Grieve."

He grasped her hips, the hard heat of him

replacing where his fingers had stroked her only moments before. He thrust what felt like a burning brand inside her, searing her insides until he filled her completely. And it felt so good.

Breathlessly, she urged him on, moaning as the molten heat that was him moved inside her. Again and again and again. Until she could no longer control the bliss she felt, and screamed his name.

Dimly, she heard her own name on his lips, before he leaned forward to kiss her.

She looked up, lost in his eyes, as she clenched around the part of him still inside her. This was what she wanted. "Marry me, Grieve," she said.

He stared at her, then began to laugh. As he sat up, he withdrew from her, leaving her emptier than she'd ever felt before. He headed for the pool to clean himself up. Only when he was done splashing, did he stop laughing.

Rhona wrapped herself in her cloak, wanting to relive the memory of his touch, branding it into her skin for every moment they were apart. "What's funny?" she asked.

"I thought a lady expected a marriage proposal before she shared her bed, not after," he said.

Rhona shrugged. "I can't imagine why any woman would agree to marry a man before knowing what sort of lover he was. When I agree to share my bed with one man for the rest of my life, it will not be a stranger who I have not touched."

He brought a dripping cloth to where she lay, and held it out. "I fear I am a messy lover. I scarcely know what possessed me, just that I wanted to possess you. I hope I did not hurt you. There is a little blood…" He pressed the cloth to her thigh, and steam rose up into the air. The cold water was chilly against her burning skin, but Rhona relished it, even more as Grieve stroked her thighs with the wet cloth in an intimate caress that promised she would know no better lover than him.

She covered his hand with hers. "You didn't

hurt me. That was…wonderful. I want you to share my bed again tonight."

He swallowed. "For warmth, like last night? For I give you fair warning, my lady. I will do my best to honour you as you deserve while I am awake, but I fear my dreams. After knowing the joy of your beautiful body, I know my dreams will be filled with you. And if my hands stray onto your body as I sleep, it is because I long to make love to you all over again."

Again? Twice in one night? Never had she heard of a man visiting his wife's bed more than once in a night. The thought was thrilling…tantalising…too much for her to resist.

"Then I insist we sleep naked. I long to feel you inside me again."

"As my lady commands."

Twenty-Seven

Three times he'd made love to her, each time more delightful than the last. If he'd had the stamina, Grieve would have loved her all night, until the dawn light kissed her cheeks, for he'd never met a girl so eager, or so angelic when she cried out his name. for the joy he'd brought her.

But would it be enough? Doubt gnawed at him, after what she'd said last night. That she wouldn't marry a man unless he was the sort of lover she wanted in her bed for the rest of her life.

He slipped out of the bed they'd made of the blankets on the floor, and headed for the pool to wash himself once more. He dressed, then headed to the cavern to see to breakfast. Perhaps he could bring it to her, so that she might break her fast in bed.

He found the bread he'd squashed last night, along with some hard cheese. If she still slept, then he could offer her a hot breakfast. Grieve set about coaxing the fire into life from the embers. When he had a decent blaze going, he set about melting the cheese and toasting the bread.

"Grieve?"

He'd taken so long, Rhona was not only awake, but dressed for the day, her fingers working to braid her hair so quickly it seemed to require no thought on her part at all.

"I'm making breakfast." He waved at the toast, which had started to burn. Hastily, he pulled the bread out of the fire and blew the flames out. "I was going to bring it to you."

"It was cold without you." Her eyes said so much more.

Grieve's mouth grew drier than the toast in his hands. He set the cheese on it and held it out. "Careful, it's hot."

She took the offering with both hands, smiling. "I like things hot." She lifted her lips for a kiss.

Grieve wiped the worst of the crumbs off his hands, then carefully cupped her face. So beautiful, and that fire in her eyes... He touched his lips to hers, and for that moment, they shared the passion of their night together. He wanted to unlace her gown and do it all over again, but he wasn't sure how long it would take to return to her father's house. Where Grieve fully intended to ask Lord Ronin for her hand, and every other bit connected to it, too.

"You must be a witch, for you have cast a spell over me," he said.

Rhona stiffened in his arms. "I have done

no such thing." She pulled away, putting several yards between them before sitting down to break her fast.

Curse his clumsy tongue. Grieve concentrated on making his own breakfast, while he tried to work out what to say to make things right.

Finally, he settled for: "Lady Rhona, if anything I have done has offended you, then I am deeply sorry. I only meant that I am so in love I cannot think straight any more, for all my thoughts are of you. If you are willing..." He turned, hoping to meet her eyes before he dropped to his knees, as custom demanded.

But Rhona was gone. She hadn't heard a word.

Grieve swore, then bit into his bread and cheese, burned his tongue, and swore some more.

He fell silent when the scrape of booted feet at the entrance alerted him that he was not alone any more.

"Rhona?" he asked tentatively, hoping she

had returned.

Instead, a child emerged from the passage, followed by another, then an older woman holding the hand of a third. "Good thing you have the fire going, young man, for we'll need it. The Albans picked a cold, clear day to attack, thinking we'd be huddled around our fires and not watching for them. More fool them, I say."

"Albans? Where?" Rhona appeared on the stepping stones, concern wrinkling her forehead. "Candace, where is my father?"

The woman looked grim. "He set off yesterday for Isla. Something about a declaration of war from Alba. This is the start of it, I'm sure."

Rhona nodded, watching more people enter the cave – some of them the women Grieve had met in her father's kitchens. The whole household was here.

"Where is Lady Doireann?" Candace asked.

The cook shook her head. "She threw a mighty fit, saying she would not leave a scrap for the Albans to steal. We left her trying to put more things in a cart than it could carry. When one of the men told her so, she ordered him away, saying she would drive the cart here herself."

Rhona swore, using words Grieve had rarely heard from a lady. "Then she's even more of a fool than I thought, for she does not even know the way. I'll go fetch her."

The cook seized her arm. "Lady Rhona, don't. If the Albans capture you, your father will never forgive us."

"He will also not forgive us if we leave Doireann to die, or worse," Rhona said grimly. "Stay here. I shall go alone."

Grieve jumped to his feet. "No you shall not! I should be the one to go."

Rhona glared at him, then subsided. "Fine. You may come with me." She trotted up the steps and returned with her cloak around her shoulders, and a bundle of cloth that she shoved into Grieve's arms. "Put this on. You'll need it."

The sweet girl who'd shared his bed was gone. In her place stood a cold-hearted warrior, like the Vikens she resembled. Grieve had never been frightened of a woman before, but right now, Rhona was terrifying.

He buckled on his sword belt, but decided to wait until they got outside to don his cloak. He wished he'd brought armour with him, but what he had was back at Lord Ronin's house, along with his other weapons. The sooner they got there, the better.

Twenty-Eight

Rhona only glanced behind her once to make sure Grieve was following her before she set off at a gallop for home. She'd be there by noon – she only hoped it would be soon enough to get Doireann to safety. Doireann had lost everything to raiders once – it would be needlessly cruel to allow it to happen again. Rhona might not like the woman, but she couldn't bring herself to hate her that much.

Her thoughts were occupied with a far more

important question: was she willing to reveal her magic to save Doireann, if that's what it took? For to do so would be to reveal that she wasn't Father's legitimate daughter, but the result of a union between him and a witch. As her father's bastard, she had no claim over Rum Isle, and neither Grieve or his father would want such a union. If she had to use magic to save Doireann, then she would lose Grieve.

But if she let the Albans harm Doireann, then her father would probably disown her, no matter who her husband was. And she couldn't live with herself, knowing she'd sacrificed another woman for her own happiness.

But if her father found out she was a bastard, he'd probably disown her anyway, so no matter what she did, Rhona would lose her home here.

Tears blurred her vision, but Rhona wiped them away. This was not a time for self-pity. She had to do what was right, and damn the consequences. She might not like Doireann, but the woman was still family, albeit by marriage, and no one hurt her family. Least of all a bunch of Alban scum.

She wove through the woods, trusting Grieve to keep up, as they neared her home. As they reached the last of the trees, Rhona dismounted, and tied her horse where it would be out of view of the house. She gestured for Grieve to do the same.

"We'll be too high if we climb the ridge on horseback. On foot, we can creep up on the house unseen. If the raiders have already arrived and we are too late…I do not want to give them any warning of our arrival," she said.

"My weapons are in the house. If I can get them, I will be more use to you than I am now with just a sword," Grieve whispered.

Rhona nodded, not wanting to voice her thoughts. If the Albans had not yet arrived, Grieve would have no need of his weapons, and all that would matter was the speed with which they got Doireann away. If the Albans had arrived before them…then Grieve's weapons were as good as lost, and nothing would save Doireann but a powerful show of magic. And that would cost her everything she held dear.

They crept up the slope, keeping low until they reached the shelter of the stones at the top. As a child, she'd traced the carvings on them and wondered what they meant, but now all her attention was on the beach at the base of the cliffs.

Her heart sank. The Alban boats had already beached themselves on the sand, and aside from a pair of boys they'd left on guard, the men were nowhere to be seen.

They might have gone inland, attacking farms and crofts. But the biggest house closest to the beach was her father's, on the cliffs overlooking the beach. They'd be fools not to go there first.

"They might already be at the house," she told Grieve. "Best we use the cover by the river to get closer."

He nodded, and followed her down the hill

to the river. Grieve was quieter on his feet than she thought he'd be – she had to glance behind her more than once to make sure he was still there, but he was, as intent as she was on making this rescue work.

If only they weren't too late.

If Doireann was dead…

Then none of the Albans would leave here alive, Rhona swore.

They'd raped Aunt Blanid, sentenced her mother Brigid to a lifetime taking care of her sister with no chance of marriage, and destroyed Doireann's home and family. She'd be damned before she allowed them to take any more from her family.

Grieve reached the willow trees first, crouching behind a trunk that still bore the marks from his axe. "We're too late," he whispered.

No. They couldn't be. Rhona dropped to her knees and peered through the forked trunk of what had been the first willow on Rum Isle.

In the yard that had always been the heart of

her father's household stood perhaps a dozen Albans, clearly recognisable in their piss-yellow tunics. They'd be pissing themselves in fear by the time she was done with them. Rhona rose, careful to keep hidden behind the seaward tree trunk. She bit her lip until she tasted blood, taking her time choosing her target.

"Bring her to me!"

The shouted command had their attention, and Rhona's, too.

Doireann appeared, marched between two men who each had a hold of one of her arms.

Rhona changed her mind about the spell, swapping fire for air, as she sent a breeze through the yard that carried Doireann's words to her.

"Please don't hurt me. I did as I was bid!" she insisted. "All the riches of Rum Isle. I know where they are!"

Maybe a fire spell was called for, after all. A fire spell that turned that treacherous bitch into a ball of flame.

"Where?" A man with fancy armour over

his yellow tunic stepped up to her.

"A cave in the woods. They're all there. I can show you…if you promise to let me go." Doireann fell to her knees. "Please, sir. You spared me on Scitis so that I could come here to find out what you wish to know."

The man laughed. "You would betray your new husband so easily?"

Doireann spat on the ground. "Lord Ronin is no husband to me, if he's even a man at all. He would not share my bed, not even on our wedding night. There's no marriage between us, and no love either. He forces me to run after his unruly brats like a servant, but won't give me a child of my own. You can have his island, and all that's on it. All I ask is that you let me go so that I might find a real man to be my husband."

"After you have shown us this cave, woman. Then we shall see."

"Let me…let me get the cart, so it will be easier to bring everything back." Doireann clambered to her feet, then took a tentative step toward the pony cart.

Rhona bit her lip, readying a fireball. The moment Doireann climbed atop that cart, Rhona would set it ablaze.

"Ooh, look, a Viken spy," a voice said behind Rhona. Then something crashed into the back of her head and darkness descended.

Twenty-Nine

Grieve had only a moment to reach for his sword, but he was too slow. One blow felled Rhona, and the second sent him half-stunned to the ground. He tried to fight, but his attacker shouted to his comrades, and soon there were a dozen Albans upon him.

"Tie them up. We always need more slaves," the Alban leader ordered, and Grieve soon found his hands bound to his feet. Another man tied Rhona's hands behind her back, then threw her over his shoulder and carried her off.

"Hey. Hey! You can't take her away. That's Lord Ronin's daughter!" he shouted.

The leather-clad leader strode up to him, leaning down so that he might look Grieve in the eye. "She looks too old to be one of his brats to me. Bring the other one."

Doireann was dragged over and thrown to the ground in front of Grieve.

"Who are these two?" the man demanded.

Doireann glared at Grieve. "The boy is the son of Lord Lewis of Myroy. She's Lord Ronin's eldest, and the most unruly of the lot. Good for ransom and not much else."

Grieve met the woman's eye. "At least I still have some honour. I'm not selling out the only people who would take me in to the enemy who killed my family!"

Doireann's eyes burned. "You're a man. You'd never understand." She jerked her head at Rhona. "She will. You'll see. Once all the Albans have had her, stolen her maidenhead and her virtue, she'll agree to anything to make them stop."

"Enough. A lord's maiden daughter is worth more intact. Nobody touches the girl. Not yet." The leader pointed at Doireann. "Get her up, and follow her to this cave. If she cannot show you, kill her."

Two men seized Doireann, ignoring her screaming protests, and took her away.

The leader turned to Grieve and the man still carrying Rhona. "These two…should be held somewhere they cannot escape from. One of the deserted isles we saw on the way. We can return for them later."

"Don't you hurt her!" Grieve shouted.

"And shut that one up," the leader said wearily.

A boot came out of nowhere, colliding with Grieve's head, and blackness embraced him.

Thirty

Rhona's head hadn't hurt this much since she drank a whole jug of wine at Sive's christening. Only she couldn't remember drinking anything this time. Instead, her mouth tasted of blood. She rolled over, and encountered another warm body, but this one didn't move.

She'd fallen asleep with Grieve after making love, and everything afterwards was a bad dream, she told herself, but even she couldn't believe the lie.

"Grieve, where are we?" she asked.

He did not respond, and only then did she dare to open her eyes. A swollen lump adorned his forehead, crusted with dark blood. But his breathing was even, and his heartbeat felt strong under her hands. Alive, but unconscious. What she wouldn't give for some willow bark now.

Rhona sat up, wincing as her head gave a warning throb. She ignored it. Better to take stock of her surroundings. The light was dim, but still enough to see. They were in a cave, but not of the same stone as Sanctuary. Rhona knew every habitable cave on Rum Isle, and this wasn't one of them. The entrance to this cavern was blocked by a latticework of thin branches, with holes too small for her to fit more than her hand through, yet large enough to see to the larger cavern beyond.

It might not be Sanctuary, but someone called this place home. A pallet in the corner for a bed, and a fire burning peat that smelled like home. A pot bubbled over the fire, but

Rhona could not smell what it contained over the smoke from the fire itself.

Her gaze swept the chamber, landing on the light source. It was no candle or lamp, but something else entirely. A swirling blue mist, trapped in what appeared to be a giant platter set against the wall. The thing glowed faintly, and Rhona fancied she saw her own face in the mist before it vanished. Whatever it was, it was magical, which meant that whoever lived here was a powerful witch.

But Rhona was the only witch in the Southern Isles. If there had been another, surely she'd have heard of her. For magic called to magic, and she would know if someone cast a spell near her. For a witch to hide herself and a powerful magical object like this one, she must be a formidable witch indeed. One Rhona did not dare to challenge by magical means.

"Please let us out. I must go home," Rhona said, drawing herself up to her full height.

"We all want to go home, but not everyone

gets what they want. The sea wanted to take you from the beach where I found you, but I rescued you from the waves and brought you here. I must keep you two together. The mirror insists." The woman who stepped into view was nothing like Rhona expected. Young and dark-haired, her eyes seemed to contain the night sky.

Rhona shivered. She buried her magic deep inside, where she hoped the woman would never find it.

"Who are you?" the woman asked.

Lost in the woods and taken prisoner by a witch. It was so like one of the tales she and Grieve had swapped that Rhona answered automatically: "I am Gretel, and that's my brother, Hansel. If you don't let us go, our father, Lord Lewis, will not be pleased. Who are you?"

"Once a queen, now a slave, loved by two men, one of whom is now dead and the other is dead to me. I am Briska, now queen of a rock that boasts little more than fearless deer and this horrible stuff called snow."

She sounded mad, though she did not look it. Maybe the magic had made her so.

"You must let us go," Rhona insisted.

"I must do nothing of the sort. The mirror says…the mirror says you must be together. But if you are brother and sister, as you say…then I am cursed!" Briska's eyes glowed blue, the same as the misty platter on the wall. "Bah, I should have known escape was an illusion. You shall not leave here until you break the curse!"

She stormed out, and no amount of calling brought her back.

Rhona slumped to the floor beside Grieve, wishing he would wake up.

Thirty-One

The first thing Grieve became aware of was something cold and wet touching his forehead. Not cold enough to numb the pain, though.

He reached for his sword, but the scabbard was empty. They must have stolen it from him, along with everything else. And Rhona.

Grieve sat up, and saw the most beautiful sight he could have imagined. Rhona's startled face as the wet cloth dangled from her hand, forgotten.

"Are you all right? Did the Albans…did they hurt you?" he asked. He prayed that the leader's promise could be trusted. Who knew with Albans?

"Someone hit me over the back of the head. But nothing else," she said. "You have a bump on your head, too – much worse than mine. Do you know where we are?"

Grieve looked around. "A cave? They didn't say where they were taking us. Somewhere we could not escape from, waiting for a ransom from my father and yours."

Rhona dropped her voice to a whisper. "I told her our father is one and the same, and that we are brother and sister. Hansel and Gretel. They were the first names I could think of. She's a witch, and names are powerful in spells. If she does not know ours, perhaps she will not be able to cast curses at us."

Grieve laughed, then winced as that made his head throb more. "Held captive by a witch, just like a story. Do you have any clever ideas for escape?"

Rhona shook her head. "She keeps saying things about a mirror, and how she is cursed, and we cannot leave until we break the curse. But I know nothing about curses. What about you?"

"I'm no witch, and nor are you. I can shoot a bow, build a house, and lift a sword to defend what is mine. If she's living in a place like this, perhaps I could make a bargain with her. It's worth a try."

He began shouting for the witch.

Rhona tried to hush him, but Grieve only shouted louder.

"Silence, boy!" the dark-haired woman hissed, stalking into the cave like a cat hunting prey. "Or I shall cast a spell on your tongue that will render it unfit for speech, though it may do other things." She smiled, and her hands glowed blue.

Grieve swallowed back the swear words that leaped to his tongue. So the woman was a witch. He would have to be careful, was all, he told himself. "What will it take for you to let my sister and me go?"

This only seemed to anger her further. "Brother and sister. The mirror lies. It will take an abomination before I can release you, and for the mirror to release me from my curse and my exile here."

None of this made any sense to Grieve, but she evidently believed it. He only knew that curses were not his area of expertise. "How would you like to live somewhere better than this cave? If I can't break your curse, maybe I can make your exile more comfortable."

She sniffed. "I do not need a lover, least of all some boy who is supposed to…never mind. I will not do it!" This last was addressed to what appeared to be a mirror on the wall. An image of Grieve and Rhona's faces appeared on it for a moment, before all it showed was the witch's reflection.

A magic mirror. Just like something in a story. And just like in a story, he must somehow trick the witch into letting them go free.

"The men of Myroy have a reputation for our skill with wood. I can build you a beautiful house where you can live. Walls where you can hang your mirror. A bed to sleep on, instead of a pallet on the floor." Grieve had her attention. Now he needed to sweeten the deal. "Much warmer than this cold cave, I promise. Just ask my sister about the other places I have built."

"Oh, he's quite good with wood," Rhona said. "You should have seen the first barn he built by himself when he was just a boy."

Grieve winced. That first barn had been a disaster. But if the witch did not know that...

"What sort of house?" the witch demanded.

Grieve spread his hands wide. "Whatever you like. Point me at the wood, and I shall build you a palace fit for a queen."

Her eyes narrowed. He had her, Grieve was certain.

"A wooden palace. If that is the best I can hope for now...then I accept. You shall build me a palace, and when I am satisfied, you shall go free." The witch nodded, then pointed at

Rhona. "But she stays. I will not have…abomination…here."

"No." Grieve folded his arms across his chest. "When the palace is complete, both of us go free."

She eyed him thoughtfully for a long time. "Very well. I shall set you both free, if you give me your solemn vow that you shall never kiss your sister, nor share her bed."

Grieve wanted to laugh, but he did not dare. "I swear by all I hold dear, by my sister's own life, that I will never kiss my sister, and I will never share her bed." An empty promise, for the only sisters he had died in infancy, and he would not share their grave, nor kiss a corpse if he could help it.

"Good. Then you may start work." The witch unlocked the door, opening it just wide enough for one person to slip through. "But she stays until your work is done."

Grieve squeezed through the gap, then heard it close behind him. "If any harm comes to her, the deal is off."

The witch inclined her head. "Agreed."

"Grieve, I don't trust her," Rhona said behind him.

Grieve didn't trust her, either, but he didn't dare say it. Instead, he ignored Rhona and followed the witch outside to plan out her new palace.

Thirty-Two

Rhona spat out a mouthful of the strange food that burned her mouth. "You are trying to poison me!"

The witch looked affronted. "I feed you the same as I eat. It is not my fault your delicate stomach will not tolerate it." As if to demonstrate, she snatched Rhona's bowl and began to spoon the contents into her own mouth with evident signs of approval. "It is perfectly good venison. I don't know what you are talking about."

Between the burning food, strange flat sheets of what the witch called bread and the gritty white liquid that the woman called milk but didn't taste like it had come from any kind of cow Rhona had ever met, Rhona wasn't sure how long she would last as the witch's captive. Forcing down every bite of food and then forcing it to stay down was a daily struggle, exacerbated by her need to hide her magic deep inside, too, lest the witch sense it.

Yet the more Rhona saw of this witch, the more she thought the woman was mad. She spent hours talking to the misty platter that looked nothing like the bronze mirrors on the islands, yet the witch insisted on calling a mirror.

More than once, Rhona had seen her own face in the mist, and Grieve's, too. She fancied she'd seen the mirror show that blissful night she and Grieve had spent together in Sanctuary, once or twice, but the witch shouted at it that such things were an abomination before storming out. Without the witch present, all the mist did was swirl, without showing pictures.

Rhona barely saw Grieve, who wasn't even allowed to sleep in the same cavern as her any more. Only when the witch was fast asleep did Grieve dare to approach the door to Rhona's prison. His hands were too big to fit through the bars, so she had to shove her fingers through to feel his touch again.

"Kill her in her sleep, and let's leave together," Rhona begged on the first night.

But Grieve had shaken his head. "I gave my word, and I will not break it. If she dishonours our deal, then I will have no mercy, but for now, stay here where you will be safe. There is no way off this island – there are no boats at all. Unless I can build one or persuade one to land here, the witch is our best chance of finding a way home. I'm working as fast as I can, but I cannot build a house in a day, so you must have patience. I swear to you, I will get you home."

The witch had awoken then, putting an end to any further conversation. "Get away from her!" she'd shouted, swatting at Grieve with a broom.

So Rhona fought her frustration, finding reserves of patience she didn't know she had. Most of her days, she spent sitting in the corner of her cell, wondering what her sisters were doing at home. Whether her father had arrived home yet. And what had happened to Doireann.

Finally, one night Grieve came in so exhausted, he flopped right down on his pallet and didn't seem to want to get up again. "Tomorrow, I shall finish my work, and you can move your things from here to your new home," he told the witch. Lifting his head so that he might meet Rhona's eyes, he added, "And then tomorrow, we shall go free."

"Yes. Good," the witch said, intent on stirring the pot over the fire. It undoubtedly contained something intended to burn through the roof of Rhona's mouth. What she wouldn't give for some normal bread, or a piece of roast pork, but the only animals the witch had were deer, or at least that's all the meat she used.

The next morning, Rhona washed with the small bucket of water in her cell, and attempted to re-braid her hair. Today, she would be free.

The witch wandered in and out of the cave, as usual, muttering to herself or the misty mirror. Rhona paid her little attention until the woman dropped the pot she'd been holding with a clang.

"It will not happen! Incest is against nature!" she shouted at the mirror.

Rhona peered through the bars of her prison. The mirror showed her and Grieve, locked in a lovers' embrace. The image brought a blush to her cheeks as she watched her own image arch her back and cry out in joy. What she wouldn't give to do that with Grieve again. When they were home, and wed, she promised herself.

"Better to kill them than let him defile her

so. Now, before it is too late!" The witch seized a knife and raced out of the cave.

Rhona shouted for the witch to come back, but the woman never heard.

She was headed out to kill Grieve.

She would have to get through Rhona first.

Rhona threw her weight against the bars, trying to pry them apart wide enough to let her through. To no avail — the latticework was too firmly fixed to come apart in her hands.

But it was wood, and wood burned.

Would it matter if the witch knew about Rhona's magic? By day's end, one of them would be dead. As long as the witch didn't get to Grieve before Rhona could warn him.

Her hands were already bleeding from her fruitless attack on the door, so the spell was barely a thought away. She pressed her bloodied hands to the wood, leaving two handprints as she backed away.

Rhona pressed her back against the wall, as far from the door as she could get, and commanded the wood to burn.

The handprints ignited, leaving blackened holes in the lattice, as flames licked hungrily at the edges. Within moments, the whole door was ablaze, and it only took a few minutes before the whole thing was reduced to ashes.

Rhona hitched up her skirts above the embers, and marched through the still-smoking remains of her prison.

"I'm coming for you, bitch," she said.

And if the witch had hurt Grieve, her death was going to be slow and painful.

Thirty-Three

Grieve heard the approaching footsteps, but he didn't look up until he'd finished hammering the shingle into place.

"Almost done!" he called. "Three more to go, and then I'll climb down to show you around!"

He'd be done already if one of the shingles hadn't split overnight, bringing down part of the roof. But that was the thing about wood. It might look perfect at first, and fit just fine with all the rest, but weeks or months or sometimes even years later, the fault deep inside would start to show, and it would crack, to the detriment of all around it. Much like people, really.

He shot a furtive glance at the witch. She was barely more than a girl herself, of an age with Rhona and Bedelia, which meant he had to tread carefully lest his clumsy tongue land him in trouble again. His care seemed to have paid off, for the witch appeared pleased with his progress on her house. Well, she had, until now. The frown on her face sent out silent alarm bells, warning him to rethink his every word before he spoke.

He hammered the last shingle into place. "Would you like to see inside your new palace, mistress?" he called from his perch on the roof. Out of reach, he thought, then wondered just how far she could cast a spell. If it was like an archer firing arrows, then he was well in range, and nowhere he stood would be safe.

Grieve climbed down the ladder and

rounded the cottage. She stood in the same spot, her frown even deeper.

Grieve strode past her and opened the door. He bowed extravagantly. "Your new palace, Your Majesty."

She almost smiled, lifting her head regally as she stepped forward.

"Get away from her! She means to kill you!"

Rhona raced into view, shouting at him and the witch.

"What?" Grieve stared at the witch, as she stared at him. He took a step back, just in case.

Rhona slowed to a halt, panting. "She said she was going to kill you." Her eyes widened in panic. "Oh, no, you don't!"

A gust of wind blew Grieve almost off his feet, it was so powerful. The same gale had pinned the witch against the door, though she struggled against it. In her hand was a curved knife with a green stone blade, like nothing Grieve had ever seen before.

The witch's hands glowed blue.

"Don't you dare touch him, you bitch!" For

a moment, it looked like Rhona held a handful of flames, before she drew her hand back and threw the missile. Whatever it was, it splashed at the witch's feet, engulfing her boots in roaring flame.

She screamed and ran inside the house, slamming the door behind her.

Rhona followed, raising her arms.

"Move, Grieve," she said. She waved her hand in his direction, and this time it seemed the very air lifted him up and deposited him at her feet. "Now, burn, bitch," she said, gritting her teeth. She turned her hands palm up, lifting them as though raising an imaginary host to heaven. But what she raised was more hellish than divine, as the house he'd painstakingly built went up in a whoosh of flame.

"Rhona!" He couldn't seem to say anything else. Couldn't think. Rhona, a witch? How?

A burst of blue light erupted from the house as the roof collapsed, so blinding they both had to turn away. It took a moment for Grieve to regain his sight, and when he did, half the house was gone, collapsed in on itself and the witch's body, no doubt, for the woman's screaming had stopped.

Rhona's breast heaved. She bent down to pick up the knife, which had magically landed at her feet.

Grieve's blood ran cold. Magically, indeed. She'd just killed a woman. What else could Rhona do?

Perhaps the witch wasn't the one he had to fear after all.

He rose onto unsteady feet. If he'd been frightened of her before…she terrified him now. A woman who could command fire didn't need him to protect her. She didn't need anyone's protection – she was a force of nature all by herself.

Rhona threw her arms around his neck and kissed him. It took him a stunned moment before he could force his mouth open to return her kiss.

It wasn't enough. She sensed that something was wrong, and pulled away.

Tears glimmered in her eyes. "I'm sorry. I couldn't let her kill you."

Grieve didn't know what to say. It didn't seem right to accept her apology, not when she was sorry for saving his life, but thanking her didn't seem right, either. Instead, he said, "How will we get home now?"

She turned and surveyed the water. "We'll need a boat." She closed her eyes and bit her lip.

Grieve felt a breeze spring up, nowhere near as powerful as the one that had carried him, but he knew it came from the same source. Rhona. A witch so powerful she commanded the elements.

Fire, air…would she part the sea so that they might walk home? Anything seemed possible.

Never in his life had he felt so small, so insignificant. Not even when Bedelia rejected him.

He was nothing next to Rhona. No one. For she deserved some great hero, a man of power and wealth and courage, while what was he? Some lord's younger son, who owned little more than his clothes and weapons, which he was competent with, but no more than that. He worked wood, but she could turn a week's work into ash with a wave of her hand.

Grieve fancied he heard voices.

"We should try in the lee of Nimbanmore. Good fishing there."

Fishermen? He glanced around, but saw no one but themselves.

"There's a curse on Nimbanmore, my grandmother says. No one who goes there ever comes back."

This voice was softer, as though whispered on the wind.

"We're not going to land there, just fish offshore. Hey, what's that smoke? Seems there's someone on the island."

That's how she was doing it, Grieve realised. Stealing the sound of their words somehow.

"Where are they?" Grieve asked.

Rhona opened her eyes and pointed. "In the lee of this island. Nimbanmore, which explains why we are the only ones here. There is a curse here, an ancient one, laid on the lake at the top of the mountain. I can feel it faintly now, but it won't hurt us. Not if we can get off this island soon." She waved her hand. "They will have no choice but to come to us. The wind in every other direction will send them onto the rocks."

Grieve couldn't believe what he was hearing. "You're going to kill some innocent fishermen?"

She tilted her head to the side and smiled. "They are hardly innocent. What man is? But no, I do not intend to kill them. If they cannot sail in this wind, they may wreck their boat, but they are Islanders and fisherman. The fishermen of Rum Isle survive gales far worse than this. They will come to the beach here, and take us home. You'll see."

It seemed to take forever before the boat landed on the beach, and the men aboard hailed them. Rhona explained who they were and how they needed a ride home, for which she would happily pay the men to make up for their lost catch.

This was Lady Rhona, Ronin's daughter, not the frightened girl she'd been for the last week in the witch's prison. How much of that had been real, and how much a pretence? Grieve truly didn't know the woman at his side at all. Witch, woman, wonder…but she could never be his wife. He wanted to worship her, not ask her what was for dinner.

Exactly as Rhona had foretold, Grieve found himself beside her on the fishing boat, headed home to Rum Isle. Standing beside the woman who held his heart, when he would never have hers.

Thirty-Four

Lord Ronin wept when he saw Rhona, and he couldn't seem to stop thanking Grieve for bringing her home. He either didn't hear or chose to ignore Grieve's protestations that he'd done nothing, and embraced him like a son.

Doireann was dead, murdered by the Albans, and Ronin had feared Rhona had suffered a similar fate.

"If not for you, I would have lost everything," Lord Ronin said with an enormous sniffle.

He still had his house, all the supplies in Sanctuary, and three of his daughters unharmed because of their early retreat to the caves, Grieve thought but didn't say as the three girls lined up to hug Rhona and drop an awkward curtsey each in his direction, at their father's command.

Grieve wanted to turn and run right out of the house, then maybe take up an axe and vent his frustration on a dozen trees, but Rhona would not approve. So he stayed and tried his best to look the part of the hero, though he felt like the opposite.

"And I would like to say that Rum Isle will always be home to the man who saved my daughter. May you always be here to keep her safe, for I am sure Rhona will want to marry you as soon as possible, and I give my hearty blessing to you both!" Ronin said with a watery smile.

"Father..." The warning in her tone made Grieve want to run more than ever.

The one woman he wanted for his wife, who could never be his.

"There's my boy! They say you've saved one girl, and I could ask no less than a hero for the quest I have in mind." Father entered the hall, arms spread wide to embrace his son.

"Father, I need to speak to you," Grieve muttered as his father hugged him.

Lord Lewis clapped him on the back. "Let's leave them to their family reunion, so we can have one of our own." He led the way into the yard.

Grieve went further, walking all the way down to the river. He knew Rhona would hear him if she wished it, but perhaps her father might not.

"Father, I saved no one. Lady Rhona saved herself. She is…" Grieve lowered his voice to a whisper. "She is a witch. She has power over the elements of fire and air. I saw her reduce a house to ashes in minutes. Surely her father must know, for how could she keep that hidden from her own family? Yet he seems to believe I saved her, instead of the other way around!"

Father scratched his chin. "It always was a mystery that Lady Blanid fell pregnant so quickly after her wedding, for she was not one to take her husband to bed earlier than needs must. Especially after…well, Lord Ronin nearly lost her to Alban raiders, too. Her sister saved her, or so 'tis said. I always wondered how a slip of a girl could take on a whole party of raiders like that. If what you say is true, then your girl must be the sister's daughter. But still Ronin's, for he would not have acknowledged her if she were not."

"I don't care whose daughter she is!" Grieve exploded, struggling to keep his voice quiet. "She's a witch. A sorceress. A woman who can burn me where I stand with a wave of her hand. I cannot marry her!"

Father stared. "She seems a lovely enough girl. If you can but keep from provoking her, there is little to worry about on that account."

"I'm not worried for me! I'm worried for

her! What do I have to give her? I'm not fit to lick the ash from her boots! I'm no hero – I'm no one. She deserves far more than anything I can give her." Grieve gazed at his father, begging him to understand. "You should have sent me to war first, not here, so I might be a war hero, at least. Someone with something to offer her."

"So you like the girl, but she thinks you're not good enough, hmm?"

Grieve shook his head. "I do not know what she thinks. I…she…when she kissed me, it seemed like she liked me…but I…"

"You will not be the first man who did not feel ready for marriage. Even I hesitated once…but the right lady will have her own way of making her heart known. Perhaps it is best to take you away from here for a while, until you are ready." Lord Lewis held Grieve's gaze, so he could not look away. "The Alban king has sent a letter that is tantamount to a declaration of war. He demands Lord Angus' eldest daughter and heir, Lady Portia, as bride to one of his sons."

Grieve spluttered. "We can't give her to Alba. Handing over Isla to them is tantamount to giving them all the Southern Isles."

Father grinned. "So you do understand a bit of strategy, after all. Yes. Giving them the girl is to give them everything. But there's more. The Council sent an envoy to the Viken king, asking for him to honour our alliance and send troops to fight the Albans when they come. Lady Portia…will be the price of that alliance. A marriage bargain between her and the Viken prince, when he lands on our shores." He cleared his throat. "But she must be kept safe, never be without a bodyguard at all times. Lady Portia is no witch. She needs protection, and the Council agrees. That's why we all had to send a member of our family to form her bodyguard. I need Mahon on Myroy, so I must send you."

Leave Rhona? The very thought cleaved Grieve's heart in two. "Father…"

"Fools like Calum are sending suitors for

her hand, seeing this as a chance to take Isla for their own. But any man who marries her is doomed to die, if he is not either the Alban prince or the Viken one. The alliance will be written in her maiden's blood, or her husband's lifeblood. I need one man among them who can lead them, forge them into the bodyguard the girl needs. Before she shoots the lot of them. She's a keen archer, I've heard." Once again, Father's eyes captured Grieve's. "You are the only man I trust. That is why I sent you here first. If your heart is here, then there is no way you will lose it to Lady Portia. And when you return, you will be a war hero – Lady Portia's valiant protector. Surely Lady Rhona cannot turn her nose up at that."

Grieve closed his eyes. "What sort of girl is Lady Portia?"

"She is her father's daughter, and her mother's, too. Passionate to a fault, but she knows her duty. Catriona married for love, but she also married the only man who could lead us. Angus says Portia will do the same. Your job is to make sure she gets a choice, though my money's on her picking the Viken prince."

"Very well, Father. I shall go to Isla. For how long?"

Father shrugged. "Until the war is over, and the girl marries her prince. War is a messy business. No one can be sure how long it will last."

Grieve bowed his head. "Then we must tell Lord Ronin, and Rhona."

Father grinned. "Want me to bring a bucket of water to put the fire out?"

Grieve wished he could laugh, but there was nothing funny about deserting Rhona now. She might not need him, but that didn't change how much he cared about her. If war was coming to the isles, the Albans would return in even greater numbers, and she could be caught unawares again. But he'd been as good as useless, anyway. Better to go to Lady Portia, and be useless among a dozen other men, hoping they would be enough to protect the girl.

Grieve took a deep breath and marched up to the house. This would not go well.

740

Thirty-Five

"Rhona, wait!" Grieve called, but Rhona didn't.

She intended to set fire to something and watch it burn to ashes before she'd do anything for Grieve again. One moment he was ready to marry her, and the next he intended to head off to guard some girl on a faraway island? Who was this Lady Portia to him, anyway?

She wanted to run into the woods and hide where he'd never find her, but the sea was closer. Something on the beach would surely burn. But the tide was in, licking at the sand, and the rock the seals liked to sun themselves on was now surrounded by dark water. Rhona didn't care. She summoned a gust of wind to carry her to that rock, where no one could reach her until she willed it.

"Rhona, come back! Please," Grieve said, as he slowed at the water's edge. "I have to do this."

"You have to protect Portia, do you? And why is she so special?" Rhona reached for the beach, for the tiny specks of dried seaweed and sawdust between the sand, and ignited them. The shore lit up like a grassfire.

Grieve jumped back onto a rock. "She's Lord Angus's daughter. His eldest. The heir to Isla."

The fire died for lack of fuel. Rhona cursed. "So? What's Isla to you? Why kiss me, make love to me if you intend to go off and marry this other woman so you can be lord of her island instead? Is Rum Isle not good enough for you? Or is it me? I am not good enough for you, now you know I am a witch and a bastard."

Grieve shook his head. "It is I who is not good enough for Rum Isle, or you. You are…a powerful sorceress, who will one day be the lady of prosperous Rum Isle, able to protect this place without needing a husband. As for Angus' daughter…Lady Portia and the lordship of all the isles is as far beyond me as the very heavens above. The Albans want her as a wife to one of their princes, and I have no doubt the Vikens will offer for her as well."

"Women are not prizes to be carried away like the spoils of war," Rhona snapped.

Grieve sobered. "No, you are not. And nor is she, which is why I must go. Alba will not have her without a fight."

Rhona swallowed. "Is she more important to you than I am?"

"No," he admitted. "She is perhaps the most important woman in the isles right now, because with her claim to Isla comes a chance at kingship, or so the Council says. I should want to defend her with my life because if Alba gets her, then they will conquer us all, and no one will be safe. I would give anything to stay here and marry you like I promised. But war is coming, and I am honour bound to fight and defend what is ours, as is every man of the isles. And you…you are not mine. Not yet. I don't deserve you. You saved us both on that island, and you have no need of me as your defender. When war comes to Rum Isle, as it will to Isla, I know you will save your family without me. My place is where I am most needed, and my father says it is on Isla, guarding the last of the Three Little Pigs."

It was Rhona's turn to laugh. "You mean THAT Lady Portia of the little pigs tale? She cannot be much to look at, if she is likened to a pig. I imagine she is kept cloistered like some princess in a tower, waiting for her prince to come and claim her."

"Perhaps. I do not know, for I have never seen the girl. My father says that she has inherited her father's instinct for politics, and that she is fond of archery. Perhaps he is sending me to her to be her bowyer and archery instructor, more than her bodyguard. I will not be alone, either — all the lords are sending men to guard her. It will not be forever. Only until the war against the Albans is over, or the girl chooses a husband."

Rhona jumped off her rock, splashing through the shallows to shore. She was too tired to use magic, and too tired to argue any more. Grieve was right, though it pained her to admit it. "Fight with honour, and don't let the Albans touch her. And when your duty is done, come home to me. I will wait for you."

Grieve ventured onto the sand, crossing the distance between them without hesitation. "Truly, I do not deserve you. But I will do as you command, for I live in hope." He kissed her, the moment stretching as Rhona tasted longing, desire and duty in that kiss. Longing and desire wanted to continue, but it was duty that ended it. "Farewell, my lady. If it is our fate to meet again on these shores, then I will marry you."

Then he turned and was gone. Rhona waited until he was out of sight before she sank to her knees and let the tears flow. If fate didn't bring him back to her, she'd burn that bitch's bones to ash. Just like the witch. And every Alban who thought to stand between her and vengeance.

Thirty-Six

Rhona didn't return to the house until she knew they'd sailed away. Her eyes were probably red from crying, but no one would notice if she kept her head down. If her father asked, she could say they were tears of grief for Doireann.

She entered the Great Hall, expecting to find it empty.

Of course, it wasn't.

Lord Lewis lifted his cup to her. "My son

tells me you are a witch, Lady Rhona. We haven't had one here on the isles in many years. We may need your help to drive off the Albans if it comes to war."

Father slammed his cup down. "No, man, you may send your sons to war, but leave my daughter be. Women protect their homes, with force if need be, but they do not go to war. We need her here at home."

"You're holding her here, just like you did to Brigid. I don't know what you did, but no matter how much she wanted to marry me, she stayed here with you! You had a wife. You didn't need her!" Lewis said, pouring himself another cup.

"Lady Brigid loved her sister, not me. Maybe not even you, either. I could not have kept her here against her will. The woman took on Alban raiders thrice, with not a survivor among them. If she were here, Doireann would not have died." Father peered into his cup.

"Doireann was a traitorous bitch who

deserved to die. The Albans only spared her on Scitis because she promised to tell them the location of the riches of Rum Isle. They killed her here because she could not lead them to Sanctuary." Rhona folded her arms across her chest. "I would have killed her, had they not knocked me unconscious before I could. I heard enough to damn her before they did. My mother would not have protected her."

Father peered blearily at her. "Did Blanid tell you? She was the only one who knew, except Brigid and me. I was too drunk on my wedding night to know the difference – drunk because I couldn't bear to see the bride I loved flinch every time I touched her, after what those bastards did to her. The second time, I knew she wasn't my wife, but, God forgive me, I lay with her anyway. She said she would do what her sister couldn't…to pretend…and I did. Blanid claimed you as hers, and I knew you were mine. Brigid wanted to give me a son, though, so we tried again…and again, but the babies did not live long enough, and then, nor did she. And Blanid…it took years before she would tolerate my touch, but she promised her sister she'd try…but we never had a son. When she died, I swore I'd never lie with another woman, and be grateful for the children I had. Doireann was a widow, I wanted her to be a nurse to my girls, but she refused to live under my roof unless we were married. So I took another vow, but she was never a wife to me. My daughters are enough."

"You mean you knew I was a bastard?" Rhona asked.

"You are my daughter, the heir to Rum Isle, until I say otherwise, and there are no bastards under this roof. I swore to Brigid on her deathbed, and I keep my oaths." Father rose. "I will hear no more of this matter. As the Lady of Rum Isle, you will protect it as your mother would."

Rhona slumped into a seat and poured herself a cup of wine. "Yes, Father."

Father nodded, took his leave of Lord Lewis, and left.

"Now how did he know you were thinking of running away to Isla, and Grieve?" Lord Lewis asked.

Rhona glared at him. "I most certainly was not!" she lied.

Lord Lewis sipped from his cup, then set it down. "My son tells me you are fond of stories. May I tell you one? One I do not think even my son knows, though he will, in time."

Rhona inclined her head. "Go on."

"Have you heard the story of the Three Little Pigs?" At Rhona's nod, he continued, "And do you remember who saves the little girls?"

"Their nurse," Rhona said slowly. "Like Candace saved my sisters."

"What if I told you it was the wolf?"

Rhona eyed him. "Then I would think you a fool, Lord Lewis, which my father tells me is not true. But if you have had as much to drink as my father, perhaps it is the wine talking."

Lewis laughed. "Wine does not talk, but it does make men talk. Too much, sometimes.

Like the day Lord Angus told me about his little wolf, the prince we have all pinned our hopes on." His shrewd eyes peered at her over the rim of his cup. Lord Lewis was as sober as Rhona herself.

"What if I told you Lord Angus took a Viken fosterling, a young prince, his blood as royal as both the king's and the crown prince, as a favour to his father? And on the day of the feast meant to welcome the boy, Lord Angus's own daughters went missing. Little Portia, the leader of the three, wanted to go swimming, she said, but her nurse said no. So when the nurse wasn't looking, she led the girls out of their father's house and down to a pool she'd heard the boys speak of… And when no one could find the girls, the young prince went searching. He found the girls in the mud, and raised the alarm so the nurse came running. Two girls came when the nurse called, but little Portia refused. He waded into the middle of that mud in his best clothes, heedless of the damage he did to them, and coaxed her out. A different man might have thrown the little girl over his shoulder and carried her out, but that boy offered her his hand and they walked out of the woods together, hand in hand."

"Why are you telling me this?" Rhona demanded.

Lewis smiled. "My son adores you, Lady Rhona, and I know he will return to Rum Isle for you. Much like I know the Viken Wolf Prince is in love with Lady Portia, and he will return to claim her. My son will do his duty, for he is honour-bound to uphold his oath. I knew your mother, and she would never desert her family, not for love or her own happiness. She would fight to the death to protect those she loved. Including you."

Rhona's eyes blazed. "Are you telling me to stay home, like a good little girl?"

To Lord Lewis' credit, he did not back down. "No, Lady Rhona. I am suggesting you do everything within your power to protect Rum Isle and its people, including yourself. For the only man who can end the war against

Alba is that Viken prince, and until he arrives, you are the best Rum Isle has. Just as I am all Myroy has, and Grieve must keep Portia safe for the Viken. We all must endure until our allies arrive. But that doesn't mean we won't fight. On the contrary. We will be defending our homes, more fiercely than any Alban raider can imagine." Lord Lewis rose from his seat and bowed. "Lady Rhona, I would hope you burn every Alban you see, before he even reaches the shore of your lovely isle. I have no doubt you will make your mother proud." He headed off.

Rhona sipped from her cup, deep in thought. She wasn't sure what to think, or to do. Too many revelations in too short a time. And yet…somehow, she thought it would all turn out all right in the end. How, she did not know, but all the best stories did, and hers…would be the best she could make it. Making her mother proud did have a lovely ring to it.

Thirty-Seven

When war came to Rum Isle, her people came to Sanctuary. So it was, and so it always would be. After the initial attack, though, the Albans had left no garrison on Rum Isle, so most of her people had returned to their homes. All except Lord Ronin's family, for their home had been burned along with the Albans and their boats. Rhona had learned her lesson – after the first attack, she'd burned the boats at sea. No Alban would set foot on her shore while she lived.

There had been whispers at first, until her father insisted that his daughter had Lady Brigid's blood in her veins and the magic that ran with it, and she would defend the island alongside its men. After watching what she could do, the men heartily embraced this idea, and the whispers ceased.

So Sanctuary echoed with emptiness, until a boat was spotted approaching Rum Isle.

The watchmen reported this to Rhona, while the people of Rum Isle filled Sanctuary again.

"We have visitors," Rhona announced to her family. Her sisters huddled closer together, looking fearful. "Don't worry, I shall see them off shortly."

Father caught her arm. "Don't go out there alone. I shall come with you. Remember what happened to Doireann."

Rhona gently pulled out of his grasp. "Doireann got what she deserved, luring Albans to our home. As will our latest intruders. Don't worry, Father. They will tell no tales once I am finished with them."

But Father would not be dissuaded. He buckled on his sword and shouldered his crossbow. "Once we both are finished with them. I am not so old that I cannot defend Rum Isle."

Blowing out a frustrated breath, she waited for him to lead the way out of the cave and onto the ridge, where he took up his accustomed spot behind a boulder that was just the right height to rest his crossbow on.

Two figures beached a coracle, before one climbed the rocks above the beach and started shouting. Shouting her name.

Rhona swore. "It's Lord Lewis. With another man."

Her heart leaped. Was it finally time to stop hiding, and start fighting?

"I have a proposition for you!" Lord Lewis bellowed.

Rhona squinted at the second man. Only one man had a proposition she might want to hear, and Lord Lewis' companion did not look like Grieve.

"Stay here and defend the girls, Father. I will speak to him."

Bless the man, he looked like he wanted to argue. As though two men would be any match for Rhona and her magic.

She bit her lip. Sparks erupted from her fingers. "I will be fine, Father."

He nodded. "And I will keep them in my sights."

She let the wind carry away the sound of her footsteps, so that the men would not hear her approach. Lord Lewis's companion dressed like a man of Isla, with a coracle to match, but no Islander ever wore a sealskin so fine over Isla wool, except perhaps Lord Angus. Lord Angus was closer to her father's age than this man, who could not be older than thirty. And Lord Angus had no sons, least of all this giant.

Lord Lewis shouted his offer again.

"I'm already betrothed, and not to that beast of a man." Rhona stepped out of hiding.

She'd surprised the Viken, for that's what he must be. Was this the man Lewis had promised would come to their aid?

Lewis' impassive face told her nothing. Instead, he gestured for the Viken to speak.

He inclined his head with what appeared to be genuine courtesy. "I am no beast, lady." The rumble of his delightfully deep voice said otherwise, as he continued, "I am Rudolf Vargssen, Prince of Viken. I have come from my cousin, King Reidar, to cast the Albans out of the Southern Isles." His eyes flashed with something like battle-fire.

One man's fire would only go so far.

Rhona dismissed him with a flick of her fingers. "Just you and old Lewis here? You have no chance, Prince of Viken. Not without an army that can match the Albans."

A faint smile curved his lips. The Viken liked a challenge. "I have three ships." Rudolf pointed.

Still Lewis said nothing. Did he think she was a politician like Lady Portia, able to read men and their true intentions before they knew themselves? Lady Portia dealt in subtleties. Rhona did not.

"Is this the wolf we are waiting for?" Rhona demanded.

Lewis inclined his head. "He is."

She wanted to breathe out a sigh of relief, but the Viken had his eyes on her. Instead, she inspected him right back. "What is your stake, Prince of Viken? What do you get out of saving the Southern Isles?"

For just a moment, Rudolf looked lost, like a boy looked out through his eyes. Then the moment was gone and he stood as stoic as before, almost as though she'd imagined it. But she hadn't.

"He wants Lady Portia," Lewis supplied.

Good luck, Viken. If Grieve was to be believed, and he usually was, Lady Portia would be no easy conquest. She might not be a witch, but she had her own weapons. If this man sought to bully Lady Portia into a marriage she did not desire, Rhona would defend her alongside Grieve and the others. "Lady Portia is no prize, like the women of other lands. She is the Lady of Isla, and if she does not like you, may heaven help you, for no one else will."

She expected him to defend his title, his suitability as a suitor. His right to conquer a woman.

What she didn't expect was his laughter.

He wiped his eyes and shrugged. "Portia liked me well enough before I left. If she likes me still...well, I guess we shall see. As long as the lady is safe, I will be satisfied."

She stared at him for a long moment. He spoke the truth, she was sure of it. And that look in his eyes...yearning, that's what it was. But for Portia or her claim?

Slowly, Rhona said, "She is safe enough. My betrothed guards her with his life."

Rudolf relaxed just the slightest bit. Relieved. Rhona bridled. If he dismissed Grieve and his men so easily, she would give him a piece of her mind.

"My son has sent word?" Lewis asked eagerly, interrupting her train of thought.

Rudolf would keep, Rhona swore, as she answered, "When he can. His letters are carried in secret and left in a place only he and I know. The lady lives, and so does he."

Lewis' grin was positively devilish. "How goes the hiding, Lady Rhona? Are your sisters sick of fish yet?"

Rhona turned her glare on Lewis. "They complain constantly. The sooner this war ends, the better." If she could play a part in it, it would be over much sooner.

The two men exchanged a glance.

"Would you like to help with the war, Lady Rhona?" Rudolf ventured. He almost sounded like he wanted her to refuse.

Fat chance of that. "My father will not approve."

Lewis laughed. "Old fool. He thinks my son should save you, for what man would follow a hero who got himself saved by a maiden?"

No, her father worried about her.

Needlessly. "Something of that sort." It was Grieve she worried about. If she went to war…Grieve agreed with her father. He would not forgive her for going to war, when it was his place to fight.

Lewis jerked his head at Rudolf. "We can blame the victory on the Viken. I'm sure he won't mind."

The Viken looked affronted. A proud prince, this one. "I prefer to fight my own battles, but I am not such a fool as to refuse the help of an ally. There are shieldmaidens among my people, Lord Lewis's late mother among them, who fight alongside their men. If you can assist my army…"

He didn't believe she could. Then he was a fool.

Rhona bit her lip, and the bush behind Lewis burst into flame.

He yelped and ran down to the water, but she sent the fire racing after him, blistering the very sands to glass until the sea steamed around him. "I told you! This witch can burn anything! With her on your side, you can't help but win!"

Witch. Rhona didn't like that word. She fought to find more that would burn in the sand at Lewis's feet, but all she found was a clump of seaweed that sent up a satisfying cloud of steam. She would not help this man conquer her countrywoman. They were Islanders, not Vikens or Albans who used women like slaves. And Lewis was a traitor who deserved to die with them.

There was a whump as Rudolf fell to his knees on the sand. "Lady Rhona, I beg you to help me free the Southern Isles from the invaders. I will give you anything you ask."

It was so easy to say no, but then she would be as much a fool as Lewis. If this man with his three ships prevailed, he would face Grieve. And Grieve would die to protect Portia.

Rhona took a deep breath. "I want all I've ever wanted. My husband. Free him from his oath to Portia, so that he can come home and marry me."

The Viken bowed his head. Understanding lit his eyes. This man had known love, too. Time would tell if it was for Lady Portia, and whether she shared his love. And Rhona would be at his side when it did, to protect her own people if it came to it. Damn Grieve and his stupid pride. It was time for this war to end, and this wolfish Viken had the power to do it. With her help.

Rhona took a deep breath. "What would you have me burn first?"

"Myroy Isle, and every other island where Albans seek to hide," Lewis said, splashing out of the sea. He shrugged. "What? I'm the Lord of Myroy. I can burn it if I want to." Lewis produced a jug from under his cloak and lifted it in a toast: "To winning this damned war!" He drank deeply.

Rudolf held out his hand. "Do we have an accord?"

If Rudolf was to live up to his name, he would have to win this war. Perhaps Grieve need never know the part she'd played. Rhona placed her hand in his. "We do, Wolf Prince."

His fingers closed around hers with a delicacy she had not expected. If it weren't for Grieve, she might actually like this Viken. Perhaps Portia would, too.

But it was too early to think of such things. First, she had a war to fight, and win.

Thirty-Eight

Rhona had seen death and destruction enough for a dozen lifetimes. She'd seen men die screaming, burning, and she'd enjoyed it. Prince Rudolf was the only man who dared stand at her side, or anywhere near her, and he did his best to arrange his face into an expression of battle-hardened watchfulness. But he was still a man, and sometimes he'd feared, sometimes he'd despaired, but more often he cheered in triumph as their growing army won yet another victory over the diminishing Alban army.

For he might be a Viken, but the Islanders treated him like one of their own. What Lord Lewis had told her was true – Rudolf had grown up on the Isles, Rhona had learned, fostered by Lord Angus, though none had known he was a prince then. And he'd fought alongside many of them as a boy, which even Rhona had to admit made him one of them. For who but an Islander fought to defend the Southern Isles?

Albans ran at the sight of him, for his reputation flew faster than an eagle. He slaughtered and burned everything in his path, they screamed, little knowing it wasn't Rudolf at all they feared, but Rhona herself. And she didn't slaughter and burn everything. Just Albans. But she let the stories spread, as stories always did. She laughed when her own people called her the Viken witch, thinking she had arrived with Rudolf. Better that they believe a lie than that she was one of their own. The men of Rum Isle knew the truth, but they kept their lady's secrets. As did Rudolf.

Twice Rhona had seen Rudolf's spirits rise at the sight of a red-haired woman on Isla, only for them to be dashed the moment the women opened their mouths. They were Lady Portia's sisters, identical in all but name and disposition. Rudolf had two of the Little Pigs, but he really wanted Number Three. Who was kept captive in a castle the Albans had dared to build on Council Isle.

When he'd heard that, he'd ordered them to ride without rest until they arrived at the loch. No one had dared argue with the hard Viken. Not even Rhona. This war had gone on too long – they all wanted it to be over.

The sisters rode with Rhona all the way to Loch Findlugan, which made the men keep their distance. They needn't have — the pregnant one, Arlie, spent most of the journey describing the gowns she wanted to make for Rhona. If it hadn't been raining, Rhona didn't doubt the woman would have had a needle in hand, making a start on the first gown while she rode. Rhona had half a mind to take her up on the offer. It would be nice to have a new gown again.

Lina had little to say, except when answering her sister's questions about the cloth bales in Lord Angus' storerooms. But Rhona could feel her eyes everywhere, sizing up the army and the land and everything they encountered. No doubt taking stock so that she might report to her husband, Lord Angus' steward.

Rudolf stayed away when the women were with her, which suited Rhona fine. Every time he looked at them, his eyes burned with a desire that forced him to look away. He burned for Lady Portia, hotter than any blaze Rhona had kindled. If Portia refused him…Rhona wasn't sure what he'd do. That's why she would see this through to the end. Prince Rudolf, the Wolf Prince of Viken, as he was now known, had fought too long and too hard to just give up, and with an army at his back, Rhona might be all that stood between him and Portia, if the girl refused him.

But Rhona would stand, for this war would be all for naught if Portia was forced into a marriage against her will. For the women of the Southern Isles fought for freedom as much as their men, and Rhona would not yield.

When Rudolf sent his envoys across the loch, against Rhona's advice, she considered returning to her tent, not wanting to see if the Albans opened fire on the two helpless women in the tiny boat. But something within her could not turn away, so she stayed. A whisper of magic sent a breeze behind the boat, speeding it to the castle, then swirling back to her, carrying the voices of those inside.

But not the words she wanted to hear.

For the first time in years, she heard Grieve's voice again: "I don't care if they're her sisters or not. If they are soldiers in disguise, then they die on our swords, but if they truly are Lady Portia's sisters, then we'll send them up to the tower with her, where they'll be safe.

God knows she could do with the company of a woman again. Keeping her amused is more than I have the wit or energy for, I fear."

Grieve's loyalties had shifted, as Rhona had known they would. He served Lady Portia now. He'd forgotten Rhona had ever existed.

Rhona bowed her head, wiping away a tear before anyone could see it.

"What is it? What's wrong? Is it Portia?" Rudolf seized her shoulders, forgetting in his panic who she was.

Rhona eyed him coldly. "Your Lady Portia is in the tower, soon to be joined by her sisters. So safe her guards have little to do but amuse her."

Rudolf's breath whooshed out of him. "Thank the heavens for that. For a moment, I thought…"

He remembered himself and released her.

"Forgive me, Lady Rhona." The Wolf Prince bowed regally. "By this time tomorrow, our alliance will be over, and the war will be won."

Rhona wiggled her fingers. "I could set fire to the castle from here, if you want it to be sooner. The walls are stone, but there is enough timber in there to burn."

His eyes widened in horror. "You cannot! Portia is in there, you said. Safe. You can't risk…and what of your man? The bargain we made? If he is dead, then he is freed of his vows, and I release you from yours."

Oh, the bitter gall, that both Portia and Grieve lived, and neither she nor Rudolf would be reunited with the ones they loved, for the pair no longer loved them. She had killed plenty of men, but she would not be the one to rip Rudolf's beating heart from his chest.

"He lives, too," Rhona said shortly. "Until tomorrow, then, Wolf Prince."

Thirty-Nine

It was strange to have a tent to herself again, but Rhona lingered there as long as she dared the next morning. She toyed with the idea of avoiding the noon peace council, but in her heart she knew she could not.

The Wolf Prince believed the cowardly Albans would surrender Portia. If she was lucky, Grieve would be among the girl's honour guard. Rhona could remain in the background and watch unseen as she saw how things played out between Portia, Grieve and Rudolf.

But when the boat landed, there were three armoured men aboard – no women.

Rudolf appeared as impassive as ever, not showing the surprise Rhona knew he must feel at not seeing Portia with them.

They came ashore, removing their helms as Rudolf did. That's when Rhona clapped both hands to her mouth to stifle her cry. The cowardly Albans had sent Grieve to treat with Rudolf in their place, without Portia. They'd sent him to his death.

Rhona had chosen a place where she could not hear them, and no magical breeze would carry their words across the whispering of half an army. She began to shove her way through the men, intent on hearing what was said. Grieve's last words, if that's what they were.

She would not let them be, she vowed. Even if he now loved Portia instead of her, she would not let him die.

A sword scraped out of its scabbard and

Rhona lost patience. She sank her teeth into her lip, and magic blew a path for her to the lakeshore.

"Sheath that thing, you bloody fool!" she shouted, running toward Grieve.

His eyes widened. "Rhona?" Down came the sword, and his eyes lit up.

Rhona could feel the fire inside her, ready to burn the world twice over in Grieve's defence. Thrice, if he loved her still.

"You lay one finger on this man, Wolf Prince, and our alliance is over!" She marched past Rudolf and took her place at Grieve's side. No man in Rudolf's army would rise in his defence against her.

Even Rudolf hesitated. He looked at Grieve for what was likely the first time. "Who are you?"

Before Grieve could speak, Rhona snapped, "He's Grieve Lewisson, my betrothed, and the head of Lady Portia's personal guard." She half expected him to wince at her words, but Grieve merely nodded. Rhona turned to

Grieve. "Why have the Albans sent you to negotiate?"

The men behind Grieve burst out laughing. "What Albans? They've all fled, like the cowards they are. Even Mason, when we shut him out. Council Island and the castle belong to Lady Portia."

"No. It belongs to my husband."

Everyone turned to stare at the newcomer. Her red hair was a banner of flame brighter than anything Rhona could conjure, marking her as the lady herself. But as she approached, Rhona found it hard not to laugh. The third Little Pig indeed, for Lady Portia's gown was caked in mud to the knees.

Then Rudolf's eyes lit up, brighter than her hair. He mustn't have noticed the soiled gown as his oh-so-majestic lady made her muddy way along the lakeshore. He'd gone to war for her. Men had died for her. More men would die for her, if this war went on. One muddy girl.

A girl who hid behind her guards, and

Grieve. No longer. Rhona fixed her gaze on the girl, willing her to show some sign of why they had all fought so long and so hard.

"My husband." When Portia repeated the words, she laid her hand on Rudolf's arm. She'd placed herself opposite Rhona, so that their eyes met.

Rhona expected curiosity, or hostility…something that told her Portia had no idea who she was facing.

But Portia's face lit with a friendly smile. "Lady Rhona." Then she offered her cheek.

But she did not leave Rudolf's side or take her hand from his arm, all the while her gaze held Rhona's. In order to give Portia the kiss of peace custom demanded, Rhona would have to approach and bow her head to kiss the shorter girl.

Portia knew nothing about Rhona. Not her power or her rank or…anything. Every man present feared her, holding their breath as they waited to see Rhona's response, yet Portia smiled on, oblivious.

"It is a pleasure. I have heard so much about you," Portia said, glancing at Grieve.

Or not oblivious.

With one glance, she said it all. She knew all about Rhona's magic, for Grieve had told her, but she was Lord Angus's daughter. A politician, like her father before her. In her father's absence, Portia stood as ruler of the Isles, but she recognised Rhona's power over Rudolf's army. Between them, they held the power to end this war, unite everyone present, and bring peace.

Rhona would drop to her knees and kiss a pig for that. But Portia was no pig. She was a lady who outranked Rhona. A lady who winked, the moment Rhona's lips left her cheek, as though they were the best of friends sharing a secret.

They had done what countless fighting men could not do. Two women had ended a war with a kiss.

"I look forward to your wedding. You must sit beside me at the feast to celebrate mine. Of course, you and Grieve must sit with us at the high table. I insist." Portia's eyes were on Grieve as she said this. Either she enjoyed his pain or…was there nothing between her and Grieve, after all?

Rhona dared to hope.

"My lady," Grieve breathed. It wasn't clear which lady he was speaking to, as his eyes darted from one to the other.

Portia lifted her eyebrows. "I hope you mean Rhona, for I'm not yours any more. Protecting me is Prince Rudolf's job now."

Of course. Her marriage released him from his vows. Grieve was free.

Portia lifted her and Rudolf's linked arms, raising her voice in a warcry that would have made any general proud. "Isla is ours!"

The army – her army – echoed her words, over and over until the valley rang with a woman's warcry. As it should be.

Rhona felt a timid tap on her shoulder.

Grieve stood there, the only man among them not cheering. "I am no longer needed. Is there any chance…would you still be willing…I mean…"

"You'll marry me today, or not at all, Grieve Lewisson. I've waited long enough, and there's a priest hereabouts who will say the words for us, or I'll light his boots on fire," Rhona said.

"But what will your father say?" Grieve asked.

"Who cares, as long as you say yes?"

Of all the men present, Grieve alone had the power to crush Rhona entirely.

She moistened her lips. "If you don't say yes, I give you fair warning I'll light your boots on fire. I'm getting really good at that."

Grieve laughed. "You need no magic to light me on fire, my lady. But you have always known that. If you wish to be married today, then I will do everything in my power to grant your wish. The war is over. It is past time that you are wed."

"You're telling me." Rhona would have said more, but Grieve caught her in his arms, and her mouth was soon too busy for anything as dull as words.

Forty

Father Fintan was only too happy to perform the ceremony, boasting that he'd officiated in the prince's wedding to Portia, only last night. When Rhona finally said the words that she'd dreamed about for so long, she wasn't sure who was happier – her or Grieve. The priest pronounced them husband and wife, then dropped his voice to a whisper to tell Rhona he would happily counsel her on the duties of marriage at any time, especially after the wedding night.

Rhona just laughed. "If my husband has forgotten how to please me in bed, I'm not the one you'll hear it from, Father. I'm not sure Grieve will confess it to you, either." She seized Grieve's hand. "Come, husband, we have a wedding feast to attend."

The camp was strangely empty, though the tents crouched like ghosts in the moonlight. Everyone else was in the castle, and the sounds of merry feasting carried across the water without the help of a breeze, magical or otherwise.

"The only feast I want is you." Grieve's words hung in the air, tantalising, tempting. Too much to refuse.

He tugged her into his arms. His embrace and the kiss that followed felt as natural as breathing – all things she wanted to do for the rest of her life.

"To my tent, then," she said, leading the way. She entered, waving her hand to light the braziers that turned the tent from chilly to bearable. She heard a clink behind her. Grieve's sword belt, most likely. He would not need it here.

"I have some wine here somewhere. It is not a bottle of Father's best, but…"

"Perhaps after, my lady. I am drunk on you already."

No one spoke to her as sweetly as Grieve. Oh, how she'd missed that. Rhona whirled, wanting to see the love in his eyes as he looked at her.

He tugged off his hose and stood naked in the firelight. Her husband. War had only improved him, turning lean, boyish muscle into the harder, muscled man before her. Everything she could ever want.

Grieve laughed. "I seem to remember I was the one lost for words, seeing you naked. Have the tables turned?"

"I…" The fire began in her belly, coursing through her veins until it flamed in her cheeks. She'd never needed a man more than she wanted Grieve now. "I need to feel you inside me, Grieve. Now."

"Then let's get you out of this gown, for I've dreamed of you every night since the day I left." His hands didn't fumble as he unlaced her gown and had her out of it before he'd finished kissing her. Her shift vanished, and now she was naked before him. He carried her to the bed, fingers caressing her even as he kissed her. There was none of the boyish nervousness from before. Now, he played her body with the deft strokes of a masterful man.

Rhona arched her back as she cried out for joy, begging for more. Grieve had anticipated her, once again, thrusting deep into her before her first blissful orgasm had finished. On the second thrust, her hips rose to meet him, ever equal to anything he was willing to give.

They moved together, one body in more than mere words, until they uttered twin cries of joy as they reached their peak together, too.

It wasn't until they lay tangled in each other's arms later, that Rhona thought to say, "Remember that witch on Nimbanmore Isle?

She would be horrified at what we've just done. She thought we were brother and sister, remember."

Grieve traced a circles around her nipples, grinning as she shivered at his touch. "There's only one witch whose opinion I care for. My lovely Lady Rhona, you never did tell me…what sort of lover am I?"

Her hands slid down his belly, stroking him into readiness. Only then did Rhona flash him a wicked smile. "I'm sure I've forgotten. But I'd love to be reminded."

Grieve rolled over, settling between her thighs. "What sort?" he demanded.

"One who likes to tease me," she grumbled, reaching for him.

He leaned forward and kissed her breasts. "If you will not say, then I will tell you. I am the sort of lover who will love you with every breath until the day I die. The sort who wants to hear my name on your lips as you cry out for pleasure, over and over again." He thrust into her, as if to punctuate his words. "And what sort of lover are you?"

She couldn't think, too intent on the pleasure of feeling the heat of him inside her again. Deep inside, where he belonged. "I'm yours," she said simply. "And as long as we're together, we get to live happily ever af....oh, Grieve!"

Grieve chuckled. "As my lady wishes, of course."

Forty-One

Briska stamped out of her boots, but the blazing leather had already set the floor alight. Swearing, she bit down hard and fought to cast the only spell that could save her. The circle of blue light flared and died, once, twice…but on the third time it seemed to stay, wavering a little, but enough. She stepped through the portal, which collapsed behind her. She peeled off her singed stockings, to find her feet red and blistered with burns. She stuck her feet in the water bucket, moaning as the icy water numbed the pain.

The mirror unclouded for a moment and a face appeared. "Well done," the woman said.

"What do you mean, well done? That brother and sister almost killed me!" Briska snapped.

The woman laughed. "Brother and sister? You are too easily persuaded. That's what got you into this mess in the first place, but I will help you. This pair are matched, and so you will move onto your next quest. Your new assignment is in the icy north, I'm afraid. You will need warmer things."

Ice and snow? Perfect for burned feet.

Briska lifted her arms. "I am ready when you are, Mistress." The last word came hard for a woman who had once been a queen, but she had little choice now. Slavery to the mirror and its mistress was all her life held now.

A portal opened before her, and Briska stepped through. The mirror, her chest of belongings, and her precious sack of spices landed in the snow behind her.

Another day, another couple. Though she shook her head when she thought of Hansel and Gretel. That pair would not have an easy time of it, she was certain. She might have made a match of them, however unwillingly, but they had a lot of work for even a hope of happily ever after.

Her mistress's face appeared in the mirror. "Next, you must match Kai and Gerda," she said.

Briska sighed as she saw the picture of the pair. At least these two had clothes on, unlike the fornicating brother and sister. Thank the heavens for small mercies. And snow to cool her feet.

From queen of a kingdom to queen of the snow, Briska's work was never done.

But first, she would need a place to live, for her new palace was gone. And all the ice and snow gave her an idea…

About the Author

Demelza Carlton has always loved the ocean, but on her first snorkelling trip she found she was afraid of fish.

She has since swum with sea lions, sharks and sea cucumbers and stood on spray drenched cliffs over a seething sea as a seven-metre cyclonic swell surged in, shattering a shipwreck below.

Demelza now lives in Perth, Western Australia, the shark attack capital of the world.

The *Ocean's Gift* series was her first foray into fiction, followed by her suspense thriller *Nightmares* trilogy. She swears the *Mel Goes to Hell* series ambushed her on a crowded train and wouldn't leave her alone.

Want to know more? You can follow Demelza on Facebook, Twitter, YouTube or her website, Demelza Carlton's Place at:

www.demelzacarlton.com